# A Bittersweet Decision

Without thinking, Jake reached out, his knuckle catching the solitary tear as it began to trail down her cheek. "I swear if you married me, I'd do everything I could to make sure you never regretted it."

"And what about you? What if you regret it?"

He gave her a small smile, shaking his head. "I won't regret it."

Rebecca studied the rugged contours of Jake's face limned by the light of a full moon. A lifetime. A lifetime with this man. To accept now that Brett wasn't coming back or that if he did, it would be too late. She swallowed her uncertainty, giving him a smile in its place.

"I'd be honored to become your wife and go with you to Texas."

"You sure?"

"I'm sure," she said without hesitation.

Watching her stroll towards the house, Jake felt as though his heart would break out of his chest. That beautiful woman was going to be his wife.

# SWEET LULLABY

## LORRAINE HEATH

DIAMOND BOOKS, NEW YORK

This book is a Diamond original edition,
and has never been previously published.

SWEET LULLABY

A Diamond Book / published by arrangement with
the author

PRINTING HISTORY
Diamond edition / March 1994

ISBN: 1-55773-987-0

Diamond Books are published by The Berkley Publishing Group,
200 Madison Avenue, New York, NY 10016.
DIAMOND and the "D" design
are trademarks belonging to Charter Communications, Inc.

PRINTED IN THE UNITED STATES OF AMERICA

10  9  8  7  6  5  4  3  2  1

To my sons, Brandon and Alex,
who taught me that a child's faith is unwavering
and that
a child's belief in dreams is strong enough
to make them come true

# SWEET LULLABY

# *P*rologue

THE FLAMES FROM the tiny candles flickered, sending illuminated fairy dancers through the paned glass window to perform on the thickening blanket of snow. The boy had been hunkered down in the middle of the yard that surrounded the white-framed house for some time now, close enough to see the beauty of the candles, but far enough away that he didn't think he would be spotted.

Large flakes of snow continued to cascade down from the heavens but he paid them no heed, just as he ignored the icy pain beginning in his sodden feet where the snow had melted and soaked through the thin soles of his boots, just as he ignored the numbing beginning in his legs. In all of his eight years upon the earth, he didn't think he'd ever seen anything as beautiful, and he was mesmerized as the candles sent their light out to play across the sparkling whiteness.

He fervently hoped his mother could see the candles. She had always enjoyed pretty things. He thought the sight before him now would bring a smile to her face, even in Heaven. And he had so loved her smiles.

A shadow darkened the window. The boy held his breath, waiting as the shadow quivered and was replaced by a boy older than the one hunched in the snow. The boy inside gazed out of the home, a fire burning brightly in the hearth filling it with warmth. The boy in the snow wondered if the boy standing by the window would tell his father what he saw. He released his breath knowing in his

1

heart it would make no difference. The thick leather strap across his skinny backside for being where he was forbidden to be was worth the few moments he'd spent enjoying the movement of the candles.

The boy inside the house turned, puffing out each solitary candle while the boy outside watched the dancing flames slowly be put to sleep. When he had completed his task, the boy inside glanced back out into the blackness of the winter night. Then he disappeared.

Outside, the boy stood up, shards of pain racing up and down his legs as the blood was restored to his feet. He waited for the large man to come storming out the door. Leaving the scene now would be useless, for the man would not ask him if he had been disobedient; he would punish him based solely on the word of his son. And although this time it was the truth, other times it hadn't been.

The snow continued falling around him, circling on the wind that was beginning to howl as the night wore on. Finally, with a slight shrug of his small shoulders, he turned and walked slowly towards the barn while the snow worked to cover his tracks.

He trudged to the last stall and sat down to remove his icy boots, setting them up carefully. He removed his wet socks, laying them on top, hoping they would be dry by morning. Tucking his chin into his coat, he brought the collar up high around his neck and went to the corner of the stall, picking up the blanket that he had folded and placed there with care that morning.

He ducked down under the wooden slats used to separate the stalls in the barn and crawled into the adjacent stall where he began rubbing the belly of the chestnut mare.

"Lay down, Lady. Please . . . it's awful cold tonight. Please lay down."

The mare complied as she always did to the soothing tone in his voice. Drawing the blanket up tightly around him, he lay down beside the horse, moving in close to her side. He was careful to place his frozen feet near enough to her for warmth, but not so near that she'd protest.

"They had a real purty tree, Lady, with candles. Bet it

didn't look as purty from the inside, though. Weren't no snow on the inside.''

He snuggled in closer to the warm beast.

''Merry Christmas, Lady,'' he whispered.

The mare nickered and moved her head in closer to the boy as he drifted off to sleep, the scent of hay and livestock surrounding them.

# Chapter One

Kentucky, 1883

WITH THE EASE of a man who has spent the better part of his life in the saddle, Jake Burnett herded the untamed horses into the waiting corrals. When the gates closed on the last of his rambunctious charges, he dismounted from his weary horse, walked to the watering trough, and poured a bucket of water over his head. His hair, the color of a muddy river after a rain, curled as it absorbed the clear liquid.

"Jake!"

He turned to greet the foreman, his smile fading when he saw the expression on Bassett's round face.

"Anderson wants to see you up at the house."

Apprehension took root in the pit of Jake's gut. Being called into the owner's office usually was not a reason for rejoicing. The last man called up there had been fired, the man before that arrested. Jake rubbed his hands down his thighs. "What about?" It didn't ease his discomfort any to see the stocky man's eyes fill with sympathy.

Bassett had always liked Jake and he wished he could offer some encouragement to the young man, but he couldn't. During the past three weeks, John Anderson had been in one foul mood: nothing was done correctly, even though it was being done exactly the same way it had been done for years. Anderson had criticized everyone and everything until yesterday evening when he'd barked out

Jake's name. Whatever the hell Jake had done, Bassett was certain the man would be off the ranch by sunset. He pulled off his hat and ran his weathered hand through his thinning blond hair. "Don't know. He just said he wanted to see you as soon as you got back. Reckon you're back. Reckon you'd best get yourself up to the house."

Jake nodded before beginning the long walk to the two-story house. He'd just returned from three weeks of gathering horses for the Lazy A. He certainly hadn't done anything while he was gone to warrant a meeting with John Anderson. It had to be something he'd done before he left, something Anderson didn't know about until he was on the trail. But what?

It didn't help matters to see Anderson's personal servant open the door for him before he arrived at the steps.

"Mr. Anderson is expecting you," Giles said.

As Giles escorted him down the long narrow hallway Jake wondered if the whole damn ranch knew John Anderson wanted to see him. Giles rapped gently on an oak door. Anderson bid him to enter. Jake removed his hat and stepped into the paneled library. The door closed quietly behind him, making him feel like a trapped animal.

Anderson stood before the window, gazing out on the corrals. As always he was dressed in what Jake would call his Sunday best—a brown jacket matching his brown pants, his white shirt pressed straight as a board. His silver hair was the only indication that he was aged. He stood slender, straight, and tall, his movements those of a man who had earned his place in the world.

"Well, Jake, appears you got some good horses in this lot."

"Yes, sir, we did."

"Fine, fine," he commented absently as he turned from the window. "Have a seat, son." He indicated the brown leather chair in front of his massive oak desk.

Jake sat without hesitating, not removing his eyes from the man before him, trying to judge his mood, finding the task impossible.

"Would you care for something to drink after that long drive?"

"No, sir."

"Hope you don't mind if I have one." He didn't wait for a response but went to the small table set in the corner and poured himself a liberal glass of whiskey. He downed half of it, refilled it, and then sat down behind the desk.

"Tell me, Jake," he said, studying his glass as if it contained all the answers to life's immense problems. "What do you think of my daughter, Rebecca?"

"Rebecca?"

"Yes, Rebecca. Do you think she's pretty?"

Relief coursed through Jake's body. First, Anderson mentioned the horses and now Reb. He obviously wanted to discuss the stallion Jake had promised he'd break for her.

"I think she's about the prettiest thing I've ever seen."

Anderson stopped studying the glass and began to study Jake. "Do you like her?"

"Oh, yes, sir." Under Anderson's intense perusal, Jake forced a smile. "Reb, uh, Rebecca is the kindest person I've ever met."

Anderson's eyes narrowed. "She's pregnant."

Jake came up out of the chair, knocking it over, sending it crashing to the floor as he stumbled back. "I swear to God! I've never laid a finger on her, Mr. Anderson! I danced one dance with her at the last barn raising, but other than that, I swear to God, I've never touched her!"

Anderson stood up, shaking his head in disgust. "I know you're not the father. Sit back down." He walked to the window, draining the amber liquid from his glass on the way.

Jake righted the chair, and sat back down on the edge of the seat. His fingers unconsciously worked the brim of his hat as he wondered why the hell Anderson was telling him all this.

"I know who the man is," Anderson said quietly. "She thinks he loves her and that he's going to come back for her, but he doesn't and he's not. He did this to spite me."

Going to come back for her? That meant the man wasn't here now. She hadn't looked pregnant when he'd left to round up the horses so she couldn't be very far along. Three men had left within the last two months. Willie Thompson, who had the mind of a child; Daniel Wright, who was old enough to be John Anderson's father; and Brett Meier, tall, coal black hair, sparkling blue eyes, and a smile that flashed white teeth, straight and true. He was a gentleman cowhand, all right.

Jake wondered if Anderson wanted him to kill the man who had defiled his daughter. But Jake would have to talk to Reb first. She wasn't one to give herself lightly. If she loved the man, Jake wouldn't want to kill him. On the other hand, if the man had taken advantage of her, Jake wouldn't hesitate to deliver a just punishment.

Anderson returned to the chair behind his desk, his eyes hard on Jake. "There's no way in hell I'm going to let Rebecca bring a bastard child into this world. I'm not going to be put to shame in this community."

So Anderson wanted him to locate the man and bring him back. He could do that, but again only after he had talked with Reb.

"I've thought long and hard about it," Anderson said. "When I die, Rebecca will inherit this ranch. She needs someone I can trust to help run it, someone young enough to be here with her in later years."

Anderson got up, refilled his glass, drank the fiery liquid, and then turned to face Jake. "I'm asking you to marry her."

Jake caught himself before he came back up out of the chair. Lord, marry Reb? Beautiful, wonderful Reb as his wife? Sweet Jesus! He had dreamed someday he would find a woman willing to marry him, but not even in his wildest dreams had he dared hope she would be someone like Rebecca Anderson. Hesitantly, he asked, "How does Rebecca feel about this?"

"She doesn't know, and even if she did, it doesn't matter how she feels. I'm not going to become the laughingstock of this community. She'll do what I tell her to do."

Inhaling deeply, Jake wiped the sweat from his palms. "I'll ask her."

"No need to do that. If you're agreeable, I'll tell her tonight at supper."

Jake stood up, took a deeper breath and, at the risk of losing his position at the ranch, said, "If you don't mind, sir, I'd prefer to ask her."

Anderson waved his hand in the air. "Fine. Just do it soon. I don't want anyone thinking that baby's not yours." He turned back to the table and refilled his glass, dismissing Jake in the process.

Wearing a small smile, Jake walked through the Victorian manor, the hardwood floors echoing his passing footsteps. Reb as his wife? Sweet Jesus, wouldn't that be something?

He stepped outside, raising a hand to shield his eyes from the glaring sun. The whirling dust, the resonant sounds of horses and cattle, the stifling heat brought him back to reality. Damn ugly bastard, he berated himself. Even if you get up the courage to ask her, she'll say no. She'll say it kindly, but it'll be no just the same.

Jake stormed out of the bunkhouse, slamming the door behind him, the men's laughter still ringing in his ears. They'd been pestering him, wanting to know what Anderson had told him that had made him lose his appetite. They'd said it wasn't natural for a man fresh back from a drive to sit before a full plate of food and not eat. He sure as hell hadn't answered them. But his silence hadn't stopped the men. They'd just started ribbing him for the hard scrubbing he'd given his body, the trimming he'd given his hair. He had enough on his mind without their badgering intruding on his thoughts.

In the moon-shadowed night, he walked to the corrals, leaned against the whitewashed fence, and watched the horses move restlessly within the confines. He knew without a doubt which of the horses Reb would select for herself. The black stallion had a fiery disposition, but Jake knew how to bend a horse without breaking his spirit.

That's what she'd told him the first time she'd watched him tame a horse.

"You bend 'em, you don't break 'em. I want you to bend my next horse. I don't like 'em too tame." She had smiled that special smile of hers, her deep blue eyes flashing with delight.

She was the most down-to-earth woman he'd ever known. Not that he'd known many women. He wasn't the type to attract women, and he knew he hadn't attracted her, but she was easy to talk with, knew horses and cattle and how to run a ranch.

She wore a pair of man's pants cut down to fit her slender hips and, if trouble was brewing, a custom-made Colt revolver strapped to her thigh. Jake had seen her use it once, amazed at the speed with which she had drawn the gun from its holster. She was a fair shot with a rifle and could keep an unruly herd on course. Had she been a man, she would have had the respect of every rancher in Kentucky.

She had been eighteen when he'd first come to the Lazy A, and even then she was beautiful. But her beauty went beyond her long black hair, her little button nose, her golden skin browned over the years as she rode the range. Her real beauty resided in her spirit, a spirit that couldn't be contained, that like the black stallion required the freedom to run. She needed a highborn man who wouldn't try to break her. And Jake Burnett was certainly not a highborn man.

Resting his elbows on the top rail of the fence, he rubbed the uneven bridge of his nose. If his mother had lived, she would have no doubt been disappointed to see how he and Mother Nature had managed to mar the perfectly shaped child she had struggled so hard to bring into the world. The child she had labored to keep alive when smallpox, with its unforgiving temperament, had struck their community. He had only been five at the time, but twenty years later, he could still hear her crooning to him, speaking words of love, her voice stronger than death's. She had poured all her energy, all her strength, all her will to live into him, so when she had come down with the menacing disease, death had taken her instead of her son. The disease had left its mark on him, as it was wont to do, marring his face with shallow valleys, not many, but enough to make him self-conscious.

The black stallion snorted and edged towards him. Reaching out, he rubbed the animal's sleek nose. "No doubt about it. She's going to think you're a handsome sight. Sure as hell wish I was, too."

Earlier in the evening, he'd studied every last man in that bunkhouse. Most were better looking, some were better hands, but none loved Reb as much as he did. He'd felt the tender stirrings of love when she'd bestowed that first smile upon him. His love had grown as he'd spent more time with her, but he'd kept his feelings locked away because to do otherwise would cause him great pain. He'd always planned to leave before she got married because he hadn't wanted to watch her being given away to another man. And now that man might be him. Whatever was her father thinking?

As dawn eased over the horizon, Jake shaved and put on his best working clothes—a pair of brown pants and a light brown shirt. He knew, pregnant or not, Reb would be out on the range. She wasn't one to sit inside waiting on anything. She'd probably just get off her horse, have her baby, and then get back up in the saddle and go chasing after strays. With any luck, that's what he'd find her doing this morning, away from everyone else.

When he came up over the ridge, the early morning mist slowly rising above the ground, he saw her sitting in the morning shade of a towering oak tree, her shoulders against the hard trunk, her head tilted back slightly, her eyes closed. He rubbed his thighs and took a deep breath. He had been up most of the night thinking about what he wanted to say to her, practicing hiding his disappointment when she said no. He had even come up with a list of reasons why she ought to take his offer seriously.

As he dismounted, Rebecca opened her eyes, smiling up at him. "Morning, Jake."

Her voice was a soft caress. What a wondrous sound it would be to wake up to each morning.

Jake tethered his horse to a low-growing bush and walked over. "What you doin', Reb?" he asked, striving to keep the nervousness out of his voice.

"Just enjoying the cool of the morning," she answered. He didn't need to know she'd just brought up her breakfast and was waiting for her stomach to settle before she got back on her horse.

Taking off his hat, Jake hunkered down beside her, balancing himself on the balls of his feet. He had the largest, most expressive velvet brown eyes she had ever seen, framed by long thick black lashes. It didn't seem fair for a man to have such beautiful eyes.

"Fine herd of horses you brought in. Guess you know which one I want."

He smiled at her, a lopsided smile, the right side invariably going up higher than the left. Boyish, a little shy, it was a smile that always warmed her heart.

"Yes, ma'am, I reckon I do. Took me three days to find that black one. Thought I might try and break him Saturday."

She raised a finely arched eyebrow. "Bend him, you mean."

"Yes, ma'am. Bend him."

He turned his hat in his hands, studying it a minute before looking back at her, stating softly, "Reb, your father told me about your situation."

She dropped her head back against the tree, closing her eyes as she released a heavy sigh. "For something he's so damned ashamed of, he sure isn't wasting any time letting people know."

"I think he's concerned you've convinced yourself the man is gonna come back. Your father thinks he won't."

She opened her eyes, blue meeting brown. "And I suppose *you* know he's not coming back?"

"No, ma'am. I don't. I do know people can get ugly,

say mean things to and about someone in your situation. I know what it's like to be called a name you weren't given by your mother when you were born, a name that has nothing to do with anything you could have controlled.''

His eyes held hers as he took an unsteady breath. "I know I'm not much to look at, but I'm a hard worker. I got some land in Texas. I've never seen it, but from what I hear Texas has good ranch land and that's what I'm hoping for. I figured to work here two more years to get together enough money for a good start, but I've got enough saved now so if I decided to go, it wouldn't be too hard a beginning.'' He hesitated, lowering his voice. "I'd be real honored if you'd go with me as my wife.''

Feeling the sting behind her eyes, she smiled tenderly. "Jake, I'm carrying Brett Meier's baby.''

"Figured the baby was his.''

"And I love him.''

"Figured that, too. I'd never expect more from you than you were willing to give, and the child would never know he wasn't mine unless you wanted it that way.''

"And if I could never willingly give you my love?''

*I'd die*, he thought. *I'd just curl up and die.*

"I'd hope maybe you could in time . . . but . . . if you couldn't, I'd understand. See, I figured we'd have more of a partnership than a marriage. Not many women in Texas. If a man doesn't bring a wife, he usually goes a long time before he finds one. I know how to handle the cattle and horses, you know how to handle the books . . . '' He stopped, the remaining reasons irrelevant as he saw the rejection in her eyes. "Anyway, you can just think about it. Offer'll stay open for a while. If you decide no, you don't have to say anything. I'll . . . I'll just know.''

She placed her hand over his. "Thank you, Jake. Thank you for asking and for being such a good friend. And for not condemning.''

"Nothing to condemn. You love him. Reckon he loves you, too.''

She smiled. "He had some prospects he had to check

on. We didn't know I was carrying his child when he left. I do think he'll come back."

Jake nodded. "Man would be a fool not to."

He stood up, looking out across the land. "Think I might bend that horse today." He returned his hat to his head, bringing the brim down low. "See ya 'round, Reb."

The morning breeze rustled the leaves above her as she watched him ride away. She'd liked Jake Burnett the first time she'd set eyes on him. He didn't act the way most of the men who worked the ranch did, strutting their wares and their talents before her. He was quiet and went about his work without stirring up a ruckus, but she noticed him anyway.

They had spent a great deal of time together the last three years, keeping an eye on her cattle, talking about ranching and different odds and ends, not really revealing much of themselves, but never lacking for something to say.

He shied away from social gatherings so she had been surprised to see him attend the last barn-raising dance. It had taken him most of the evening to gather the courage to ask her to dance. She had almost decided she was going to have to do the asking, because she was determined to have at least one dance with him. She had watched him approach two young ladies during the evening, one accepting, the other rejecting his offer for a dance. And watching him dance, she had found herself wanting to be the one in his arms.

He was long gone before the tears started trailing down her cheeks. So far, she hated being pregnant. Throwing up every morning, being tired every afternoon, and crying at the least little thing like a man asking her to marry him. But, Lord, it had been a sweet proposal. Almost worth accepting.

# Chapter Two

IT OCCURRED TO Rebecca that her pregnancy might not be the only cause for her bouts of nausea in the mornings. The strain, tension, and utter madness that was filling the house she and her father had lovingly shared was more than enough to make her ill.

All her life, she had ardently confided in the man who now sat at the table ignoring her. He had always been understanding, always been kind, always given good advice. So it had been natural for her to trust him with this latest bit of news. She had realized her mistake when she saw his hand in the air, a second before it made contact with her cheek, slamming her to the floor. She had been surprised his bellowing hadn't started a stampede. And he hadn't said one word to her since. Not one damn word. Not good morning. Not how are you feeling. And she hadn't said one word to him. They took turns glaring at each other. She'd never thought it would be possible to hate him, this house, this ranch, but she did.

And what if Brett didn't come back? She'd never doubted his love for her, and had never contemplated a future without him in it. And yet he had left, exacting from her no promises, giving her none in return. How long should she wait for him? How long *could* she wait before her present circumstance forced her to leave? She thought she'd go insane if she stayed here much longer.

So what was her alternative? She owned cattle that she had raised and bred. But where could she take them? She no longer cared as long as it was away from here. She thought if Giles looked down his nose at her one more time she'd poke his eyes out. And the little tut-tut noises made with his tongue against his teeth made her want to shriek.

She shoved her plate out of the way, setting her elbows on the table and her chin on her intertwined fingers. "Jake Burnett asked me to marry him today."

Without lifting his eyes from his china plate, her father said, "Good. I told him not to wait too long. I have the marriage ceremony scheduled for a week from Saturday. The Reverend Mitchell will perform the ceremony here at the house."

Rebecca felt the hairs on the back of her neck bristle as her eyes narrowed. "I said he asked me. I didn't say I said yes."

Her father laid down his fork and for the first time in three weeks looked her straight in the eye. "He wanted to ask, but regardless of how you feel, your answer is yes. I will not have you give birth to a child out of wedlock. And Burnett is your best choice. He may not be as fancy a man as you'd like, but he has an innate ability when it comes to ranching."

"You can't force me."

His eyes became as hard as stone, and for the first time in her life, she actually feared her father.

"Rebecca, I have not acquired all that I have by being tenderhearted. I have overlooked a great deal of your transgressions, not saying no when I should have, letting you run free when I should have harnessed you. Believe me, daughter, if you think these past weeks have been miserable, embarrass me a week from Saturday and you'll discover that there is indeed hell on earth."

"I don't believe I'm hearing this from you."

"Believe it. I came here with nothing. More than this ranch, more than you, I value the respect the people in this area give me. I will not have it shattered because one night you decided to become a whore."

She blinked back her tears. "How can you hate me so much?"

Anderson began eating. "I don't hate you. I'm just deeply disappointed in you. Once you have fulfilled your obligations regarding this marriage, I'm sure everything will return to normal. You'll wear your mother's wedding dress."

"May I be excused?"

Her father gave a curt nod and Rebecca left the table, willing herself not to run screaming out of the house.

She found Jake in the barn, kneeling in a stall and cooing to a troubled mare. He was so intent on his task he didn't hear her approach. She knew it was unfair but she clasped her hands together and pounded on his back, sending him sprawling over the mare, who protested by kicking him.

"What the—" He scrambled up, holding his side, glaring at her. "What the hell did you do that for?"

Her fists were rolled into tight balls, her chest was heaving, her eyes were ablaze with cerulean fire. "My father said your proposal was no such thing! It was a command! I have no choice but to marry you!"

Jake released a weary sigh. "Well, he was wrong." He dropped to his knees, his hands comforting the distressed animal. "The foal is breech. I gotta turn him. Will you hold the mare's head?"

Rebecca knelt down, laying the mare's head on her lap, stroking her gently. "So I don't have to marry you?"

"Hell no. I wouldn't marry a woman who didn't want to marry me. He told me he wanted me to marry you and I said I'd ask. But that's all. I'd ask. The final decision is yours."

She watched as he struggled to turn the foal. Would any other man have accepted an offer of John Anderson's ranch and daughter only if she was willing? "He doesn't know about your land in Texas, does he?"

"No." He continued working, the strain evident in his voice. "I didn't tell him. I was afraid he might offer—" He shot her a quick glance, wishing he was better with words as she arched a brow.

"Might offer me to someone else?"

"Might tell someone else about your situation before I got a chance to ask."

Satisfied with his efforts, he began to caress the mare, his bloodied hands gentle on the great beast, his voice tender. "All right, girl."

The foal was born, struggling to stand. Rebecca watched Jake's face fill with tenderness and awe in the miracle he'd just witnessed. He scooted back against the wall, watching the newborn creature.

"Why?" Rebecca asked quietly. "Why did you ask me to marry you? You've offered me your name, a piece of your dreams. What do you get?"

He had slept so little last night and the day had been long, filled with chores. Then the mare had gone into a difficult labor. How could he explain his reasons when he hadn't thought about them yet himself? If not her love, what did he get? Her eyes were so blue and her ebony hair cascaded about her, creating the perfect frame for her face, so beautiful. His voice was low, his eyes warm.

"It's a rugged land, filled with the voices of men, the wild cries of animals. I'd have the soft, sweet music of a woman's voice. When winter browns and deadens the earth, I'd only have to look across the room to see the beauty of spring. I'd have friendship in the place of loneliness. I'd have more than I ever hoped to have."

He wasn't usually such a flowery speaker. But the words, like him, were honest and they touched her heart. If a woman couldn't marry the man she loved, she should at least marry a man she liked. And Rebecca did like Jake. She enjoyed his company, the emotions reflected in his eyes, the gentleness he bestowed upon the animals. But to decide now . . .

"Would you take a walk with me?" she asked.

Offering her a small smile, he nodded.

They strolled out of the barn and Jake detoured by the water pump to wash his hands. Then they continued on into the night, skirting around the buildings until they were walking along the dirt path that led to the house, a comfortable silence enveloping them. A warm breeze blew across the land. Rebecca reached back and grabbed her hair, draping it over one shoulder before slumping against one of the many trees that lined the path. "How did you come by your land in Texas?" she asked.

Jake rubbed the side of his nose. "Man who raised me left it to me when he died."

"He must have thought a great deal of you to leave you something as precious as land."

He shook his head. "To tell you the truth, Reb, I don't know why he left it to me. He had two sons. Seems like he should have left it to one of them."

She moved her hands behind her back and pressed against the tree. "So why are you here and not in Texas?"

"Because the land is the only thing Thomas Truscott ever gave me. I started heading that way . . . then I realized I needed money." He shrugged. "Your father was hiring."

Rebecca looked up into the black heavens, distant stars twinkling. If she were a little girl, she'd latch onto one of them and make a wish. But she wasn't a little girl anymore. In Brett's arms, she'd become a woman, and soon she'd become a mother. Her heart believed that Brett would return to take her as his wife, to be a father to her child, but her father's words, his anger, and the endless days with no word from Brett had begun to plant seeds of doubt within her mind. During any other time in her life she would have listened to her heart. But now she had a life more precious than her own to consider.

"Oh, Jake, I don't know if Brett's coming back," she said in a hoarse whisper, fighting back the tears that accompanied the acknowledgment of her fears, angry at herself for being so weak. "He didn't say he would. He just said he had some things he had to take care of."

Jake shoved his hands into his pockets, not certain what he'd do if those tears gathering in her eyes started rolling down her cheeks. "Maybe we could track him down."

She gave him a tremulous smile. "I thought about that, but I don't even know in which direction he headed. And after two months, even the best trackers would have a hard time finding him.

"I've made such a mess of things. A month ago, all I worried about was whether or not you'd find me a black stallion. And now . . . I've never had anyone as angry at me as my father is. It's as though he hates me.'' She released a ragged sigh. "Tonight was the first time in three weeks he's spoken to me, and it was to tell me that if I didn't marry you, he'd make my life hell.''

Without thinking, he reached out, his knuckle catching the solitary tear as it began to trail down her cheek. "I swear if you married me, I'd do everything I could to make sure you never regretted it.''

"And what about you? What if you regret it?''

He gave her a small smile, shaking his head. "I won't regret it.''

She studied the rugged contours of Jake's face limned by the light of a full moon. A lifetime. A lifetime with this man. To accept now that Brett wasn't coming back or that if he did, it would be too late. To spend a lifetime gazing into velvet brown eyes instead of blue. To be greeted with a lopsided grin instead of a straight full smile. To live with a man willing to give so much and ask for so little. She swallowed her uncertainty, giving him a smile in its place.

"I'd be honored to become your wife and go with you to Texas.''

"You sure?''

"I'm sure,'' she said without hesitation.

He bestowed upon her his lopsided, endearing smile and extended his hand.

She slipped her hand into his rough, callused one, a hand that gentled the horses, a hand that might bring her child into this world. Stretching up, she placed a brief kiss on his cheek. "Meet me in the morning where you found me today and we'll work out the details.''

Watching her stroll towards the house, Jake felt as though his heart would break out of his chest. That beautiful woman was going to be his wife.

Hearing the retching sounds as he dismounted, Jake headed for the bush where Rebecca was standing, feet braced apart, her body bent over at the waist.

"You all right?" he asked, concerned.

"Will be—" She gestured him away as another wave of nausea broke through bringing up the remainder of her breakfast. Taking three great gulps of air, she stood up as a canteen of water was thrust in front of her. Smiling, she took the cool water into her mouth, swishing it around before spitting it out. Then she faced Jake, who had broken out in a light film of sweat watching her.

"You should have left," she said.

"Did you do this yesterday?"

She walked over to the tree and sat down. "And the day before that and the day before that."

Jake dropped down beside her. She looked at him with woeful eyes.

"I don't know how the human race continues. Having babies is no fun as far as I can tell. Growing up on a ranch, I'm used to birthing but I didn't know about this. I've never seen a mare bring up her breakfast . . . or a dog . . . or a pig . . . or a chicken."

Jake started laughing and she hit him on the arm. "It's not funny."

"I know." He tried to stop laughing. "I'm real sorry you're feeling poorly but . . . the world would be a mess if animals were throwing up all over the place."

"But it's not fair!"

"No, I reckon it's not. Maybe it won't last long."

"It's already lasted too long as far as I'm concerned." Sighing, she leaned her head back, closing her eyes. "My father has our wedding set for a week from Saturday. I'd like to get married here if that's all right with you."

"We'll do this however you want."

She opened her eyes, fixing them on his. "My father isn't going to be happy we're leaving. I don't want to tell him until we're ready to go. And I want to leave the day after we're married."

That gave them ten days to get ready. "You sure you should be traveling?"

"If I weren't used to riding, I'd worry. But I think as

long as I don't do anything I don't normally do, I'll be fine. I want to leave now.''

''I'll have to get into town to get my money and some supplies. I could do that this Saturday.''

She leaned forward, resting her elbow on an upturned knee, the luster returning to her eyes. Lord, but he loved that sparkle in her blue eyes, like the sun reflecting off a mirrored lake.

''I have five hundred Herefords we can take with us. My contribution to the partnership. We can use the old line shack on the north side to store our things until we're ready to go.''

''We'll have to hire a few men to help us with the herd,'' he said. ''Guess I'd best start figuring up everything we'll need.''

''Everything's happening kind of fast, isn't it?'' she asked.

''Yep. But that's probably for the best. We'd probably both run off in opposite directions if we stopped to think about it too long.''

He stood up, helping her to her feet. It was a warm day, the wind blowing across the sea of tall grasses, teasing the leaves in the majestic trees. And it occurred to Jake that they had just finished planning the beginning of their life together.

The men inside the bunkhouse were tittering like little old ladies, but Jake ignored them as he sat on his bunk trying to make a list of all the supplies they'd need. He could thank Thomas Truscott for his ability to read and write. As long as he had kept up on his chores, he had been allowed to attend the one-room schoolhouse that had serviced their community. Allowed—as if it were a privilege instead of a right that everyone should have.

He had left the Truscott ranch unprepared. He didn't plan to leave this one the same way. He'd learned a lot in three years, and he intended to put all his knowledge to good use. He drew an unplanned line across the paper as his arm was roughly nudged.

"Did you know, Jake?"

He glanced up and smiled at Frank Lewis, the only person besides Reb he'd ever considered a true friend. The red-haired youth had been raised in the city. In search of adventure, he'd signed on at the Lazy A shortly after Jake had. Knowing how much experienced ranch hands liked to pick on city boys, Jake had taken it upon himself to teach Frank the things he'd need to know to survive life on a ranch.

"Know what?" He hadn't been listening, and he really couldn't have cared less, but he didn't want to crush Frank's excitement. Considering the fresh nicks on Frank's face, he figured Frank was going to announce that he was having to shave every day now.

"Know about Reb getting married?"

He felt the heat warming his face and he just hoped the red creeping up it wasn't visible. "Yeah, I knew."

"Goddamn! So it is true! Goddamn! Reb getting married! Wonder who the lucky son-of-a-bitch is. Any idea, Jake?"

Along with shaving, Frank thought the use of "goddamn" was a sign of manhood. Jake refrained from smiling at his overabundant use of the word. Once would have sufficed to get his message across.

Jake hadn't given any thought as to how he would tell people he was marrying Reb, and he wasn't exactly sure how to tell Frank now without sounding as though he were bragging. He was given a momentary reprieve when the door to the bunkhouse opened.

"Jake!" Bassett's bellowing voice filled the room.

Jake peered around Frank. "Yes, sir?"

"Anderson's expecting you up at the house for supper at seven. Be on time, boy."

"Yes, sir."

Frank's eyes widened. "Why's Anderson having you up to the house for supper?"

Although Jake had told Frank about his plans to be a rancher, he'd never shared his past or his feelings for Reb with his friend. Self-consciously, he cleared his throat.

"Reckon it's because I'm the lucky son-of-a-bitch that's marrying Reb."

Frank's eyes widened further, and Jake wondered how they managed to stay in his head. "Goddamn! Reb's marrying you?"

Jake couldn't stop the smile from spreading across his face. "Yep."

Frank's face fell and he looked like a mongrel pup that someone had just kicked out into the snow. "But what about your land in Texas?"

Jake threw a glance around the bunkhouse before motioning Frank closer. "We're still going," he said in a hushed tone. "Only now Reb's going with us."

"Is her father gonna like that?"

"Probably not, which is why we need to keep quiet about it."

Nodding his understanding, Frank straightened his lanky frame. Then his face broke out into a broad smile. "Goddamn! You are a lucky son-of-a-bitch!"

Jake had never seen so much cutlery set out beside one plate in his entire life. One fork, one knife, that's all a man needed to eat a meal. He realized sitting at this table that all the decisions he and Reb had made that morning regarding their leaving had been easy. What was difficult was trying to decide which damn fork to pick up. It wouldn't be so bad if they all looked the same, but they didn't. If he picked up the wrong one, everyone would know. Dear Lord, she must have grown up making these decisions at supper every night.

She cleared her throat and Jake's gaze snapped from the silverware to a pair of blue eyes. She twirled a fork in her hand. Jake nodded slightly and picked up an identical fork. Lord, he hoped she wasn't planning on bringing all this cutlery with her on the trail.

"Now then, Jake," Anderson began. "I had a meeting with my lawyer today and out of fairness to you, I have had my will rewritten to leave this ranch to any children that you and Rebecca have together, thereby assuring this unfortunate offspring takes nothing away from your own children.''

Jake saw the fire ignite in Rebecca's eyes. His own temper heated up, but he controlled it.

''Mr. Anderson, I've always considered you a fair man, but this here doesn't sound fair to me. With all due respect, sir, this child is Reb's and is entitled to a part of this ranch.''

''This child is another man's leavings. Rebecca is damn fortunate you have chosen to overlook her transgressions and for that I intend to show my appreciation.''

The fork clattered as it hit the china and Rebecca shoved her plate back. ''I'm finished. May I be excused?''

''No, you may not be excused. You'll wait until your betrothed is finished before you leave this table.''

Carefully, Jake set his fork down. ''Actually, sir, I'm finished. I'm not used to such fine fare, and I need to be checking on that foal. If you'll excuse us . . . ''

Anderson nodded. Neither Jake nor Rebecca could leave the table fast enough. Jake took her elbow when they reached the hall. ''Let's get some fresh air.''

They walked outside, heading for the corral.

''Has he been like that the whole time?'' Jake asked.

''When he talks to me. I guess I should be grateful he says as little as he does.'' She spun around. ''You understand why I can't stay, don't you?''

''I understand,'' he said solemnly.

''Even though I'm getting married, he'll never accept this child. He'll always single him out. . . . I don't want this child feeling different, Jake.''

''He won't.'' He looked off into the night. It dawned on him that since he didn't walk around with a large ''B'' branded on his forehead his parentage might not be as evident to everyone else as it was to him. Out of fairness, he realized he should at least tell Rebecca. He forced his gaze back to hers. ''I'm a bastard, Reb. My mother was a . . . '' He swallowed. It was just a word, but it was a word that should never be associated with a mother, especially his mother. ''She was a prostitute. I don't know for sure who my father was. I have an idea but I can't be positive.''

Resting her hand on his arm, she searched his eyes.
''That's what you meant about being called names. Oh,
Jake, I just thought you meant children's teasing. You know
firsthand what this child would go through growing up.''

A sadness crept into his eyes. ''What they say about
words not hurting . . . it's not true. I would have preferred
the sticks and stones.''

She studied his face. He may not have had sticks and
stones, but she was certain he'd had some fists. ''Did you
get into fights because of your background?''

Self-consciously, he rubbed the uneven bridge of his
nose. ''Yeah.''

She touched the scar above his brow, wondering how
many other things she didn't know about him. Things she
would learn in time, things about her that she supposed he
would learn.

He wrapped his fingers around hers, bringing her hand
away from his face, and they continued walking towards
the corral.

Rebecca rested her arms on the fence, her chin on her
arms. ''He's giving us ten of these horses as a wedding
present. Pick out the best and we'll take them with us.''

''Speaking of what we're taking with us. . . . '' Jake gave
her a hard stare. ''You're not planning on taking all those
forks with you, are you?''

Her laughter filled the night, washing over him like a
summer storm. ''No. Two should do it. One for me and
one for you.''

Jake released a sigh of relief. ''Thank God.''

She slipped her arm through his as they started walking
back towards the house. ''What are all those men doing
outside the bunkhouse this time of night?'' she asked.

They stopped walking a few feet from the house. Jake
rubbed the back of his neck. Some of the men had seemed
downright disgruntled when the news of his marriage to
Reb had spread through the bunkhouse. Others had thrown
threatening glances his way. He couldn't blame them.

"Well, they heard you were marrying me and most of them ain't believing it."

"And why not?"

"Because they have the same opinion I do."

"Which is?"

Oh, Lord, he was going to lose her now. "That you're a beautiful woman and could marry any man you wanted. All you'd have to do is let him know. As a matter of fact, Reb, I was thinking . . . if there's someone else—"

She put one of her slender fingers to his lips. "Don't you think they're going to think it a little strange if you don't give me a good-night kiss?"

"Would you mind?"

"If they thought it strange?"

"No." His eyes lovingly caressed her face. She was offering him more than he'd hoped for. "Would you mind if I gave you a good-night kiss?"

Her smile was warm, her lips inviting. "No, I wouldn't mind at all."

He removed his hat. Placing a roughened hand on the nape of her neck, bringing her close, he leaned down to brush his lips against hers, feeling the softness, the fullness of them against his own. He lingered only a moment before pulling back, afraid the temptation to taste the sweetness of her mouth would overpower him.

"Good night, Reb." His voice was drowned out by the catcalls and kissing sounds of the men at the bunkhouse. "Damn cowboys," he muttered.

Smiling up at him, she turned and started skipping back towards the house. "They'll be worse at the wedding!" she called out over her shoulder.

Jake headed towards the bunkhouse, shoving his hat down low over his brow, ignoring every question that was asked since every question was the same, only asked in a different voice. How had he managed to convince Rebecca Anderson to marry him?

Rebecca blew the lamp out before walking to the window of her bedroom. Looking out over the east side of the ranch, her gaze fell onto the bunkhouse. As she traced the outline of her lips with her finger, she wondered if Jake was already asleep. Although the kiss had been brief and as light as fairy wings, she could still feel exactly where his lips had covered hers. She had been surprised to feel her heart beating so hard, to hear its thundering in her ears, and to realize she felt disappointed when he had said good night.

A lifetime. She wrapped her arms around herself and smiled. A lifetime.

# Chapter Three

IT DIDN'T TAKE long for the black stallion to learn who was master, although Rebecca knew it would take a few more months for the sinewy mustang to adapt and become the first-rate cutting pony she wanted. His training would begin on the trail when they left for Texas.

"I'm going to call him Shadow!" Rebecca called out, smiling at Jake. Her smile was even broader than the one she'd given him when she'd first watched him work with the horses. She felt a swelling of pride in her chest that threatened to burst the buttons on her shirt.

Her eyes were as bright as the sun and Jake couldn't resist giving her his own smile, which had nothing to do with his success in taming the horse, and everything to do with that gorgeous expression he'd been able to bring forth on her face. He removed his hat and hit at the dust on his pants. When he looked up, she placed her hand on the back of his head, planting a kiss on his lips to the hoots of the few men who had come to watch the horses being broken.

His smile became as broad as hers. "Do that every time I break a horse, and I'll break the whole herd instead of the ten that belong to us."

Rebecca laughed, a sweet, melodic laugh as she released him and turned her attention to the restless horses prancing in the corral.

"Which one do you want next?" he asked her.

"The palomino."

He rolled his eyes. "Not going after any without spirit, are you?"

"No need to when I got you."

Her words warmed him as much as her lips pressing against his. He plopped his hat back on his head. "Okay, boys, she wants the palomino!"

After witnessing the hostility Anderson had been directing at his daughter, Jake had decided breaking the horses might be what Reb needed to take her mind off her troubles. And it certainly did seem to be doing the trick. The tension lines he'd spotted beneath her eyes that morning were gone and the smile had returned to her face. He intended to make sure she understood that she was no longer carrying her burdens alone.

The days before the wedding flew by like a flock of birds heading south for the winter. Jake bought a wagon and some supplies, storing everything at the north line shack.

One evening he took Rebecca into town to have dinner at the hotel so they could have a relaxed meal without her father. It was comforting to find that despite the strain of the coming marriage, together, alone, they were at ease with each other. For appearance's sake, he would kiss her good night because eyes were always watching somewhere, but the kisses remained chaste. Not a night went by that he didn't go to sleep without his last thoughts concentrating on eyes of blue and all he would do to keep them sparkling and happy.

Rebecca sank down into the tub, leisurely washing herself with the scented soap her father had imported from France for her. She leaned back, the warm waters creating a mist around her. The groom wasn't the man she'd spent countless nights dreaming about, wasn't the man she loved, wasn't the father of her child. But Jake Burnett was a good man. In all the time she'd known him, he'd never shown her anything but kindness.

She stepped out of the water and dried herself off with soft towels before sitting down before her mirror. She gazed at her reflection, somehow expecting it to look different.

But it didn't. She took a deep breath and began to prepare herself for the most important day of her life.

When she was satisfied with her efforts, she moved to the window, looking out at the familiar view. She had once found comfort here. All her future comforts resided with the man awaiting her downstairs.

She stepped into the hallway.

"My God, girl, you look just like your mother standing there," her father said as he approached her.

It was the first time he had ever indicated she resembled her mother, although she had suspected it. He kept no portraits of her mother, had only on rare occasions even mentioned her. Her death during Rebecca's delivery had shattered her father. Until this moment, it had never occurred to her that she was a constant reminder of the woman he had loved.

Anderson extended his arm to his daughter and she slipped her hand around it.

"All these years," he said, "I thought she had left me, and this evening, I see that she was with me all along. What a wonderful gift you are." He kissed her cheek. "You're a beautiful bride."

Tears sprang to Rebecca's eyes at her father's kind words, words similar to so many he had spoken over the years. His harsh treatment after she told him about the baby had hurt her terribly. Her tears were also brought on by the knowledge that in a small way she was betraying him. She gave him a heartfelt smile. "I love you, Daddy. Remember that. No matter what happens. I love you."

They descended the sweeping stairs and stepped into her father's study. The sea of guests parted. She saw Jake, wearing a crisp white shirt and a black tie, standing before the window. Beside him stood Frank Lewis, looking more nervous than the groom.

Jake's mouth went dry at the sight of his bride, the white silk dress adorned with tiny pearls fitting her as though she had been molded inside of it. She wore a wreath of tiny flowers, her long, black hair cascading down her narrow back. The long skirt whispered across the floor as she came to stand beside him.

Tentatively, she released her hold on her father and slipped her arm through Jake's as her father moved away.

Jake cupped her cheek with his palm, his eyes searching hers. "If you've changed your mind, I'll step aside." His voice was low, his words for her alone.

"I haven't. Have you?"

Slowly he shook his head, his gaze delving so deeply into hers, she felt their souls touching, mating, taking vows stronger than the ones that were about to be spoken aloud.

Reverend Mitchell studied the young couple standing before him. He had spoken at length with Jake earlier. Jake had confided the special circumstances surrounding his marriage to Rebecca. Mitchell knew beyond any doubt that Jake loved Rebecca. He wasn't certain of Rebecca's feelings. He knew she cared for Jake. Her actions in preparing herself for the exchange of vows was a testament to her feelings. But he also knew she carried another man's child, which would always give her a strong bond to that other man. He had married many couples whose marriages were not initially brought on by love. He knew love tended to sneak up on people. He read a passage from Corinthians, hoping the words that so effectively described love would guide Rebecca so she would recognize love when it came to reside in her heart.

When the passage ended, he asked the couple to hold hands while they faced each other repeating their vows after him.

Her blue eyes held his brown ones as Rebecca began, her voice soft and sweet. "I, Rebecca Lynn Anderson, take thee, Jake Burnett, to be my lawfully wedded husband . . ." She stopped, not expecting Mitchell's next words of "honor and cherish." Her eyes searched the reverend's. "I thought it was supposed to be 'love, honor, and obey.' "

Reverend Mitchell smiled, lifting a brow. "Jake didn't think you would obey."

She blushed, the heat warming her face. "He knows me too well."

Mitchell leaned down and spoke softly. "And Jake didn't want you to exchange empty vows. I thought these would give you a good foundation upon which to build your life together. Honor him as your husband, cherish him as your friend."

She turned her attention back to Jake and squeezed his hands. "To honor and cherish, in sickness and in health, for better or worse, through richer and poorer, forsaking all others, as long as we both shall live."

Jake cleared his throat before following Mitchell's voice with his own, deep and true. "I, Jake Burnett, take thee, Rebecca Lynn Anderson, to be my lawfully wedded wife, to love, honor, and cherish, in sickness and in health, for better or worse, through richer and poorer, forsaking all others, as long as we both shall live." He reached out, took a gold band with tiny roses engraved on it from Frank, and slipped it on the third finger of Rebecca's left hand. It fit perfectly. "With this ring, I thee wed," he added.

Reverend Mitchell clasped their hands in his own. "What God has joined together, let no man put asunder. You may kiss the bride."

Rebecca tilted her face up to Jake and she felt his lips brushing lightly against hers. Then his lips were beside her ear, whispering, "A lifetime of happiness, Reb, I promise."

She felt the stinging behind her eyes, no longer certain she was worthy of this man, promising herself she would do everything in her power to be.

Handshakes, kisses, and congratulations were profusely offered. The din of conversation circled around Rebecca and there were moments when she felt like she was a little girl again, holding her arms straight out and whirling until the earth seemed to move about her. She felt flushed and breathing became difficult. Then she felt a strong hand clamp down on her waist and found herself being led away from the well-wishers.

She stepped onto the veranda and inhaled deeply before looking up into her husband's face. "Thank you."

"It's a little overwhelming."

She laughed softly. "It is, isn't it?"

Jake moved his hand away from her waist and leaned against a pillar. "Think you'll miss it?"

She shook her head. "There was a time when I couldn't imagine leaving. And now . . . Now I can't wait to leave."

The guests began trickling outside where tables and benches had been set up. Food was served. Toasts were made. The sunset burst forth its hues of lavenders and pinks, oranges, and blues as the husband and wife sat side by side entranced with nature's gift on their wedding day.

As day bid its final farewell to night, the guests departed. Rebecca found herself standing alone with Jake in the study, not certain where her father had discreetly disappeared to, but grateful he had. Jake was watching her as though he were waiting for something. Then she realized he wouldn't be sleeping in the bunkhouse. He was her husband now. He had married her, had earned the right to sleep in her bed. She inhaled deeply, strengthening her resolve. "I guess we'll sleep in my room tonight."

Jake nodded and followed her up the stairs. She opened the door to her room and stood within the threshold, waiting, uncertain. It didn't seem real, but this was her wedding night. Her wedding night and she didn't have a special nightgown. She wasn't even sure if she needed one or not. She had always expected her wedding night to be a little different. She thought she'd be swept off her feet, carried to the bed. . . .

"You going in?" a deep voice asked behind her.

She jumped into the room, wringing her hands, looking at everything that had once been so familiar and now seemed so foreign. She heard the door close quietly behind her and moved further into the room.

Jake glanced around, his eyes falling on the pink ruffled bedspread that covered the bed.

"This is your room?" he asked.

She turned, blushing as she saw where his gaze was directed. "Yes, what's wrong with it?"

Smiling, he looked at her. "Nothing. I just didn't expect it to be so frilly."

She tilted her chin up defiantly. "Just because I like cows

doesn't mean I don't like feminine things as well.''

''No, I suppose it doesn't.'' He moved to the bed and sat down.

She turned and began to study the flowered wallpaper. It wasn't that frilly. She heard one boot thump to the floor and then the other. Then she heard the sound of his shirt being tugged out of his pants.

''Reb?''

She spun around, eyes wide. ''What?''

''Come here,'' he said as he patted the bed.

She walked over, standing in front of him, feeling the familiar tug on her heart as he gave her a lopsided grin.

''Sit down.''

She sat down on the bed, her back straight as a board, her hands clasped together in her lap.

''You seem a little nervous,'' Jake said.

She swallowed. ''Aren't brides supposed to be nervous on their wedding night?''

He placed his large, warm hand over her trembling ones.

''Not this bride and not this wedding night. I told you why I asked you to marry me, and I told you what I expected—no more than you're willing to give.''

''Don't you want to consummate the marriage?''

''No, I don't. I want to make love to you. But not until you're ready. Not until it's what you want.''

Her hands unclasped and he slipped his fingers through hers. ''It's been a hell of a week and a long day,'' he said. ''Tomorrow is going to be even longer. I think it'd be best if we both got a good night's sleep.''

Her eyes shot up to his, expressing gratitude. He ignored the pain her obvious relief brought him.

Her cheeks took on a pink hue. ''I need to get my nightgown.''

She lifted herself off the bed and walked to her dresser. As she fumbled around in the drawers, she wondered why she couldn't remember in which drawer she kept her nightgowns. She finally located a plain white one and spun around triumphantly.

Jake was laying on the bed, eyes closed, the covers

drawn over him. She tiptoed to the bed and stared down at him. He had fallen asleep.

After lowering the flame in the lamp, she undressed and slipped the gown over her head. Lifting the covers, she began to ease herself into the bed. Jake's arm came up and she froze.

"I thought you were asleep," she scolded.

"I know," he said, and she could hear the smile in his voice.

"Did you watch me undress?"

"No."

She looked at his hand lifted in the air, outlined by the dim light of the moon. "What are you doing?"

"I thought I might hold you."

"Oh." The thought brought with it a measure of excitement. It would almost be as though they were husband and wife, but she wondered how close he intended to hold her. "Are you completely unclothed?"

"No. Only took off my shirt and my pants."

"And your boots."

"And my boots."

She wondered if he'd ever dreamed about his wedding night the way she'd dreamed about hers. The reality of the night was far removed from the dream.

She lay down, drawing the cover over her as his arm slowly came around her shoulders.

"You could put your head on my shoulder, if you like," he said.

Tentatively, she rested her head in the crook of his shoulder, her cheek pressed against his bare chest. She could feel the warmth of his skin, hear the pounding of his heart. She placed her hand on his stomach and felt him stiffen. She smiled. He was as nervous as she was about their sleeping together. She relaxed against him, fingering the unfamiliar ring on her hand. "Where did you get the ring?"

He ran his fingers lightly over the sleeve of her gown. "It was my mother's. Not her wedding ring. She was never married. It was just a ring she had. I always liked it. It's the only thing of hers that I have. I wanted you to have it.

Hope you don't mind . . . I mean it not being a real wedding ring and all.''

"I don't mind. It's beautiful. So delicate. It means a lot to me that you'd give it to me.''

"Means a lot to me that you'd wear it.''

They lay in silence for a few moments before Jake spoke again.

"You looked beautiful this evening, Reb.''

"I wanted to do something special for you.''

"You did. You married me.'' His hand stopped moving. "That dress fit you like a glove. You sure don't look pregnant. When is this baby due anyway?''

"January.''

Jake counted back the months and asked quietly, "Last barn raising?''

Rebecca sighed. "Yes.''

He had a hundred questions he wanted to ask her, but he had no right to the answers. "Good night, Reb.''

"Jake?''

"What?''

"Will you give me a good-night kiss? You know . . . the kind of kiss brides usually get on their wedding nights.''

Jake shifted his body until they were both lying on their sides, facing each other. He trailed his fingers along her jaw. "I don't know much about the kinds of kisses brides get . . . but I know the kind of kiss I'd like to give you.''

He worked his other hand out from underneath her and cupped her face, bringing his lips against hers, pressing firmly against her soft flesh. She sighed and he slipped his tongue through her parted lips, tasting her for the first time, their tongues introducing themselves as they slowly waltzed around each other.

Rebecca felt a warm stirring deep within her, not certain she wanted the kiss to end, not certain she wanted to roll over and go to sleep. His kiss was as undemanding as his proposal. So different from any kiss Brett had ever given her. It was different from any kiss she'd ever received, touching her deeper than any kiss before it.

His breathing was labored as he ended the kiss and

placed his lips lightly on her forehead. "Go to sleep now, Reb."

She complied and Jake took her soft hair between two of his fingers, rubbing gently. He had just stepped into purgatory. Whatever had he been thinking when he'd promised not to take more than she was willing to give? What if she never wanted to love him emotionally or physically? He was lying in bed with the woman he loved . . . a woman he couldn't make love to. He closed his eyes. More than anything in this world, he wanted this woman to be happy. He'd give her anything, do anything to make her happy. Even if it made his own life hell.

Rebecca squinted against the early morning sunlight filtering into the room. Languorously, she stretched her body before opening her eyes fully and catching sight of the shirtless man standing at the table. He was splashing water on his face, using the water in her washbasin. She had seen him bare-chested before, but somehow knowing he was now her husband made everything about him seem different. She had never noticed how his lean frame showed a strength brought on by years of herding cattle and working on a ranch. His skin was taut across his muscles, the absence of hair on his chest lending a smoothness to his form as his muscles rippled with his movements.

Glancing over at her, he reached for his shirt. Rebecca felt herself redden from the top of her head to the tips of her toes, and she brought the covers up to her neck.

He gave her a small smile. "Morning."

Relaxing her grip on the blankets, she returned his smile. "Good morning."

"Half a dozen of your father's men want to come to Texas with us. Thought I'd go on out and get them moving."

She watched the way his hands worked the buttons on his shirt, wondering how it would have felt to have had those hands work the buttons on her wedding gown. "That's probably a good idea."

He reached for his hat and walked to the door. "You

just come on down when you're ready." His smile increased. "I won't leave without you."

"I wouldn't want you to," she said softly.

Sitting on her horse, Rebecca listened as Jake issued the orders to take the ten horses he had broken and then to round up the cattle that bore her brand, the Rocking R. As the men rode off, she heard a distant door slam. She turned towards the house, watching her father storming down the walk, his silk robe flapping in his wake, his fist pounding at the air high above his head.

"What the hell is going on here, Rebecca?"

"We're leaving, Daddy. Jake has some land in Texas. We're going to have our own ranch there."

Jake sidled his horse up beside Rebecca's, not wanting her to face her father's wrath alone.

"Dammit!" Anderson's face reddened and the veins in his neck threatened to explode as he glared at Jake. "Dammit! You son-of-a-bitch, I didn't give you my daughter so you could take her away! I'll have this marriage annulled."

"That's going to be a little hard to do," Jake said calmly. "Considering she's carrying my baby."

Anderson took a step towards Jake, controlled rage evident in his voice. "That baby is not yours."

"Can you prove it?" Jake asked.

Rebecca felt the warmth spread throughout her heart. He was claiming the child as his even before it was born.

Anderson glared at his daughter. "Get down off that horse, girl. You're not going anywhere. I'll get you an annulment. I won't make you marry anyone. We'll put it up for adoption when it's born."

*It*, she thought, *it*. As though the child wasn't already flesh and blood growing inside of her. Tears brimming in her eyes, she shook her head.

"Dammit, girl. I raised you to take over this ranch when I died. I won't have all my hard work go to nothing. You're my daughter and you'll do what I say!"

"She's my wife and she'll do what she wants."

The words were wrapped in compassion and understanding, a gift Rebecca accepted into her heart. Her gaze met Jake's and she recognized all that he was offering beneath the words. She had but to dismount and he'd ride away, leaving her his name.

"I'm going with Jake."

Anderson reined in his anger, his blue eyes assessing his daughter as he laid down his final card. "Leave with him, Rebecca, and I'll disown you. You'll be dead to me. You'll never know my love again, girl."

"Your love, Daddy? Is this love talking now?"

"I only want what's best for you, girl."

"And I want what's best for my baby. I'm going to Texas with Jake. We're taking my cattle and the horses you gave us. When the time comes, I'll let you know if you have a grandson or a granddaughter."

"Don't bother. I'll never recognize the child or any that comes of your union with this man." He nodded towards Jake. "You're a fool, Rebecca Anderson."

"The name is Rebecca Burnett. And I think, Daddy, that you're the fool." She gave the man she had loved for twenty-one years of her life a last look before turning her horse and galloping out of his life.

Jake followed her, and when the house was no longer in sight, he reached over and grabbed the reins of her horse, pulling them both to a halt. He dismounted, then walked over and pulled her off her horse, bringing his arms around her as she sobbed against his chest.

"Oh, Jake, why is the whole world turning ugly?"

"Not the whole world. Just a few people, a few moments. I reckon we need the ugly to appreciate the beauty."

He wiped the warm tears rolling down her smooth cheek with his thumb. Her skin, unlike his, was flawless, and her blue eyes, hurt and confused, overflowing with tears, were looking up at him.

"You can stay, Reb."

"I know. But I'd rather go with you."

He pressed his lips to one swollen eyelid and then another. "I'll never hurt you the way he did. I swear it." His lips followed the trail of tears until they reached her mouth.

He opened his mouth over hers and she welcomed him, needing his closeness. The kiss was not passionate. It did not take her breath away or make her tremble with desire the way Brett's had, but instead filled her with a sense of security, a sense of belonging, of being important to one human being. All the things her father had taken away from her, Jake was giving back.

He rubbed her cheek, his smile sincere. "I think it's time we headed for Texas."

He helped her mount her horse and when he had mounted his own, she reached over and squeezed his hand.

"I think I'm going to like being your wife."

He leaned over touching one corner of her small smile. "I never want you to regret it, Reb. We'll make it a good life."

As they began their journey, Rebecca didn't look back. Her future lay ahead with the man riding beside her. In such a short time, her world had been shattered. But beside her rode a man who would help her rebuild it with love and trust and sacrifice.

# Chapter Four

Texas, 1883

LADENED WITH SUPPLIES, the wagon creaked as it rolled over the fertile land. Jake halted its progress, set the brake and jumped down, then walked out past the horses.

Rebecca knew he was anxious about the land, about coming to Texas knowing as little about the place as he did. The closer they'd come to arriving, the less he'd talked. They'd discreetly left camp as the sun peered over the horizon because Jake wanted to see his land without the other men milling around.

She watched now as he removed his hat, looking out over the rolling expanse of green that was visible for miles, clumps of trees dotting the landscape. She saw his back straighten with pride and knew, even though she was only staring at his back, that he was pleased with what lay before him. So she was quite surprised when he turned around and she saw all the doubts plaguing his face.

"It's not much—" he said, as he began walking back towards the wagon.

"I think it's beautiful," she said.

His face broke out into the biggest grin she'd ever seen. "It is, isn't it?"

"Help me down, Jake, so I can set foot on your land."

He plopped his hat back on his head. "No, ma'am. I'll help you down so you can set foot on *our* land."

He placed his hands on her expanding waist, lifting her down to the ground. She leaned back against him and his arms came around her, drawing her close.

He pointed towards an oak tree, its branches uplifted and spread wide, the dense greenery providing shade to the earth beneath it. "I figure we can build our first house beside that tree there. It'll be a small house, probably just one room so we can get it up quick. But later, later I'll build you the kind of house you deserve. And over there, we'll build the barn and corrals. And right there I want to build a windmill."

"A windmill?" she asked. Windmills were a rare sight in the West.

"It'll help us pump water into the house and if we build the well deep enough, we should be able to keep our stock watered during dry spells. And over there," his arm swept in a semicircle, "we'll build a bunkhouse and a cookhouse. Hell, eventually we'll have everything we need." He placed warm lips against the back of her head. "It's going to be good here, Reb."

Placing her hands over his and giving them a squeeze, she knew in her heart that he was right.

Two men guarded the cattle that were released on the open range, while the other men built a hasty corral for the horses. Then they began building the one-room house where Jake and Rebecca would live. Where eventually, she would undoubtedly give birth.

As the days passed, she watched their progress, giving little aid except to bring them water and assist the cook they'd hired just outside of Kentucky.

From time to time, Jake would leave the men, slip his arm around her and ask her a question about the house. Where did she want the windows, the fireplace, the door? At night, their pallets laying side by side, they'd talk about the ranch. What he wanted it to be. Their relationship had remained chaste. In the open air, with seven cowboys and a cook along with them, little opportunity had existed for intimacy. Jake seemed content with their relationship, which more closely resembled that of two age-old friends than that of a husband and wife.

But each day, she felt her feelings for this man becoming deeper. His kindness was unlimited, not only to her and the men, but to the animals as well. She watched him now as he directed the men's efforts. With any luck the house would be completed in the next day or two.

Rebecca lifted her hand to her brow to shade her eyes from the glaring sun and looked out into the distance. Since they'd been here, they'd not had one visitor. But it certainly looked as if they were getting at least one now. A wagon was pulling up.

The wagon came to a halt not far from where Rebecca stood and all work on the house momentarily stopped as curiosity was piqued. A young man roughly Frank's age held the reins, and a rotund woman wearing a white bonnet was pushing a younger woman out of the seat.

"Come on, Ruth, get down. We got new neighbors and, thank God, a woman among them."

Unexpectedly, Rebecca found herself pressed against the older woman's ample bosom, the woman's thick arms jiggling as they came away from Rebecca's back.

"Lord, child, this state can use all the women it can get. My son Luke there said he saw some new folks and I said no but sure enough he was right. I'm Carrie Reading and this here's my daughter, Ruth. The rest wouldn't come, couldn't give up a day of work." She hit Rebecca's arm. "You know how menfolk are. And Land O'Goshen, if you ain't with child!"

Rebecca laughed. Carrie Reading was a true rambler and her sentences were so disjointed, it seemed as if she had been saving up her conversation for years and was trying to throw it all out in one go. Rebecca extended her hand.

"I'm Rebecca Burnett."

"Hell, girl, I don't see enough women to want to shake their hands!" Then her arms were back around Rebecca, hugging tightly.

Jake had ambled over, keeping a safe distance, and Rebecca couldn't blame him. Public displays of affection were foreign to him, and she hoped Carrie wouldn't press him to her bosom.

"Mrs. Reading—"

"Carrie, darling. Call me Carrie. We were friends before we even met."

"All right, Carrie. This is my husband, Jake."

The woman turned, with arms outstretched, taking a step towards Jake who took a step back and tilted his hat. "Ma'am."

"Oh, a shy one!" She punched Rebecca's arm again. "I like the shy ones. They usually make the best lovers."

Rebecca brought a hand to her mouth as she watched the heat suffuse Jake's face.

"If you'll excuse me, I gotta get back to work," he said with a duck of his head.

"No, wait!" Carrie called out. "I take it you're the owner of this spread."

"Yes, ma'am."

"And you need a barn. Tomorrow night, we're having a dance for my Ruth here to celebrate her sixteenth birthday. We'd just love for y'all to come—all of you. Give you a chance to meet your neighbors and next Saturday I'll get all their lazy carcasses out here to build your barn. What do you say?"

"That's real nice of you to offer, ma'am."

"We'd love to go to the dance, Carrie, but I think we have enough men to build our own barn," Rebecca said, noting Jake's discomfiture with the situation.

"Not in your life, girl. Hell, we all build each other's barns around here. Only way to get it done. We'll see you tomorrow night at sunset. Just go south. You can't miss our spread, the Triple Bar."

She gave Rebecca one last hug before heaving herself up into the wagon and hitting her son's arm, her signal that it was time to go.

"Now don't disappoint me!" she called out. And Rebecca wondered if all the women here were like her.

"Did that invitation include me?"

Rebecca turned to Frank. "I think it included everyone."

"And that Ruth's going to be there, that pretty girl?"

"Yes, she is. The dance is for her."

"Goddamn. I need you to teach me to dance."

She pulled his hat off his head and tousled his hair. "I'd be happy to, Frank."


Rebecca watched the hues of the sunset cross the sky. One thing she loved about Texas was its sunsets. Caught unaware, she screamed when she felt herself being lifted into Jake's arms.

"What in the world are you doing, Jake Burnett?"

"Taking you home."

He carried her to the house, up onto the porch and through the threshold of the simple wooden structure, then set her down on the puncheon floor of flat cedar logs. The walls were built of twelve-inch, rough-hewn cedar logs, chinked with clay. The only door was made of heavy boards. It fastened with a latchstring.

"It's not much," he said, waiting for her disappointment to show. It was far nicer than the building he had grown up in, but it was nowhere near as nice as the home in which she had been raised.

Rebecca pivoted slowly on the balls of her feet, her eyes taking inventory and assessing each feature of the single room. The wall to the right of the door housed the stone fireplace. The wall across from it held the stove. To the back of the house was space for their bed. Because Rebecca liked the sun to visit inside as much as it did outside, each side of the house had two windows, protected by heavy wooden shutters that hung on handwrought hinges. She completed her circle, smiled up at Jake and slipped her arms around his neck.

"I love it."

His eyes lowered to her lips. Yes, Jake, she thought. I want you to kiss me.

Frank stuck his head in the door. "You want us to start hauling the furniture in before it gets too dark?"

Sighing, Jake released her. "Now it's your turn to work, Reb. Just tell them where you want everything."

It didn't take long as they had brought only the barest

of necessities. They set a sofa before the fireplace, a table and four chairs before the stove, and beside it a pine cupboard. A four-poster bed was set in the corner in the back so one window looked down on it. A dresser and a mahogany wardrobe rested against the back wall. They would add more as time went by, but for now it was enough to get them through.

When they were finished, they sat around the campfire and ate supper with the men, listening as Lee Hastings sang ballads in a deep resonant voice. The stocky man had beefy arms and curly black hair touching his shoulders. When he stood, his short legs rounded out so he always looked as though he were still sitting upon a horse. He began to sing "The Cowboy's Lament." The song was Rebecca's favorite. She snuggled back against Jake as his arms encircled her. When the last note was sung, the couple said good night and walked side by side back towards their house.

Jake closed the door behind them and brought a plank of wood down against the door barring entrance. He set the lantern down on the table and smiled at his wife. It was the first time they had been alone since the night they had gotten married.

Rebecca lifted her shoulders, spreading her arms out. "It's our house."

Jake looked around, smiling at the towels she had hung over the windows. "Guess we need to get some curtains. Men don't think of things like that."

"You seem to have thought of just about everything else."

"I tried. Are you tired?"

"Yes, I am."

He went to the back of the house and brought out a hammer and some nails.

"I thought we could tack up a quilt to give you a little more privacy."

"I'd like that." She moved to a chest and took out a faded quilt. "This one should do."

Standing on a chair, Jake nailed it up. He stepped down, admiring his handiwork. It was crooked.

"I'm not much of a carpenter."

"You built the house."

"With a lot of help." He studied her standing there, her eyes as big as the moon. "Why don't you get ready for bed?"

She nodded, then slipped behind the quilt. After removing her clothes, she wiped her body with a damp rag and pulled her nightgown over her head. She was five months pregnant and she didn't want Jake to see her body in its present state. The little mound of her belly seemed to be doubling in size every day. Another aspect of pregnancy that didn't thrill her. Then she felt the flutter of butterfly wings inside her, and smiled, rubbing the small mound. She didn't feel it often, and at first she hadn't been sure what it was, but now she recognized it as the baby moving inside her. It was one thing about pregnancy she loved. She unbraided her hair and brushed it vigorously before braiding it again. Then she shrugged, unbraided it, ran her brush through it and poked her head around the quilt.

"I'm ready for bed."

Jake was sitting on the sofa, his long legs stretched out before him. He turned his attention from the empty fireplace to her.

"Good night, Reb. Have sweet dreams."

She was unexpectedly hit with disappointment. "Good night," she said softly.

Rebecca climbed into bed, drawing the covers up over her. Then she threw them off and clambered out of bed. She marched across the tiny room until she was standing in front of Jake, hands on her hips.

"What do you mean by 'Good night. Have sweet dreams'? For months now, I've been lying on the hard ground, my pallet beside yours, resting my head on your shoulder with your arm around me. Every night I've thought how nice it'd be when we could sleep in a soft bed again and now you're telling me 'Good night' like you're not planning on sharing that soft bed with me! Get yourself up off that sofa and get into that bed now!"

He stood up, giving her a big lopsided grin. "I just wanted to make sure that's where you wanted me." He touched her cheek. "You looked scared as hell when I closed that door behind us. I don't want you to ever be afraid of me, Reb. I'd never hurt you, and I'd never do anything you didn't want."

"Then come to bed and hold me so I can get some sleep."

She climbed into bed, and lay on her back with her eyes squeezed shut while he undressed. Then she felt the bed dip under his weight. She scooted over, placing her head on his shoulder while his arm came around her.

"This is as nice as I remembered it," she said.

"I didn't know you liked this."

"Actually, Jake, there's not a lot about you that I don't like."

"What is something you don't like?"

She drew her brows together in thought. "Well . . . do you promise not to get your feelings hurt if I tell you?"

"I promise."

"Well, then. I thought you should have given Carrie a great big hug and a kiss smack dab on the lips."

Jake laughed. "She was something else, wasn't she? Do you think she's always like that?"

"Probably. I bet her husband is quiet."

"Makes sense. You got a quiet husband. I have a loud wife."

"I am not loud!"

"Shh. The men will hear you."

"What are you going to have them do next?"

"Since we'll have help with our barn, I'm going to have them start on the bunkhouse. The weather seems pretty mild here, but you never can tell, and I don't want them shacking up with us if it gets cold."

Rebecca snuggled against him.

"What was that?" he asked.

"What?"

"Be still," he ordered.

"Did you hear something?"

"No, thought I felt something. Was it the baby?" he asked.

"Yes."

He rolled her over onto her back and came up on an elbow. They had slept in all their clothes every night, and since their first night Jake hadn't been able to feel Reb's body, let alone the tiny movements within her. He moved the covers off, gazing down at her.

"Oh, Jake, don't look at it."

"Why not? It's beautiful. Can I put my hand on your stomach?"

She nodded.

He placed his hand lightly on her stomach and waited. Through her cotton gown, he felt the baby kick.

And waited.

"Will he move again?" he asked.

She heard the disappointment in his voice and wished she had the power to make the baby move. "I don't know. He doesn't move very often." She took his hand and moved it to her left side. "He seems to like this side." She placed her hand over his and pressed it against her side. And they waited.

And waited.

Then Jake felt the slightest tremor beneath his palm.

"Lord, how long has he been doing this?"

Rebecca smiled, surprised by the joy she felt at being able to share this moment with him. "About three weeks. At first I didn't know what it was."

"Does it hurt when he moves?"

"No. Actually, it's the one part about being pregnant that makes me think all the rest is worth it."

"What's it feel like . . . inside, when he moves?"

She glanced down at her stomach. How could she explain it? It was really like nothing she had ever felt before.

"Have you ever cupped your hands around a butterfly?" she asked.

Jake nodded.

"That's what it feels like."

His hand roamed over her stomach. "I hope we meet the doctor tomorrow night."

"You could deliver the baby."

"If you were a horse."

"It's the same principle."

His eyes came back to hers. "If I have to, I will. But I'd prefer to have someone here who knows exactly what he's doing."

He lay back down, drawing her up against his side. She was too precious, too important to risk losing.

Slowly, Rebecca opened her eyes as the sunlight filtered in through the towels hung in the windows.

"Put the woman in a soft bed and she sleeps the day away," Jake teased.

"I don't see you up and about."

Oh, he was up, and when she unconsciously moved her leg up his thigh, he rolled out of bed and into his pants.

"Thought we'd take a ride over the land today," he said to her over his shoulder.

"I'd love to, but what would I wear?" She splayed her fingers on her stomach. "I can't get into my pants or my split skirts anymore, and I don't ride sidesaddle."

"Find your split skirt while I saddle our horses."

He walked out before she could protest. A few minutes later, he returned with biscuits and grits. Then he took a knife and her skirt and ripped open the front seam. He poked two holes in her now open waistband and drew a thin rope through them. Rebecca watched with interest while she downed the breakfast. He held up his creation.

"That ought to do it."

Rebecca's eyes widened. "I'll be poking out!"

"Exactly. You can wear one of my shirts over it and no one will be able to tell."

She chewed the last of her biscuit, contemplating the idea. Then licking her fingers, she scrambled out of the bed and took the skirt from him, brushing him away to the other side of the quilt.

A few minutes later she came out from behind the quilt looking like a little girl with her hair braided and her face freshly scrubbed. She placed a hand on her tiny mound.

"Won't you be embarrassed to have me beside you?" she asked.

His eyes were warm as he shook his head. Smiling, she shrugged. "All right. I'm ready if you are."

She longed to break her horse into a run but understood the foolishness of the idea. They guided their horses around the outskirts of the ranch, now and then coming across the remains of an abandoned campfire.

"I think you've got people using your land," she said as they stopped beside a site that showed evidence of recent habitation.

"Our land," he corrected her. "And I'm sure of it. Until recently, most of Texas was open land. A lot of it still is. Many small ranchers own only the cattle. They use whatever land or water is available without worrying about who owns it." He surveyed the land stretching out for miles before them. Then his gaze turned to her. "Partner, what do you think of fencing?"

Rebecca's eyes held his honestly. "I don't like what the barbed wire does to the cattle that are stupid enough to run into it. But I believe it's the only way a man can effectively protect what's his. I believe one day every ranch in this country will be fenced off."

Jake nodded. "Several of the larger ranchers have already begun fencing in their land. I want to breed your Herefords—"

"Our Herefords," she interjected with a pointed look.

Jake smiled. "Our Herefords. I want to breed them with the longhorns that are being raised here now. If I don't fence in the land, I can't control the breeding, and instead of getting better stock, we'll end up with something nobody wants."

"A lot of people are against closing off the ranges, Jake. It won't make us popular people. It might bring a lot of anger our way."

"I've considered that. In some parts of the state there've been outright wars fought. The Rangers are supposed to back the cattlemen who own the land, but out here, we have to be able to depend on ourselves. Whatever trouble comes is ours to handle. I won't put up the fence if you're against it."

"I didn't realize you knew so much about Texas."

He grinned. "I know about the state. I just didn't know about our land. I was worried sick when we passed through that stretch of tall pines that our land was going to be sitting in the middle of it. But it's not. It's wide and it's open. Our cattle can roam it and so can anyone else's. We'll need more hands to keep the cattle from wandering. Come spring roundup or fall sorting time, we'll have to invest a lot of time separating our cattle out from the others. In the long run, I think the fences will save us trouble. But in the beginning, it's likely to bring it. We just have to decide if we want to sit in the present or step into the future."

She lifted her face to the sky, feeling the warmth of the sun filtering down to her and she laughed, sending her voice out around her. Then she eyed Jake.

"A cowboy poet is what you are, Jake Burnett. When you want something, you ask for it with the prettiest words I have ever heard. Put up your fence, and I'll shoot anyone who tries to take it down."

Leaning over, he took her fingers and brought them to his lips. He couldn't have chosen a better partner.

# Chapter Five

REBECCA WAS BEGINNING to wonder if the six men sitting in the back of the creaking wagon had ever been to a dance before. They were cackling like a bunch of chickens going after the solitary rooster in the henhouse, and the thick fog created by the sweet-smelling water they had doused themselves with was making her nauseous. Jake pulled the wagon up beside one of a half-dozen others and helped Rebecca down. The men took off in search of easy prey. They had been too long on the trail. She pitied any woman, young or old, who happened to be there tonight— she would be danced to death.

As soon as she and Jake entered the barn, she found herself pressed against a soft bosom. Carrie could strike from anywhere. Her roundness muffled the sound of her approach, but her voice gave her away.

"I was beginning to think y'all wouldn't come!" She turned to Jake. "Now don't you be shy with me tonight, boy! I expect at least one dance."

Jake nodded and smiled. For all her bossing, he liked Carrie. "Yes, ma'am."

Carrie held up a finger. "Now you two wait right here."

Rebecca laughed as she watched Carrie tromp off, hands set into loose fists, arms swinging. The band began to strike up a tune and she stopped them. Couples had already started to dance, but Carrie couldn't have cared less.

"My family—get yourselves to the front of the barn right now!"

She gave the band of odd players a curt nod and the men once again began playing. A host of people started gathering beside Jake and Rebecca as Carrie bounced back over.

"Line up!" she ordered.

"Oh, Ma!" A dark-haired young man looked imploringly at the rotund woman. "Somebody's asking Mary to dance."

"As long as you get the last dance, it don't matter. Now get in line or I'll swat that hide of yours."

Begrudgingly, he stepped back. Standing a good head taller than the first young man, he took his place as the second in the stair-step line that consisted of an assortment of boys and one girl.

"Now, then. These are our new neighbors, Rebecca and Jake Burnett, mister and missus to you unless they tell you otherwise. You are to make them feel welcome."

She turned with evident pride on her face. "These are my children." She stuck out a pudgy finger, going down the line, "Matthew, Mark, Luke, John, Ruth, James, Ezekiel, Micah."

"The books of the Bible?" Rebecca asked softly.

"That's right." She reached around behind her, pulling forward a short dark-haired man. "And this here is my man Michael."

To Jake, Michael Reading held out a weathered hand that matched his weathered face. But set within the creases created by sun and wind were the kindest pair of blue eyes Rebecca had ever seen. They twinkled like the stars overhead and when he nodded at Jake they gleamed in welcome.

Jake firmly shook his hand. "We appreciate your inviting us."

Michael nodded and smiled before releasing Jake's hand.

"He can't talk," Carrie explained. "Got wounded during the War Between the States, shot in the throat. So I talk for both of us, don't I, darling?"

Michael rolled his eyes, and Rebecca knew the man might not talk but he could communicate.

Carrie nudged her arm. "See what I mean about the quiet

ones? And I enjoyed making every one of them."

"Oh, Ma!" Ruth wailed. "Can we go now? Please!"

"Go on, get out of here."

In less than a second, the only thing visible where the children had been was a cloud of dust settling back to the ground.

Carrie and Michael walked off when the band started up another tune. Rebecca stood tapping her foot, waiting for Jake to ask her to dance. He didn't get the chance.

A man with startling green eyes and blond hair introduced himself with confidence. As a young girl Rebecca had envisioned the gods of Greek mythology looking very much as he did. His name was William Long, and he said he was a cattle baron. When he asked Jake's permission to escort his wife out onto the dance floor, Jake could do no more than nod and step back. He couldn't help thinking William Long was the kind of man Rebecca Anderson should have married.

Feeling out of place, Jake wandered outside. The sounds of banjos, fiddles, and guitars filtered into the darkness of the night. He stood watching the horses prance around each other, his elbows resting on the wooden corral. Jake rubbed the uneven bridge of his nose, knowing if he smiled, it would be an uneven smile that matched his uneven skin. He would never be polished, he would never be flawless, and if he were ever in a position to call himself a cattle baron, he would still look like an old cowhand.

It wasn't long before he felt Rebecca come stand beside him. He didn't turn to face her. He hated himself for being jealous, and he didn't want her to see what he was feeling.

"Looks like they got some good horses. We might consider breeding ours with theirs," he said, his eyes never leaving the animals playing before him.

She set her arms on the top rail of the fence, gazing out. "The last dance we had, it took you most of the night to gather up the courage to ask me to dance." She looked at his profile. "Will it take you that long tonight?" she asked softly.

"Lot of handsome men in there who'd like to dance with you."

"And I just want to dance with you."

His head snapped around, his eyes searching her face for the truth.

"I'm your wife, Jake. The first dance, the last dance, and every dance in between is yours. And you don't even have to ask me. All you have to do is slip your hand in mine."

"Would you want me to ask you if you weren't my wife?"

"I wanted you to ask me at the last dance. I want you to ask me now. I enjoy dancing in your arms."

"I stepped on your feet."

"Only at first. How many times had you danced before then?"

"Once."

"Ask me to dance," she prodded softly. "Not because I'm your wife . . . but because you want to dance with me. Because I want to dance with you."

Even in the darkness, she was beautiful. And she wanted to dance with him. He intertwined his fingers with hers.

"I thought you'd never ask," she said, smiling, her hips swaying in motion to the music as they walked back into the barn, hand in hand.


"Don't you think you've had enough whiskey?"

Frank turned around, his jaw set. "I'm a grown man."

"And you're going to look like a grown fool if you keep drinking like that," Rebecca said.

He studied his boots—polished earlier, now scuffed— before he brought his eyes back up to her. "Goddamn, Reb. She won't even dance with me. That Ruth. I asked her real polite like you told me to and she just laughed and said no. Why won't she dance with me?"

Rebecca understood some of his frustration. She had been attracted to Brett the first time she saw him, riding in from the north. "I don't know, Frank. Some women in this world can't look beyond the surface of a man. And it's usually their loss. I notice she spends a lot of time sitting on the side, waiting. I'm not sure I'd want to spend my life with someone who sat on the side. I'd rather have someone who was right in the middle, whooping it up every time."

Frank's brows drew together. "But she sure is pretty, Reb."

"Pretty fades in time. And when it's gone, you're only left with what was underneath."

Frank nodded, his mouth puckering. "I'm going to ask her one more time anyway."

Watching him tromp off, she realized how fortunate she'd been. Brett had returned her feelings in equal measure.

"It's about time beautiful women started coming to Texas," said a voice that was resonant and suave. Rebecca turned, feeling an immediate aversion to the man as his brown eyes slowly traveled the length of her, assessing her attributes.

"And unfortunately, it appears I'm too late. I assume you're married?"

She gave him a small smile that was as cold as she could muster. "Yes, I am."

"Don't worry, my dear. That won't be a deterrent to our relationship. It will only make it more challenging."

Rebecca released a short laugh. "I assure you, sir, we will never have a relationship." Turning on her heel, she walked off and went to find Jake.

"Carrie says the doctor in town is sober one day a week," he said as soon as she walked up. "I'm not having a drunk deliver your baby."

Jake looked so disgruntled that Rebecca touched her fingertips to the corner of his turned-down mouth, trying to force his lips into a smile.

"It'll be all right. I know you can do it."

"Reb, this is different. You're not a horse that means almost nothing to me. If I do something wrong—"

"Well, look what the devil drug up. My father's bastard. Come to claim your land in Texas, have you?"

Jake felt as though he had been poleaxed as he slowly turned around, coming face to face with Ethan Truscott, the nemesis of his past. Brown eyes met brown and Jake was surprised that after three years, he could still feel so much hatred directed towards him.

"You know, pretty lady, you really ought to show more common sense in selecting the company you keep. I don't imagine your husband would be pleased to find out you're spending time in the presence of this bastard."

Rebecca took great pleasure in realizing the man she had recently snubbed was standing before them now. It would give her the chance to really put him in his place. "On the contrary, I don't think my husband would mind at all." She pressed up against Jake's side. "Would you, Jake?"

Jake slipped his arm possessively around his wife. He'd never felt so proud in all his life. "No, I wouldn't mind at all. Can't say I'd be pleased, though, if I found you in the company of Ethan Truscott."

Ethan shifted his eyes from Rebecca to Jake. "She's your wife?" He snorted. "What whorehouse did you pick her up in?"

Jake released his hold on Rebecca and she quickly moved her hand to his chest to stay him. "Jake!"

He looked at her.

"It's not worth it," she said quietly.

He blew out a deep gust of air, nodding before turning back to face Ethan. "I got no quarrel with you."

"No? Then you have a different recollection of our childhood than I do."

"Don't be causing trouble tonight, Ethan." Another brown-eyed man joined the group.

"Dammit, Zach. He got the land and we got the debts."

"Maybe he deserved the land."

"Like hell he did. You're just too damn forgiving, you know that? Just like Father."

"I don't remember Father being so forgiving where Jake was concerned." He extended a hand to Jake. "I've got no hard feelings."

Jake hesitated. He could count all the acts of kindness that had been directed his way during the years he had lived on their ranch on one hand. But Zachary Truscott had never singled him out for ridicule or abuse. He put his hand in Zach's and received a handshake firmer than he had expected.

Zach tilted his head towards Rebecca. "Ma'am." Then he hit his brother on the shoulder. "Let's go."

"I gotta—"

Zach grabbed Ethan's shirt front. "You start a fight here and I'll side against you. And I imagine everyone else will, too. You're the bastard here tonight. Now let's go."

The expression on Ethan's face announced louder than any words that matters weren't settled between him and Jake. He abruptly turned and stormed out of the barn, shoving aside anyone who, in his opinion, was standing in his path. Close behind him, Zach followed.

Moving the towel curtain back slightly so the full moon could shine into the room, Rebecca gazed out upon the peaceful star-filled night sky, knowing her husband was feeling very little peace. They had come home and gone through the motions of getting ready for bed without a word. Now he lay staring at the ceiling, one hand behind his head. She rolled over and touched his arm. He gave her a small smile as he lifted his arm to welcome her.

"Sorry," he whispered.

His hand idly rubbed her arm as she waited for him to reconcile his feelings.

"Tell me," she finally said softly.

His hand stilled, and when he answered his voice was unsteady and low. "Those two men are my half brothers. I never knew for sure before tonight. There were times when I thought the man who took me away long after my mother died was my father. But then I'd think no man could treat his son, his own flesh and blood, the way he treated me. When he came and got me, I was like a little puppy that's being taken to a new home, its tail a-waggin', its mouth open and its tongue hanging out in anticipation. Then when we got there, I got hit because in my excitement, I hadn't sat still enough in the wagon."

"How old were you?"

"Seven. He set me up in a stall in the barn. I had one blanket to keep me warm at night. When winter rolled in, to keep warm, I'd sleep next to whatever animal I could coax into laying down. I got Ethan and Zach's hand-me-downs. Their clothes never seemed to fit right. I always looked like somebody that nobody wanted."

"And you were too young to leave," Rebecca stated softly.

"But I tried. When I was nine. It was November. It had just turned cold and I wanted to go somewhere that was warm. But he came after me. He paraded me around, stark naked, in front of the entire ranch so I'd learn what I'd have if I didn't have him. He tied me up in the barn for three days, alone, without any food or water. Without my blanket. I couldn't get to the animals for warmth. I couldn't go anywhere to relieve myself. I wanted to die when he came to the barn to release me, to make sure I understood how grateful I should be. I was sitting in this mess that I had made and Ethan doubled over laughing. And I got hit for making the mess."

She tightened her hold on him wishing she could take away his pain. "When I met Ethan tonight, I took an instant dislike to him. And now I know why. He's a cruel, ugly man."

Rolling her over to her back, Jake splayed his fingers on her stomach.

"I'll never beat this child, or humiliate him, or make him feel like he's nothing."

She touched the scar above his brow. "I know. You're such a good person. I don't know how they could have treated you like that."

In the moonlight, she saw a smile cross his face. "Do you know when I first thought I might be worth something?"

She shook her head. "No."

His eyes held hers. "This crazy brown mustang had been trying to throw me for pretty close to half an hour, and I thought for sure I was going to have to give up on him. Then he just calmed down and let me ride him." His hand moved from her stomach to her cheek. "And I felt this warmth coming at me, and I turned and saw this beautiful girl leaning over the fence. Her dark hair was caught up in a long braid hanging over her shoulder, her black Stetson was tipped up off her forehead, her blue eyes were shining, and a wonderful straight smile went from one side of her face to the other. Then she spoke to me—me, the bastard who had never received a word of praise since his mother died—and she told me she wanted me to break her next horse. I realized for the first time in my life that I might have something of value to offer another human being."

"Jake, that was over three years ago. How can you remember all that?"

"Why did you remember?" he asked in a low voice as his mouth slowly moved downward to cover hers. She raked her fingers up the nape of his neck, into his thick curling hair, pressing him down on her as her lips parted. He groaned as his tongue slipped into her mouth, exploring the sweet depths he had denied himself since they had left Kentucky. His thumb gently caressed her soft cheek. He wanted to touch the softness of her entire body, but didn't dare. He knew she had lain with a man she loved, had felt another's loving arms around her, had experienced that man's expression of love and had returned it in kind. How could he ask or expect her to settle for less, to be intimate with him, a man who loved her, a man she cared for but did not love. He needed to at least feel she wanted him, even if just a little, before he made love to her.

Rebecca felt the warmth of his kiss seep deep down within her. His tongue retreated and hers followed, exploring his mouth at leisure. She could taste the one whiskey he had sipped earlier in the evening. She felt the roughness of his tongue, and the sleek underside. How nice it would feel to have that tongue touch more than her mouth. But she contented herself with the kiss, for she felt anything more would be a betrayal of her love for Brett.

He rolled them back to their sides before his mouth released hers. She snuggled up against him, the child within her moving against him as well. She couldn't believe Jake had remembered that day in such detail. And why *had* she remembered it?

She could recall everything as vividly as Jake had. She could still see him keeping his balance as the horse tried to throw him. She had gasped three times when the horse had bucked with such intensity that she was sure the rider would be thrown, but he wasn't. Then the horse had calmed and she'd spoken to the man. She had expected a broad smile to cross his features, and waited for him to dismount and saunter up to her, introduce himself and proclaim to be the best hand in the state. But instead, he'd given her a small smile, a smile so small that she didn't know one side tilted up higher than the other. Then he'd dismounted and asked Bassett what he was to do next. She had known then he'd never come after her like the other men. She'd wanted to get to know him so she'd had Bassett assign him to her cattle. Rebecca had always enjoyed talking with him, working by his side. And now she was his wife. Her arms tightened around him. She was his wife. And she promised herself she'd never hurt him.

But promises are easily made when one knows not what the future holds. And promises given only to one's own heart are easily forgotten.

# Chapter Six

THE RIDER HESITATED a fair distance from the group assembled to build the barn.

Standing beside her husband, Rebecca watched as Jake's eyes narrowed. Then he lifted his arm, signaling the rider to approach. She felt the familiar tug on her heart, only this time, the tug was a little harder, touched a little deeper. What she was beginning to feel towards him went beyond simple affection, but she wasn't sure it was love. She slipped her arm behind his back, welcoming the pressure of his arm as it came around her, drawing her near.

Zach Truscott drew his horse up beside Jake.

"Heard you were building a barn today. Thought you could use some help."

"We can always use a good man," Jake said.

"Can't say I'm that. But I can hammer a nail into wood."

Leaving the group of women who were preparing the noon meal, Rebecca walked to the oak tree beside their house where Zach was lifting a ladle of cool water to his lips.

"Must have been difficult to come here today," Rebecca said.

Zach returned the ladle to the bucket of water, his eyes meeting Rebecca's. "No, ma'am. What was hard was extending my hand the other night. I wasn't sure he'd accept it, and I didn't realize how badly I wanted him to until he did."

He allowed his gaze to roam towards the barn, which was half completed. "Your husband intrigues me. You can't begin to comprehend the amount of hate that surrounded him when he was growing up. I don't understand why he doesn't seem to harbor any bitterness."

"He's told me a little."

Looking askance at her, he said, "I imagine it was only a little." His eyes went back to Jake. "My mother hated him because he was visible proof of her husband's infidelity. My father hated him because he saw Jake as his fall from Grace. I think my father thought if he showed God he had no feelings for the boy, God would forgive his transgressions and welcome him into the Kingdom. Ethan hated him because he was living testimony that our father was human. Ethan worshipped Father as he worshipped God, questioned nothing the man said or did. Jake's presence shattered his illusions."

"But you didn't hate him," Rebecca said softly.

"I hated him with a passion that made me tremble. It scared the hell out of me to know I could feel any emotion that deeply or that powerfully."

Rebecca was surprised by the impassioned confession. "Why did you hate him?"

Removing his hat, Zach used the sleeve of his shirt to remove the sweat that had collected along his brow. He heaved a deep sigh. "For all his coldness, Ethan was the perfect son. I, on the other hand, was the one who questioned, the one who didn't always do as I was told. Father took a strap to me a couple of times and I just laughed, saying it didn't hurt. Then he brought Jake home."

Zach shook his head. "I can't even remember now what I did, but Father grabbed my arm and dragged me out to the barn. Jake was asleep on the straw, looking so peaceful. My father yanked him up and tied him to a beam, jerked his pants down and applied his strap with a vengeance that my backside had always been spared.

"When my father was done, he asked me if that had hurt and told me that in the future when I disobeyed him, Jake would get the beating. Then he walked out, leaving me to cut him down. Jake looked at me with those big brown eyes of his filled with tears and whispered, 'What'd I do wrong? If he'd tell me, I wouldn't do it again.' And I told him the truth. 'You were born.' So I toed the line as best I could, which probably wasn't good enough.''

"I hope you'll understand my feelings," Rebecca said, "but I do hope your father is burning in hell.''

Zach gave her a sad smile. "I'll do you one better, Mrs. Burnett. I hope someday Ethan and I join him.''

He sauntered off towards the barn. Rebecca turned, leaning her head against the rough bark of the tree as the tears wandered down her cheeks. It had been long ago and Jake had survived it. Her Jake, her sweet, gentle Jake.

Jake slipped back into his shirt and took the plate Rebecca offered.

"Do you mind if we go sit over there?" He nodded towards the tree that was offering Zach shade.

"No, I don't mind.''

Together they walked over.

"Mind if we join you?" Jake asked.

"Not at all," Zach said as he moved over to allow more room against the tree.

Jake helped Rebecca lower herself to the ground before dropping his own lean frame down.

"Ethan said you got the debts. What debts were those?''

Zach laughed. "Seems Father not only enjoyed whoring, but gambling and drinking as well. Ironic, I thought, since I think one of your beatings came about because I got caught with a bottle of sour mash. Anyway, he owed just about everyone in town and they came to collect. We had to sell everything to pay off his debts.''

"Sorry to hear that. You had a real nice ranch.''

"Mother died pretty soon after that. The humiliation was too much for her.''

"So you and Ethan came out here?''

"Yep. Went down to Mexico, bought a few longhorns, stole a few, too. Been grazing them on the open range.'' He eyed Jake. "Mostly your open range.''

"I'm fixing to fence it off."

"Figured you would. I'd better warn you, Ethan won't take kindly to it. Despite the fact the deed's in your name, he thinks he has a right to this land. I don't agree, but I've stayed with him so far because we've had no troubles."

"How many head do you have?"

"Fifty."

"How can you make a profit with so few?" Rebecca asked. "By the time you drive them to market, you'd be lucky to break even."

Zach looked around Jake at Rebecca, then amused, his eyes came back to Jake. "I thought you married her because she was beautiful."

"I married her because she's the best damn rancher I know." He glanced over at his wife. "But now that you mention it, I guess she's not so hard on the eyes."

Rebecca acknowledged Jake's compliment by placing a hand on his thigh, a subtle action that did not escape Zach's notice.

"You're avoiding my question, Mr. Truscott," she said.

"Call me Zach. A lot of men own only a few cattle, graze them on open range. We make a profit by combining our herds when it's time to get them to market."

"We brought Hereford cattle from Kentucky," Jake said. "I want to breed them with longhorns. Would you be interested in selling yours?"

"I'll think on it. I doubt Ethan will want to sell. I hear that ranchers are willing to pay seventy-five dollars a head for Herefords up in the Panhandle. You'd best guard yours well."

The meal ended and the men went back to work finishing off the barn, completing the project as the sun dipped down to touch the horizon. The men threw buckets of water on each other, washed down and slipped away to change into clean clothes as Carrie set the band up in one corner of the barn.

Rebecca felt the warmth of Jake's hand surrounding hers as music began to fill the newly built barn. She smiled up at him as he escorted her to its center, took her in his arms and began to waltz with her in time to the music.

Zach had a difficult time keeping his eyes from straying to Rebecca. Her eyes danced as much as her feet as she was held in her husband's arms. She was a beautiful woman. She could have had any man and she had chosen Jake.

Zach had known many beautiful women, women who flirted, who looked at him through lowered lashes, laughed at a secret joke. Women who were married and still played the role of coquette. But Rebecca was unlike any of those women. She was never far from her husband's side. Zach had only seen her dance with two men other than Jake. He strolled over and asked her for a dance.

"You're a beautiful woman, Rebecca," he said once he had her safely on the dance floor. He grew serious. "When Jake puts up his fence, he won't be able to avoid the war that will follow."

"And which side will you choose?" she asked.

"I won't. I'll take my cattle and go somewhere else. You should probably do the same."

"Is that a threat?"

"No, ma'am. I just wouldn't want to see you get hurt. There's no reason for you to be exposed to the dangers."

She met his gaze levelly. "Mr. Truscott, if something touches Jake, it touches me. I assure you if I wished to avoid the trouble, I'd need only ask Jake not to put up his fence. He explained to me what would happen if he fenced in his land. But it's his land, every acre, and if he wants to fence it in, he has the right to do so and I'll stand by him."

Zach smiled, shaking his head. "I didn't mean to offend you. I find myself in an unusual position. I never expected to envy Jake anything. But I envy him for having you."

The dance ended and Rebecca pulled away. "Thank you for the dance."

Zach took her arm. "I hope we can still be friends."

She gazed into brown eyes similar to Jake's, but the shade was not as deep nor the reflection of emotion as rich. "I'd like for us to be friends, but I want to make sure you understand my position. I told Jake if he put up his fence,

I'd shoot anyone that tried to tear it down. I meant it. I was raised on a ranch. I was raised to be a rancher. And I was raised to fight for what is mine. Side with Ethan and you not only go against Jake, you go against me.''

''Jake is a lucky man.''

''Funny,'' Rebecca said as she turned to leave, ''I've always considered myself the fortunate one.''

Watching her return to her husband's side, Zach gazed longingly after her. Jake deserved some good in his life, but he had outdone himself when it had come to choosing a wife.

He waited patiently until Frank escorted Rebecca out to the dance floor. Then he took a deep breath and walked up to Jake.

''Don't suppose you could use another ranch hand on your spread, could you?'' he asked, wishing his palms weren't sweating.

Jake studied the man standing before him. The handshake they'd exchanged at the Reading Ranch couldn't erase the memories of all those bitter years, but working beside Zach today had seemed to forge a fragile bond between the two men. ''Helping me build my barn is one thing. Working for me is something entirely different. Don't you think it'll cause hard feelings between you and Ethan?''

''I can handle Ethan.''

''What about your cattle?''

''I'll take my share from Ethan, graze them with yours. If I don't turn out to be the best hand you ever hired, you can keep them.''

''You seem to forget I know exactly how good you are.''

Zach smiled. ''Then you'll win either way, won't you?''

Jake wanted to make sure Zach understood what his position would be if he came to work for him. ''Lee Hastings is my foreman. You'd have to take orders from him.''

''I've got no problem with that.''

''And Reb. She's my partner. Her word's the same as mine.''

"Figured as much."

"Well then." Jake extended his hand. When Zach took it, he smiled. "Welcome to the Rocking R."

Gray-haired men swore the route of the Shawnee Trail was determined by the town of Pleasure. Silver-haired women swore Pleasure chose its location because of the route of the Shawnee Trail. Neither side could prove their case, but one certainty remained: the town of Pleasure took its name from the reason for its existence.

Andrea Shanley had come to the barren land with one purpose in mind: to make herself wealthy. She hired carpenters and, in what at that time seemed to be the middle of nowhere, she erected a large house.

One week after the carpenters left, the residents of her establishment arrived and the place opened for business. Its business was to bring pleasure to the men who drove the herds up from the bowels of Texas to the shipping centers in Kansas.

Jake pulled the wagon up in front of Pleasure's only general store, then helped his wife down as a flurry of dry dust swept through the main street. Frank and Lee Hastings hopped out of the back of the wagon, promising to return in an hour to help Jake load up the supplies. Jake followed his wife into the general store and then headed over to talk to the owner.

Strolling through the store, Rebecca was surprised by the amount of finery, satin cloths, and fancy feathers that adorned the shelves, wondering who in the world would need such things. She stopped beside a bolt of blue calico, running her fingers over it, turning around when she felt her husband's presence beside her.

"Would you like blue curtains?" she asked.

Jake studied the cloth without touching it. It was marked at ten cents a yard. The first thing Reb had asked for and he wasn't going to be able to give it to her.

"Would you prefer another color?" Rebecca asked, noting his hesitancy to commit himself to blue.

"No, blue will be fine. But . . . " His forlorn expression told Rebecca something was amiss.

"What's wrong?"

"Reb, we're going to have to go back over this list of supplies and decide what we really don't need."

"Why?"

Jake ran his hand down his thigh. "Because I was expecting to be able to buy on credit, and Mr. Abrams says I'll have to pay cash. I need to hold onto the cash as much as possible."

She looked past her husband to the man standing behind the counter, a man who obviously dipped his hand into the candy jar. He was smacking his lips as though he were tasting sugar. She wondered how long it had been since he had been able to see his feet. She brought her eyes back to her husband.

"Why won't he extend us credit?"

"Because I'm not worth anything."

Jake hadn't seen anger flare up in those blue eyes so intensely since her father had announced her child would not inherit his land. "Did he tell you that?" she hissed.

"Yes, ma'am. But he's right. I only have eight hundred dollars left." He once again ran his hand down his thigh. "I'm thinking I might have to look for work on another ranch."

"You're going to work another man's spread so you can finance your own? You married me to handle the books. Guess it's time I started earning my keep. Introduce me to Mr. Abrams."

As they walked to the counter, Rebecca ignored the way the man watched her. He looked like a child running his tongue slowly over an all-day sucker.

"Is it true you won't extend us credit?" Rebecca asked.

"It's like I told your husband. We've had a dry summer and cattle aren't doing well. People owe me and they aren't paying."

"Do we owe you?"

"No, ma'am."

"So you're judging us on others' abilities instead of our own. I assure you that's not a wise business decision. My husband has only just begun working his spread, but he brought five hundred head of cattle from Kentucky, and we have not suffered from a drought. For anyone that knows him, his handshake serves as adequate collateral. Since you don't know him, I'll overlook the insult you've leveled against him this time, and I'll trust it won't happen in the future.''

Samuel's face turned as red as the candy sitting in one of his glass jars. "I'm real sorry, ma'am. But I just can't extend you credit."

"Is there a bank in this town?"

"Yes, ma'am. Four storefronts down."

"And if we bring you a letter of credit from the president of the bank, will you extend credit to us?"

Samuel chortled. "Ma'am, if you can get a letter of credit from tightwad Harry, I'll give you the store."

"May I have that in writing before I leave?"

Samuel's mouth dropped open. The woman was serious. "No, ma'am."

"Mr. Abrams." Rebecca extended her hand which he hesitantly shook. She and Jake turned to leave. Then she turned back. "Is there somewhere in town where we can get something to eat?"

"The hotel across the street serves up a good meal."

"Thank you, Mr. Abrams. We'll be back shortly."

Rebecca walked quickly out of the store. Jake followed more slowly. His wife waited on the boardwalk, tapping her foot, her arms crossed under her chest, her jaw set as he had never seen it set.

"I'm sorry," he said.

Her eyes snapped up to his. "What are you apologizing for?" She shook her head and released her pent-up breath. "It's my fault. I'm used to dealing in a state where everyone knew me and my father's name was as good as a bank draft." She slipped her arm through his. "Before we leave today, though, you'll be able to get credit anywhere in town that you want it." She smiled up at him. "Let's go get some lunch and I'll explain it all to you."

In a few minutes they were sitting at a small table covered with a red and white checkered cloth. They ordered

steaks, and after the waiter left, Rebecca rested her elbows
on the table, setting her chin on her intertwined fingers.

"Did Truscott only teach you the backbreaking work?"

"Not everything I do is backbreaking."

"Did he ever show his books?"

"Hell, no."

Rebecca shook her head. "He leaves you land but
doesn't give you the knowledge to run it. It's almost as
though he wanted you to fail, even from the grave, causing
you undue hardship."

Jake's eyes bore into hers. "I'm not going to fail."

She laid her hand over his. "I know that, Jake. But you
would have succeeded with a lot more sacrifice than was
necessary. You would have done without, you would have
worked another's spread. You would have done the best
you knew how and it would have gotten you through. Now
I'm going to teach you what Truscott didn't."

Reaching into her reticule, she pulled out a piece of paper
and a pencil. She put the tip of the pencil on the tip of her
tongue before whisking the pencil down the paper, drawing
a vertical line.

"Now, then. Do you know what an asset is?" she asked.

"A fancy name for what I'm sitting on?"

She laughed. "No. An asset is what you have that is of
value."

His eyes grew warm. "So you're an asset."

She blushed. "That's a matter of opinion, but I thank
you for thinking so. The first thing we need to do is tally
up your assets. You said you have eight hundred dollars
cash, right?"

"Right."

She wrote the amount down on the right side of the line.
"Now then, you have land valued at six dollars an acre."
She wrote land to the left of the line, its value to the right.

"So these are *our* assets," Jake said.

She looked up at him. "All right. Our assets. Now then,
we have five hundred head of cattle. Zach said you could
get seventy-five dollars a head further to the west so we'll

value them at seventy. How many longhorns have you acquired?''

Jake had given the men he found grazing their cattle on
his range the option of selling him the cattle or moving on.
Mavericks, cattle bearing no brands but roaming the range,
were fair game and he had acquired a few, burning the
Rocking R brand into their hides to establish ownership that
would not be questioned. ''Forty-three.''

Rebecca wrote down their value. ''We brought ten horses
with us and you have rounded up fourteen strays so we
have twenty-four horses not being used to work the ranch.
We won't count the horses the men ride since you let them
take the horse with them if they leave. We have a house.''

''It's only one room.''

''But it protects us from the elements of nature,'' she
said without looking up. ''A barn, a bunkhouse that's close
enough to being finished to count. When you get that cookhouse built, we'll add it. Now let's see . . . '' She stuck the
pencil in her mouth, her eyes gazing at the ceiling. ''As-
sorted livestock,'' she said, returning the pencil to the paper. Then her eyes snapped to his. ''Anything else?''

''I think that's about it.''

''All right.''

He smiled, watching her brows draw together in concen-
tration, the tip of her tongue touching the top of her lip as
she ran the pencil down the figures, adding up the amounts.
He had a strong desire to plant a kiss on that mouth.

Her face relaxed when the figuring was done. She drew
three circles around an amount and shoved the paper under
Jake's nose.

''That, Mr. Burnett, is what you are worth.''

Astounded, Jake stared at the number she had circled.

''But I don't have it in cash. I can't spend it.''

''No, but if you sold everything you would and could.
So we can use it as collateral.''

''How does that work?''

''When we go to the bank, we're going to ask for a loan
and put part of your land up as collateral. That means if
you don't pay the money back, the bank gets the land.''

"I'll pay the money back," Jake declared emphatically.

"Of course you will. Which is the whole point. The bank gives us the money. You use it to purchase more cattle, improve your ranch so you can make more money. Then we pay back the loan plus interest. But we come out ahead. We still have the land, you have more cattle and you work your spread instead of someone else's."

Jake looked doubtful.

"My father ran his ranch exactly like this. I doubt he even had eight hundred dollars in the bank. All his assets were tied up in the land and the cattle. He borrowed the money, invested it, paid it back, and borrowed it again."

Resting his hands on the table, Jake clenched them into tightened balls. "God, I feel stupid."

She placed her hand over his. "You're not stupid. How could you know if no one ever bothered to show you?"

"You knew."

"Because my father pulled me by the hand, kicking and screaming, to every meeting he ever attended. I met bankers, investors, businessmen. I learned how my father ran the ranch and how he depended on others to help him get where he wanted to be."

The tension lines Jake had worn since they'd gone into the general store eased away. "Your father raises shorthorns. What made you take an interest in Herefords?"

She smiled in remembrance of a happier time. "My father took me to the Centennial Exposition in Philadelphia. The cattle were on exhibition there. I thought they were cute."

His eyes widened. "Cute?"

She shrugged. "I was fourteen at the time. That's how I judged things."

"And how do you judge things now?" he asked.

"Differently."

Jake's mood lightened considerably before the meal was over. They left the hotel, crossing back to the boardwalk that ran in front of the general store. A sturdy man with windswept white hair was leaning back in a wooden chair, his newspaper held just low enough so he could watch all the passing activity. As the couple approached, he dropped his chair down, stood up, and put away his paper. He removed his spectacles and put them in his pocket, then extended a hand to Jake.

"Doyle Thomas, Attorney-at-Law. You must be the new folks."

"Yes, sir, we are," Jake said as he took the man's hand. "I'm Jake Burnett and this is my wife, Rebecca."

Doyle reached for his hat and shrugged. "Must have left it inside. Going to the bank?"

"Yes, sir," Jake said.

"Most people do. If you ever need a lawyer"—he pointed to the shingle above his door—"come see me. I'm not only the best, I'm the only one in town." He chuckled at his own joke as Jake and Rebecca walked past him.

"Either of you see my eyeglasses?" he called after them.

"Your pocket," they both said at once, grinning at each other.

"Oh, yeah," Doyle said as he took them out and slipped them on. He turned around twice before remembering where he'd left his newspaper.

When they found the bank and were waiting for an audience with the president, Rebecca slipped her hand into Jake's.

"You see that little desk back in the corner, behind the little gate?"

Jake nodded.

"Just think of it as a corral and the man sitting at the desk is the stallion you're getting ready to bend."

In less than half an hour, they returned to the general store. Jake handed Samuel Abrams the letter of credit along with his list of supplies while Rebecca picked out the cloth she wanted for curtains.

"I like the blue," he said, coming up behind her. "Do you sew?"

She smiled. "I sew as well as you hang a quilt."

Frowning, he rubbed the bridge of his nose. "That good, huh?"

She patted his arm. "Don't worry. I'm not going to make

them. I've asked Ruth to do it.''

Rebecca made a point of giving Mr. Abrams an especially sweet good-bye as they left the store. He managed a small smile in return.

They found Frank and Lee waiting for them in the wagon.

On their way out of town, they drove past a large house that seemed to slumber in the light of day.

"I wonder who lives there," Rebecca commented. "I'd love to see the inside."

Frank sat up. "It's real pretty inside. It's got—" He stopped when Lee hit him in the shoulder. "What?"

Lee scowled at the youth and Frank pulled himself back down into the corner of the wagon. Rebecca watched the crimson color creeping up her husband's face.

"Jake, have you been inside that house?"

"No, ma'am."

"But you know about that house."

"Yes, ma'am. It's the reason this town is called Pleasure."

Rebecca nodded. "I see. Well, at least now I know why Mr. Abrams carries such fancy cloths." She looked askance at her husband. "I guess we both learned something today."

Jake glanced her way, smiling. She might not be in love with him, but she had shown today that she would be loyal and stand by him. That was more than many wives did for their husbands. "Yes, ma'am, I reckon we did."

# Chapter Seven

FRANK SAUNTERED OUT of the barn, his long limbs moving haphazardly, then stopped dead in his tracks. Ruth Reading was reining in her horse in front of the house. Abruptly, he changed directions, ambling towards the house and pretty Ruth, completely forgetting whatever errand had sent him out of the barn to begin with.

Stepping out onto the porch, wiping her hands with a coarse towel, Rebecca greeted Ruth and her brother Luke.

"I'm ready to make your curtains today, Mrs. Burnett."

"Come on in then. I've got the material ready and waiting. If Luke needs to head home, I can have one of the men escort you back later."

"I'll be happy to escort her home," Frank said, leaning around Ruth and taking the reins of her horse. "I'll see to your horse, too."

Without noticing that his smile was not returned, he led the horse away while Luke, with a polite tip of his hat towards Rebecca, headed for home.

In no time Ruth was sitting by the window, her nimble fingers making meticulous stitches in the cloth. The sun reflected off her blond hair and her blue eyes danced as she talked about her brothers and other ranchers in the area. Then her fingers and tongue stilled as she peered out the window with increasing interest as a rider came into view.

"Zach Truscott is heading in. What do you suppose he wants?" Ruth asked.

Rebecca shrugged slightly. "He's working for us now."

"He is?" She set her sewing down. "Will you excuse me a minute?" She lifted her hand, curling and uncurling her fingers. "I need to rest my hands." She hurried out the door and almost ran to the barn.

When she got there Zach was lifting the saddle off his horse. He began brushing the animal down while she nibbled at the oats he'd placed before her in the last stall.

"Hello, Zach."

Tilting his hat up off his brow with a thumb, he peered over his horse's rump. "Well, hello, Ruth. What are you doing here?"

"Making curtains for Mrs. Burnett. Would you escort me home when I'm finished?"

"Sure."

She peered at him through her lowered lashes. "I need to get back to those curtains. See you later."

He flashed her a smile and Ruth felt her insides warm as she scurried back to the house.

Rebecca noticed less than perfect stitches began showing up when Ruth returned from her outside excursion. Her nimble fingers were working as quickly, but not as carefully. Rebecca was certain the girl's mind was no longer on the task at hand but was centered around something or someone else.

A short time later, Ruth laid the final curtain down. "There, all done."

Rebecca handed her two dollars, the agreed-upon price. She would have gladly paid anything to get out of making the curtains herself. Her most meticulous stitch did not come close to the perfection of Ruth's worst one. "I appreciate you doing this for me."

"If you need anything else done, just let me know. I enjoy sewing."

Ruth brought herself up on her toes, holding her hands behind her back. Then she lowered her heels back down to the floor. "Well, I'd better go find Zach."

"Zach?"

"He's going to take me home."

"I thought Frank offered."

"He did but . . . well . . . I'd just feel safer with Zach."

Raising herself back up onto her toes, she spun around and went searching for Zach leaving Rebecca with the distinct impression that trouble was brewing.

Ruth was standing under the eaves of the porch, swishing her hips back and forth, waiting for Zach to saddle up their horses when Frank sauntered over.

"You ready to go?"

Keeping her eyes on the barn, Ruth said, "Zach is taking me home."

"Goddamn! I asked first!"

Bringing the horses out of the barn, Zach caught Frank's words, imagining most of the ranch had heard them, he'd yelled them so loudly.

Frank turned on Zach. "I'm taking her home." Frank clenched his fists almost as tightly as he'd clenched his jaws.

With trepidation, Rebecca stuck her head out the door. "Frank, I need some help hanging these curtains."

"Dammit! I said I'd take her home."

Frank glared at Zach as though everything was Zach's fault. Ruth hopped down off the porch, gazing up at Zach with adoration in her eyes, adoration that Zach knew could eventually mean trouble. She was too young for a man of his experience. Smiling apologetically at Ruth, he handed the reins of his horse to Frank. "I'll help Rebecca with the curtains."

Zach walked over to the crestfallen girl. "I'm sorry, Ruth, but men have a code of honor. If Frank asked first, I have to step aside."

"But I like you."

"You barely know me. You can't judge a man by a couple of dances."

"You're Mr. Burnett's brother and I like Mr. Burnett."

"I'm not Jake's brother. I want to be, but I'm a fair distance away from being that right now." He hoisted her up into the saddle. "Frank'll see that you get home safe."

Ruth glowered at the beaming Frank and sent her horse

into a gallop. Frank mounted Zach's horse and took off after her.

Rebecca wrapped her arms around one of the rough beams supporting the roof. "Poor Frank."

"Yep, the boy's in for heartache that's for sure. I'd say she was his first love. Funny how the first time around, a person can fall in love with someone they hardly know." Zach moved up onto the porch. "Do you remember your first love, Rebecca?"

An image of hair the color of midnight, eyes a deep blue flashed through her mind. Her first love. Every man before Brett had been in awe of her beauty or her father's position. But Brett had taken her down off her pedestal, had made her feel touchable.

She had been in the stall tending her horse. She turned around and found him towering above her. Without a word, he'd pressed her against him, his mouth opening to devour hers. She'd whimpered and his arms had tightened around her. Before Brett, she'd been kissed by young men whose tongues had dashed around her mouth without the courage to touch anything. But Brett had touched everything, every nook and cranny, exploring her mouth, slowly, deliberately. It had been pure heaven.

"I remember him." She sighed wistfully.

"First loves are hard to forget," Zach admitted. "I think no matter how many times a person falls in love, the first love and the last love are the only two that really matter. Now you had some curtains that needed hanging?"

Nodding, she walked into the house. For her, the first love and the last love were one and the same.

Frank sat straight in his saddle, his chest swelling with pride. Ruth had slowed her horse down to a trot and then to a walk, for which he was extremely grateful. Traveling at a slower rate allowed him to gaze upon her beauty. And Lord, she was beautiful.

Only one thing was spoiling the moment. There was no one to see him with this woman by his side. There was nothing but open space between the Rocking R and the

Triple Bar. He wished they could detour through town.

Twilight was setting in as they arrived at Ruth's house. Ruth dismounted before Frank had a chance to help her. Then she was hurrying up the steps to the house. Frank rushed after her, grabbing her arm. She jerked free and glared at him. Frank smiled.

"I was wondering if you'd like to go riding with me sometime."

"I just went riding with you."

His smile grew. "Yeah, I know. And I thought it was kinda pleasant. Thought maybe you'd like to do it again."

"No."

The smile left Frank's face. "Why the hell not?"

"Because you're a boy."

"I sure as hell am not. Hell, I shave every day!"

Ruth rolled her eyes. "I've got to get inside."

Dumbfounded, Frank watched as the door closed, taking her away. He tromped down the stairs and mounted his horse. Ruth was nearly as beautiful as Reb. He wondered how Jake had managed to make Reb love him. He thought of the way Jake looked at Reb, the way she looked at him. The man made her feel special. Frank smiled. He'd just have to think of a way to make Ruth feel special.

Laughter escaped Rebecca's throat as she pressed both palms against her aching side, trying to ease the spasms brought on by the antics of the cowboys preparing themselves to ride into town. She wondered why they had even bothered to bathe when they were coating themselves with all the dust they were stirring up. Jake was smiling, shaking his head, and she wondered if he wanted to go with them. She couldn't recall ever seeing him go off on a Saturday night when they had lived in Kentucky, but then she hadn't really paid that much attention back then. The dust settled and the two of them were left, moving towards the chores that awaited them without speaking.

Life had settled into a pleasant routine. Each day, she and Jake would ride the range, keeping a watch on the cattle, inspecting the progress of the barbed-wire fencing that was being strung up with mechanical stretchers. Their journey was slowed because of Rebecca's expanding girth. Jake would pick up their meals from the cook and they would eat together at the rough oak table in their house. They'd discuss plans for the ranch, Jake's desire to build tanks to catch the rainwater, windmills to pull up the water that the earth hoarded like a miser deep below. He had been toying with the idea of growing his own hay so he could feed his cattle if the winter turned harsh. It was a novel idea in a state known for its mild winters, but Jake didn't trust Mother Nature and didn't want to be dependent on her moods. Rebecca greeted all his ideas with excitement and enthusiasm, adding a few ideas of her own, suggesting he lease some of his land to farmers who would use part of their land to plant, harvest, and bind the hay that Jake wanted.

On Saturday afternoons, they did what they were doing now—washing their clothes. Jake scrubbed them in the big wooden tub and handed them to Rebecca to drape over the line he had strung up. The first time he had dipped her undergarments in the water, he had turned beet red, and though she had offered to wash her own things, he had insisted he do his share.

She draped his shirt over the line and turned back towards him, laughing as she did so. He was surveying the sky with great intensity and she knew he was washing some personal article of hers.

When they finished with the laundry, they cleaned the inside of the house, sweeping and dusting and straightening up. Then they went for a walk, hand in hand. When they got back, they cooked supper together. Jake brought two chairs out onto the porch, and they ate the worst meal they'd had in a while, laughing over it as they tried to remember what it was they'd fixed. They sat back quietly and watched the setting sun.

After it got darker, they washed up the dishes. Then Jake excused himself to take care of some chores. More and more often lately he claimed to have work to do in the evenings. Rebecca curled up on the sofa with a book, wait-

ing for his return, wondering why he was finding reasons
to be away from her when he hadn't before.

The copy of *Treasure Island* that her father had given
her for Christmas the previous year lay open on her lap.
But she couldn't concentrate. She wished Jake hadn't chosen this particular night to leave her alone. It was too quiet
without the men around, and she found her thoughts drifting hauntingly more and more often to Brett.

As always, it was the rich hue of his blue eyes that came
to her first. On more than one occasion, she had felt herself
falling into the depths of those mesmerizing eyes. Then he
would smile and she would become lost, the world narrow-
ing down until it was only the two of them.

Even when they were surrounded by people, she'd only
see Brett. Brett and his blue eyes. Blue.

The night he'd taken her into the city to watch a play,
she'd worn a silk gown that matched the shade of his eyes
perfectly. He'd looked so handsome in his black suit as
they'd strolled through the opulent lobby, crystal chande-
liers reflecting the gaslights. He'd escorted her to a private
box in the balcony. Her eyes had been on him as she'd
taken her seat. As soon as she sat down, she'd popped back
up, and spun around. Sitting on the chair was a small
wrapped package, the box adorning it flattened.

She'd snatched it up, sat down and begun to unwrap it.
"What is it?"

He'd laughed, the sound rumbling out across the balcony. "If I'd wanted you to know right away, I wouldn't
have gone to the trouble of having it wrapped."

Inside, she'd found a necklace, diamonds and sapphires
more dazzling than anything she'd ever seen.

"Where in the world did you get these?"

"Royal flush."

"You won them in a poker game?" she'd asked in
amazement.

"No, I won money in a poker game."

"And you spent it on me?"

"Who else am I going to spend it on?"

Her father paid a fair wage but it didn't allow for luxuries. She'd thought of all the things Brett could have bought for himself. She'd felt as precious as the jewels because he'd chosen instead to buy something for her.

He'd draped the necklace around her neck, then used his fingers to outline it along her flesh, his fingers straying down to the exposed curves of her breasts.

"I sure do like this gown," he'd said, his voice low and deep, sending shivers racing up her spine. "Someday, Rebecca, you'll be wearing me the way you wear this gown, next to your body, and I'll feel so much finer than silk."

The curtains had opened. He'd slipped his hand beneath her hair, rubbing her neck, moving his fingers around to tease her throat, her shoulders, the sensitive places behind her ears. So much of *Hamlet* had been lost to her.

And now Brett was lost to her as well. She closed the book, setting it down on the sofa, and walked out of the house.

Darkness surrounded her and a warm breeze whistled through the scattered trees. The baby moved. Already, she loved this little life growing inside her, this little life she had created with Brett. For the remainder of her years, she would be grateful to him for leaving a part of himself with her.

She wondered if Jake, if any man, could truly love another's child as his own.

She stepped off the porch, feeling a strong need to be with Jake at that moment, hoping he would understand.

She walked across the narrow yard to the barn, realizing she had no idea where he was. She stepped into the barn, relieved to see his chestnut stallion content in the stall. She was peering in stalls, wondering where he could possibly be, when she heard the gritty sound of wood being sanded. Stepping into the doorway of the back room where extra supplies were kept, she saw him sitting on the floor, Indian style. He was sanding and blowing a piece of curved wood, holding it out to inspect it, then beginning the process over again.

"What are you doing?" she asked.

Her words startled him and he jumped. Not wanting to

anger him, Rebecca threw one hand to her mouth to stifle her laughter. He placed a hand over his heart.

"You looking to become a widow? Jesus, you almost made my heart stop beating."

"I'm sorry." But the giggles in her voice rendered her apology insincere and he pierced her with narrowed eyes. "I really am sorry. I was just . . . getting lonely."

He pointed towards a low stool in the corner. "You want to sit in here?"

"Do you mind?"

"It beats having you sneak up on me," he said with irritation in his voice but a smile in his eyes. She plopped herself down on the stool.

"You never go into town with the men," she said.

He jerked his head up from his task to eye her warily. "I'm a married man."

"But even before that. I don't remember ever seeing you go."

He shrugged and went back to sanding the wood. "A man spends money in town on Saturday night. I was saving my money for this place."

She stuck her hands between her knees. "You think the men are visiting that big house on the edge of town?"

"Probably," he answered without looking up or stopping his work.

"Have you . . . have you ever been to a . . . a whorehouse?"

His eyes snapped up to hold hers. Her cheeks were flushed, and he knew she was having one hell of a time maintaining eye contact with him.

"Once . . . a long time back."

"Only once?"

He gave a light shrug. "I didn't like the way it made me feel."

She leaned forward, her eyes wide, disbelieving. "You didn't like the way it made you feel?"

Now the flush ran through his face, and he was the one having one hell of a time maintaining eye contact.

"Oh . . . not that. I mean . . . I liked that . . . it was afterwards that I didn't like. I didn't like feeling like I'd had to pay a woman to want me.''

"Ohh.'' She sat back up, nodding her head as though she understood. "I see.'' Her brows drew together. "Most men don't care, do they?''

"I reckon not.'' He went back to sanding the wood, hoping that was the end of that subject.

Rebecca allowed her gaze to wander around the room. Harnesses hung over pegs in the walls. A saddle in need of repair sat in a corner. Except for the boxes and odds and ends stacked haphazardly at the back, the room was neat and orderly, leaving ample room for a man to work.

She turned her attention to Jake, his head bent as he worked. He'd rolled up his sleeves, exposing his forearms. They were firm, even when he relaxed them, a product of hard work. He lifted his arm, wiping the sweat from his brow with the sleeve of his shirt. She tilted her head, one way then the other picturing him in a black suit. He'd need to wear brown.

"Have you ever been to a play?''

"Once.'' A teasing glint came into his eyes, and he tilted up one corner of his mouth. "A long time back.''

She smiled and leaned forward. "Did you like the way it made you feel?''

"I suppose. Made me laugh a couple of times, made me sad for a while, but in the end, it made me feel good. You like the way plays make you feel?''

She felt the heat flush her cheeks and nodded, afraid if she tried to speak her voice would sound husky and betray her feelings. She had indeed enjoyed the way she'd felt when she'd watched the play with Brett.

Jake studied her a minute and then went back to sanding his wood, for which she was grateful. She'd come in here to take her mind away from Brett, and her conversation with Jake had brought about the opposite effect. She was once again remembering the feel of Brett's presence beside her, the touch of his fingers. She shook the thoughts away and tried to imagine what it would be like to attend a play with Jake. He'd no doubt leave her in peace to enjoy the staged performance. For some reason, that thought left her disappointed.

She watched as he moved his large hands over the wood. She knew from experience that his long fingers felt almost as rough as the sandpaper. And yet the sandpaper left no evidence of its coarseness. Instead the wood looked smoothed and polished as though it had been caressed. She realized that Jake was indeed caressing the wood, touching it lightly, taking great care to ensure the rough texture of the paper caused no damage. His deliberate movements created a rasping sound that was as soothing as any lullaby.

"Thought you said you weren't much of a carpenter?"

"What?"

"The night you nailed up the quilt you said you weren't much of a carpenter."

He pointed the piece of wood at her. "I said you could sit, not talk."

The unexpected sternness in his voice sent her emotions reeling. She straightened her legs out, lifted her feet, then set them back down. Nodding her head, her eyes large and round like those of a chastised schoolgirl, she turned her face away.

Leaning over, he touched her knee. "I'm sorry," he said softly.

Shaking her head, she kept her face averted. "It's okay. It's just because I'm pregnant. I get moody." She rubbed her closed eyelids, hoping when she looked at him he wouldn't know that tears had sprung to her eyes. Sometimes she felt like a heavy black rain cloud that could burst forth showers unexpectedly anytime.

"It was supposed to be a surprise, but I'll show you now if you want," Jake said.

Her head snapped around, unshed tears filling her eyes, and a big smile gracing her face that melted his heart.

"A surprise?"

He returned her smile before getting up to haul supplies out of the way. He pulled forth a wooden chair. Her eyes flew from the chair to the piece of carved wood he had been working on.

"A rocking chair?" she asked.

"I thought a mother should be able to rock her baby."

"Oh, Jake," she whispered, her fingers pressed lightly to her lips. She lovingly touched the chair's back, the delicately carved spindles trailing down. Then she ran her hand over the armrests before pressing her palm to the seat. "You did all this?"

"It's not—" The look in her eyes stayed his words.

"If you say it's not much, I'll whack you."

He grinned at her.

"It's the most beautiful thing I've ever seen," she said. "Why did you make me think you didn't have any carpentry skills?"

"I started planning this before we left Kentucky. Thought the surprise would be more fun if you weren't expecting anything."

"And was it?"

"Yep, but that's not all."

Incredulously, she looked at him. "What else have you been up to?"

He cleared more obstacles out of the way before turning back to her, holding a small wooden cradle. He set it down at her feet. She dropped to her knees and he knelt beside her.

"I made the bottoms curved so you can rock him in here if you want to."

She tipped the cradle and released it, watching it rock back and forth. But it was the tiny headboard that fascinated her. Intricately carved mustangs adorned it. In wonder, she outlined one of the horses rearing up on his back legs.

"Did you carve all this?" she asked, awed.

"I didn't know what to put on it. I wanted something that would be okay whether you had a boy or a girl and then I figured with your love for horses, your child's bound to love them, too. But if you want, I can redo it if the baby's a girl and you want something a little more dainty."

Amazed, she said, "Jake, do you have any idea how many fine things I've been given over the years, how many expensive things? And not one of them is as valuable as this. It's so obviously from your heart." She squeezed her eyes shut to stay the tears but they burst forth anyway. Her hands flew to cover her face as she released a loud sob.

His arms came around her. "This wasn't supposed to make you cry."

"You're too good to me. You give me everything and I don't give you anything."

"Married people aren't supposed to keep a tally of what they do for each other, Reb. It all evens out in the end. Here." He pulled back, wiping her tears from her face. "You stop crying and I'll finish the rocker so we can take it inside the house and you can try it out. Okay?"

She nodded and went back to sit on the stool, watching the love and care he poured into his work, wondering if there was a limit to how much he could give.

# Chapter *E*ight

TEN-YEAR-OLD JOHN READING slowed his galloping horse down to a trot. He didn't want to spook the cattle that Mr. and Mrs. Burnett were moving along. Growing up on a ranch, he was familiar with the dangers a spooked cow could unleash. His father's temper was one of them if any of his boys were to blame for a stampede.

Recognizing his dilemma, Jake and Rebecca moved away from the few unbranded strays they'd run across. The boy was laughing so hard they were afraid he was going to fall out of his saddle.

"Ma says you're to come over right now!" He guffawed, pressing a tightened fist into his stomach. "Funniest thing I ever did see'd! Geese flew in and started eating Pa's corn out in the field. Aggravated him so much he threw them the corn he'd been soaking in whiskey. Geese ate it!" He inhaled deeply. "Now, they're so drunk they can't fly! They're acting like Matthew did last time he went to town, and Ma said we're gonna catch 'em and eat 'em before they throw up like Matthew did! Ma says it don't matter you got work to do. You gotta come!" He took off without waiting for an answer. He had four other ranches to visit and he wanted to get back while the geese were still flapping their wings. Besides, when Ma said to do something, it got done.

Jake glanced over at Rebecca. "Does that woman ever ask?"

"Would it make a difference?"

"Reckon not. Let's get these cows to Zach so he can brand them, and we'll round up the rest of the men and get over there."

Leaning into Jake, Rebecca wiped the tears from her eyes. They had stopped off at the house and she had changed into a light blue cotton dress. She had no desire for Carrie or any of their other neighbors to see the atrocious clothing she wore when she rode a horse these days. She and Jake had come in the wagon, some of the men riding with them. Others, anxious to see the drunken geese, had opted to ride their horses so they could get to the Triple Bar quicker.

"Funniest thing I ever did see'd," Rebecca crowed and Jake thought he was going to have to hold her up. He couldn't recall ever seeing her laugh this hard. Rambunctious children rushed after the geese who could remember no more about flying than the flapping of their wings. The geese emitted garbled honks and fumbled over webbed feet that didn't take them where they wanted to go. Less daring children settled for picking up the geese that had passed out in the field.

Some of the adults were turning the geese on skewers over the open flames. How Carrie had managed to prepare in so short a time for so many people was beyond Rebecca's comprehension, but prepared she had and everyone felt welcome. Tables were set up with benches, quilts were spread beneath trees. There were even burlap sacks stuffed with goose feathers for anyone who wanted them for mattresses or pillows.

When the meal was done and all the greasy fingers had been licked or washed, Carrie announced that the boys wanted to have a tournament. Rebecca was standing near Zach when the proclamation was made. She glanced over at him, raising a brow.

"A tournament?"

"They had one at the Fourth of July picnic. It was pretty interesting." He took a step closer, relishing the opportunity to be near her. "The boys pretend they are knights of old attempting to win a fair maiden's hand. See the poles Michael is putting up?''

Rebecca nodded as she watched Michael poke a pole in the ground every sixty feet or so. The poles each had an arm that extended out and held a ring even with a mounted man's shoulder.

"The boys use wooden lances to take the rings off the poles. They each get several passes and someone keeps tally of the number of rings each boy manages to hook and keep on his lance. The one who gets the most is proclaimed the champion knight and is given the honor of selecting a queen.''

One behind another, the young men lined up on their horses, Frank among them. People gathered on both sides of the three hundred foot track where the horses would run.

Matthew Reading galloped to the center of the track holding up a tightened fist and made the first announcement in a deep clear voice. "Knight of the Triple Bar, ready, ride!''

Luke Reading lowered his lance, spurred his horse and galloped down the line. He knocked the first ring to the ground, hooked the second. He galloped to the third, hooked the ring but it slipped off his lance. He continued the ride to the end, missing the last two rings, then turned around and galloped back to Matthew, presenting him with the solitary ring that had managed to stay on his lance. Carrie wrote the number down and Michael hung the rings back on the arms of the poles.

Matthew made the next announcement, "Knight of the Rocking R, ready, ride!'' and Frank took off, gathering all the rings along the way to the chant of beginner's luck.

More than anything else, Jake enjoyed watching his wife when she was enjoying something. Her face was alight, her eyes pools of blue taking in everything that was happening before her. Slowly, he eased his way up through the crowd to stand behind her. Slipping his arms around her, he brought his mouth close to her ear. "No.''

Rebecca's smile increased. She turned slightly, poking her finger into his chest.

"As soon as this baby is born, Jake Burnett, I'm going to do it."

He laughed. "It wouldn't be fair to the boys." He lowered his voice. "You know you'd win."

She returned his laughter. "In private then." She leaned back against him. "But I am going to do it, one way or the other."

Jake looked over at Zach. "You should see her when she's not riding for two. Those boys wouldn't stand a chance."

The riders rode the length three times. When the numbers were tallied, Frank was declared the Champion Knight and given the privilege of selecting someone to be his Queen. Searching the crowds, he spied the woman he wanted and his smile grew. Now was his opportunity to make her feel special. "Ruth Reading!"

Ruth groaned. Only at her mother's persistent prodding did she move forward to receive a kiss from Frank. Frank hadn't known he'd be expected to kiss her. He decided he was being offered the ideal opportunity to show Ruth that he was indeed a man, and not some gangling boy. Taking her in his arms, he leaned her over backwards, intending to impress her with his romantic embrace. But just as his lips reached hers, he lost his balance and they both plummeted to the ground.

Jake lowered his head moving it slowly from side to side. Rebecca covered her face with her hands. Zach walked off, laughing.

The velvet darkness had descended over the land and the people gathered around the campfires. They were singing ballads and listening to tales. Rebecca was sitting beside Jake, her hand in his.

Zach leaned against a tree and watched as Jake said something to Rebecca, something that made her smile. She tilted her head up and said something to him. Of all the couples sitting before the dancing flames, Rebecca and Jake seemed to have the most to say to each other, and Zach was fascinated watching how easily Jake could bring a smile to her face. Jake's fingers splayed across the top of Rebecca's stomach. Zach saw a softness sweep over both their faces simultaneously, and he knew they had felt the baby move. He stomped down the green monster that threatened to rule him. He had hated Jake when he was a boy because a son wasn't supposed to hate his father. He wouldn't envy him now because he was married to Rebecca. He shoved himself away from the tree and walked off into the night.

Sitting outside the ring of fires, Frank wondered what the hell he could do to make Ruth like him, to make her want to be with him. He had intended to sweep her off her feet with his kiss that afternoon. Well, he had certainly swept her off her feet, but not the way he had intended. He had wanted her to take notice of him and she certainly had when he'd dropped her before falling down on top of her. He'd made a real fool of himself and he hadn't even been drinking. Solemnly, he went to get his horse. There was nothing for him here.

Dropping down on the bed, holding out a buttonhook, Rebecca stuck a foot up, batting her eyelashes several times. "Please?"

Jake took the buttonhook from her and she pressed her foot against his thigh. He had such firm thighs. She watched his fingers struggling with the buttons on her shoes.

"Why do they make these things so tiny?" he asked.

"I don't know. Here I'll do it," she said as she reached for the hook.

He pulled it back. "No, I'll do it."

She lay back, resting up on her elbows. "I enjoyed today."

"I could tell. I don't think I've ever seen you laugh so hard. Felt sorry for Frank, though."

Rebecca sighed. "I wish he would leave Ruth alone. She's obviously not interested in him."

Jake pulled her shoe off and dropped it to the floor. She rubbed her stockinged foot up and down his thigh, enjoying the feel of his hardened muscles against her instep. His hand came to rest over her foot, stilling her actions. She looked up into his intense gaze, wondering what she had been thinking, realizing she hadn't been thinking at all.

"I'll do the other one," she squeaked before clearing her throat.

"I'll do it," Jake said as he patted his thigh.

She lowered one foot to the floor and replaced it with the other. His eyes left hers to concentrate on his task. He dropped the second shoe to the floor and pressed her foot against his thigh.

"Did you need to rub this one?" he asked, his intense gaze back on her.

She closed her eyes, trying to think. To breathe she had to bring air into her lungs and then blow it out. She could do that. She opened her eyes and he stepped back, her foot dropping to the floor.

"Maybe another time," he said. He turned, breathing deeply.

"Jake?"

Turning back around, he gave her a small smile. "What?"

"I'm sorry," she whispered. "I shouldn't have . . . "

Reaching out, he touched her cheek. "Don't apologize. Partnerships aren't easy."

"But we should have a marriage."

"Maybe someday we will."

"I'm your wife. You have the right—"

Quickly, he pressed his finger against her lips, silencing her words. "Lord, Reb, I can't think of anything that'd be more degrading to either one of us."

"Don't you want to?"

"Do you?"

"I don't know," she replied honestly.

A banging on the door made them both jump. Jake gave her a small smile before moving around the quilt, heading for the door. Rebecca followed him, wondering what exactly it was she did want.

Jake lifted the bar and opened the door slightly. He peered out and then ushered Zach into the house.

"I'm sorry to bother you so late," Zach began, "but coming home, I ran across Frank's horse, still saddled, about a mile from here. Looked like it had done some pretty hard riding."

Rebecca sidled up to Jake and he put his arm around her, his hand resting on the small of her back. Zach wondered if these two were even aware of how much they touched each other.

"I take it Frank's not in the bunkhouse," Jake said.

"Nope. No one's seen him since he left the Readings'."

Jake released a deep sigh. "If Ethan's harmed that boy, he and I'll be settling up."

"The line starts behind me," Zach said.

Jake nodded acceptance of Zach's feelings, knowing, however, that if Ethan were involved, no one would get to him before Jake did. "Go get the men. We'll split up into groups and go searching for him."

The two men walked out of the house without another word and Rebecca went to change clothes.

Moments later she stepped out onto the porch, closing the door behind her.

"Where the hell do you think you're going?" A harsh voice sounded and she turned to confront Zach. His face was set in stark lines, his lips pressed so tightly together they were almost invisible, his brown eyes almost black.

"I'm going with you," she said.

"The hell you are."

Taken aback, Rebecca stated calmly, "Zach, you're overstepping your bounds on this."

Zach turned to Jake. "Tell her she's not going," he demanded.

Jake handed the reins to his wife. "Why would I do that?" he asked as he helped her mount. "She's the best tracker I know."

The three rode out together. The absence of a moon was a hindrance as their horses plodded along. All they could see was what surrounded them—a black abyss. Jake and Zach each held a lantern which aided them in their search as much as the moon did. No breeze whispered across the land to bring them any scents, the occasional howl of a coyote raised the fine hairs on the back of their necks. Their quest for the missing Frank seemed hopeless but each rider was equally reluctant to turn back.

Rebecca reached out to touch Jake's arm.

"Over there. I think I see some burning embers."

Jake squinted towards the blackness. "I think you're right. Let's check it out."

Zach stared in the direction they had both looked and all he could see was the darkness.

Frank lay on the solid ground, his hands tied to his ankles, his ankles bound together. He hadn't been brave but he didn't think he had been a coward either. What man wouldn't have reacted the way he had under the circumstances?

Trouble had come in the form of galloping riders, brandishing torches, shouting, and firing random shots that whizzed by him so close he was certain they were meant for his skinny hide. He had urged his horse into a full gallop back towards the Rocking R but he had known his actions were futile. He heard the whistling of the lariat before the circle of rope closed around him, pinning his arms to his body. His horse continued galloping towards the ranch as Frank was jerked out of the saddle by the unrelenting master of the rope. The air was painfully knocked out of his lungs as his body made contact with the hard ground. Descending on him like starved vultures, the men had tied his hands before him and dragged more than walked him back to their camp.

Their small camp had had a temporary look about it. A fire set in the middle was heating up a branding iron. Frank had thought as he'd watched the metal glowing brightly that it was a damned odd time of day to be branding cattle. In the firelight, he'd noticed all the men were wearing their bandannas drawn up over their noses and wondered if they were cattle rustlers.

One of the men had dismounted and started untying his hands.

"Got us a maverick here," he'd said in a raspy voice that sounded like someone had scrubbed his throat with a stiff-bristled brush.

The man closest to the fire had lifted the red-hot iron out of the flames and said, "Then I guess we'd best brand him."

The full impact of those words had hit Frank like a bucking bronco. Yelling his usual curse, he had managed to break free. His dash for freedom had been cut short as a man near the fire had sent out a twirling rope and lassoed him. Laughter had echoed around him as the men trussed him up, worked his pants down and applied the fiery hot brand to his tender, young flesh. His agonizing scream rent the still night air.

And now with his backside still bringing tears to his eyes, he lay alone wondering what he was going to do to get out of this unjust predicament, hoping those howling coyote weren't hungry, wishing he'd stayed at the Reading Ranch. Ruth's snubs hadn't hurt his pride as badly as the beating that had just been delivered to him.

He saw the flickering light of lanterns, heard the riders and, praying it wasn't the men returning, he lifted his head to get a better look. Goddamn, it was Rebecca.

"Oh, Frank!" Rebecca wailed with tears in her eyes when she caught sight of him.

"Get her away from me!" he yelled. He looked imploringly at Jake as the man knelt down beside Rebecca and started to cut the bindings. "I'm exposed!"

"Relax, Frank," Rebecca said as she ran her fingers along his brow. "I've seen your bare backside before."

"The hell you have! I swear, Jake, I've never shown her anything!"

Zach sat on his haunches, intrigued. Whether she had seen Frank or not, she had the young man so upset that he wasn't paying any attention to the ministrations she was now carefully bestowing upon him.

"Sure you have. At the watering hole at the Lazy A," Rebecca explained.

Frank's eyes widened.

"That's right," she said as she carefully examined his burn. "When you cowpokes were supposed to be out watching the herds, you'd sneak off when you got too hot and go swimming in my watering hole."

"How did you know?" Frank asked, trying desperately to remember everything they'd said and done. Hell, men might say or do anything if they thought no women were around.

"Because I was swimming there first and had to get out when the bunch of you showed up. So I decided to stay and watch the show."

"Is that all you did?" Frank asked. "Watch?"

"Nope. I listened too. And you know that story Lee told about that contortionist woman he said he bedded?"

Two harsh curses were uttered at once, and Zach worked hard to stifle his laughter, making a mental note to ask Jake about this particular story.

"I didn't believe a word of it," Rebecca said. She turned to Jake. "I think we ought to cut the backside out of his pants and take him home. I can tend him better there."

"But these are my best pants!" Frank wailed.

"I'll buy you another pair," Jake said as he set about the task before they began the long trek back.

Rebecca tended Frank's burn and then returned to the house while Jake took some time to talk with the returning men. She sat on the bed, her legs curled up, her stomach protruding out as far as it could. She heard Jake come in and saw the light before the quilt dim, but he didn't come to bed.

"Are we still friends?" she asked as she came to stand before the sofa where he was sitting, elbows on his knees, his shoulders hunched over, his head bowed. His head shot up.

"Why the hell wouldn't we be?"

"Because of what I did earlier when you were taking off my shoes . . . the things I said."

Leaning forward, he took her hand in his and pulled her

down to the sofa. He brought her head to rest in the crook of his shoulder.

"We'd be in a sorry state if our friendship was that fragile. Our marriage didn't come about like most. But I haven't changed my mind about anything I said when I asked you to marry me." Jake rubbed a hand down his thigh, and then said softly, "Don't take offense at what I'm going to say." He looked down at her, and she was looking up at him with such concern that all he wanted to do was ease the worry lines between her brows. "You've been with a man . . . a man you love. I imagine there's nothing finer than when two people who love each other—" He moved a hand slowly through the air as though it were a blanket covering two lovers. "What I have to offer you . . . it won't be as fine . . . so it has to be what you want."

"It seems so unfair to you."

He shook his head. "You were honest with me about your feelings when I asked you to marry me. I got no cause to complain. Besides . . . winter's coming soon and you can start earning your keep."

Rebecca put her hand on her expanded girth. "Somehow I don't think I'm going to look very springlike."

"Close enough to keep me happy."

She snuggled up closer. "You're a good friend, Jake. Always have been."

He pressed his lips to the top of her head. "Zach and I are going to ride out first light and see if we can figure out what was going on tonight."

"Promise me you'll be careful. Men that would do that to Frank are capable of doing anything."

Jake hunkered down before the barren ashes watching as the wind caught and swirled the dry remains of the campfire. He lifted the iron that had been heated to a redhot glow and pressed against Frank's backside. A wellspring of anger, too long suppressed, gushed forth.

"It's a poor imitation," he said, his voice harsh.

Zach knelt down beside him, his eyes studying the offending object.

"Guess they chose your brand to make a point."

Jake nodded as he slowly twirled the stem of the brand.

"I don't think Frank was sought out," Zach added. "I think he just happened to be the unlucky one passing by. Whoever did this would have probably preferred someone who wasn't one of your men."

"Lord, I'm thinking of John Reading riding all over the place, laughing, telling people about those geese. What if they'd happened upon him first?"

Jake dropped his head wondering if he was at fault. Was someone making a statement against him, his fencing? Or were the men who had attacked Frank just mean bastards with nothing better to do than harass decent folks? Jake looked off into the distance. They hadn't found one thing to tell them who was responsible. And yet he couldn't help but feel that somehow Ethan was involved.

He'd been twelve the first time Ethan had told everyone within hearing distance the crude things his mother had done with men for money. He'd delivered a blow to Ethan's chest; Ethan had responded by plowing his hardened fists into Jake's face. The raised ridge on the bridge of his nose and some scars on his backside from the lashes he'd received from Truscott's belt served as a reminder of that day. Ethan had received no lashes. The lesson to be learned was to turn the other cheek. This had made Jake laugh since he hadn't been able to sit down on either cheek for a week.

Other fights had followed, Ethan always claiming victory. Until the day they'd put Thomas Truscott in the ground. Jake had pummeled his fists into Ethan until the man couldn't move, until there could be no doubt who'd won. But standing over Ethan with bloodied fists, he'd realized he hadn't won anything at all. He'd found no victory, no pride, only emptiness.

"What ever happened with Lisa Sue?" Jake asked quietly, turning his gaze towards Zach. His head snapped around so fast Jake heard his neck pop.

"Lisa Sue?"

"Thought you two were sweet on each other."

Zach lifted up the dust and threw it into the wind, watching it sail away until it was nothing. He shrugged. "She wasn't too keen on marrying a man who had nothing to offer. Told her I'd come for her once we got settled here, once I knew we could make a go of it. Three months later, she married Joe Raskins."

"Joe Raskins?"

The look of horror on Jake's face made Zach laugh. It was the first time he'd thought of Lisa Sue without hurting.

"Good Lord. If she wasn't going to marry you, at least she didn't have to lower herself to Joe Raskins. 'Less he's changed considerable since I knew him."

Zach shook his head, his eyes twinkling. "Same as he was when we went to school with him. Obnoxious as hell. Only comfort I got from knowing she'd married him was knowing it wouldn't take her long to regret it. But then . . . after a while, that thought held no comfort either. I loved her. Hate thinking she'll spend the rest of her life unhappy."

"Because I got the land and you got the debts?"

Zach's expression hardened. "I don't resent you getting the land. I figure every stroke of his strap bought you an acre of land. No, what I resent is his burying us in debt up to our necks and not leaving a spade for us to dig ourselves out with."

"I'm sorry about Lisa Sue."

Zach forced a small smile. "It's probably just as well. Got to admit, though, I envy the hell out of you. Married to Rebecca."

"I don't think you'd envy me if you knew the cost."

"I'd pay any price for a woman like Rebecca."

Jake studied the sleek nose, the hollow cheeks, the firm chin, the deep brown eyes of the man before him. He looked back at the iron that was growing heavy in his hand. "You probably wouldn't have to pay the same price." He fought for a while against saying the words but last night had made him remember how true they were. "She doesn't love me."

"You're crazy. The woman adores you."

Jake said nothing. He wouldn't argue what he knew in his heart to be true.

Zach shook his head. Lee had told him that Rebecca was pregnant when Jake married her. But then, based on the story Lee had related with relish about the contortionist, Zach wasn't certain Lee could be trusted to tell the exact truth. "Rebecca doesn't strike me as the type of woman who would lie with a man she didn't love."

Jake dropped the iron and brought himself to his feet. "She didn't."

Zach wanted a further explanation of what that remark meant—had she loved him and stopped? Was she carrying another man's baby?—but Jake pulled himself up onto his horse. "I'm going to go check the west side. Why don't you head east and we'll meet back here?"

Zach could do no more than nod, and envy was the last thing he felt at the moment.

It was late in the evening before a weary Jake and an exhausted Zach walked into the house. Rebecca poured two cups of black coffee and set them down before the men as they dropped into chairs. Rebecca moved around behind Jake and began kneading the muscles in his shoulders.

"No luck?" she asked.

"There's not even an unbranded stray calf on our land today," Jake said.

"Think it was Ethan?" she asked Zach.

"Hard to say. Frank said they were masked and he didn't recognize any of their voices." He sighed. "Ethan's grievances are against Jake. I don't think he'd take them out on someone else."

Rebecca sat down. "I just don't understand what they were doing with one of our branding irons."

"I locked them all up when I was done," Zach said. "The one we found today wasn't one of ours."

She sighed. "I guess there's not really a lot we can do. Do you want to join us for supper?"

"What are you fixing?" Zach asked.

Jake laughed. "She doesn't cook. She goes and picks up

a couple of plates from the cook.''

She patted his shoulder. "Not tonight. Tonight it's your turn to go pick up the plates."

Jake scooted his chair back. "Three plates?"

Zach nodded and Jake stood up.

"Why don't you see if Frank wants to join us?" Rebecca asked.

Jake nodded as he went out the door. Rebecca got up to fetch some utensils and Zach moved in quietly behind her.

"Is there anything I can help you with?" he asked.

She turned, not a whisper's breath separating them, knowing she needed to give him a task to get him to move back.

"You can take these to the table," she said, extending a hand holding forks and knives.

Zach's hand closed over hers. "You and Jake were friends before you got married, weren't you?"

"Yes. Very good friends."

"It shows. I can tell the two of you like each other. I'm not sure my parents ever really liked each other. If they did, it was way before Ethan and I were born. Did you and Jake meet at the Lazy A?"

"Yes, we did."

"What did you do there?" he asked, wanting to know everything about her, about Jake, about how they had met.

Rebecca smiled. "Same thing I do here."

"No, here you're the owner's wife. What were you there?"

"The owner's daughter."

Zach's face went flat. "You're John Anderson's daughter?"

"Do you know my father?"

"By reputation only," Zach said as he took the utensils from her and began laying them on the table. When he was finished, he turned around facing her.

"Don't take this wrong. I like Jake. Even before when I hated him, I liked him, if that makes any sense. But you're an incredibly beautiful woman, Rebecca, and your father is one of the wealthiest ranch owners in Kentucky. You could have married anyone. Why Jake?''

Closing her eyes, she tilted her head back and released a deep sigh. "I have been asked that question so many times in the past few months and generally I ignore it." She brought her gaze back to Zach. "But I like you, Zach, so I'll tell you why I married Jake."

He leaned his hips back against the table, folding his arms over his chest, a seductive smile playing at his lips. "I'm listening."

"Last night when you came to tell us about finding Frank's horse . . . Do you remember the conversation that filled this house?"

"Sure."

"What did Jake say to me?"

His dark brows drew together. Was this a trick question? "He didn't say anything."

"And when I went outside, dressed to ride, where was my horse?"

Zach's head dropped down. "Saddled and waiting."

"That's why I married Jake. Most men see me as a porcelain doll. Something to be put up on the mantel, shown off, taken down and dusted once in a while. The closest Jake has come to treating me like a porcelain doll was the night I met Ethan. And I would have gladly played the role for him if it had been what he had wanted."

Zach brought his eyes back to hers. The truth was so evident. Why couldn't Jake see it? The envy had returned and Zach was surprised to find he was glad of it. He wanted Jake to have something in his life that a man like Zach would envy. His voice was sincere as a warm smile spread across his face. "I'm glad Jake has you."

The door opened and Jake walked in holding two plates, followed by Frank holding two more.

Rebecca moved forward. "How's your backside, Frank?"

"Just fine," he said as he moved to the side of the table away from her.

"Let me see it."

"Goddamn! Jake already looked at it. Hell, people have

been looking at it all day! It's fine!''

Rebecca's eyes went to Jake and he nodded. The men set the plates on the table, and they all sat down to eat. Jake looked at Frank and Frank gave him a curt nod.

''Reb,'' Jake began. ''About those conversations at the watering hole . . . ''

Rebecca laughed. ''I didn't believe a one of them. Not a one.''

# Chapter Nine

FRANK KICKED THE unsuspecting rock, sending it sailing a good forty feet, wishing it had sailed clear to the Reading Ranch and popped Ruth Reading on top of her stubborn head. He had bumped into Ruth, literally, outside the general store, recovered enough to tip his hat and ask after her health. She had tilted up her pert little nose and told him it was none of his business. Damn females! If more women were in the area, he'd find one to make Ruth jealous. Yes, sir, the girl didn't know a good man when she met one, that was for damn sure. He'd show her. Someday, she'd be begging him to notice her and then he'd tilt his freckled nose up at her.

Rebecca watched him as she waited for whatever Jake was scrubbing to death. "Why didn't you let Frank go into town with the others? It's not his turn to watch the herd."

Jake plopped the wet shirt into her hands. "Because he's looking for a fight. He ran into Ruth Reading in town this morning and he's been huffing and puffing ever since."

Rebecca looked back at the sulking Frank as he kicked at the dust, unable to find any more rocks. She sighed. "I wish Frank could meet someone to take his mind off of Ruth."

She walked to the line and slung the shirt over it, feeling a sudden, warm sticky wetness between her legs.

"Jake!"

The panic in her voice sent him flying to her. "What? What's wrong?"

"I think I'm bleeding."

He lifted her arms, searching her face and body. "Where?"

"The baby," she said, trembling.

His eyes dropped down below her waist and then he scooped her up in his arms, carrying her towards the house.

"Frank!" he yelled. "Go into town and get the doctor! Quick!"

Frank's eyes almost came out of his head. The doctor now? It wasn't time. He moved like lightning, adding a string of oaths to his usual.

Gingerly, Jake laid her down on the bed.

"Do you hurt anywhere?" he asked.

"No, nowhere."

"Are you cramping or uncomfortable?"

"No. But I'm scared. It's three months too early."

"Don't be scared. Everything's going to be all right." He looked so calm, so sure that she almost believed him.

"Reb, honey, I need to see if you are bleeding and I need to see how much."

She nodded. Now was not the time to concern herself with exposing her body to him. He left her side briefly to retrieve some cloths and towels and set them down on the bed. Then he went to wash his hands, taking deep breaths as he did so to stop his trembling. He was shaking as badly as she was and it wouldn't do for her to know he was scared as hell.

Coming back, he gave her a small smile of reassurance.

"I'm going to be real gentle, honey, but I want you to let me know if I hurt you."

"I will," she said in a meek voice.

He squeezed her hand. "Reb, honey, don't be afraid."

Releasing her hand, he very gently lifted her skirt back before removing her undergarments. She felt a hot flush sear her face, and inwardly she chastised herself. He'd see a lot more than this when he delivered the baby. If he didn't deliver it today. Instinctively, she jerked when he tenderly placed his hand beneath her hip to lay some towels under her. His eyes sought hers.

"I won't hurt you, honey. I swear it. But I need to look. You just relax and close your eyes." His voice was a soothing balm as she lay back on the pillow and closed her eyes.

"I like the way you say that," she said with a sigh.

"Say what?" he asked, confused.

"Honey. It sounds just like warm honey dripping over hot biscuits on a cold morning."

"I didn't realize I was saying that."

Her eyes opened briefly. "I know."

He watched her for a brief moment, listening to her breathing, listening to his own heart beating. God, he didn't want anything to happen to her.

"I'm going to touch you now, okay?"

"Okay," she said quietly.

And she felt his touch, as light as a wind blowing through the tall prairie grasses.

"Reb, honey, are you feeling any pain at all now?"

"No."

"I'm going to touch you again now so just stay relaxed."

She opened her eyes, watching his face as his large hands examined her with all the gentleness and loving care he could bring forth. Her mind drifted back to all the things he had done for her over the months since he'd first taken her as his wife, his patience, his understanding, his willingness to accept so little from her. And she felt something grow within her heart that she had never felt before, not even for Brett. She had married one special man, one very special man. And she was almost certain that he had not told her the main reason he had wanted to marry her. He loved her. She closed her eyes to stay the tears that accompanied her feelings of guilt. He wouldn't want her pity or her sympathy. And she didn't know why she couldn't give him her love.

He slipped her skirt back down, releasing a deep breath.

"You're not bleeding much at all. And since you don't have any pain, I don't think you're in danger of losing the baby." He sat down on the edge of the bed. "I've seen this happen with mares before. I don't know why . . . if maybe they just get too active or their body gets confused

. . . but anyway, I think all you have to do is take it easy. No more riding out with me, no more lifting, or cleaning, or working.''

"I'm just supposed to sit around for three months?''

"I know it's not in your nature, Reb, but I think it's going to have to be if you want this baby. Do you want me to make you some of that tea you're fond of?''

She nodded and turned her head to gaze out the window. Three months of sitting around. She'd go insane.

He brought her the tea, then propped pillows up behind her back and helped her sit up. He removed her shoes and sat down on the end of the bed, rubbing her feet.

She looked at him through woeful eyes. "You think I need to take it easy the entire time?''

He was sympathetic but realistic. "To be safe. Unless the doctor tells you different. I just don't know that much about women having babies.''

She sipped from the cup, the warm liquid calming her.

"I'm wondering when you're going to decide I'm too much trouble,'' she said.

"Never,'' he replied.

Frank came rushing into the house after the sun set, his face flushed, his breathing heavy. Jake looked up from the sofa, Rebecca from the rocker, and he skidded to a halt.

"Did you bring the doctor?'' Jake asked.

Frank shook his head. "Town ain't got no doctor. Goddamn, but the man got killed last night playing cards. He was cheating and a man called him for it. Shot him dead center in the chest. They don't know when another one will be coming to town but the marshal said he sent a wire out today.'' He took a breath to spare his lungs exploding. "You all right now, Reb?''

"I think so. Jake took good care of me.''

His shoulders slumped forward. "I sure as hell am glad to hear that.''

The barbed-wire fence was going up at a steady pace and just as steadily it was being pulled down. Men with cattle cut the wire to let their cattle drink from water holes they'd used in the past. Men on horseback wanted a direct path to their destination and cut the wire to achieve it. Others cut it down just to oppose its going up. Most just cut the wire and went on their way. Sometimes the posts were burned, the fires seen in the distance at night.

Moving slowly across the land, the six riders felt their actions were justified as the man they had beaten stumbled behind them. His hands were tied behind his back, the ropes cutting into his flesh. A rope around his neck chafed the skin.

Jake and Frank stepped out of the barn just as the riders drew up. The man wanted to drop to his knees but he wasn't certain the journey was over yet. If it wasn't, he didn't want to be on his knees when the horse started moving because he knew he wouldn't be able to bring himself up to his feet before the rope tightened around his neck.

Rebecca stepped out of the house. Quickly, she crossed the yard, flinching when she saw Zach's swollen face. He stood motionless between the riders. Jake gave every rider a hard look, settling his impenetrable gaze at last upon Lee Hastings.

"We moved the cattle this morning like you told us," Lee explained. "This afternoon, the wire was cut and the cattle chased out. Zach told his brother what we were planning on doing and that's how he knew where to strike us so it'd hurt. He's here spying for his brother, working to destroy us."

Jake's jaw clenched and his eyes narrowed. "You got proof?"

"No, sir, but—"

Jake grabbed Lee, pulling him off his horse and throwing him to the ground. "Untie him now," Jake said in a low hiss.

"But he was the last one with the branding irons the night Frank was attacked," Lee argued.

"Untie him," Jake said.

Lee started to protest again but thought better of it and set about cutting the ropes holding Zach prisoner.

Jake's gaze locked firmly on the six men before him. His

voice emanated controlled rage. "You men listen and listen good. I won't have any man beaten for something he didn't do. The next time something like this happens, you're off this ranch. And numbers won't make a difference. If all of you are involved, all of you go." His eyes fell on Lee. "And standing by watching is the same as doing."

Rebecca put her hand on Zach's arm. "Come on in the house and I'll tend to you."

He shrugged her off. "I can take care of myself."

"Don't be so stubborn," she scolded. "Come on."

He squinted at her through his one good eye and followed her back to the house. He sat in a chair at the table while she retrieved a bowl of water and some salve and bandages. When she started cleaning the cut above his brow, he flinched.

Jake walked in, pulled out a chair, turned it around, and sat straddling it. "Think you got any broken ribs?" he asked.

"No," Zach said, not looking at Jake.

"Would you tell me if you did?"

"No." He gave Jake a small smile. "But I imagine your wife's planning on poking around to make sure." He studied the man sitting across from him. "Why didn't you ask me if I did what they said?"

"I only ask questions when I don't know the answer."

"You expect me to believe you haven't thought the same thing?"

"It crossed my mind you might be working with Ethan against me. But I don't think you are. Want some coffee?"

Zach nodded, wishing he hadn't when the pain in his head intensified.

Jake got up and poured two cups. "Want some, Reb?" he asked.

"No, thank you. Unbutton your shirt," she instructed Zach.

Zach smiled. "My ribs are fine. I swear they are."

"All right." Rebecca closed up her box.

Jake set the cup of coffee in front of Zach as he sipped from his own cup. Zach took a swallow, then closed both hands around the cup, concentrating on the black liquid. "I'm not working with Ethan. I did go talk to him earlier in the week to tell him to leave, which just made him angrier. I do think he's the one that ran off your cattle today. I also think he's the one that's responsible for most of the damage done to your fencing."

Jake nodded. "It's going to get a lot uglier before it gets better. Ethan's in the wrong and sooner or later, he's going to pay for it. I'll understand if you're not here in the morning, and if the cattle you brought with you and ten of my own are gone. I won't send my men looking for them."

Zach thanked Jake and Rebecca, then walked with a single-minded purpose to the bunkhouse. He ignored the men, not wanting to see their suspicions, doubts, or sympathy. He lay down on his bed without taking his clothes off, having no desire to let them see the full extent of his injuries. He had lied to Rebecca. His ribs weren't fine. He didn't think they were broken, but he was sure several were cracked. He supposed he should have let her help him, but at that moment he had wanted to avoid contact with anyone. He hadn't deserved the beating, and it had left him filled with impotent rage. For the first time he fully understood why no one had been able to drag Jake off of Ethan when he had laid his fists into him the day of their father's funeral. Jake had collected many undeserved beatings over the years, most instigated by Ethan's careful wording of the truth. Sighing, Zach laid a wrist over his eyes, his mind drifting.

The moment he was born, he idolized Ethan, always tagging after him, trying his older brother's limited patience. Cuffs about the head were delivered playfully when he became too much of a nuisance, secrets were whispered through a knothole in a board along the wall that separated their rooms. It was through that knothole that they had first discussed Jake.

The harsh words inflicting pain and anger had begun long after they'd both gone to sleep. How long the words had been flung back and forth between their parents or what had initially prompted the voices to raise to a fevered pitch they never knew. They had sifted through the argument hoarding bits and pieces of information like miners searching for gold. They were just able to figure out that their father had another son, a son he was going to bring home the next day, a son their mother didn't want.

Another brother. Zach had always longed for a brother to tag along after him and worship him the way he worshipped Ethan. He was certain his father would tell them about their brother in the morning. When he did, he would offer to share his bed with his newfound brother. He'd stayed awake the remainder of the night thinking of his younger brother and anticipating his own rise in status to that of a big brother.

But things hadn't worked out the way he'd hoped. His father had hitched the wagon and rolled out of sight without a word, leaving Zach sitting on the porch steps the rest of the day waiting for his return. It didn't come until evening.

Zach had seen the young boy clutching his small bundle, looking uncertain. He had hopped off the porch ready to make him feel welcome, but his father's stern face and hard voice when he had told the boy to get down off the wagon stopped Zach. Ethan had moved up beside him, his face a reflection of their father's.

Still clutching his bundle, the boy had followed their father as he took long sure strides towards the bunkhouse, the two older boys falling into step behind.

His father had opened the door to the bunkhouse and pulled the boy in. "This is where the men sleep. When you can work like a man, you can sleep in here." Then he had pulled the boy out and marched him back to the barn, stopping beside the last stall.

"This is where you'll sleep until then. Do you understand?"

With large, somber eyes, the boy had looked up at him and nodded.

"You speak when you're spoken to. Do you understand?"

"Yeah," he said in a near whisper.

"Yes, sir. You say, 'yes, sir' and 'no, sir' to me."

Blinking his eyes, the boy said softly, "Yes, sir. I understand."

"Good. These are my sons, Ethan and Zachary. You'll address them as you do me. Do you understand?"

"Yes, sir."

The boy had turned, and for the first time, both Truscotts had gotten a good look at their brother. Zach had watched his lips move as though he were going to smile.

"What's wrong with his face?" Ethan had asked.

The boy had flinched but he didn't turn away, keeping his eyes on Ethan, studying him.

"He had smallpox," Truscott had said.

"That's like the plague, isn't it?" Ethan had asked. "Like what God sends down to the sinners to punish 'em and mark 'em?"

"Indeed, son, it's a plague. You boys head on to the house. I'll be there shortly."

"Why can't he sleep in the house with us?" Zach had whispered to Ethan as they walked out of the barn.

"Because he's a child of sin."

They had eaten their supper, an uneasy suffocating silence hovering around them. When they had finished the meal, their mother had placed a bowl in the center of the table for the scraps from their plates and Ethan had carried the bowl out to the barn, Zach tagging along behind.

Jake was sitting in the corner, his bundle resting beside him, his arms crossed over his upturned knees, his head laying on his arms.

"Here's your food, you ugly bastard," Ethan had said and Zach's eyes had snapped to his brother's. Ethan had never talked to him in that tone of voice or thrown unkind words at him.

Jake had cautiously lifted his head, eyeing Ethan warily.

"Come and get your supper."

Jake had slowly risen to his feet and walked towards them, his eyes never leaving Ethan's.

"Say 'please, sir,' " Ethan goaded.

Jake shook his head, his lips pressed tightly together, his eyes still studying the older boy.

"Wonder where a whore's bastard got such pride," Ethan had said and walked out of the barn holding the bowl.

Zach had looked at his newest brother. "You don't have to say 'sir' to me."

"Reckon I'd better."

He'd turned around, heading back to his corner. Zach had seen the two streaks of blood on the back of his shirt, recognizing the marks made by a switch. His father had used one on him once. He hadn't drawn blood, but he had managed to leave raised welts.

"I'll tell my mother you're hurt. She'll come tend your back."

Jake had smiled. "Is your ma nice?"

"Oh, yeah," Zach had reassured him. "And she's real good when it comes to dealing with hurts."

"So was my ma."

"She's dead, isn't she?"

Jake had nodded. "I sure do miss her."

"I'd miss my mother, too, if she was gone."

Zach had run to the kitchen where his mother was drying the last of the dishes.

"Father took a switch to Jake and his back is bleeding. Will you help him?" Zach had asked the woman who had always been there for him.

"I will neither help nor hurt him," she had said with finality. "Never mention him to me again." And she had walked out of the room, but not before Zach had seen the lie. By not helping Jake, she was hurting him.

Later that night, Zach had crept into the kitchen, filled a bowl with leftovers and taken it to the barn. He'd set it down beside the sleeping boy, wishing he couldn't see where the tears had cleaned his face. He had nudged the boy's shoulder. Jake had opened his eyes, lifting his head and staring at him.

"Here," Zach had said and walked away leaving the bowl. He'd taken several steps before he turned to look back and saw the boy wipe his eyes before thrusting his hands into the bowl and stuffing the food into his eager mouth. Zach had felt the first stirrings of hatred begin. He had wanted to rail at his father, his mother, and his brother. Every Saturday night their mother scrubbed the grime from their bodies. Every Sunday morning they dressed in their finest clothes and went to church so the grime could be scrubbed from their souls. At that moment he had known that all the scrubbings in the world wouldn't be enough to cleanse him.

"You gonna be all right?"

Zach lifted his wrist and peered out, smiling at Frank's concerned face.

"Yeah, I'll be fine."

"I figured after what they did to you today, you might decide to leave tomorrow. I just wanted you to know that I don't believe anything they accused you of doing. I know you didn't have nothing to do with my branding."

"Thanks, Frank."

Frank nodded. " 'Night."

Zach closed his eyes wishing he had let Rebecca prod around. He was sore as hell.

The following morning, as the sun sent streaks of orange across the horizon, Zachary Truscott, with a swollen face and aching ribs, saddled his horse and set out to tend his younger brother's herd.

# Chapter Ten

THE WOODBOX WAS empty. The stove smelled of ashes. The discarded clothes needed to be washed and ironed.

Yet Rebecca rocked back and forth, a feather pillow at her back, her feet elevated on a tiny stool Jake had somehow found time to make for her. She was reading *Black Beauty*, a book he had bought the last time he went to town because he thought the story would cheer her up. Dropping the book on the floor and bracing her hands on both armrests, Rebecca pushed herself to her feet.

It wasn't fair to Jake. He was carrying his load and hers. She had told him if he put up his fence, she'd shoot anyone that tried to take it down. War permeated the air as silent warriors used stealth to attack, cowardice to avoid direct confrontations. They must know in the darkest recesses of their conscience they were in the wrong. Meanwhile she sat safe and secure inside the house, aiding and abetting the enemy because she wouldn't risk the health of her child by offering Jake substantial aid. He left before the sun came up, returned after the sun had set. He would have stayed out all night, but he didn't trust her to keep her due date. The past two nights, he had fallen asleep right after supper, last night shortly after he had dropped his weary body down on the sofa.

She stomped out onto the porch and surveyed the area. No one was in sight. Good. She'd just fill up that old woodbox. When she was through she started a fire in the stove, deciding to cook Jake a good meal. He always came home around noon to see how she was doing. Today she'd surprise him with something special when he came traipsing in through the door.

"What the hell are you doing?"

Spinning around, she faced the tall man standing in the doorway, legs wide apart, hands pressed to his hips, jaw set. She had seen Jake angry before, just never angry at her.

"Fixing you lunch," she said, lifting her chin up.

"Who the hell put the wood in that box?"

"I did," she said, lifting her chin higher. She had never seen him work so hard to control his temper, and the fact that he was having to work so hard made her rethink her earlier desire to surprise him. She was no longer certain her actions carried any merit.

"You could have waited and I would have gotten the wood for you. And I can fix our lunch if you've grown tired of eating grub."

Deciding his stance was more intimidating than hers, she braced her legs apart and her hands flew to where her hips used to jut out.

"It's not fair, Jake. You're wearing yourself out carrying your load and mine. You're losing weight and you look like a raccoon with those dark circles around your eyes. You can barely make it to bed before you give in to exhaustion, and last night you didn't even get that far."

"I'm not complaining."

"And you never do! I could hit you over the head with a cast-iron skillet and you wouldn't complain. You'd probably think you deserved it whether you did or not!"

"I thought you loved Brett. I though you wanted his baby." He took a menacing step forward. "Well, let me tell you, wife, you lose this baby because of your stubbornness, don't come crying to me. I'll have no sympathy for you. None whatsoever! I don't want to see a tear! Not one goddamn tear!"

He stormed out of the house, slamming the door shut behind him. Rebecca dropped into a chair, resting her elbows on the table, digging the heels of her hands into her watery eyes. Was that their first fight? She felt lonely and desolate, far worse than she had when she began the useless day. The wood of the table darkened where her tears splashed upon it.

Nature was as fickle as a woman with too many beaux. The men had gone out that morning leaving vests and jackets behind because the warm sun was shining down on the land. But now the sky had enticed the arrival of heavy black clouds that only occasionally allowed the sun to peer through. Rebecca stood on the front porch and felt the gust of icy wind hit her full force, sending shivers through her body. Did winter come this quickly?

She watched as Zach and Frank scurried towards the barn. She knew they would be needed on the range because a stampede was imminent with the weather that was brewing. A horse snapping a twig in the still of the night was enough to start a stampede that could send the cattle rushing forward without thought for a distance of a hundred miles or more. And there was more than a snapping twig coming now.

Frank hustled out of the barn, sending his horse into a gallop. Zach detoured by the house.

"There's no way there won't be a damn stampede!" he cried, the wind carrying his voice towards Rebecca. "Guess you'll stay home this time!"

"Only because I have no choice! You be careful!"

He tipped his hat. "Will do! I'll see that Jake does the same!" He spurred his horse into a hard gallop leaving Rebecca standing alone on the porch.

He'd barely left before thunder roared in the heavens above and lightning flashed across the sky, illuminating the clouds. Rebecca stood mesmerized, gazing at the spectacle above her, feeling as though Nature were showing off. The wind blew against her, the temperature rapidly declined and then the icy rain began to fall. She wrapped her arms around herself and, like an old woman who has already experienced all life has to offer, walked back into the house to sit in her rocking chair and listen to the rain beating down on the roof.

The initial crack of boisterous thunder sent the first timorous steer bolting, the remainder of the herd following in its path.

No orders were shouted; the men worked like the mechanized wheels of a finely crafted watch. Each knew what he had to do, where he had to be in order to stay the herd and turn it into itself.

Jake heard the sickening crack of splintering bone and knew his horse had dropped a leg down a prairie dog hole, something every man feared when he was forced to push his horse unmercifully. The horse screamed out in agony and lurched forward, throwing Jake out of the saddle. As he sailed through the air, he reflexively pulled his Winchester rifle out of the scabbard. He landed in the open, no hope for protection as an errant bull rushed towards him.

Time slowed down to an eerie crawl as he watched the bulge of brawny muscles stretch and bunch to move the animal forward with the greatest speed. He could see the power of the beast, the smoky air escaping flared nostrils, the wild look of terror in the longhorn's dark eyes.

Scrambling to position himself, Jake fired his rifle. The bull fell into a crumpled mass near enough that he could hear the animal's last shaky breath. But he knew he couldn't shoot the entire herd, and he couldn't outrun it. The animals' path was being channeled by the men on horseback, and, unfortunately, it was being channeled to cut across him. Swiftly, he turned and fired a shot to put his faithful horse out of his misery, wondering if he should do the same for himself.

He saw a rider break free of the mayhem, sending his horse into a frenzied gallop. The man controlled the reins with one hand as the other was extended to Jake. He grabbed the man's arm tightly and swung himself up behind the saddle just as the cattle thundered across the sodden land.

They rode hard towards the cook who was following along behind the stampeding herd. The man had no experience at turning a herd, but he kept the extra horses easily accessible to the men and searched for any man who might have fallen from his horse and been trampled.

Time allowed only a brief word of thanks and a slap on the shoulder to Zach as Jake dismounted. He climbed up onto the horse waiting for him and headed back towards the herd.

He and the men worked together as the heavens boomed, the lightning flashed. The bitter cold seeped down to their weary bones. Finally the cattle were heading into themselves, following a concentric path, the circle becoming smaller and smaller as the men regained control. The beasts would circumnavigate the forced path until they came to an exhausted halt. But even then, it would take little to re-awaken the nightmare of another stampede.

After pulling off his boots, Jake hesitated on the porch. Then he pushed open the door, expecting to see a skillet fall down on his head. He was worn out, even before the storm hit, and he was worried, his worry triggering the harsh words he had shot at Reb earlier. Pleasure had yet to obtain another doctor. Jake knew he could deliver the baby if there were no complications, but keeping Reb from doing anything was like trying to stop the storm from advancing across the land. He had no experience in handling a woman he had just angered. Standing just inside the door, wet and shivering, with his teeth chattering didn't do much to build his confidence.

He hung his hat and slicker on a peg before daring to glance at his wife.

"How did you get so wet?" she asked.

"Waited too long to unroll my slicker and put it on."

"Jake Burnett, you know better than to do that."

"And you know better than to be hauling stuff around."

Rebecca lifted herself out of the rocking chair and headed for the chest in the back corner of the room.

"Get by the fire and take those wet clothes off," she ordered.

He didn't hesitate to obey. He had heard cold weather could arrive unexpectedly, he just hadn't known it happened that drastically in Texas.

He had stripped down to his sopping underwear when she returned, dropping one blanket on the sofa, holding another up above her head, letting it unfold itself.

"Get out of everything," she said, "and wrap that blanket around your waist." For a married couple, they had seen little of each other's bodies, and there were times when it was a damn nuisance.

"I'm decent," Jake said as his teeth hit together.

She draped the blanket she had been holding over his trembling shoulders and pushed him down on the sofa. Then she climbed up on the sofa and began rubbing his body vigorously. "I was so worried when that storm blew in. I was very careful not to strain myself when I built the fire," she said quietly.

His hand came out from under the blanket to stay hers. "Reb, I'm sorry about what I said earlier. I had no right."

"You had every right. You knew I carried another man's baby when you married me and you accepted it as your own. I'm the one who should apologize. You've been nothing but kind and good to me and this unborn child. Besides"—she shrugged—"if you hadn't scolded me, I would have saddled a horse and joined you out there."

"I didn't mean what I said about losing the baby."

She placed a finger on his lips. "I know. We both spoke in anger. The words are best forgotten."

She started rubbing him again, trying to get him warm. "Did the herd stampede?"

"As soon as the lightning filled the sky, they took off. Thought I was going to regret putting up the fence. We barely got them turned in time to prevent them running into it."

"Are you going to keep all the men out there tonight?"

"Yes, I just wanted to make sure you were all right and get some dry clothes on. Then I'll go back out."

"You need to get warm first. Let me inside the blanket."

He opened the blanket and she slipped inside, pressing her body against his. Through her cotton nightgown, the warmth of her body penetrated him. She continued to rub his arms with her hands, and his body ceased its quaking.

"Better?" she asked.

Leaning his head back, he answered, "Uh-huh."

And before she could say another word, he was asleep. She stilled her hands, and curled up beside him, feeling safe and secure within the cocoon they had created.

The rumbling seemed to begin at the earth's core and move outward until the ground, the trees, the buildings were rumbling as well. Jake's eyes snapped open the same instant that Rebecca's did. He helped her move herself off of him, then he went to the back of the house for a dry set of clothes.

"They're coming this way!" he shouted as the noise and rumbling increased in intensity. He came running back. Rebecca was standing beside the door holding up his coat to help him into it. He turned to face her, hesitating.

"I've never given you an order," he said, "but I'm giving you one now. Stay in this house."

He opened the door and she stopped him, throwing her arms around his neck. "Please be careful," she whispered, her voice trembling.

He wrapped his arms around her. "You just stay here so I don't have to worry about you and I'll be fine."

He released her and rushed out. She dropped the plank of wood across the door, knowing if a steer decided to come through, the plank would probably not change his mind.

Rebecca dimmed the flame in the lantern and peeked out the window. The thundering herd stormed through, hooves pounding the earth. They were up to six-hundred-and-fifty head of cattle now, and she was grateful they had no more. In two years, Jake would have two, maybe three thousand head of cattle. That kind of stampede could level everything that surrounded them. She had been in the midst of a stampede before and it hadn't frightened her, probably because her mind had been bent on turning the herd. But sitting beside the window, gazing out, she decided everyone who dealt with cattle was insane. It was frightening to watch the beasts, terrified and wild, running past as a few determined cowboys tried to control them.

The storm and cattle raged until noon the following day. Periods of tranquillity settled across the herd, only to be interrupted when thunder or lightning unexpectedly cut through the stillness. When the storm moved on, it left behind a bitter cold in its wake.

Rebecca scattered seed along the ground for the few chickens Carrie had brought their way shortly after she'd discovered her new neighbors. It was one chore she could manage without straining herself or endangering her child.

She waved at the riders guiding horses back into the corral. The men had had to set them loose. If the cattle had knocked down one side of their corral, they would have been trapped.

"Looks like you got most of them," she said to Frank as he dismounted.

Frank beat his hands together, then blew on them. "We got about half of them."

"I watched you from the window last night. You did really well."

She was surprised Frank didn't give her the smile he usually did when she praised him.

"I was scared as hell . . . after seeing Jake get thrown and nearly trampled to death. . . . "

He shuddered and Rebecca knew it wasn't from the cold. She felt her knees grow weak, and it was with the greatest of efforts that she kept her voice calm. "Jake got thrown from his horse?"

"Goddamn, yes. First stampede. We were just getting the cattle turned and damn if he didn't get thrown right in the path. Never seen a man ride as hard as Zach did to get Jake out of the way."

Someone hollered at Frank. "Guess I'd better help these no-accounts get the rest of the horses." He pulled himself back up into the saddle. "Reckon they're rethinking their opinion of Zach this morning."

"Yes, I imagine they are."

It wasn't until he rode away that Rebecca walked with

stiffened legs to the barn. She found Jake in the last stall brushing down Shadow for her. She wrapped her hands around a beam and rested her head against the rough wood. What would she have done if something had happened to Jake? If her last memory of him had been the argument they'd had before the storm? She couldn't imagine her life without him in it.

Jake turned from his task, giving her a smile, a smile that quickly faded at the expression of fear on her face.

Her legs lost their ability to hold her up and she slid down to the ground. His heart stopped at the sight of her slumped outside the stall and he ran towards her. He skidded to a halt and dropped down to his knees.

"Reb? What's wrong? Are you hurting? Is it the baby?"

Opening her eyes, she searched his concerned face.

"Where's your horse?"

"My horse?"

"Your chestnut stallion."

He dropped his head. "I lost him last night."

"And I almost lost you."

He slowly brought his eyes to hers. "Reb, it wasn't—" He stopped. "It's over now. There's no point in dwelling on it."

She braced his face in her hands, bringing his mouth down to hers, and gently kissed the man who had come to mean so much to her.

Jake eased her over into the next stall and laid her down, his arms encircling her as he sought to reassure her, his mouth never leaving hers. No one had cared this much about him since his mother had died. Her concern gave him hope for the future.

The sound of a throat clearing made the two jump apart as though they were children caught behind the schoolhouse. His grin spreading from one corner of his face to the other, Zach looked down at them.

Jake brought himself to his feet and helped Rebecca as she clumsily struggled to get off the hay-covered floor. Her face was flushed with warmth as she leaned up and kissed Zach on the cheek.

"Thank you," she said.

"What for?" Zach asked.

"For taking care of Jake last night."

He watched as she ambled out of the barn before leading his horse into the stall. He peered over the wooden slats. "Brother, you and I have a different definition of the word 'love.'"

Zach quickly turned away, embarrassed by the familial endearment he had used without thinking. He had yet to earn the right to call Jake brother. And he knew, as Jake went back to the task of brushing Shadow, that the term had made him uncomfortable as well.

As the days passed, the cold diminished. But the milder weather didn't stop people from getting in the Christmas spirit.

It was impossible to tell who wore the biggest smile, Frank or Zach, as they trudged into the house, startling Rebecca. She threw her hand to her mouth and her smile rivaled theirs in brilliance.

"Jake sent us to find one," Frank said as he and Zach struggled to stand the monster pine tree in the corner. They rolled their eyes realizing that in their desire to please Rebecca they had failed to take into account the size of the house. At least a fourth of the tree was going to have to be cut off.

Glancing around the small house and then back to the tree, Rebecca said, "Let's set it up in the barn. Then we can all enjoy it and celebrate Christmas together."

By nightfall, the men were all gathered around the tree singing off-tune carols that sent tears of mirth rolling down Rebecca's cheeks.

Gifts had magically appeared under the sparsely decorated branches. Frank was like a little boy, giving out the gifts, anxious to get it done so he could see what Rebecca had given him.

He handed Rebecca her present from Jake. She lovingly ran her fingers over the brown paper and clumsily tied string, knowing Jake had wrapped it himself. She tugged at the string, and the wrapping fell into what remained of her lap. She was left holding a small wooden box with a tiny carved mustang raised up on his hind legs carved in the top. She ran her finger over it, tears in her eyes when she looked up at Jake.

"You made this," she said.

"But not what's in it."

Slowly, she opened the box. Nestled inside was a tiny silver drum with seemingly random bumps running over it. Thin metal teeth touched the drum.

"A music box," she whispered.

"I was going to buy you one already made, but none of the boxes opened to show you the music, they only showed you another box. Thought you'd like to see the music being made. You wind it up back here."

Rebecca turned the box around and twisted the tiny knob. She listened and watched in delight as the tiny creation tinkled out the notes to "The Cowboy's Lament."

Placing her palm on Jake's cheek, she turned his face towards hers and brushed a kiss across his lips. "Thank you. It's beautiful."

"Open yours, Jake!" Frank said. "You're the only one left that hasn't opened his gift." He and the other men had already unwrapped theirs.

Jake untied the ribbon on the perfectly wrapped gift, revealing a pair of thick gloves.

"Goddamn! She got us both the same thing!" Frank said, holding up an identical pair, wondering why she hadn't given Jake something special. It was a thought that didn't cross Jake's mind.

"They're supposed to be really tough . . . for handling barbed wire," Rebecca explained.

"With all the wire we're stringing, Frank and I sure can use them. Thank you."

"Try them on," Rebecca prodded. "If they don't fit, we'll have to send them back."

Jake slipped his hand inside one and froze, then he

slowly pulled his hand out, clasping a gold pocket watch, its gold chain trailing behind.

"Open it," Rebecca whispered.

Jake looked at her. "Open it?"

"The watch. There's something inside for you."

Inside, carved letters said, "To the one I cherish. Reb."

"It's not as special," Rebecca said. "I didn't actually do the carving."

Jake ran a finger across the etched words. "It's very special," he said in a hoarse voice, wishing all the men would head back to the bunkhouse now. He needed time to adjust to receiving such a wondrous gift.

"Goddamn! You could at least kiss her!" Frank exclaimed. "She didn't put nothing in my gloves!"

Laughter filled the barn and Jake was grateful the spell was broken. He turned to his wife and gave her a light kiss. "Thank you."

"Now, it's our turn," Lee said as he stood up, holding a sprig of green over his head. "We had one hell of a time finding this." He extended a hand to Rebecca. "Come on, Reb, don't let us down."

Laughing, Rebecca put her hand in his, allowing herself to be pulled into his arms. "You must really be desperate," she teased.

"Yes, ma'am, we are," Lee said as he leaned over to kiss her. "Night, Jake," he said with a smile as he handed the mistletoe off to the next man.

Frank was the last one in line. He placed his kiss on Rebecca's cheek, then said, "Thanks for giving me something so fine. Made me feel special."

"You are special, Frank."

"Merry Christmas," he said with a duck of his head as he headed out the barn door.

One small gift remained under the tree. Jake picked it up and slipped it into the pocket of his jacket.

"I'm going to take a quick ride out to check on the herd," he said.

She slipped her arms around his waist, turning her face

up to gaze at him. "I'm sorry he didn't come."

Jake nodded. "Maybe next year."


The night began to turn brisk as the wind picked up. The moon illuminated the herd as the cattle stood bracing themselves against the chill. Zach brought the collar of his jacket up to protect his neck and brought his hat down lower. Jake had said he thought the cattle would be fine with no one watching them tonight and had invited everyone to join them in the barn for a small Christmas celebration. And Zach had wanted to go. He knew what Jake was giving Rebecca, and he had wanted to see her face when she opened the gift. He heard a rider approach, surprised to see Jake drawing up beside him.

"You would have been welcome," Jake said as he pulled on the reins of his horse.

Zach shook his head. "Just couldn't do it."

"The men—"

"It's got nothing to do with the men." Zach leaned his head back, felt the wind hit his neck and tucked his chin back into the jacket. "When I was ten, Mother put candles on the branches of our tree, something she had never done before because she was afraid of fire. We were laughing and unwrapping gifts, eating all the food she had cooked. Having one hell of a good time." Zach turned to Jake. "Then Mother told me to go blow out all the candles. Before I did, I looked out the window and there you were, squatting down in the yard, staring at the tree, the flames from the candles throwing light across your face."

"It was a beautiful tree," Jake admitted, remembering the sight of the candles flickering in the window and reflecting on the snow.

"I was on the inside looking out; you were on the outside looking in. Well . . . now, you're the one on the inside and you deserve to be."

"There's room on the inside for you, too, Zach. Reb would have liked for you to have been there with us."

Zach smiled. "That's reason to go, I suppose. If you both

feel the same next year, I'll join you.''

Jake reached into his pocket and extended the small gift to Zach. ''It's just a little something I picked up.''

Zach unwrapped the gift and smiled at the harmonica he found inside. He wished he had thought to get something for Jake.

''I heard you playing on a harmonica one night. I liked the way it sounded,'' Jake said.

''Unfortunately, Father heard it, too.''

''Your father called it Satan's noise.''

Zach turned the instrument over in his hand and said quietly, ''He was your father, too.''

Jake shook his head. ''Takes more than planting the seed to make a man a father.''

And it took more than having the same father to make two men brothers, Zach thought.

''Besides,'' Jake continued. ''I'm not convinced he was my father. Hell, Zach, my mother was a whore. Any drifter passing through could have sired me.''

Zach's gaze intensified as he studied the man before him. ''She wasn't a whore before she conceived you,'' he said, his voice low as though he were revealing something he had been sworn to secrecy not to tell. ''She was my mother's sister.

''She had come to live with us after our grandparents died. After she got pregnant, she moved into town, went to work at the local bordello. It was years before Father knew why she'd left, years before my mother knew who had fathered her sister's baby.''

Jake had no words to express what he was feeling. Zach expected none. He sighed, lightly tossing the harmonica in his hand. ''We weren't allowed music. Father gave you twelve lashes because I played this damn thing.''

''It was only ten. And he's not here now. Good night, Zach . . . and thanks for telling me. I always wondered.''

As he galloped away, the strains from ''Amazing Grace'' filled the air, replenishing a tortured soul with peace.

Standing beside the bed, Jake looked down on his sleeping wife. She was lying on her back, her hands palms up resting on her pillow, the music box sitting on her stomach. He caressed the etched letters on his watch with his thumb. She cherished him. He wondered how close that came to love.

Slowly, she opened her eyes. "Did you find him?"

Jake sat down on the bed. "Yes. He wouldn't come because I wasn't allowed to celebrate Christmas with his family."

She shook her head. "In many ways, I think Zach suffered almost as much as you did. Maybe Ethan did, too, although I find it difficult to feel any sympathy for him. You're the one who should have been bitter, who should have grown into an angry man."

Jake smiled in remembrance. "I can probably thank my mother that I didn't. I was only five when she died, but I can still hear the softness of her voice, feel the gentle touch of her hand. I carry her with me always. Only thing that got me through sometimes."

"That's the kind of mother I'd like to be," Rebecca said.

"I have no doubts that's exactly the kind of mother you will be."

Rebecca lifted the music box off her stomach. "I was letting him listen to it."

"You think he can hear it?"

She shrugged. "I hope he can hear what's going on out here, otherwise I've spent a great deal of time singing lullabies to myself these past few months."

He opened his hand, revealing the watch. "I want to thank you for the watch. I never had such a fine gift before."

Rebecca sat up, brushing his hair up off his brow. "I wanted you to know how much you mean to me. You're my best friend, Jake. Under the circumstances, I don't think there's anyone else I could have married." She slipped two fingers up the cuff of her gown and retrieved the sprig of green. "Did you think I wouldn't notice that you didn't get in line?" She held the mistletoe over his head. "Don't disappoint me," she whispered.

And he didn't.

# Chapter Eleven

PRESSING TIGHTENED FISTS into her lower back, Rebecca arched her spine trying to ease the dull ache that had begun early that morning. They were five days into the new year. According to her estimates, she had nearly three more weeks of waddling like a duck and feeling the increased discomfort she was fighting now.

Jake walked into their home holding two plates heaped with vittles, the weary lines etched on his face deepening as he caught sight of his wife.

"Are you all right?"

"Yes," she sighed. "My back is just aching. I feel like this baby turned into a steel cannonball today and fell from my ribs to my knees."

"You think a hot bath would help?"

A hot bath would be heaven, and if she weren't an invalid, she'd take one. But she wasn't going to ask Jake to prepare one for her.

"It's too much trouble," she said, trying to keep the longing out of her voice and succeeding, but her eyes failed her efforts.

Jake set the plates on the table and tugged on his shirt. "There's no way I can lay in that bed with you tonight smelling the way I do, and washing up's not going to do me any good. I'd like a bath, too."

Once the dishes were cleared away, Jake brought out a large wooden tub and set it up behind the quilt. Then he began hauling water in and heating it up. When he had filled the tub with steaming water, he stepped out from behind the quilt and bowed, extending an arm towards the bath.

"You first."

Laughing, Rebecca walked past him. "I won't argue this time."

Leaning back against the wooden tub, the warm water lapping around her body, Rebecca closed her eyes and sighed. She longed to sit in the water all night, but she knew Jake would use the same water when she was finished. It was too much trouble to empty the tub and refill it. She had felt guilty the first time they had used the tub because she hadn't realized that he would use her water, and it was cold by the time she clambered out.

Picking up the lard soap, she began rubbing it between her hands, thinking of French soaps and other things that were rarely found out here. The hard soap went slipping out of her hands, thudding and skidding across the floor, beneath the quilt and into the other side of the room. She froze. Should she climb out of the tub and try to get it herself? Should she ask Jake to get it for her?

Jake looked at the uneven ball of soap as though it were something alien, something he had never before seen. Should he step outside so she'd feel free to get out of the tub and get it herself? Should he kick it back under the quilt? Dammit! She was his wife, he'd see her body and a whole lot more before the next month rolled around. Jake got up and walked towards the quilt, bent down and picked up the soap. He weighed it in his hand as he weighed his options.

He stepped around the quilt. Her back was to him and she glanced at him over her hunched shoulders. She tentatively held out a hand, while the other ineffectually covered her upper body. Her dark hair was piled on top of her head, dampened tendrils framing her face. He took a step forward and placed the soap in her outstretched hand before turning and heading out of the house.

Standing on the porch, he inhaled deeply. Handing her the soap was not what he had wanted to do. He had wanted to scrub her back, to ease that ache in her lower back. Sweet Lord, but he wanted to touch her the way a man touches his wife, the way a man touches the woman he loves. He bowed his head, wondering if she would ever want him the way he wanted her. But he realized he was being unfair. Right now, she was swollen and miserable and the last thing she probably wanted was a man touching her.

The door squeaked behind him and Rebecca stuck her head out.

"I'm finished," she said quietly.

Turning, Jake gave her a small smile and went into the house to scrub the grime off his own body.

Sitting on the sofa with her feet drawn up under her, Rebecca listened to the muffled sounds of Jake's movements behind the quilt. She heard the gentle lapping of the water as he set his lean frame down into the tub. Then drawing in a deep breath, she got up, and shoving the sleeves of her gown past her elbows, she moved around behind the quilt.

He was scrubbing his face, and she watched the play of muscles across his back. Then she knelt down behind him and placed a finger on his shoulder. All his actions, including breathing, ceased.

"I'll wash your back," she said, extending a hand forward to receive the soap.

He glanced back over his shoulder. "I can do it."

She shook her head. "You've been working hard. It's the least I can do, and I won't strain myself doing it." She shook her hand. "Give me the soap and lean forward."

He did as she asked. She lathered up the soap and began washing his back, rubbing it and massaging it in the process. Had anything ever felt so nice?

"I wanted to do this for you," he said quietly.

"Why didn't you?"

"I wasn't sure you'd want me to."

She continued to wash his firm back, rinsing the soap off and then re-washing until she heard his steady, slow rhythmic breathing.

"Jake?" She pressed two fingers into his back. "Jake?"

His head snapped up, his eyes trying to focus, his mind trying to remember where he was.

"I'll finish," he said groggily.

Handing him the soap, she got up and without looking back went straight to bed. She lay on her side, watching the moonbeams ease in through the tiny cracks in the closed shutters. She pulled the covers up more closely about her, trying to stave off the chill of the room. She listened to Jake's movements, tempted to roll over and watch him. She heard his wet feet hit the floor, conscious of his rapid movements as he dried off and slipped on his long johns.

The bed dipped with his weight. She rolled over, snuggling up against him, his body bringing her warmth. There were moments when she was nestled within his embrace that she wanted more than his arms around her, craved more than the idle movements of his fingers up and down her back. His fingers stilled and she heard his deep rhythmic breathing. She closed her eyes until her breathing matched his.

The loud clamoring of iron against iron brought Rebecca and Jake out of a sound sleep and the words "Fire!" brought Jake out of bed. He threw his pants on.

"Stay put!" he shouted, pointing a finger at Rebecca. He grabbed his jacket and shoved his arms into it before he rushed out.

She slipped her feet out of the warm bed and set them on the icy floor. Her body swayed from side to side as she moved to the front door. She opened the door, fully intending to just stand there and watch, but then she saw the fire consuming the barn and Jake rushing in behind Zach to save the stock trapped inside. She released a bloodcurdling scream and tore out into the yard.

Someone stayed her progress, and she sought to control her panic by issuing orders to anyone within hearing distance. She had the men form a line and buckets of water were sent uselessly down it. She heaved the buckets alongside them, her eyes never leaving the barn as flames licked at the structure and shot upward towards the black heavens. The horses began galloping out. As far away from the struc-

ture as she was, she could still feel the heat emanating from
its core, searing anyone that came too close. She saw Jake
and Zach both run out, wrapping water-drenched blankets
around themselves and shouting directions to each other
before storming back into the inferno.

The red-hot flames surrounded the two men as they huddled together trying to determine if any animals were left
trapped inside the barn. A frantic neighing was heard in the
distance, and Jake ran a quick list through his mind of all
the animals he and Zach had released. Then without
thought, he headed towards the rear of the barn. Abruptly,
he was halted and spun around.

He felt as though his skin was blistering, his eyes were
watering, and he knew he and Zach couldn't stay inside
much longer.

"Where are you going?" Zach shouted over the roar of
the fire.

"Reb's horse is the only one left! He's in the back
stall!"

"I'll get him!" Zach said. "You head back out!"

"It's my responsibility!"

Zach jerked Jake until his head snapped. "Dammit! I
don't know why you don't think she loves you! But she
does and she needs you a hell of a lot more than she needs
a damn horse! You never learned growing up that you have
to obey your older brother, so you're gonna learn now! Get
the hell out of here, little brother, or I'll carry you out and
the horse can stay!"

Jake stared into eyes of brown, emotions running through
him that conflicted with everything he'd known growing
up.

"Leave the horse!" he yelled as he grabbed onto Zach's
coat. "Let's just get the hell out of here!"

The roof to the barn began caving in, and burning beams
began falling around them. Jake ducked down, throwing his
arms over his head. When he stood back up, Zach was
gone.

Jake stumbled out of the burning building. Bending at

the waist, bracing his arms against his knees, he inhaled deeply of the outside air, trying to force the smoky air out of his aching lungs.

When he straightened, he saw Reb coming towards him. Then she doubled over, and screamed. Jake ran towards her, catching her before she hit the ground. Another pain hit her before the first one left and she lifted fear-filled eyes up to his.

"Oh, God! The baby's coming! He's coming now!" she cried.

Jake scanned the area for someone he could trust.

"Frank! Make sure Zach got out!" he yelled. Then the barn, the fire, everything else was forgotten as he carried Rebecca into the house.

Gently, Jake laid Rebecca down on the bed as she doubled up, another pain hitting her. She grabbed his hand, squeezing hard.

"They're coming so fast! Oh, God! It hurts!"

"Reb, honey, I gotta go scrub up. I'll be right back. Just try to relax, honey."

"But it's too soon, Jake. After all this, I'm going to lose him."

"No, you won't. I promise, Reb. Everything's going to be all right."

He pulled his hand free and turned to go, stopping and rubbing her back as she doubled over on her side when the onslaught of pain caught her again. As soon as her breathing started slowing, he ran to the bowl of water and began to scrub his burned hands. Dammit! They thought they had three more weeks to get ready!

He pulled a sheet out of the chest and ripped it into pieces, tying one piece on each end of the bed, handing the cloths to her.

"Just pull on these when the pain comes," he ordered. Then he lifted her gown and laid batting under her. He watched in wonder as her muscles visibly tightened and she clenched her jaw.

"Reb, honey, don't hold it in. Scream. Scream all you want. I gotta see if his head is down. It might hurt, honey."

"It hurts now, Jake." And then she filled the house with a scream that escaped out into the night and startled the men who were still battling the fire.

"I can feel his head. He's real low down. Next time, just push, honey. Bear down and push. It's going to be all right, Reb."

His voice was soothing and calm, his hands gently rubbing her stomach, and for a minute she almost believed him. Then an unbearably hard contraction hit her, followed rapidly by another. When she thought she could stand it no longer, it subsided. She opened her tear-filled eyes and between the valley of her raised knees, she saw Jake smiling.

"What the hell are you smiling at, Burnett?" she snarled.

He looked at her with innocence. "I can see his head. He's got black hair."

"Black hair?" she asked in a softened tone.

"He's almost here, honey."

Then the pain gripped her again, even more intense than before, and she slipped into blissful blackness. She felt as though she were swimming through a dark tunnel, and at the end a tiny wailing sound was calling her. Painstakingly, she opened her eyes. Jake was hovering over her, cradling a tiny bundle in his strong, protective arms.

"We have a son, Reb," he said in a quiet voice as he laid the child on her chest.

Her fingers lightly brushed the dark hair as she studied the crinkled face. How odd, she thought, that we start life so wrinkled and end it the same way.

In wonder she said, "He looks just like—" She stopped herself from saying Brett, for the boy did look just like his father. "Just perfect," she amended.

"I'll clean him up as soon as I've taken care of you," Jake said. Her body expelled the afterbirth. He washed her, padded her, and changed the bedding without moving her from the bed. The entire time, she admired her perfect son, touched the five tiny fingers on each of his hands, his ten curled-up toes, the faint brows over his eyes, the hair that already promised to be thick and full. Jake helped her slip into a clean, soft gown, and then he took the baby to clean him up. Rebecca closed her eyes, Jake's words echoing through her mind, "We have a son."

He brought the clean, sleeping infant back to her. "He's more presentable now, but he fell asleep. Guess it was hard work for him, too. Do you want to hold him?"

She reached out her arms. "Just for a minute."

He gave the sleeping child to his mother and Rebecca's eyes fell on Jake's hands.

"Oh! Your hands!"

"Bad night to have a fire."

"Bring me the salve and dressing."

"I'll be all right."

"Do it, Jake Burnett!"

It hurt like hell to carry the jar of salve and the dressing to her. She sat up and laid the baby down on the bed, gently taking Jake's hand in her own.

"How in the world did you manage to deliver a baby?" she wailed.

"Actually, they didn't start hurting until I stopped."

She applied the salve and lightly wrapped his hands, wincing as she did so, knowing he was doing the same. She wondered how the hell he could not help feeling pain while he was delivering the baby. And how many times had she squeezed his hand?

When she was done, he laid the baby in his cradle and tucked Rebecca into bed before returning outside to herald the good news and assess the damages done by the fire.

Rebecca was surprised she couldn't sleep. After all she'd been through, she thought she'd fall into a deep slumber and never wake up. From time to time, her eyes caressed the sleeping infant, finding it difficult to believe the little mound that had been her belly was that beautiful child who was now part of her world. Already, she could not remember what it was like not to have him in her life. She heard the door open and waited for Jake to come to her. When he didn't, she eased herself out of the bed. He was sitting on the couch, head back, eyes closed.

"What are you doing?" she asked.

His eyes snapped open. "You should be in bed."

"So should you."

"I thought you'd be more comfortable if I slept here," he said.

"Well, you thought wrong. Come to bed."

"In a while."

The woefulness in his voice caused her to sit down. "What happened?"

Jake sighed. How could he tell her? How could he explain not only what had happened but how he was feeling about it? He released a ragged sigh, sorrow-filled eyes turned her way. "Zach didn't make it out."

Raising herself up onto her knees, she drew him against her bosom, her arms encircling him, tears filling her eyes. "I'm so sorry, Jake," she said quietly. "It wasn't your fault. When you came out of the barn, the flames were already too high for anyone else to go back in."

His arms came around her, squeezing tightly. "I didn't want to like him, Reb. But I did. We were just beginning to know each other, to come to an understanding about the past."

"How do you think the fire got started?"

"I'd bet my life Ethan started it."

"Life's little ironies. He started it to destroy one brother and ended up destroying the other." She raked her fingers through his hair. "Come to bed, hold me, let me hold you."

They lay in each other's arms, mindful not to hurt each other, listening to the soft breathing of their son.

"What do you think I should name him?" Rebecca asked in the stillness of the night.

"Thought you might want to name him after his father."

"I'd like that," she said, as tears of happiness mingled with the tears of sadness brought on by Zach's death. Jake Burnett was the most unselfish man she had ever known. "We'll call him Jacob. Jacob Burnett."

Jake was hurting, emotionally and physically, and he was exhausted. He stared at her in wonder.

"You're going to name him after me?"

"I don't see any other father in this house."

Ignoring the pain throbbing in his hands, he drew her

close, holding onto her tightly. It was the most precious gift she could have given him.

The meager group of scruffy men looked up from the campfire they were huddled around, the overcast sky adding to the dreariness. Ethan unfolded his body and sauntered confidently over to the rider who had dared to enter their midst.

"Where's your men? Or did you come to your senses and decide to leave this state?"

Jake studied the man. As much as he disliked him, he took no pleasure in bringing him the news.

"Someone torched our barn last night."

Ethan gave the man a knowing sneer, pleased to take note of the burns on his hands. "And I guess you came to accuse me of the wrongdoing?"

Jake shook his head and sighed. "No. I came to tell you that Zach died helping me get the livestock out of the barn."

Ethan stumbled back as though someone had rammed a hardened fist into his chest.

"I've set aside some land. Thought we'd bury him there tomorrow. Seemed appropriate since your father bought the land. If you prefer to bury him somewhere else—"

Ethan turned away, walking past his men and the fire, walking until he was surrounded by emptiness. Then he dropped to his knees and railed against the forces that had destroyed the only person left in the world who he had loved.

The small, somber group gathered around the grave, the men standing with their hats in their hands, giving the only thing they had left to give, their deepest respect.

Ethan rode up and without a word dismounted and took his place opposite Jake. His eyes bore into Jake during the minister's recitation. When the minister closed his Bible, he looked between the two men, wondering who would throw the handful of dirt onto the wooden casket that had been lowered into the cold ground.

"You do it," Ethan snarled. "You're the reason he's dead."

Before anyone could respond to the accusation, Rebecca stepped forward, picked up a handful of dirt and dropped it on the casket. "Good-bye, Zach," she whispered. "I'm glad Jake had you." Then she stepped back and slipped her arm around Jake, leading him away, the other mourners following, leaving Ethan to bear his grief alone beside the gaping hole.

The bunkhouse had been cleared to provide room for all the food the thoughtful neighbors had brought. Rebecca and Jake walked to the house where someone had offered to watch the sleeping babe while they attended the funeral. When they entered, they saw that the woman had been replaced by Carrie. A large smile crossed her face as she turned to them. She immediately trudged over to Jake and threw her arms around him.

"I know this is a sad occasion, but there's still reason for rejoicing. You done good, boy. You got one handsome son."

Jake worked his way out of Carrie's embrace. "We're proud of him," he said.

"And with good reason."

Jake left to accept condolences from the mourners, and Rebecca picked up her son. Carrie watched her as she sat down to nurse him.

"So much for your lying-in period," Carrie said.

"I barely had time to have the baby," Rebecca said, "much less stay in bed and recover."

"I never believed in staying in bed myself. Hell, half the peoples of the world go back into the fields right after their babies are born." She gave Rebecca a knowing look.

"You'll be surprised how over the years he'll come to resemble Jake. He'll pick up Jake's mannerisms and no one will ever guess," Carrie said.

Rebecca's eyes snapped to Carrie's, wondering what she meant by that comment. She saw in Carrie's eyes that she meant exactly what Rebecca was afraid Carrie had meant.

''Takes a special man to accept another's child as his own,'' Carrie said.

Rebecca felt the tears stinging her eyes. Would everyone know?

''Which one of my sons do you think wasn't fathered by Michael?''

The shock of the question stopped Rebecca's tears from falling. Her eyes widened, then narrowed as she ran all the Reading boys through her mind. ''That's a trick question,'' she said. ''All of them are Michael's sons.''

Carrie leaned back. ''That's true enough. But he didn't plant the seed that brought forth Mark.''

''Does he know that?'' Rebecca asked.

Carrie laughed. ''Course he knows. He was off fighting the damn Yankees. War was coming to a close, raids were increasing. Men were deserting, taking whatever they could. We had lost everything. All I had left was Matthew and the hope that Michael would return safe. Then one night, five men came on a raid. Only thing to raid was me. Got no idea which one got lucky, and I don't want to know. I hadn't seen Michael in a year when he returned, and I was so full of baby that I hid from him.'' Carrie smiled at the memory. ''But he found me. And we came here to start over. Course, Mark doesn't know. We never saw any point in telling him.''

''Do you think everyone else will know he's not Jake's?''

Carrie stood up and patted Rebecca's shoulder. ''But he is Jake's. I knew that the minute Jake walked in the door and his eyes focused on the boy.'' She touched Jacob's hair. ''No one else will look as closely as I did. I apologize, Rebecca. Since Mark was born, I always wonder.''

''It would be nice if he had Jake's smile,'' Rebecca said. ''I've always liked his smile.'' Her eyes caressed the sleeping child.

It was a week before Jake's hands were healed enough that he could carve out the marker for Zach's grave. Rebecca accompanied him on his trek to Zach's resting place

and stood silently watching as Jake worked to set the
marker in the ground. She thought of Zach with great fond-
ness, missing him more than she had thought she would.
She hoped fervently that he had not been disappointed to
find himself embraced by the powerful arms of the Lord.
Hell was not the final destination for men like Zach, regardless of his desire to join his father.

His task completed, Jake stood up. When Rebecca
moved to stand beside him, he put his arm around her waist.

"Seems like there ought to be something more I can
do," Jake said in a pained whisper.

Rebecca pressed her head against his chest. Turning, they
slowly walked away from the marker. The epitaph carved
deeply into the wood silently proclaimed what voices had
been given no opportunity to declare:

ZACHARY TRUSCOTT
Beloved Brother and Friend
1857–1884

# Chapter Twelve

JOHN IRELAND, THE governor of Texas, called the legislature together for a special session. In January, shortly after the fire that took Zach's life, they passed a law making it illegal to cut a barbed-wire fence.

The Rocking R had experienced less trouble, although Jake was certain that Ethan stopping his troublemaking had nothing to do with the law. He felt the man was simply biding his time and would make one last bid for ownership of his land.

But Jake had more on his mind than worrying about when Ethan would make his move. He set his horse into a gallop, eager to reach the Reading ranch. He was hoping to avoid Carrie's embrace, but he was willing to endure it if the woman would help him. He had caught Rebecca crying too many times lately not to know something was wrong. But when he'd asked her what was the matter, she'd said she didn't know. He thought it more likely she didn't want to admit the truth to him: she regretted marrying him now that the baby was born.

He reined in his horse as Carrie came out the door.

"Land O'Goshen, boy. Did you finally come to your senses and want a hug?"

Blushing, Jake tipped his hat. "No, ma'am. But I was wondering if I might have a word with you."

"Sure. Come on in."

Jake dismounted and followed her into the house.

"Pour you some coffee?" Carrie asked, watching as Jake waited for her to sit down.

"No, thank you."

She plopped down in the unvarnished wooden chair. He sat down at a right angle to her, laying his hat on the table.

Jake's eyes left hers as he contemplated how much to say. He decided to begin with as little as possible.

Carrie reached over, placing her plump hand over Jake's forearm. "Tell me what's bothering you," she said warmly.

Jake returned his gaze to her. "It's Reb. Lately . . . lately she's been crying a lot. I ask her what's wrong, and she says she don't know. How can a woman not know why she's crying?"

"How old's that boy of yours?"

"Little over two months."

"Then that's the problem," Carrie said confidently, leaning back in the chair, her arms crossed under her full bosom.

Jake eyed her warily, wondering what he was missing. It couldn't be that simple, whatever the hell it was. "What's the problem?"

"It's natural for a woman to cry after a baby is born, to get all sad and not know why. A woman's body spends nine months changing to make a baby and then bam!"— she slammed her hand down on the table and Jake jumped—"All of a sudden she's done making the baby and her body says what the hell do I do now. And it gets confused trying to be like it was before."

"What do I do to help her? I don't like to see her crying."

Carrie leaned forward, conspiratorially. "Do something special. Take her on a picnic."

"A picnic?"

"Certainly. Tomorrow's Sunday. Do it then. Give her a change of scenery. A beautiful spring day, flowers in bloom, bees a-buzzin'. It'll do her a world of good."

"Sounds too simple."

She patted his arm. "Most things in life are just that

simple, and we work like the devil trying to make them hard.''

All the commotion in the house brought Rebecca out of bed. She padded across the floor, hands on her hips, and glared at her husband.

"What the hell are you doing?" she asked harshly.

Jake turned, his face beaming, and she regretted the harshness of her words.

"Working on a surprise."

Smiling, she ambled over to his side, peering down at his busy hands. "What are you working on this time?"

"A picnic."

"A picnic?"

"I found a real pretty spot I want to take you and Jacob to this morning. Thought we'd just be lazy and watch the clouds roll by."

"What can I do to help?" Rebecca asked with an enthusiasm she hadn't shown in weeks, and Jake promised himself to find a way to thank Carrie Reading properly.

It didn't take them long to pack everything they needed into the wagon and set off. They drove slowly up a small hill. At the top Rebecca gasped, squeezing Jake's arm. The hill, coated in blue flowers, swept down to a tiny pond. Near the pond, a giant oak tree, its opulent branches majestically spread, offered the perfect shade for a picnic. The hill wasn't steep and Jake guided the wagon cautiously down the slight incline.

Jake jumped down and helped Rebecca out of the wagon, then reached back to pick up the basket holding Jacob. He handed the bundle of food to Rebecca and brought out a frayed quilt. He spread the quilt in the shade and set Jacob's basket down. Rebecca turned slowly, admiring the view.

Jake headed back towards the wagon and returned with ropes and a tiny cradle. He hung it from a low branch of the towering oak.

"Thought we could swing Jacob," he explained.

Rebecca smiled. He had been true to his word, treating Jacob as though he were his own flesh and blood. Jake held him every evening, sometimes getting up in the middle of the night to bring Jacob to her when he was hungry. She knew his feelings for the boy weren't false. One night she had been so exhausted that she didn't hear Jacob until he was contentedly suckling at her barely exposed breast. Jake was looking down on the boy with such love that tears had sprung to Rebecca's eyes. Tears were becoming an everyday occurrence in her life lately and she didn't know why. She'd think she was pregnant again if she didn't know that was an absolute impossibility. She gasped as Jake began to climb the tree.

"What are you doing?"

"Gotta hang this," he called down.

She watched, holding her breath as he inched out on a bulky tree limb and began tying a rope to the branch overhead. When he was done, he shoved a plank of wood off the bough and a swing fell down.

Her hands flew to her mouth. "I haven't sat in a swing since I was a child."

Jake dropped to the ground and strode towards the quilt. "Let's eat first, then I'll push you."

In her excitement, Rebecca had eaten very little. Jake watched as she strolled through the tall grasses and among the flowers. She had regained her slender figure, and her rounded hips swayed back and forth as she walked. Her breasts were fuller than they'd been before because she was nursing her son. She bent over to pick up a flower and Jake groaned, beginning to wonder at the wisdom of having this picnic. He had been a fool to marry her and tell her he'd never touch her, to knowingly make his life a living hell. Had he thought he was a saint for Christ's sake?

It had been difficult enough to restrain himself while she was pregnant. Her expanding girth should have been a deterrent, but instead he'd found her waddling adorable. It had warmed him to the roots of his soul to watch her unconsciously rest her hand on her stomach and smile. But now that she was once again shaped like a delicate hourglass, he ached to do more than hold her in his arms. The few times he had allowed himself the privilege of kissing her, he had hoped he would awaken feelings in her, feelings that would make her want him just half as much as he wanted her. But he hadn't stirred anything within her. He had little doubt she had been kissed by the best. And Jake Burnett was not the best.

"Do you know what they call these?" she asked, dropping her lithe body down beside him.

"Carrie says they're bluebonnets. See"—he pointed—"they're shaped like that white bonnet she wears."

She smiled up at him, her eyes dancing. "Will you push me now?"

He knew he shouldn't. He shouldn't touch her. Why had he made the damn swing?

"Sure," he said.

She jumped up and ran to sit on the swing. He moved around behind her. Her back was so narrow, so tapered. He lowered his eyes and cursed under his breath. He had made the swing too small and she was sitting too far back, leaving none of the wood exposed. He'd have to place his hands on her backside. Gaining a temporary reprieve, he grabbed the rope just above her hands. He pulled the swing back as far as he could and released it, hoping her weight would give her the height she wanted.

"Higher!" she called out, giving him no choice but to set his large hands on her small, firm buttocks. She squealed and leaned back, her hair almost brushing the ground. God, she looked radiant. She returned to him and he pushed again. Damn Carrie and her ideas.

"That's enough!" she called down and gratefully he moved back, unable to tear his eyes off of her.

The swing slowed and she ran around and grabbed Jake's hands. Pulling him after her, she charged halfway up the hill. She twirled them in a circle until she lost her balance and stumbled, falling to the ground, bringing Jake with her.

She was nestled among the bluebonnets, her dark features highlighted by their blueness, a blueness that almost matched her eyes. Her eyes were alight with joy, her lips parted as she drew in deep breaths, and he was lost. God help him but he was lost.

His mouth came down on hers, his tongue delving deeply

into the succulent area between her parted lips. He allowed his hand to cup her breast, feeling the taut nipple through her dress, rubbing his palm over it and pressing down. He shoved his knee between hers, pressing the hardness between his loins against her thighs, imitating the movements he would be making if he were buried deep inside her.

Suddenly, the wailing, painful cry of a baby broke through to Jake's consciousness, and he hauled his disappointed body off her. She jumped up and ran to the child. He buried his head among the flowers, gulping great breaths of air as he sought to control his quaking. She hadn't fought him, but then he had to admit he hadn't given her a chance.

Jake pulled himself to his feet, and walked over to where Rebecca stood. She was lightly shaking Jacob up and down, cooing to him. Her face crimson, she averted her eyes as he approached.

"He got stung by a bee," she explained softly.

"We'd best get him home then."

Jake packed up the picnic. They rode home in silence. When they arrived, Rebecca assured Jake she could tend to the boy's needs and took Jacob into the house. Jake saddled his horse and rode out.

Drawing the shawl over her white cotton nightgown, Rebecca stepped out into the cool night breeze, to wait on the porch for Jake to come out of the barn. She hadn't been at all surprised that he'd returned so late in the evening. She had noticed it was his habit to ride out when he was burdened, the heavier the burden, the farther he traveled, not so much to escape his troubles, but to face them.

His behavior that afternoon had taken her by surprise, but not nearly as much as her own reaction to his body pressing down on hers. She had actually cursed under her breath when Jacob had begun wailing. Leaving Jake's sturdy arms to tend to her son's needs had taken every ounce of motherly instinct she could collect. She had been filled with such guilt, she had been unable to face Jake. Wasn't a mother supposed to willingly put her child first? But she hadn't wanted to. She had wanted to put her

husband first and more, she had wanted exactly what was
happening in that field among the bluebonnets.

She saw Jake step out of the barn. He stopped beside a
large tub of clear water and pulled off his shirt and his
black, broad-brimmed hat. Then he dipped his cupped
hands into the cool water and splashed it over his body,
scrubbing his face and upper body, shaking the drops free
like a puppy. He slipped back into his shirt, not bothering
to button it, and used his hat to slap the dust off his pants
as he walked towards the house.

He stopped abruptly when he saw her, every emotion he
carried within his heart reflected in his deep brown eyes.
The pointed toes of his boots were touching the edge of the
porch, his feet still on the ground, placing Rebecca on eye
level with him. She watched as his Adam's apple bobbed
up and down and he rubbed a hand unconsciously down a
thigh.

"About this afternoon," he began.

"Jacob is just fine," she interjected. "The swelling on
his cheek has already gone down."

He nodded. "Good. . . . About what I did . . . "

"Taking us on a picnic was a wonderful idea. We both
enjoyed it very much," she said softly.

He closed his eyes, his throat visibly working to swallow.
He opened his eyes, meeting hers squarely. "About what
happened when we were laying on the ground. I . . . I took
liberties I shouldn't have. I'm sorry. It won't happen again.
I swear it won't."

She placed her palm on his cheek. "Jake . . . "

His hand came up, taking her wrist, moving her hand
away from his face.

"You'd best not do that, Reb. As a matter of fact, I was
thinking maybe I ought to start sleeping in the barn . . .
until we can get a bigger house built . . . one with more
rooms." He had considered sleeping in the bunkhouse, but
he didn't want the men to know what his relationship with
his wife entailed. He had some pride.

"In the barn . . . with the rest of the animals?" she asked.

His gaze dropped to the ground. He remained silent because she was right. He had behaved like an animal. If a bee hadn't decided to pay Jacob a visit, Jake probably would not have regained control of himself, and his promise to her would have been broken.

"I wouldn't like it at all if you slept in the barn, Jake."

Slowly, his eyes came up to meet hers. "I don't think you understand, Reb."

Her free hand came up to cup his cheek, and her shawl slid to the ground. "I want you in my bed."

She watched him contemplating her words, his brows drawn together, his lips tight, and she knew he wasn't sure that she understood.

"For eight months, I've been laying in your arms at night, sleeping in your tender embrace. Tonight, I want more than that," she said quietly. In invitation, she slipped her arm around his neck, bringing her lips to his, running her tongue along the well-defined edges of his lips. Unconsciously, his hold on her wrist tightened as his lips parted and her tongue slipped inside to greet his. It wasn't a passionate or fiery kiss; it was designed to reassure. She ran her hand down his arm, placing her hand in his. "Come to bed, Jake." She walked towards the door, stopping when he failed to follow.

His eyes searched hers. "Are you sure?"

She moved back to him and pressed her cheek against his, speaking softly into his ear. "I'm sure." She leaned back to meet his gaze squarely. "I wanted to kill that damn bee this afternoon."

The right side of his mouth tilted up, and she leaned over, pressing a kiss against one corner. "I love your smile," she whispered.

He wondered if it was possible to love part of a person without loving the whole person. "Let me take off my boots," he whispered. "I don't want to wake Jacob."

Smiling, she whispered back, "No, we don't want to wake Jacob."

Silently they crept through the house, his hand gripping hers. They stopped when they were hidden behind the hanging quilt, facing each other.

Breathing was difficult, and Jake was certain she was

waiting for him to take the first step. He had often thought about this moment, wanting it perfect for her. He rubbed his hands down his thighs. Where to begin?

"Remember when you asked me about my going to a whorehouse?"

"Jake, now is not the time to tell me about all your exploits."

"That's just it. There was just the one time, ever, with any woman. And I was so damn drunk, I don't remember most of it."

She brushed away the hair at his temple. "There's only been one time for me, too. Do you want to get drunk again?" she asked quietly.

"No, ma'am. I want to remember every moment of this." His fingers lightly traced the outline of her face, his eyes lovingly caressing her features. "I love you, Reb. With all my heart, I do."

Then his large, roughened hands cupped her silky smooth face, tilting it slightly as his lips pressed against hers. The tip of his tongue slowly circled the contours of her lips, before slowly slipping between the softness into the hot, wet recesses of her mouth. His mouth opened wider, bidding hers to do the same, their tongues probing and withdrawing only to probe again. She was everything he had ever been denied—beauty, kindness, tolerance, understanding—washing over him like a summer storm, drenching him, cleansing him, ending the emotional drought brought on by his mother's untimely death.

Slipping her small hands under his open shirt, she pressed her palms against his taut skin, slowly moving them upwards, easing his shirt off his shoulders. Without breaking off the kiss, he brought his arms down, his shirt falling to the floor. He pressed her close to his bare chest. Through the thin cotton gown, he could feel the curves of her body, her warmth. He was stepping out of purgatory into heaven and wanted to savor the journey.

Stretching up onto her toes, Rebecca pushed herself closer to Jake, the warm, tingly feeling running rampant through her body. It was so much nicer than the sensations she had experienced in the field when layer upon layer of clothing had separated them.

With trembling fingers, he worked on the buttons of her nightgown. She placed her hands over his, stilling his actions.

"You've seen me without clothes. After Jacob was born, you bathed me."

"But I didn't look at you then the way I'm going to look at you now."

Bringing his hands to her lips, she placed a light kiss on each callused fingertip.

"It's only me."

"It's because it's you," he said. "I wouldn't care if it was anyone else."

She released his hands, brushing her fingers up into his hair as he returned to the glorious task of disrobing her. When he had slipped the last button through its hole, the one resting just below her navel, he put his hands on either side of the parted material, widening the crevice exposing her body. His hands touched only the cotton of the gown. She felt her entire body quivering in anticipation as he slowly removed the gown, never touching her. His slow movements created the gentlest of breezes whispering across her skin. Just his presence so near had tautened her nipples, and her breasts, bounteous from childbirth, were full and firm. She was surprised to find how much she ached for him to touch her.

"Can I loosen your hair?" he asked.

"You can do anything you want," she said as she turned, giving him access to her bound hair.

For a moment, the braid was forgotten as he gazed at her in wonder. The tip of the braid rested against the small of her back, touching a tiny dimple just above her dainty, rounded backside. He remembered the feel of his hands pressing against her when he had pushed her in the swing. He loosened her braid, combing his fingers through the long, thick, ebony strands. She shook her head, releasing the scent of roses as her long mane fell gracefully around her narrow shoulders.

"Will you turn around? Just a little?" he asked.

She presented him with a partial profile. The moon peeking in through the curtains cast a halo around her, and his eyes lovingly roamed the length of her from her crown to her toes. Each feature warranted its own attention, its own praise. And his eyes did praise her.

"Lord, but you're beautiful," he said softly.

Lifting her hands, she cupped the air around her breasts. "I'm afraid some of this is going away when I stop nursing."

"I know. I remember how you were shaped before. Just as beautiful as you are now."

She had seen his compassion, felt his tender touch the day she thought she was losing the baby. She remembered his gentleness the night Jacob was born. But those moments paled in comparison to the gentleness he bestowed upon her now. His touch, as he ran his hands along the contours of her flesh, was as light as newly falling snow, and like the snow that coated the ground, his touch stayed with her after his hands moved on.

She pressed both palms against his flat stomach, then moved splayed fingers up his chest, admiring his lean form. As she gradually brought her hands back down, her eyes locked into his. She felt his body stiffen, his breath catch, as she began to push the buttons of his pants through their holes, one by one. She slipped her hands around to his backside, gliding them until they rested firmly between his clothes and his skin. Averting her eyes, she brought his pants and all he wore underneath down, helping him step out of them before removing his socks. Resting on her knees, she straightened her back. Lifting her gaze, she beheld him for the first time. She ran the tips of her fingers up his inner thighs, and then down, the hair covering his skin as soft as the down of a newborn duckling, the muscles firm and hard, and she relished the feel of them under her caresses.

"I almost envy your horse," she said, "because these thighs hug him all day."

She tilted her head up, her eyes holding his as her hands

took separate journeys up his thighs, meeting and molding themselves around their final destination.

Releasing a low groan, he pulled her up, his mouth locking onto hers as he backed her towards the bed. The back of her knees hit the mattress, jolting both of them, and she fell back onto the bed, with him falling down on top of her.

Slipping his arm under her, he scooted her over until they were laying lengthwise on the bed, her head pressed down into the feather pillow. Then he began his loving sojourn along her flesh, inhaling her sweet feminine scent, pressing kisses to her neck, behind her ear, down to the hollow of her throat, along her collarbone. Deliberating with himself, he placed a kiss in the valley between her breasts, hesitating before kissing the side of the breast he had cupped in his hand, not daring to go further.

"It's all right," she whispered.

His eyes snapped to hers. "I don't want to hurt you."

"You won't," she said.

His mouth came back to hers, the sweet cavern growing warmer with each sweeping thrust of his tongue. His mouth had never touched, never tasted a woman's body, and there had never been any woman he wanted to taste as much as he wanted to taste her. Her body was so different from his, soft in places where his was hard, smooth where his was rough.

Tenderly, he kneaded her breast as his mouth left hers, trailing hot kisses, not stopping until he had pressed a kiss on the tightened, darkened orb. He covered it with his mouth, his tongue laving it at a leisurely pace as he sought to memorize the varying textures of her flesh.

She gasped, her back coming up off the bed, her hands digging into his scalp, pressing him closer. Unschooled in the art of love, he reveled in her reaction to him as he sought to show her with his hands, his mouth, his tongue how much he loved her.

She felt a warmth centering in the pit of her stomach cascading through her body and a hot wetness beginning between her thighs. His mouth moved to her other breast, and she released a small cry. Without releasing his hold, he gazed up at her, grateful to find she didn't look as if she were in pain. He took his mouth completely around her breasts before returning his lips to hers. He slipped a knee between her thighs, and she opened herself to him. Bringing the other knee in, he braced himself up above her, and looking down on her with love, reaffirmed his feelings with tender words before burying himself deep inside her. He found instant release . . . and mortification.

She felt him shudder, releasing a small anguished cry, and her arms tightened around him. She wondered how long he had wanted this moment, how much he had wanted it for his release to come so swiftly. The moon cast a silvery glow over his back, illuminating the crisscross of scars on his backside. Tears welled up in her eyes for the boy who had been beaten for expressing excitement, paraded around before others because he sought warmth. And for the man who had thought no woman could ever want him.

"I'm sorry, Reb." His voice was thick beside her ear.

"For what?" she asked quietly.

Lifting his head away from her sweetly scented neck, he gazed down into her eyes. As inexperienced as he was, he had heard enough talk in the bunkhouse to know he had left her unfulfilled. "I should have waited. You should have . . . I just should have waited."

Cupping his face in her hands, she brought his lips back down to hers, kissing him tenderly, accepting an apology when none was necessary.

"Do we have to stop now?" she asked gently. Firmly placing her hands on his scarred backside, holding him in place, she thrust her hips down. He had grown limp nestled inside of her, and her actions brought the blood rushing back to his loins. Slowly, she moved down and back up. "Do we?" she asked.

"No, ma'am." He grinned down at her. "I reckon we don't."

His mouth came down on hers, his hips slowly moving in circles. She sighed, flattening her head back against the pillow while he covered the tip of her breast with his

mouth, sucking gently, and her gasps began again. He deepened his thrusts and her gasps began in earnest, her throat
emitting little cries that ebbed and flowed with his movements, her hands bearing down on him, digging into his
flesh. He hoisted himself above her, watching the expressions change on her face, her mouth softly agape, her eyes
closed, now and then her brows drawing together and then
relaxing. Her gasps became more audible, and then she released a cry as her back arched away from the bed bringing
her body up to his. She seemed suspended in a realm of
sensations. He had never witnessed anything so beautiful
in his entire life. She slid down to the bed. Languorously,
she opened her eyes, the blue liquid pools reflecting a depth
of feeling that catapulted him into the same realm, this time
without guilt, without shame. He dropped down to his elbows, wondering if he'd ever breathe normally again.

Rolling to his side, he brought her with him, pressing
their bodies together. He ran his fingertips idly up and down
her arm. He wanted to thank her, but somehow it seemed
inappropriate. So instead, he drew her closer, bringing his
arms tightly around her, trying to hold onto the moment as
they both drifted off to sleep.


A dark cloud passed before the moon, casting eerie shadows across the landscape. Standing before the window,
holding the curtain back, Rebecca stared out into the distance. Jacob had awakened for his late night feeding, and
now she couldn't go back to sleep. The last she wanted to
do was compare Jake with Brett but she was standing here doing it anyway.

Her father had wanted a bigger, more prestigious barn.
It had taken two days for the neighbors and hands to build
it. To celebrate its completion, he had ordered the biggest
dance ever held in the state. Three bands took turns playing,
cattle were slaughtered, beer and whiskey were served all
afternoon and evening and far into the night. She had just
finished dancing with Jake when Brett had asked her to take
a stroll with him. The warmth of Jake's hand in hers, the
sight of his lopsided grin, the smile in his eyes as they'd

circled the dance area were still with her when Brett had slipped his arm around her waist.

They had walked out into the moonless night, away from the lights of the ranch, away from the music, away from the din of people talking and laughing. They had walked until the only thing visible was the star-filled black velvet sky. He had taken her in his strong arms without warning and had kissed her in a way no man had ever kissed her, his tongue plunging deeply, sending ripples of sensations coursing through her body. Then he had laid her down, and his mouth had continued its assault on her senses. He had hesitated not at all in putting his mouth on the flesh he had wanted to taste. She hadn't even been aware that he had removed their clothes until his mouth had closed around her nipple, tugging at it until it hardened. And then he had placed himself between her thighs, creating sweet sensations, whispering words of love.

He was a smooth, practiced, polished lover. She had fallen in love with his startling blue eyes and his easy smile, his deep voice that constantly caressed, and his hands that turned her body to fire.

But the fire he had ignited had never been like the fire that had burned through her tonight. She had felt everything Jake had done. Nothing had taken her unawares. She had felt every button being released, had felt the gown slowly leaving her body. She had felt his uncertainty and his hesitancy. And his disappointment when his body had reacted against his will. With Jake, the act of love would never be completely smooth. Her clothes would not melt away without her knowledge. No, Jake Burnett was not Brett Meier.

"Are you all right?" a gentle voice asked and she turned. He was standing beside her, wearing his pants, half the buttons done up. She had drifted so far away in thought that she hadn't heard him leave the bed.

"I'm fine. Jacob woke up and then I couldn't get back to sleep."

"Are you sorry?"

She searched his concerned countenance until the meaning of his question hit her. She placed a hand on his chest.

"No. No, I'm not sorry at all."

"I know I'm awkward . . . "

She brought her hand to his lips.

"Jake, how can you have so much confidence when it comes to running a ranch and handling the livestock and so little when it comes to women?"

He sighed. "Reckon cause I've never had a ranch or livestock laugh at me." His eyes held hers. "I know Ethan put the girls up to laughing at me . . . but there was never one that didn't . . . until you."

She touched his cheek. "I think those girls were probably just jealous."

"Jealous? Of what?"

She brushed the hair up off his brow. "Your eyes. You have the most beautiful eyes."

He gave her a sad smile. "There's nothing beautiful about me, Reb."

Pressing her hand to his heart, she said, "Here you're the most considerate, generous person I know, Jake Burnett, and it's all reflected in your eyes. Don't you tell me I don't know beauty when I see it."

He ran his knuckles down her cheek, speaking softly. "You're the beautiful one. You could have married anyone."

"I know," she said with warmth in her eyes. "Of all the things my father did for me, I'm most grateful he asked you to marry me." She reached down to unbutton his pants. "I appreciate you not buttoning them all up. Next time, don't even bother to put them on."

Groaning, he pressed her back on the bed, managing to slip out of his pants in the process.

# Chapter Thirteen

THE BELL SUSPENDED above the door emitted a tinny, tinkling sound as Jake entered the general store.

"Be with you in a minute, Jake," Samuel Abrams said as he turned impatiently back to his waiting customer.

A boy who was no older than six stood before the counter longingly eyeing a glass container filled with confections. Jake watched as he tentatively moved four small fingers towards the glass, shot a glance to the man standing before Samuel, and then withdrew his fingers. If Jake had been allowed into town when he was a boy, he had no doubt he would have stood looking at the jar of candy as intently as the small boy standing there now, and he knew he would not have been allowed to have any. He hunkered down beside the boy. "Want one?"

The boy smiled shyly. "Nay, me da says they're not for buying—just for lookin'. But if I owned me a store, I'd sell everythin' in it."

"Is that your father?" Jake asked, nodding towards the man at the counter.

"Aye. He's a blacksmith. You know what a blacksmith is?"

Jake smiled at the pride reflected in the tiny face. "Yes. Are you settling here?"

The boy shrugged, the corners of his mouth turning down. "Don't know. Me da says they got too many smiths here. Da said 'twould be better here, but it ain't. I never been so hungry in me 'ole life."

169

Jake's heart ached for the boy.

"Where did you come from?"

"Ireland. We came over on a big boat. I was sick the 'ole time. 'Twas no fun at all. Da had to pay extra to bring his smithy tools and now he can't find work. Me mum used to work in people's houses but there ain't no fancy folks here what needs a servant. I'm thinking 'twould have been better to stay in Ireland."

Jake's interest perked up at the news that his mother worked in people's houses. "What did your mother do in those houses?"

The boy shrugged. "Worked."

Jake held out a hand. "I'm Jake Burnett."

The boy put his small hand in Jake's, and it was swallowed up. "Sean O'Hennessy."

"I'm happy to meet you, Sean O'Hennessy."

"Damn it, man! I got five hungry children. I'm only asking for a little credit—"

Jake kept talking to Sean, trying to keep him from hearing his father's argument.

"You've got no job and no prospects. I'm sorry, Mr. O'Hennessy, but where do you think I'd be if I gave credit to everyone that asked?"

"Look, man. I'll sweep your store, I'll haul your boxes—"

"I've already got a boy that comes in to do that. I wish I could help. But you've just told me you spent the last of your money getting your wagon fixed, which sounds to me like you're planning on moving on. Where would that leave me?"

"I wouldna leave without paying you, man!" O'Hennessy bellowed.

"So you say." Samuel Abrams reached in a drawer and brought out a handful of crumpled papers. "These men all said the same thing. I'm sorry."

"Mr. O'Hennessy?"

The man glaring at Jake was well-muscled from years of working with iron, sledging a hammer atop an anvil. His red hair was almost nonexistent except for a patch that circled just above his neck. Jake thought it was worn thin from constant rubbing. In the few moments he had been observing the man, he had run his hands across his shiny pate no less than a dozen times. Jake extended a hand. "My name's Jake Burnett."

Brian O'Hennessy studied the hand extended to him, then he studied Jake's eyes. He liked what he saw and shoved his hand out. "Brian O'Hennessy."

"Your son tells me you're a blacksmith."

"That I am, man. And a damn good one when I got the work to do."

"Your son also tells me your wife used to take care of people's homes."

"That she did. Cleaning, scrubbing, watching babies, whatever was required."

"I own a ranch a few miles south of here. I could use a blacksmith. It's damn inconvenient having to come into town when I need a horse shod or a tool mended. For a while, until I get my herd to market, I could only give you and your family room and board. If you're interested, the job is yours."

Brian rubbed the top of his head. Room and board wouldn't make him a rich man, but it would keep his children dry and their bellies filled.

"Yes, sir, I'm interested."

"I also have a three-month-old son. Do you think your wife would be interested in caring for my house and son a few hours each morning? I'd pay her for it."

"She would."

Jake could barely contain his excitement. "Then we've got a bargain," he said, extending his hand again. "Where are you staying?"

"In a wagon, south end of town."

"I'll pick you up in two hours."

Jake handed a piece of paper to Samuel. "I'll be back to pick these things up in an hour. Put Mr. O'Hennessy's supplies on my account, too, will you, Sam?"

"Sure thing, Jake."

Jake reached into a glass jar, careful not to take from the

one that had been deemed for looking at only, and withdrew five sarsaparilla sticks. "And these, too."

He handed them to Sean. "Share these with your brothers and sisters, okay?"

Sean's eyes widened at the unexpected gift. "Yes, sir, I will."

Jake opened the door and the little bell tinkled. He turned back. "Oh, Mr. O'Hennessy. I'd appreciate it if you and your family wouldn't say anything to my wife about your wife coming to help out in the morning. I want to surprise Reb."

"We'll keep quiet."

Jake walked out the door, his smile broad.

"Now, that's a good man," Brian O'Hennessy commented to the air.

"Won't find one finer, not in these parts," Samuel said. Then he gave Brian a hard stare. "But he wouldn't have given you credit either."

Brian had taken an instant liking to Jake, but still he was surprised to see such a beauty run out of the house and fling herself into Jake's arms as soon as he jumped down off the wagon. He didn't know why, but he just hadn't envisioned Jake Burnett with a woman who could take a man's breath away.

Jake lowered Rebecca to the ground before releasing his lips from hers. "I hired a blacksmith."

"A blacksmith. Do you honestly think we have enough work here to keep a blacksmith busy?"

"We will in time. And until then he'll help out with odd jobs."

Her eyes narrowed.

"Hell, I don't even know if he'll stay, but he's got five hungry kids and at least here they won't be hungry."

He slipped his arm protectively around her. "Come on, I'll introduce you."

As soon as Jake turned towards the O'Hennessy wagon, a mad scramble began as Brian tried to get his family into some sort of condition to meet people. He lined them up by age, then rearranged them by height, rearranged them by sex, and started to rearrange them again before his wife shoved him aside.

"The man's not the king, Bri. I'll not have you behaving like a fool. Line up," she said and the children rearranged themselves by age. "That's how it's done," she said, giving her husband a curt nod.

Rebecca had studied the activity, and she stifled her laughter. She supposed she'd be nervous under the circumstances as well.

"Brian, this is my wife, Rebecca. Reb, this here's Brian."

Brian removed his hat, his shiny pate reflecting the setting sun. "Ma'am. 'Tis a pleasure to meet you to be sure. You don't know how much we appreciate your fine husband givin' us a chance here."

"Believe it or not, Brian, I probably do. Jake was saying just the other night how much simpler life would be if we had a blacksmith living on the ranch." Jake pinched her waist and she shot a conspiratorial glance his way.

"Well . . . did he now? 'Tis interesting how life works, is it not? Now I'd like to introduce you to the pride and joys of my life. This is my wife, Maura."

The tiny woman with the bright red hair and hazel eyes took a quick curtsy. " 'Tis glad we are to be here."

Rebecca suddenly felt as though she had stepped back in time to her first encounter with Carrie. Now she fully understood how her friend had felt.

"It'll be nice to have a woman around, Maura. As you'll soon learn, we are in rare supply here."

"And these are our children," Brian said. "Our eldest son, Kevin. He's nineteen. He'll be helping me. He's learning the trade, he is."

Kevin took a small step forward and gave a slight nod of his head.

"My daughter, Arlene."

When Kevin stepped back, Arlene stepped forward and curtsied. At seventeen, she was unaware of her attraction. Like her brothers, her hazel eyes changed with her moods, turning a speckled green when she was happy.

Patrick, age fourteen, stepped forward next, followed by Neil age ten, and lastly Sean, who produced half a sarsaparilla stick out of his pocket. His face gleamed as he tilted his head back to look up at Jake.

"Saved half o'mine, I did."

Jake tousled the boy's hair. "We'll get more next time we go into town."

"And this one," Brian said, patting his wife's stomach, "I'm hoping is a girl."

"Bri!" Maura slapped his hand away. "You'll bring us bad luck, you will."

Frank had been unloading Jake's wagon during the introductions, not paying much attention. But as he started to turn towards the house with a sack of flour he saw the girl curtsy. The girl? He almost dropped the load he was carrying. Why the hell hadn't Jake told him there was a woman among the lot? Her hair was pulled back, but most of it had worked its way free and was framing her face like the sparks from the sun. He dropped the bag of flour and ambled towards the wagon of newcomers. It'd be impolite not to introduce himself.

He forcibly cleared his throat and Jake turned to him.

"Having trouble with the supplies?"

"No, sir. You just forgot to introduce me earlier."

"I did, didn't I?" Jake made the introductions.

Frank removed his hat, tilting his head towards Arlene. "Ma'am. That's a right pretty name you got. Goes with your face."

Arlene blushed and lowered her eyes.

Jake nudged Frank. "Finish up with the supplies."

Frank donned his hat, running his finger slowly along the brim. "Glad to have you folks here with us. Let me know if there's anything I can do to help you get settled."

He ambled back to the wagon, rarely taking his eyes off Arlene as he hauled in the last of the supplies. She was a pretty thing. Ruth Reading was going to get a taste of jealousy before Frank was finished.

\*      \*      \*

After making a final notation in the ledger, Rebecca set the pencil down and closed the book. Her eyes tenderly lit upon her husband and son as they lay before the hearth. Jacob was intently studying the large hand with wiggling fingers that was moving towards him. His smile broadened and his feet began kicking vigorously as the fingers moved closer until they landed on his tummy and tickled him. His father's smile was just as broad as he moved down to replace his wandering fingers with his lips. He blew air against his son's soft stomach, and Jacob gave his first burst of laughter. Jake's head snapped around to find Rebecca.

"Did you hear that?" he asked.

"Yes," she said, chuckling as she moved to join them on the floor. "You sure are good with him."

"He's so good-natured. He's a real joy to have around."

Rebecca moved in closer to Jake, slipping under his arm and batting her eyelashes at him.

"Tell me, Jake, does my name go with my face?"

Jake blew out a gust of air. "Where the hell did that boy pick up that kind of talk?"

She laughed. "I don't know. I hope that girl doesn't get hurt."

"I don't think Frank would hurt her."

"Not intentionally maybe. But he's so fixated on Ruth it worries me sometimes."

Jake kissed the top of her head.

"I noticed you sent three extra men out tonight. That leaves five empty bunks in the bunkhouse," she said, her eyes twinkling. "If I were to take a look inside, I wouldn't find four O'Hennessy sons and one father filling those bunks, would I?"

"You would. Hell, Reb, the women have been sleeping in the wagon and the men on the ground since they got off the boat. It won't hurt for us to have extra men out at night."

"Just as long as I don't find you giving up your bed."

"Never," he said as his wiggling fingers moved towards her, bringing tickles and laughter to his wife.

*     *     *

The sun filtered into the room and Rebecca squinted her eyes before turning her head to look up into Jake's smiling face.

"What are you grinning about, Jake Burnett?"

Reaching over, he dropped a hand down on her bottom. "Get up and get dressed to ride." He slid out of bed. "Wear pants."

She arched a brow. "And what, pray tell, am I to do with our son?"

"We'll take him with us if we have to. Just get ready."

She had just buttoned her shirt when she heard the door open and Jake announce they had company. She slipped on her boots and came around the quilt, greeted by two smiles.

"Good morning to ya," Maura said.

"Good morning. What can we do for you?"

Maura looked questioningly up at Jake, whose smile broadened.

"She's come to look after the house and Jacob. She's going to help out every morning for a few hours."

Rebecca put her hands on her hips, shaking her head. "And just what am I supposed—" She shrieked and threw herself into Jake's arms. "It wasn't the blacksmith you wanted!" She laughed.

"Shh, woman, there's a man's pride at stake," Jake whispered. He plopped her hat on her head before taking her hand in his and leading her out to the horses. She mounted Shadow. With a challenge set in her eyes, she laughed and galloped away with Jake in hot pursuit.

The wind blew in her face, the smell of cattle assaulted her nostrils, the sun warmed her, and she rode as though it were the last time she would ever be allowed to do so. She had missed riding, the feel of a horse beneath her. She pulled her horse up short at the crest of the small hill where Jake had hung the swing. He pulled up beside her. She smiled, her chest heaving as she tried to regain her breath.

"Thank you, Jake."

Reaching over, he ran his fingers down her cheek. "You weren't meant to mind a house, Reb." His gaze swept the far-reaching horizons. "This is where you belong. Out in the open where you can run free."

He dismounted. Slipping his hand around hers, entwining their fingers, he escorted her along the hill to a spot where the bluebonnets grew thick and abundant. He lay her down among them, his mouth descending on hers with a deliberate purpose, his tongue sweeping her welcoming warmth. He worked his fingers down beneath the waistband of her pants until he found the haven he sought, gently caressing as her hips pressed up against him. She unbuttoned his shirt, gliding her hands along his flesh.

Pulling himself free of her hold, he pushed himself to his knees and reached down to release the buttons on her pants. She lifted her hips, while he pushed the pants down her thighs, past her knees, then unbuttoned his own pants, entering her as his lips returned to hers. His thrusts were hard, deep, her fervor equaling his until their passion built beyond its limits.

Lying among the cool grasses and flowers, Rebecca opened her eyes. She laughed, earning a darkened scowl from Jake.

"You didn't even bother to take off your hat," she chided.

"I didn't bother to take anything off," he said as he nuzzled her neck.

"Your arms are trembling." She pulled against them. "Lay on me."

"I'm too heavy for you," he said as he rolled over and adjusted her clothes to make her presentable before doing the same for himself. Lying on his back, he brought her to his side.

"You are the politest man I know, Jake Burnett."

"Had politeness beat into me."

"I suspected as much."

He opened his eyes, searching hers. His hand cupped her chin. "I'm sorry. I shouldn't have said that. It was a long time ago."

"Which means it was when you were a boy. When I think—"

He pulled her face closer to his. "Don't think. Don't think about it." He brought her lips down to his, kissing

her tenderly, smiling to himself as he yanked her hat off
and tossed it aside.

"Morning!"

Jake looked down at the towheaded boy, his smile filling
his face. The sun had almost passed the horizon, filling the
sky with pinks and lavenders, and the promise of a beautiful
day.

"You're up early," Jake said.

"Cowboys get up early," Sean explained, his face taking
on a seriousness that belied his youth. "You riding out?"

"Yep. Gotta check on my herd."

The boy looked down at the ground, burying his toes in
the dirt, shot a look up at Jake as though about to ask a
question, thought better of it, and went back to covering
his feet with dust.

"Want to come with me?"

The boy bobbed his head up and down so fast that his
hair was up when his head was down.

"Go ask your mother."

Sean tore off towards the wagon, coming back wearing
a bright smile. Jake leaned down from his horse, and
brought the boy up with one arm.

"Where's your shoes?" he asked.

"They got too small."

"You don't think your feet got too big?"

"That, too," Sean said as he leaned forward in anticipation.

Jake placed his hat on top of the boy's head.

"A real cowboy wears a hat," he said as he put his arm
protectively around the child and sent the horse into a slow
gait.

Rebecca's nose twitched as it touched something soft,
and a familiar fragrance surrounded her. Opening her eyes,
she smiled, reaching out to touch the bluebonnets resting
beside her pillow. She wondered when Jake had gone to
gather them. Looking out the window, she saw him riding
out, his arms protectively circling a small rider. Rolling

back over, she buried her face in the bluebonnets. She had come to care deeply for Jake, at moments wondering if perhaps she did love him. But what she felt for him was so different from what she had felt for Brett.

Brett had filled her dreams, surrounded her with excitement. Across a room, she could feel his gaze touch her, warm her. She squeezed her eyes shut trying to banish all thoughts of Brett from her mind. He was like a ghost, haunting her mind, flitting in and out, always there, not always visible. She wanted to give her heart to Jake without reservations, but Brett somehow managed to keep a hold on a piece of it. She wondered what it would take to free herself of Brett so that she could truly love Jake.

She got up and dressed and moments later Maura knocked on the door.

Rebecca smiled her greeting. "Jacob should sleep for a while. I don't think he'll give you any trouble while I'm gone."

Maura's eyes widened "You're wearing a gun! You dinna wear one yesterday."

Rebecca glanced down at her attire, her pants, her cotton shirt, and her Colt hanging low on her hip.

"Yesterday I knew I'd be by Jake's side. Today, I'll be out working, riding the range, looking for strays. I have to be able to protect myself."

"You mean Jake wants me in the house so you can go be a cowboy?"

Rebecca laughed. "Something like that."

"And it's what you want to do?"

"Yes, it is. And Jake knew it more than I did."

Picking her hat up off the table, she called, "I'll be back before lunch."

Smiling, Jake watched as his wife drew even with him. She leaned over and wrapped her arms around his neck.

"Oh, Jake! I don't think I've ever been this happy!"

Slipping a hand to the nape of her neck, he said softly, "It's what I promised you when I married you." Looking deeply into her eyes, he added, "I love you, Reb," just before his mouth covered hers.

She felt an ache, unable to say the words she was certain he longed to hear.

Pulling back, she said, "I saw you riding off with Sean this morning."

He removed his hands from her. "Yeah, I gave him a quick tour. Boy's got no shoes. And his parents are too proud to let me buy him a pair. A boy shouldn't be running around out here without shoes."

She rubbed his cheek. "We'll think of something."

He grinned. "I had Frank run off some of the cattle. They headed south. Go round them up."

Tilting her head back, she laughed. "You did no such thing."

"No, but I thought about it."

She left his side, and he watched as she chased after an errant calf. Her body barely moved as her knees hugged the horse. She leaned down, riding close to the stallion, her long braid laying still against her back. She cut in front of the calf, her horse pivoting on his hind legs. The calf tried to move around them, but with the barest shift in her weight, Rebecca directed the horse to block the calf's progress. When she'd skillfully turned it back towards the herd, Rebecca lifted an arm to wave at Jake, her smile visible even from this distance. He felt a familiar tightening in his loins. How many times had he watched her ride across the Lazy A, experienced the same stirrings, and ridden away so she'd never know what his true feelings were? He didn't have to ride away today. He could watch her graceful movements to his heart's content.

After her morning working with Jake, Rebecca was eager to see the baby. She found him in the O'Hennessys' wagon, Maura jiggling him on her lap.

"Hope you dinna mind me bringing the lad over here for a while."

"Not at all," Rebecca said as she dismounted. "He needs to be outside."

Brian tipped his hat, trying to keep the disapproval off his face. The woman was not dressed the way a woman was supposed to dress. He wondered why Jake had married her. Had to be her beauty.

As the adults talked, Sean spotted the large rock, glistening in the sun. Glistening like gold. What if it was gold? He'd be rich and he'd share it with his family. He left the wagon and walked towards it, studying it as he went. He reached down to pick it up, halting when he heard Jacob's rattle. His breath stopped when he heard the scream, followed closely by the sound of an explosion. Something in front of him went flying. Then his mother was sobbing, pulling him close to her, taking him away from the gold, suffocating him in the process.

Brian looked at the gun being held firmly in Rebecca's hand, not certain he had witnessed what he thought he had witnessed. One second the woman was standing relaxed, talking, and the next the gun was in her hand and she was aiming it at his son. Had he been younger, or not so heavyset, perhaps he could have stopped her. He thanked God that he had been neither.

Rebecca walked over and picked up what remained of the rattlesnake, then brought it to Sean.

Shaking its tail, she asked, "Do you hear that, Sean?"

His eyes widened. "Yes, ma'am."

"Never move if you hear that sound." She laid the battered snake down, cut off the tail, and handed it to the boy. "These are rattlers. You keep them as a reminder."

Standing up, she faced Brian and Maura. "I know you're proud people and don't want charity, but Saturday when Jake goes into town for supplies, your children will be in the wagon with him and they'll come back wearing boots. We have no saints here to drive the snakes away."

Picking up her son, she headed back to the house.

Maura lightly touched her husband's arm. "What do you think, Bri?"

"I'm a-thinkin' Jake dinna marry her for her beauty."

Frank approached the wagon where the two women were putting away the last of the dishes.

"Evening," he said as he removed his hat, wondering at

his nervousness. He'd never felt this jumpy in his stomach when he'd approached Ruth.

Both women stopped working, Maura studying him intently and Arlene looking up at him through her lashes, trying to decide if it would be appropriate to smile at him.

"I was wondering, Miss Arlene, if you'd be interested in taking a walk with me."

Arlene looked to her mother for her approval and was disappointed to see she wasn't going to receive it.

"I'm not so sure that's a good idea," Maura said. Her daughter was young and pretty and this young man with his flirtatious ways seemed too worldly.

"We'd just walk over there to the windmill," Frank said with a flick of his head. "You'll be able to see us the entire time. I swear, ma'am, I wouldn't take advantage."

Maura blushed at being so easily read, pursed her lips, and gave her daughter permission to go.

The walk to the windmill wasn't nearly long enough, Frank discovered. They quickly reached it and stood beneath the towering structure, listening to the clacking sounds made by the wooden wheel above. The sun was setting in the distance, and Frank was determined to have Arlene back to the wagon before the sun was gone.

"Have you ever had a drink of water brought up from the earth by a windmill?" he asked.

She shook her head, wishing her tongue would come untied. She'd never had a gentleman show interest in her before.

Frank dipped his hand into the water, forming a cup, and brought his hand to her lips. She sipped on the water, and Frank felt the warmth of her lips clear down to his boots. The water dribbled down her chin and she laughed, taking a step back, wiping her chin with the back of her hand. She had a sweet laugh, and Frank tried to remember what Ruth's laughter sounded like. He realized he'd never heard her laughter, only her derisive snorts.

"Tell me, Mr. Lewis. What sort of plans does a man like yourself make for the future? I mean what does a man do here to better himself?"

In his entire life, Frank had never been called mister, and it warmed him more than the pressure of her lips against his hand.

"Well now, I'm hoping to be foreman of this spread someday."

"Foreman?"

"Yes, ma'am. See, Lee Hastings carries that title now, but he's always talking about heading out to Wyoming or Montana or somewhere. When he goes I hope to have enough experience that Jake'll trust me with the position. I been with him longer than anyone else has." He decided not to mention that the time he was counting began when Jake first told him about the land and not when they'd all started heading for it.

"Is it how long a man's been here then that'll get him the job?"

"No, ma'am. It's experience and knowledge. I'm short on knowledge, but Jake's kinda taken me under his wing and is teaching me everything he knows. He's the best man I've ever known."

Frank's impassioned speech silenced him. He wasn't used to revealing his feelings for people he cared about.

"Do you miss Ireland?" he asked before realizing that it was a stupid question. If she did, the thought might sadden her, and he wasn't ready to give up her smiles.

"Only a bit," she said. "Mostly, I miss the little people."

"The little people?"

"You know . . . the elves and leprechauns and fairies. The wee folk who are whispered about at bedtime."

Frank pushed out his chest. "We don't have no wee folk here. Everything here is as big as it can get. Now, you take a jackrabbit for instance. Why they're so big, you can saddle 'em and ride 'em."

Arlene broke out into a big smile. "I think you're funning with me, Mr. Lewis."

"Call me Frank."

"Frank," she said shyly.

"And no, ma'am. I'm not funning you. Why just last

week I saddled one up and rode him down to Mexico.''

She laughed. "You are funning me!"

"No, ma'am." He leaned down conspiratorially. "I'm spinning a tall tale."

"Is that a polite word for a lie?"

"No, ma'am!" He placed his hand over his heart. "I swear next time I go riding a jackrabbit, I'll bring you along."

Her laughter followed along beside him as he walked her back to the wagon, and it stayed with him throughout the night.


Purring like a cat, Rebecca stretched her lean frame.

"I've thought of this all day," Jake said in a husky voice as he ran his tongue down the center of her back. "I had forgotten how beautiful you look riding a horse. Your hips have spread a little since you became a mother. Those pants fit real snug now, outlining your little bottom real nice."

He nipped at her bottom and she squirmed. Straddling her hips, he brought his lips back up to her neck, giving her little love bites before running his hands and his mouth down her slender back. He spread warm kisses along her thighs, her knees, down her calves and back up again. She sighed contentedly. "Nice."

He rolled her over, trailing hot kisses along her throat. His tongue outlined the tiny shell of her ear and dipped inside, sending shudders through her body. He cupped a breast in his palm, kneading gently as he drew the tip into his mouth, feeling it harden as it came into contact with his swirling tongue. His thumb slipped under his mouth, to aid his tongue in caressing the tiny sensitive pearl. She gasped with pleasure, and her body began moving as though he were buried deep within her.

"Have you been practicing?" she asked throatily.

"No," he said as his mouth returned to cover hers. "Just been thinking about it all day, like I said."

Drawing his tongue into her mouth, she suckled gently before releasing it to allow it to roam the confines of her mouth. He eased his hand down her midriff, lightly sending it back and forth across her stomach, as his mouth sought to pay homage to her other breast. Shivers of anticipation raced through her as she raked her hands through his hair, down his neck, onto his shoulders. Then reaching down, she wrapped her warm fingers around him, his heat increasing her own. He emitted a low moan as she tenderly stroked him. And then his hand moved down, covering the tight curls nestled between her legs, his hand sliding back and forth until his fingers parted the frail barrier and touched her silky wetness. Tightening her hold on him, she thought she might die if he touched her anymore. But she didn't and he did. Slowly he explored the velvet smoothness. She gasped, lifting her hips up, her hand stilling as he continued his exploration in earnest.

Rebecca felt the heat waves rolling through her, each one more intense than the next, clouding all sane thoughts until the only thing she could think of was Jake and having him nestled deep within her. Her body was inflamed and she wanted him, needed him to extinguish the fire. She tightened her hold on him. "Now, Jake."

He thrust himself hard and deep within her, and she cried out as her body came up off the bed, her arms tightening around him. Then she lay below him, trembling violently. And it scared the hell out of Jake.

He stilled, enfolding her in his arms. "Reb? Reb, honey?"

Her trembling slowly eased, and in the moonbeams dancing across her features, he could see the blush creeping up her cheeks. She captured his face in her hands, her eyes searching his. "It was glorious, Jake," she whispered.

A low guttural moan escaped his throat as his mouth sought hers and his hips began undulating. Rebecca tore her mouth off his and began searing his neck with her kisses. She ran her tongue down his chest, until it touched and snared his nipple, then pressed her mouth against the hardened tip, alternately suckling and stroking until he was shuddering above her.

Burying his head against her neck, he sought to control his quaking body as her hands trailed up and down his damp back.

"Jake?"

"Mmm?"

"I like it when you spend the day thinking."

He brought his head up, twinkling eyes and a mischievous grin gracing his countenance.

"Reb, honey, that was just what I thought about this morning. Wait until I show you what I thought about this afternoon."

# Chapter Fourteen

JAKE STRETCHED OUT at an angle on the wooden bench suspended from the overhang of the porch. Rebecca was curled up at his side. He lazily pushed his foot against the porch, enticing the bench to sway back and forth at a leisurely pace. Beside them, nestled in his crib, Jacob welcomed nighttime by curling up into a ball and snoring softly. And over the horizon, the sun bid its final farewell to day.

Jake hadn't closeted himself off in secret when he had made the bench. Many an evening Rebecca and Jacob had sat on the porch watching Jake work. He wouldn't tell them what his project was, making them guess. Even after she had figured it out, Rebecca didn't know what he was going to do with it. Now, she sighed contentedly as his hand idly stroked her arm.

"This is nice, isn't it, Reb?" he asked, somewhat awed that life could have turned out to be so good. He'd never known such serenity existed.

"Yes, it is," she said as her fingers nimbly worked to undo a button on his shirt and her hand slipped inside to rest against his heart.

In the distance, they watched the silhouette of Frank and Arlene as they walked hand in hand towards a private destination. Men headed out to watch the herd; men headed in to bed down for the night. A warm breeze blew across the land. Kevin O'Hennessy put the last of his father's tools away, gave a final longing glance towards the horses scam-

187

pering in the corral, and made his decision. With his hands stuffed in his pockets, he walked over to the porch.

"Evening, Mr. and Mrs. Burnett," he said as he removed his hat.

"Kevin," Rebecca said, acknowledging the lad.

Kevin's eyes focused on Jake. "Mr. Burnett, sir, I was wondering . . . I mean . . . I been thinking and seeing as how Frank's as old as me and he works for you and all . . . well . . . I was wondering if maybe you could hire me and teach me to be a cowboy."

Jake studied the young man before him. Already his arms were thick, his legs sturdy from laying hammer to anvil with a poetic rhythm that rivaled many of the ballads sung around roaring campfires. "Being a cowhand is hard work," he said.

"I'm not afraid of hard work, sir."

"Thought you were going to learn your father's trade?"

"Yes, sir. Me da wanted me to, and if we'd stayed in Ireland I would have been content to do so. But here"— he threw his arm out in a circle—"there's so much more."

"Have you talked to your father about working for me?"

"Yes, sir. He understands me wanting something different."

"Gotta get up before the sun."

"Yes, sir."

"Gotta work all day."

"Yes, sir."

"Gotta go over to that corral and decide which horse you want to ride when the sun comes up in the morning."

Kevin's eyes widened. "Does that mean you'll hire me?"

"Reckon it does."

Kevin hit his hat on his leg. "Thank you, sir! Thank you. You won't regret it. I give you my word," he said as he extended a hand to Jake.

Rebecca unwrapped herself from Jake's side so he could shake the lad's hand and then wrapped herself back when Kevin walked off. His position in front of the porch was soon replaced by Patrick O'Hennessy, who having just turned fifteen, thought himself capable at least of keeping up with his older brother.

He removed his hat, crunching it in his hands as he studied the ground intently, then lifted his eyes to Jake's without lifting his head. He cleared his throat three times.

"Mr. Burnett, sir."

Jake smiled. "Go pick out a horse."

The boy's head jerked up. "Thank you! You won't regret it, you won't!" And he ran off to herald the news to anyone who cared to listen.

Rebecca began laughing. "I'm not sure whether we'll find Brian over here next asking you to take him on or demanding you find him a replacement for all the strong arms you're depriving him of."

"Boys have a right to decide what they want to do with their lives. They might not like working the range. It's not an easy life, for every moment of excitement, there's at least a hundred of boredom." He glanced down at his wife. "Your father didn't give you much choice. Think there's something else you'd rather be doing?"

Slipping her hand out of his shirt, she nimbly undid the remainder of his buttons before running a hand up his chest and catching the nape of his neck. She tilted her head up, bringing his mouth down to hers.

"Mmm-huh. There's something else I'd rather be doing. But we need to go inside to do it."

Chuckling warmly, Jake stopped the bench's swinging motions. No. Life had never been so good.

Sean O'Hennessy sat on the edge of the porch, digging his bony elbows into his knees, drawing random circles in the dry dirt with a skinny stick he had found near the tree. His lower lip jutted out, his light auburn brows drawn tightly together. He had been the cowboy in the family, riding out in the saddle with Mr. Jake every morning when the sun came up. Now two of his older brothers were going to be the real cowboys. They were each going to ride their own horse. They wouldn't have someone holding on to them. He wasn't really a cowboy, and that admission, even if made only to himself, pained him.

Jake came over, holding two pair of reins in his hands, and hunkered down beside the boy. "You gonna ride with me today?"

Sean's lower lip jutted out further, and he moved his head slowly from side to side, keeping his eyes fixed on the ground.

"Well, I'm real sorry to hear that. I was hoping maybe you could start riding Shorty for me."

The boy's head popped up. "Who's Shorty?"

Jake threw a thumb over his shoulder. "This little mare over here. All my men are too big to ride her, and I've been looking for someone who's the right size to take care of her."

Sean jumped up. "I could do it!"

Jake rubbed his chin in thought. "You'd have to ride her every day, make sure she gets fed, brush her down."

"I could do it! I'm not too big for her!"

Separating the reins, Jake handed a pair to Sean. "She's yours then, cowboy."

He helped the boy get up into the saddle, then mounted his own horse, a rope tethered to Sean's horse in his hand.

"I'll hold on to your horse until you learn to use the reins to guide her," he explained to the boy. They headed out, and behind them, Kevin and Patrick followed, grinning at each other.

Trade Market was held the second Monday of each month come hell or high water. People from around the county and the surrounding area brought their wares to trade or sell.

Although they had left the ranch before the sun was up, leaving Jacob in Maura's care, Jake and Rebecca arrived in the midst of bustling activity. Frank and Arlene, eyes wide, mouths agape, rode in the back of the wagon. The two couples separated, agreeing to meet back at the wagon when the sun set. Rebecca slipped her arm through Jake's and let him lead the way.

They stopped in front of a wagon where a man in a top hat paced back and forth on a board he had set up on blocks, a bottle in his hand. He proclaimed in a bellowing voice that his elixir was guaranteed to cure all ills. They watched him for a while, his performance worthy of any stage show Rebecca had ever seen, although she didn't believe a word of what he said. As they wandered on Jake bought Rebecca a lemonade from a young girl wearing two braids caught up in a circle on either side of her head. Rebecca steered Jake away from the women kicking their legs up in the back of a wagon while a man with a toothless grin strummed on his banjo.

Rebecca caught the glint in Jake's eye when they came to the livestock. Jake stopped to study a bull, running his hands over the animal's flanks.

The man standing beside the animal introduced himself. "Is this the result of a longhorn and shorthorn?" Jake asked.

"Yep. Wanna buy him?" Homer Price asked.

Jake shook his head. "No, just wondering. You having a lot of luck breeding them?"

"I'm pleased with what I got this year, considering it was such a dry season. Lost several calves, though. You a rancher?"

"Yeah. But I'm breeding Herefords." Jake talked on with the man, and Rebecca stood back, smiling.

"Your husband changing his mind on what kind of cattle he wants to raise?"

Rebecca turned around, smiling up at William Long. "I doubt that. Jake just likes to check out the competition. How are you, William?"

"Be doing better if I could get my hands on some Herefords. Don't suppose your husband brought any to sell?"

"No, but maybe if you asked him real sweet."

"Hey, William! Want to buy some of my stock?" Homer yelled out.

Jake looked up to see William Long standing close to Rebecca and he smiled, walking over to join them, his hand coming to rest on the small of Rebecca's back.

"Not from you, Homer," William called back. "But I'd like to buy some from you, Jake."

Jake gauged his competition. "I don't need the money. I could use the longhorns you have on your spread."

"Sounds fair. We'll swap, head for head."

Jake laughed. "Either you think I'm a fool or you don't know the value of your animals. Ten longhorns for one Hereford."

William laughed. "Somehow, it seems unfair that you should not only have a beautiful wife, but should get so many of my cattle as well. But it's a deal. I'll bring them out later in the week. Could you spare twenty?"

Jake's eyes widened. "Can you spare two hundred?"

William chuckled. "Actually, the truth is with this dry season we're having, I'll be glad to get rid of them."

The men shook hands, and William tipped his hat to Rebecca as he left. She moved in closer to Jake as they began walking along looking at the other livestock that was being offered. It filled her with a great deal of satisfaction to know that Jake's confidence in himself had grown to the point that he no longer felt threatened when she talked with a man like William Long.

Frank roughly pulled Arlene to his side, his hand clamping down on her waist.

"Well, hello there, Ruth," Frank said to the young woman looking over the bonnets. "This here's Arlene O'Hennessy. Her father is a blacksmith at our ranch. She and her family live there with us. Arlene, sweetheart, darling, this here's Ruth Reading. Her family owns a ranch near ours."

Arlene shot Frank a warning glance. Then she smiled at Ruth. "It's nice to meet you."

Ignoring Frank, Ruth smiled at Arlene. "You talk funny. Where are you from?"

"My dear Arlene is from Ireland," Frank said. "Isn't that right, sugar?" He placed a kiss on her cheek, drawing her more firmly up against his side.

"We'll have to get together sometime," Ruth said. "I'd love to hear about your country, but I have to go now."

As soon as Ruth was out of hearing range, Arlene

wrenched herself free of Frank's grasp.

"And what in God's name was that about, Frank Lewis?"

"Nothing," Frank said as he searched the crowds to see if Ruth was looking back.

"You wouldn't be trying to make the lass jealous now, would you?"

Frank's eyes came back to hers. Hers were a brown, which surprised him. He remembered them as being green.

"I wanted to give her a taste of her own medicine. She was always ignoring me before. I wanted her to see how stupid she was."

"What a fool I've been. I'll not be used, Frank. If you want to make her jealous, you find someone else with which to do it."

"That's just it, Arlene. There ain't nobody else."

Tears sprang to Arlene's eyes. She choked back a sob, then turned and darted off.

"Wait, Arlene! I didn't mean that the way it sounded!" He looked back in the direction Ruth had gone. He was free to go after her, to see if she'd have him now that she knew someone else was interested in him. But he'd just discovered that he couldn't have cared less about Ruth. At first, his interest in Arlene was just to make Ruth jealous. When that reason had changed, he wasn't sure. He got on tiptoe to look over the top of the crowd, but he couldn't see Arlene. Damn it! He had come to care for Arlene a lot. She wasn't as pretty as Ruth, but she made him feel like a man. He shoved his way through the crowd, cursing himself and his stupidity.

Frank finally found Arlene already in the wagon when it was time to meet up with Jake and Rebecca. Night settled down over the land as the wagon rolled along, headed back towards the Rocking R. Frank and Arlene sat in opposite corners, glaring at each other.

"Did you enjoy yourself today, Arlene?" Rebecca asked, wondering what had happened between the couple.

"Aye, 'twas a fine day, it was. I met one of your neighbors. A Miss Ruth Reading. Frank was kind enough to introduce us.''

Rebecca and Jake exchanged glances, both thinking the same thing.

''You and Ruth are about the same age, I think,'' Rebecca said.

''Aye. We're very close in age, but Ruth, she's the lucky one, she is. Frank here intends to make her his wife.''

''I never said that!'' Frank bellowed.

''Then why are you trying to make her jealous?''

''I wasn't trying to make her jealous!''

''No? Darling, sweets, sugar dumpling? Then what were you trying to do, my dearest?''

Frank jerked his hat off and hit the side of the wagon with it. ''Goddamn!''

''I've told you, Frank, I'll not have you taking the Lord's name in vain around me.''

''Well now, I ain't around you, am I? You're on one side of the wagon and I'm on the other, so I'll say anything I goddamn want to!'' He shoved his hat back on his head, moving further into his corner of the wagon.

''Every time I asked her to dance, she'd laugh and say 'no.' Every time I saw her in town, I'd say 'Morning, Ruth. How you doing?' and she'd either just stick her nose up in the air or tell me it was none of my business. And today, I had this beautiful woman walking around with me, and I just wanted her to know I was good enough.''

''But you used me, Frank. You used me and it hurt.''

Frank drew himself up. ''I didn't mean to hurt you. And I didn't mean what I said about your being the only one. Oh, hell, all right, that first night I asked you to take a walk with me because I wanted to get you to like me so that when we ran into Ruth someday, I could make her jealous.'' Tentatively, he reached across to touch her hand. ''But after that walk, I swear I never thought about Ruth again. I like you so much, all I can ever think about is you. I acted like a fool today. Hell, I was a fool today. I just wanted Ruth to see that someone as pretty as you could hold her head up high when she walked with me. Ruth always made me feel like I was something a cow left behind. I wanted her to see that I wasn't.''

Arlene released a ragged sigh. "I trusted you with my heart, man. And you damn near broke it today.''

Frank squeezed her hand as he whispered, "I want to hold you, Arlene. Will you let me?''

Slowly, she moved her head up and down, and Frank moved over, drawing her into his arms. "I'm sorry,'' he said. "I'm so sorry. She's nothing and you're everything.'' He tilted her chin up. "Will you let me kiss you?''

She nodded and he lowered his lips to hers, gently kissing her, trying to take away the hurt.

Rebecca rubbed her hand down Jake's thigh. "Maybe you should let Frank drive the horses,'' she whispered.

"Because you don't trust Frank, or because you want to be stretched out in the back of the wagon?''

"Both.''

"Come sit on my lap then. They won't notice.''

She moved to his lap, sitting at a right angle. She removed his hat, running her fingers up through his hair.

"You sure you won't tell me why you bought those four little wheels?'' she teased. Jake just smiled mysteriously. Not really wanting to spoil his latest surprise, Rebecca changed the subject.

"I was proud of you today, handling William Long the way you did.'' Her fingers stilled. "What did you think of him the first time you met him?'' she asked quietly.

"That he was the kind of man you should have married.''

"And now you don't think that anymore?''

"Now, it doesn't matter. You're married to me.''

"I was the night you met him.''

Jake's eyes met and held hers in the moonlight. "No, you weren't. Not really.'' His arm tightened around her. "But you are now.''

Rebecca brought her lips to his, and they welcomed her. The wagon traveled along in the moonlight, the horses nickering as Jake's hold on the reins loosened. Fortunately, they knew the way home.

* * *

Five-month-old Jacob leaned back against the feather pillows in the wooden wagon his father had lovingly built, the miniature wheels turning around and around as Sean cautiously pulled him along in front of the house. Suddenly, Sean stopped, spun around, and, with eyes wide, splayed fingers framing his face, he shouted "Boo!" And for the hundredth time Jacob went into peals of laughter.

Rebecca knew her son's ribs were aching, because his laughter was infectious and her own ribs were close to cracking. She leaned into Jake, wiping the tears from her eyes, feeling the rumbling of his body as he sought to control his laughter, a difficult task as Sean again booed and Jacob's laughter increased in intensity.

Jake moved his wife to the bench swing before both their legs gave out on them. He put his arm around her as their laughter subsided.

"He's certainly enjoying the wagon," Rebecca said.

"Oh, I think he's enjoying Sean more."

"I don't know what I'd do if anything happened to Jacob."

Jake jerked his head down, his brows furrowed, his eyes searching Rebecca's. "What brought that on?"

She shrugged. "I don't know. A mother's worries I guess."

He rubbed her shoulder. "Nothing's going to happen to him."

She offered him a small smile. "I know it's silly, but sometimes I think maybe we'll be spared any sorrows because you had more than your share when you were growing up. That maybe all you went through will protect us."

Jake pulled her in closer against him. "I don't think there's anyone sitting up above who keeps a tally on how much sorrow each person gets. Sometimes I think sorrow and joy are kept in containers like Abrams's candy, and someone just dips a hand in and throws it out. It all just depends where you happen to be standing at the time."

"Still, it would be nice if some good were to come out of all the suffering you went through as a child."

"But something good did come out of it."

She looked at him questioningly.

"If Truscott hadn't come for me, I would probably be playing a piano in a whorehouse right about now. I wouldn't have my land, my cattle, a son." He trailed his fingers along her cheek, around her jaw. "Or you," he said quietly as his lips met hers, Jacob's laughter echoing in the distance.

The star-filled sky stretched as far as a man could see, the occasional bray of a steer rending the still night air, the fire crackling as it spread its warmth. Jake took a deep breath as he lay back, bracing himself up on an elbow, and looked out at all that surrounded him. He had always enjoyed tending cattle at night, peace filtering through him. It had been a while since he had sat by a roaring campfire, but he had offered to do it tonight because one of the men was getting married and the others had wanted to take him into town for one last fling. Frank had offered to stay behind as well.

It was the first night since he'd married Reb that he wasn't sleeping with her. He knew it was silly, but he missed her, thoughts of her lying in that bed all alone filling his head. He'd do some powerful thinking before the night was over, and he'd share it all with her in the morning when he got back.

Frank hunkered down before the fire, studying it intently before throwing Jake a look over his shoulder.

"Can I talk to you man-to-man?" Frank asked.

Jake smiled. Frank had stopped shaving the peach fuzz under his nose, but still his mustache wasn't visible.

"Sure."

Frank moved back. "It's about women."

"I'm hardly the expert on women," Jake said.

"You must know something. You married Reb."

Jake couldn't argue with that flawed logic. "What do you want to know?"

Frank's face grew serious. "Well, see, I like Arlene a lot. Hell, I guess I love her. And I think she loves me. And we go for long walks and well, she's real partial to kisses, but . . . '' He hesitated, then continued. ''Well, see . . . she won't let me give her more than a kiss. If I try to . . . well, go further, she says I won't respect her. Hell, I want to make love to her. And I will respect her afterwards. I told her that, but she said no anyway. And I was just wondering, since Reb was pregnant when you married her, how the hell did you convince her . . . you know, to say yes?''

Jake sat up and put an elbow on his knee, rubbing the bridge of his nose. It occurred to him he could just tell Frank it was none of his business. He sighed. ''Do you swear that what I tell you won't go beyond this campfire?''

Frank eagerly scooted up. ''Yes, sir. I swear it.'' He made an ''X'' across his heart. ''I swear to God.''

Jake's eyes held Frank's, making sure the man understood the seriousness of what he was about to say.

''Jacob was two months old the first time I made love to Reb.''

Frank's eyes widened and his mouth dropped open in disbelief.

''You mean . . . you mean she's like the Virgin Mary?''

Jake couldn't stop the grin from forming as he shook his head. ''No. She loved someone else, and he loved her, I reckon. But he left not knowing she was pregnant. So I married her.''

Frank was astounded. Not so much because Rebecca was pregnant when Jake married her, but because Jake hadn't made love to her as soon as it was legal to do so. ''But if you were married, why'd you wait? You could have had her on your wedding night.''

''Because I didn't want to 'have her.' I wanted to make love to her, and I wanted to wait until it was what she wanted too.''

Frank digested the information. ''Hell, that sure as hell don't help me any.'' He eyed Jake warily. '' 'Less you're thinking I ought to wait until it's what Arlene wants?''

''You have to decide how much you love her, Frank. Do you just want her once or for the rest of your life? She's the one that's got to respect herself afterwards.''

Frank nodded. He had expected the answer to be simple.

Goddamn, love wasn't simple at all.

At the sound of an approaching rider, they both rose to their feet, hands resting easily on their guns. In the firelight, Jake saw his beautiful wife dismount.

"What's wrong?" he asked.

"I don't like sleeping alone," she said as she slipped her arms around his waist.

"Who's watching Jacob?"

"Maura and Brian. I gave them our bed for the night. Do you have any idea how long it's been since they've slept in a bed together? She was blushing like a bride when I left."

Jake's hands traveled up and down her back.

"Frank, there are some cattle straying off at the far end. You need to get them back to the main herd."

"Yes, sir," the youth said as he headed for his horse, knowing full well Jake couldn't see any cattle straying off.

"Take Reb's horse. It's already saddled."

"Yes, sir." Frank smiled as he mounted. "Probably take me a while to get them rounded up."

Jake's eyes met Frank's. "On the other hand, why don't you head on in. Reb can help me watch the cattle tonight."

Turning to his wife, he said, "Come join me by the fire. I've been doing some thinking."

As Frank rode away, he heard Rebecca's laughter filling the night sky. Maybe Jake was right. It certainly would be nice to know the woman wanted him as much as he wanted her.

Not long after Frank left, Rebecca was snuggled up against her husband's firm body, feeling his hands caressing her bare back. The fire crackled, throwing out its warmth. The black heavens blanketed the night.

She tilted her head back, and Jake began moving stray strands of hair from her face.

"Have I ever told you how beautiful you are?" he asked.

She reached up, outlining his brow with her thumb. "You tell me all the time with your eyes. You have such expressive eyes."

He drew his arms more tightly around her. "I've been thinking—"

She began to laugh. "Why am I not surprised?" She had enjoyed watching the herd with him in Kentucky, but it didn't even begin to compare with the pleasures of watching the herd with him in Texas.

"Oh, no, not that kind of thinking. I've been thinking about your house. Now that I understand how assets and collateral work, I'm thinking we won't have to wait as long to build your house. And I was just wondering what kind of house you wanted."

She began drawing figure eights on his chest with her fingertip. "Can it be my dream house?"

Jake smiled down on her. "Certainly."

Her foot began a slow caress of his calf. "I'd like to have a turret on each side and at least two bay windows in the front. I'd like a porch that goes all the way around the house. All the bedrooms would be on the second floor, and our room would have French doors that lead out onto a balcony."

"You don't want something fancy?" His eyes teased her as much as his words. The house she wanted was exactly what he wanted to give her, finer than anything he'd ever lived in, grander than the house she had shared with her father.

Her eyes grew warm. "I'm content with what I have, Jake. There's really no need to build a house before you take your cattle to market."

"What you have is so much less than what you had, Reb."

"No, it's not," she said softly. "In many ways it's so much more." She gave her husband a lingering kiss.

"I think those cattle are going to be watching themselves tonight," Jake said when her mouth left his and began traveling along his neck.

"Yes, they are," she admitted.

She straddled his lap as he began pressing kisses between her breasts, his tongue tasting her sweet flesh. His mouth moved slowly along the side of a breast, then his tongue circled the tip before his mouth covered it, suckling gently. She dropped her head back as her fingers gripped Jake's shoulders. He brought a hand up to the back of her head, tilting her head down towards him as his lips sought hers, his tongue delving deeply into the sweet recesses of her mouth, hot and moist. Her throaty sounds sent shivers through his body.

Gently he rolled her over onto her back, his body nestled between her legs, his lips slowly pressing hot, moist kisses along her flesh as his body traveled down the length of hers. His tongue tasted the flesh of her breasts, of her stomach, before running down her thighs.

She felt his warm breath fan her thighs, so close to the apex where they melted into her body. She felt the slight rustle between her legs, the way she imagined a tree would feel in a gentle breeze.

"I love you," he said.

Then she felt his tongue caress the most intimate of places, the gasp that escaped her lips brought on by sheer pleasure. His velvet tongue slowly stroked her silken folds, sending sensations reeling through her. She gave herself up to the sweet bliss, so intense and yet so soft, calling out his name in her ecstasy.

He moved up, kissing her fully on the mouth. She tasted herself, wanting to feel shocked, but instead finding herself wanting to give as much to him.

He lifted himself above her, and when he would have entered her, she stayed his actions with both hands pressed to his hips. She pushed him onto his back, kissing him tenderly before beginning her descent, placing kisses along his chest, down his stomach, along his thighs as he had her. He threaded his fingers into her hair, bringing her head up, his eyes locking into hers.

"You don't have—"

"I want to," she whispered hoarsely as she lowered her lips. She felt the slight shudder run through him, and his fingers tightened their grasp on her hair, his reaction thrilling her.

Jake gave himself up to the swirling sensations until he

thought he'd be able to stand it no longer. Reaching down, he lifted her, settling her back down to sheathe him, his hands helping to guide her movements. As she arched back, his mouth began to seek out new trails along her flesh.

Rebecca felt the sensations mounting, one on top of another. From the top of her head to the tip of her toes, no part of her body was spared the tingling that deepened with each thrust. She felt suddenly desperate to consume this man, and she grasped his face in her hands and brought her mouth down hard on his, his scent and her scent mingling, pressing her body as close as she could, wanting all of him, wanting to touch him the way he touched her, not just her body but her soul. His caresses touched more than just her flesh. His passion seeped down to her innermost core, always leaving her more than she was before. She cried out, her body arching away from him as his strong hands braced her back, pulling her back to him as he buried his face between her breasts and his final thrusts brought his release.

Seeking to steady his own breathing, he held her close, compliant on top of him. Their arms tightened around each other, and though she had never voiced the words, Jake was certain she loved him. How could she give so much to him if she didn't?

# Chapter Fifteen

FRANK RODE HIS horse like a posse was on his tail, and it was all Jake could do not to laugh. The young man pulled up beside him, his smile threatening to reach his ears.

"Goddamn, Jake. You'll never guess who's up at the house."

Jake shook his head, grinning. "No, I probably won't."

"Brett Meier."

The grin as well as the blood left Jake's face, and he prodded his horse into a gallop. Frank watched him ride off, his response to the news not at all what the younger man had been expecting. He found himself wondering what it was about Brett Meier that had scared the hell out of Jake.

"Hello, Rebecca."

Rebecca felt the breath leave her body as she slowly turned from the stove to face the open door. The sight of the man standing in the doorway, his blue eyes piercing her, assaulted all her senses. Her knees weakened, and her heart began pounding in her ears. His handsome features had faded in her memory. His black hair was almost blue, his blue eyes a deeper, richer hue than her own. He had grown a thick dark mustache that rested over his full lips, the ends even, raised up the same amount on each side over his sensuous smile.

"Hello, Brett," she whispered, surprised she could speak at all.

In four long, sure strides he was standing before her.

"I had one hell of a time tracking you down. Your father wouldn't tell me shit. Giles told me you were pregnant, had married Jake, and had come to Texas. You have any idea how big this damn state is?"

The sound of wood hitting wood near the hearth made him turn. Openly, he watched the baby pounding his rattle on the hard floor. Based on what Giles had told him, after a little monetary incentive, he had little doubt that the child she had been carrying when she had left the Lazy A was his. It had taken all his charms to seduce her. Charms Jake Burnett did not have. "Is this my son?"

If Rebecca had made love to a hundred men that night, she still would have known which man had fathered her son. The boy was a miniature replica of his father.

"Yes. He's six months old now," she said, as though Brett would be unable to calculate his age.

He knelt down beside the boy, who placed his tiny hand around the offered finger, taking it into his mouth and gnawing on it with zeal.

"What did you name him?"

She hesitated, uncertain what his feelings would be about the name she had chosen. "Jacob."

He nodded, releasing the child's hold on him and standing up to face her.

"I have some land in Montana, two thousand head of cattle, a house that's more than one room. I want you and my son to live there with me."

She took a step back, shaking her head. "It's too late, Brett. I'm married."

"And who the hell in Montana will know that . . . or care for that matter. People will know only what we tell them. You'll be my wife in every other way, and the boy is already my son."

"Brett, I can't. Jake has been so good to us."

His eyes searched hers, blue into blue, deep, discerning.

"I know it was cruel of me to come here. My heart and my conscience fought every step of the way." He gave her a seductive smile. "My heart won. Rebecca, I couldn't walk away, not without seeing you. If I'd left you with no intention of returning, it would have been different. But I didn't. Your father thought I wanted his land, not you, said he'd disown you if I married you. So I had to find us a better start than the one I could have offered you in Kentucky. I always planned to return to your waiting arms.''

''You didn't say you'd come back,'' she said in a pained whisper.

''I thought you knew, woman.'' His fingers lightly caressed her cheek. ''Didn't I tell you what was in my heart? Didn't I show you?''

Without warning, his lips, hot and searing, were on hers, his tongue penetrating, his mouth devouring. She released a whimper as his arms drew her against his hardened frame. Along with his handsome features, the feel of him, the taste of him had faded in her memory. Everything came rushing back . . . everything . . . every memory . . . every kiss, every embrace, the one night they had shared, the only night they would ever share. Her mind told her it was too late for them, but her heart held on with a fierce determination. She heard the clearing of a throat and jumped back, her breathing labored, her cheeks crimson. She started to move around him to face Jake, but Brett caught her shoulders, retaining her, his eyes holding hers with force.

''I love you, Rebecca. I want you to come with me to Montana. I know you and Jake have some things to work out. I'm staying at the hotel in town. I'll be there until noon on Monday. If you haven't come to me by then, I'll know your answer.'' His gaze intensified. ''I won't come for you again.''

He released her, turning to face Jake, knowing Rebecca had no decision to make. Brett had everything to offer her. Jake had nothing. He extended his hand. Jake hesitated, then wiped his sweaty palm on his thigh before shaking Brett's hand.

''I appreciate your taking such good care of Rebecca and my son. And for whatever pain we cause you, I'm sorry.''

The velvet brown eyes flew to Rebecca, but she avoided his gaze. Jake thought maybe someone had leveled a shotgun at his chest and fired at point-blank range into his heart. Brett walked out of the small house.

Bending down, Rebecca picked up her son, holding him close to her heart as she turned back to the stove.

"I wasn't expecting you back so soon, Jake. Supper's not ready. If you want . . . I can fix you something quick right now." A tear dropped onto the skillet and sizzled, followed by another. She twirled around. "I wasn't expecting Brett either. I swear, I didn't know he'd come here."

Jake strode across the room, each step he took echoing throughout the house. Why was it that everything about Jake was so noticeable? Brett had glided across the room, and she hadn't heard a step he took. Placing a callused thumb on her cheek, Jake wiped the tears from one side and then the other.

"I didn't come for supper. Frank told me Brett was here. I just . . . I just wanted to make sure you were all right."

Her eyes were glistening with unshed tears as she nodded her head. "I'm fine." Then she felt compelled to add, "I didn't know he was going to kiss me and when . . . "

His thumb fell to her swollen lips, so thoroughly kissed that even if he hadn't seen, he would have known. "I know. I should have made my presence known sooner." But he had wanted to hear her reason for staying, wishing now with all his heart that he hadn't. He placed a light kiss on her forehead, realizing she needed time to herself. "I need to get back to the herd. Will you be all right?"

Sniffing, she nodded. "Yeah. I'll be fine."

When he left, she took the skillet off the stove. Then she lay down on her bed, curled herself around her son and cried. Brett had come for her, but he had come too late.

Jake sat on the hill, looking out, but he didn't see the ripples the wind created across the pond nor the playful shadows the sun threw against the earth. All he could see was how perfectly Rebecca's body had melded against Brett's, how well matched they were standing there together, ebony hair, blue eyes, facial features shaped to perfection by Someone's loving hand. He had promised her he'd do everything he could to see she had no regrets. He dropped his head, his chin resting against his chest, wondering if she'd be there when he got back.

The sky had turned a midnight black, a thousand stars lighting the velvet darkness before Jake returned. Rebecca lay in bed, her eyes aching and swollen. She heard the door open, heard him setting his boots beside the door, and even without his boots, she heard him walking across the floor, hesitating, and then continuing on past the hanging quilt. She listened as he removed his clothes and then stubbed his toe on something. His "dammit" was followed by a "shh!" as he scolded himself. And she smiled. Even when there was no one to notice, he was polite.

The bed dipped under his weight, and she knew he was leaning up on an elbow watching her. She had come to know so much about him since the night she had married him.

"I waited supper," she said.

"One of the watering holes was poisoned. We had to move the cattle."

"How many did you lose?" she asked.

"We lost four."

She was hugging the far side of the bed, lying on her side with her back to him. Any other time, she would have shot up in bed, angered that someone would poison a watering hole, any watering hole. He reached out, placing a hand on her waist.

She sighed. "I'm really tired, Jake."

He withdrew his hand, rolling over to his other side, his back to her. He had only wanted to hold her. He knew she wouldn't want to make love with him after seeing Brett today. But, damn, he had needed to hold her.

The scent of fresh-baked biscuits brought Rebecca out of her fitful sleep. Her eyes stung, and her whole face felt swollen. Jake walked in bearing a plate of biscuits and gravy, laying it on the bed beside her as she sat up.

"Morning, sleepyhead," he said.

Rebecca squinted. "The sun's barely up. You make it

sound like I've been sleeping the day away." She fingered the plate. "I don't know why you have to be so good to me."

Because I love you, he thought, but he no longer dared to say the words out loud. Already he felt a constriction around his heart that he knew would only worsen in the next few days.

"I need to go into town today to pick up some supplies and take care of some business. Do you and Jacob want to come with me?" he asked.

"No, thank you." She didn't want to chance running into Brett. It had been hard enough not to leave with him yesterday. She gave Jake a small smile. "Not this time. We'll go with you the next time." She wanted to reassure him that there would be a next time, that what she was going through was only temporary, that it would last only until Monday.

Leaning over, he placed a kiss on the top of her head. "I'll be late. Don't wait supper on me."

After he left, she damned her eyes for the torrent of tears they were sending down her cheeks. She'd dry up to nothing, like the bleached bones on the arid land, if she kept crying this much.

Walking aimlessly, Rebecca pulled Jacob in his wagon around the corrals, through the barn, under the clattering windmill, back around the house and finally settled on their final destination, the weathered oak tree that provided shade for their small home. She set Jacob down on a blanket, which he rapidly scooted off, pulling himself up to his feet. Hugging the age-old tree, he walked around it, gleefully enjoying his independence. Watching her son, she wondered if any child had ever been as happy, any child as loved as he was. She could not fault Jake for the attention he gave the boy. If she were honest with herself, she couldn't fault him for anything. He'd given her everything he had promised. The fault lay within herself.

She had doubted that Brett would return. That was her mistake. And now Brett would suffer for it. It seemed an eternity since she had walked through the night with Jake and decided to accept his offer, decided that even if Brett returned it would be too late. But how was she to have known he would return or that it would hurt so much to see him?

Sean ambled over and hunkered down before her, a stance she had often seen Jake take, and she wondered if Brian minded that his sons so emulated her husband.

"Saw Mr. Jake hitch up the wagon this morning. Did he go into town?"

"He had some business to take care of," Rebecca told the boy.

Sean nodded. "Think he'll stop by the general store?"

She smiled. "He said something about picking up some supplies."

"Think he'll pick up some sweets?"

Her smile deepened. "He usually does, doesn't he?" she asked.

Sean bobbed his head, then reached into his pocket and brought out two coins. "Mr. Jake's been paying me one dollar a month to take care of Shorty. I sure do like Mr. Jake."

"I like him, too," Rebecca said. And she did. She always had.

Sean eyed her warily. "Don't you love him?"

"He's my husband, Sean. What do you think?"

The boy's eyes narrowed, and Rebecca wished she hadn't asked the question. Children, with their innocent abandon, were too apt to see the truth. Sean gave a curt nod.

"Yep. You love him. Want me to pull Jacob for a while?"

She plopped Jacob back into the wagon and watched as his smile stretched across his face further and further with each step Sean took. She settled herself back against the tree, wondering how she had managed to fool Sean. Children were not easily fooled. And if she had fooled him, who else had she managed to fool?

No matter how desperately she sought it, sleep would not come to her. Rebecca heard the creaking of the wagon, wishing she had fallen asleep before Jake got back. She didn't want to hurt him, she really didn't, but she didn't think she could stand his being nice to her.

Jake quietly closed the door behind him, remembering a time when more than a lamp sitting on a table welcomed him home. He hung his hat on a peg and set his boots down beside the door. He walked over to the table and sent the flame in the lamp to sleep with a quick breath of air. He didn't expect to find sleep for himself so easily. He walked past the quilt, and his eyes fell on his wife huddled on the far side of the bed. Her breathing wasn't deep enough for her to be asleep, but she didn't move as he approached, and he wondered how much of the past year she regretted. Cautiously, he slipped under the covers and very slowly slipped his arm around her, wanting her to think he thought she was asleep so he could hold her.

"My head hurts, Jake."

She felt his body stiffen.

"I only want to hold you, Reb." Then in a pained whisper, he added, "Please."

Those damnable tears filled Rebecca's eyes as she scooted over until her backside was pressed against his stomach.

He pressed his lips against the top of her head, inhaling the fresh scent of her hair. She must have washed it while he was away. It always smelled like roses right after she'd washed it, and it felt as fine as cornsilk.

"I was wondering," he said quietly, "if you and Jacob would go on a picnic with me tomorrow, out to that little pond."

"I have so many chores I didn't get done today. I was planning on doing them tomorrow."

"The chores'll wait. Please, Reb. It would mean a lot to me for the three of us to spend some time together tomorrow."

God, now she had him begging her. He who had given her everything was forced to beg for a simple picnic. She rolled over, putting her arms around him, pressing her cheek against his hardened chest.

"I think we could all use a picnic," she said.

Drawing his arms more tightly around her, he wished he couldn't feel where her tears had dampened her cheeks. Tomorrow was Sunday, and the following day, at noon, Brett Meier would ride out of town. And Jake was afraid the man wouldn't be leaving alone.

The bluebonnets had long since left the hillside, replaced with new flowers in a variety of colors. Picking at the tall blades of grass surrounding them, Rebecca sat on the quilt Jake had spread out on the thick blanket of clover. Her mind was far away from this site, wondering where she would be today, how different her life would be, if she had waited for Brett's return. He might have come before Jacob was born. Her son would have been legitimatized by his own father instead of Jake. She released a deep sigh. What-ifs never did much good, certainly never perked her up.

"Do you want something to eat?" Jake asked, wishing she'd bestow upon him a smile, a warm smile that said she cared about him. He needed this picnic, to have one last memory of them here on this hillside.

She lifted a shoulder. "No. I'm really not too hungry just yet."

"Would you like something to drink? I made you some of that lemonade you were partial to when we went to the Market."

"No, thank you."

Rubbing his hands on his thighs, he glanced over at Jacob, sound asleep on a tiny blanket nearby. Even the boy wasn't going to cooperate. Jake took a sip of the lemonade, his mouth puckering at the taste, wondering what else went into it besides water and the juice squeezed from lemons. Sugar maybe, or honey? He tossed the tart drink onto the grass, grateful Reb hadn't tried it.

"Would you like for me to push you in the swing?" Jake asked.

"No," Rebecca sighed. A bee buzzed by, circled around and landed on the tip of her shoe where it peeked out from beneath her skirt. She studied it, thinking of the first picnic they had shared here beneath the tree and the bee that had

come along and spoiled the afternoon. Jake had brought her
and Jacob back here many times since then. It was always
pleasant, always peaceful. Except for today. She snapped
her head around. "I am spoiling the day, aren't I, Jake?
Why ever do you put up with me? Yes, I'd like for you to
push me in the swing." She jumped up and he grabbed her
hand. "Sit back down, Reb. I got something to say, and I
should have said it sooner."

Rebecca sat down, dreading his words, afraid he was
going to ask her if she still loved Brett. Once Brett left,
everything would be all right, everything would return to
normal. She would even be able to talk about him, but not
now, not while he was so close, within easy reach.

"I went to see Doyle Thomas when I was in town yesterday."

"Doyle Thomas? What in the world do we need with a
lawyer?"

Jake's eyes held hers. *Please Lord, don't let her want
this, let her tell me I was wrong.* "I asked him to draw up
divorce papers."

"Divorce papers? Why did you do that?"

He took a deep breath. "Because when I asked you to
marry me, I told you I'd never expect more from you than
you were willing to give . . . that includes staying with me
when the man you love has come for you."

Rebecca's hands flew to her mouth, the life back in her
eyes. "Do you mean it, Jake?"

"Yes, ma'am. I do."

Her slender fingers couldn't hide the brightness of the
smile spreading across her face. Jake's heart soared to know
he could bring her such happiness before it plummeted to
its death. The muscles in his throat constricted, and he swallowed repeatedly, trying to get them to loosen up.

"He'll have the papers ready for us in the morning. I
figured we could go into town first thing and sign them.
It'll take about two months for the divorce to be finalized,
but you could go ahead and go to Montana with Brett. Mr.
Thomas will send you the divorce papers when they're final."

She grabbed his hand and placed a kiss of gratitude on the roughened skin, her smile lessening as she realized she was going to be leaving this good man. "I don't know what to say," she said quietly, her earlier exuberance dissipating. "I wasn't expecting this."

Jake didn't know what to say either, but he knew the picnic was over. "I reckon we ought to get back. I imagine you got some packing to do."

She dropped his hand and began gathering her things, her son included. Then she spun around and watched Jake as he brought the corners of the quilt together, clumsily folding up the picnic, looking so alone, so lonely. Tears gathered in her eyes, and she turned away, her eyes blinking back the tears until she could see clearly. What she saw before her brought the tears back. She walked over and touched the rope of the swing.

Jake waited patiently for Rebecca to say good-bye to the hillside, hoping she'd understand if their own good-bye was brief.

They rode back in silence, Jake sullen and quiet, Rebecca thoughtful as she anticipated packing for her trip to Montana. Montana. Montana with Brett. It was what she wanted, to be with Brett, to be his wife. It's what she would have had a year ago if he hadn't left, if circumstances hadn't forced her to settle for something else.

Jake stopped the wagon outside the house, helping Rebecca down from the wagon. For the briefest moment while he held her, he wanted desperately to pull her to him, to hold her, to tell her he loved her. Instead he simply released her and moved up to lead the horses into the barn. She headed for the house, her step light, and then she turned abruptly, her face uncertain.

"What should I take with me?"

He turned to face her, memorizing the image of her standing in the doorway to what was no longer their house, but was now only his. "Anything you want to. Everything was for you."

She nodded, turning and hurrying into the house. It was

a few minutes later that she heard the horse whinny outside the door.

Stepping out onto the porch, she saw Jake sitting astride his stallion, his hat pulled down so low that she couldn't see his eyes at all, a shadow drawn over the rest of his features.

"I gotta go check on the herd. I'll be back late."

She started to go to him, to receive her customary good-bye kiss, but stopped, realizing she'd probably receive no more from him. He tilted his head slightly, touching his finger to the brim of his hat, and rode away.

# Chapter Sixteen

STARING OUT THE bedroom window, Rebecca sat huddled in the bed, her nightgown pulled down over her drawn-up knees. She had effectively shuttered away her dreams of being with Brett, but all it had taken was seeing him in her doorway to bring back the dreams, the longing to be with him. Then Jake had offered her the opportunity to transform the dream into reality, and she'd snatched it up without even considering what it must have cost him. How could she have been so insensitive, so selfish? Why hadn't she taken a moment to appreciate the gift wrap before discarding it for the gift?

She had been in bed two hours now, waiting for Jake to return. In the distance, she saw the lone rider, shoulders hunched, his horse plodding along slowly. After everything he had done for her, he deserved better than she'd given him. She waited half an hour before sadly realizing that he wasn't going to come to her.

Rebecca slipped a shawl over her shoulders and went out to the barn. Pitching hay around as though his life depended on it, Jake didn't hear her approach. He jumped away when she touched his arm.

"Made me jump out of my skin. You should be asleep."

"I couldn't sleep. What are you doing?"

"Trying . . . trying to get this barn cleaned up. Seems like I never have time anymore to do the most basic things."

"Aren't you going to come to bed?"

He returned to throwing hay into an empty stall. "No. I got too much energy tonight."

She moved closer to him, resting a hand on his arm. "I know better ways to use up that energy."

He stilled, his eyes delving into hers. "No," he said softly.

"Why not? I'm still your wife."

He shook his head sadly. "I never wanted it that way."

"It was never given simply because I'm your wife. I cared about you. I still do."

His eyes caressed her face the way his hands ached to. "I don't know how to make sure you don't get pregnant."

She searched his face. "I could be pregnant now."

"I've thought of that. And if you are, I was wondering if you'd mind letting me know . . . I won't bother you or come for the baby unless you don't want him . . . then I would . . . I don't want him to grow up not feeling loved."

"I'd want him, Jake."

He gave a slight nod. "I wasn't sure. But will you let me know?"

She nodded. "And you'd be welcome anytime to come see him."

Jake shook his head. "It'd be best if I didn't. I'd just want to know."

She rubbed his arm. "Please come to bed. If nothing else, just hold me."

"Let me finish up here. Won't take me long."

Releasing her hold on his arm, she walked slowly out of the barn. The vibration of the pitchfork hitting the ground and the hay sifting to the earth were the only sounds from within.

Gazing out the window, she watched as some time later Jake came out of the barn. He shrugged out of his shirt, and splashed the cool water over his body and through his hair. Even now, he wouldn't come into the house smelling like he'd been outside all day. She wondered if he'd wash up when she wasn't here; if it was just his habit or if it was something he did for her. He turned back towards the house, and she slipped behind the quilt that still separated their bed from the rest of the house.

Sitting down on the porch, Jake stared up at the stars twinkling in the blackened sky. Silver clouds reflected the moon's faint light. Only the barest of breezes moved around him. Horses nickered in the corral. Everything appeared the same. And tomorrow, it would probably still appear no different.

He pulled his boots off before stepping into the house in his stockinged feet. He stopped beside Jacob's cradle, hunkering down beside the sleeping boy. Jacob was sleeping on his stomach, his knees drawn up under him so his bottom was sticking up high in the air. Looked damned uncomfortable to Jake but the boy's face was serene and peaceful and Jake wondered what he was dreaming.

"You won't even remember me," he whispered to the sleeping child, "but I'll never forget you." He lowered his face to the small head and placed a light kiss on the dark hair.

As he stood up, he saw Rebecca peering around the quilt.

"You need to get some sleep," he said. "Tomorrow's going to be a long day."

Rebecca slipped out of her gown before slipping in under the covers, watching Jake, his back to her, shed his clothes down to his underwear and then stop. When was the last time he had worn anything to bed? Lifting the covers, he got into bed in one fluid movement, lifting an arm, welcoming her into his final embrace, closing his arm around her.

"I'm sorry, Jake," she whispered. "I never meant to hurt you."

"I know. I got no regrets, Reb."

"How can you not?"

"You've given me enough happiness to last a lifetime."

The ache in her heart grew until she thought she'd die from it. She began whispering his name over and over as she placed kisses lightly on his chest, his neck. Jake cupped her face in his strong hands, stilling her caresses, holding her eyes with his own.

"Don't, Reb."

"Please, Jake. Please. One more time. Let me say good-bye proper. The way I want to."

"I can't, honey."

She placed her palms on the back of his hands, entwining their fingers before pulling his hands off her cheeks. She lowered his hands to his pillow, as she lowered her lips to his, running her tongue along their fullness, feeling the formation of the lopsided smile before he groaned and surrendered. Her fingers tightened their hold, keeping his hands pinned beside his head as her mouth opened over his, the kiss deepening.

Flipping her over, Jake broke free of her hold. He shed his remaining clothes before returning his hands and lips to hers, taking his turn at holding her hands in place as his mouth covered hers, his tongue sweeping the silky inside of her mouth, slowly, seductively. If this was to be the last time, he didn't want it rushed.

His mouth trailed down the slender column of her throat. His name was a litany released from her parted lips, softly echoed over and over as her hands strained against his, forcing him to release his hold on her.

Raking her fingers through his thick brown hair, she held him close as he ran his tongue around her erect nipple sending shivers coursing through her body before drawing the tightened tip into his mouth. His teeth closed down on it, tugging gently, and she writhed beneath him as his hands and mouth continued to assault her senses.

One last time, his hands traveled over her body. One last time, his mouth tasted her flesh. One last time, he raised himself above her and looked down on her with love. One last time, he buried himself deep within her, his hips slowly rotating, grinding his pelvis against hers. One last time, he listened to her cries of mounting pleasure and watched her back arch, bringing her slim body up against his with an effortless grace. And then he withdrew, spilling his seed into his own hand.

Rebecca's eyes flew open as she felt the emptiness engulf her.

"I'm sorry," he said, lifting his eyes to hers. "But if I haven't already given you a child, I didn't want to do it tonight."

Tears sprang to her eyes as she ran her fingers down his tortured face. "Oh, Jake. I am so sorry."

Rolling over, he brought her into his arms.

"Don't cry for me. All I've ever wanted is for you to be happy. For a while, I think you were happy here. But now you have a chance for more, for what you should have had to begin with." His voice became hoarse as he pushed the words out. "I want you to have it."

"I'm going to miss you so much, Jake."

"I'll miss you, too."

She didn't try to stifle the tears, but let them flow down her face onto his chest. He said nothing as his arms tightened their hold on her. He supposed he should find comfort in the knowledge that it wasn't easy for her to leave. But despite the tears, she was still leaving, and there was no comfort in that knowledge at all.


Whistling a catchy Irish tune, Frank sauntered into the barn, coming up short at the sight of Jake.

"Why you hitching up the wagon, Jake?"

Continuing his task, Jake said, "Taking Reb into town."

"On a Monday?"

"Yeah." He stopped and without looking at Frank said quietly, "You might want to tell her good-bye."

"She's only going into town. Why would I want to . . . ? She's not coming back, is she?"

"No . . . she's not."

"Goddamn!" He yanked his hat off his head and slapped it against his leg. "It's that Brett Meier, ain't it? How the hell can you let her go?"

Jake spun around. "What do you want me to do, Frank? She left me as soon as his foot crossed the threshold of our house. The only hope I have of holding onto anything we had is to let her go. Otherwise, bitterness and regret will kill everything. She'll always wonder what it would have been like if she had gone with him. She loves him, and now he's come for her." His voice went low. "Do you have any idea how loud silent tears are, Frank? They can fill the room, drowning, suffocating you and your love until there's nothing left. I love her too much not to let her go."

Frank stomped back and forth, then spun around in frustration. "Goddamn! I think this whole thing stinks. He ain't near as good a man as you. Why can't she see that?"

Jake went back to hitching up the horses. "Just go tell her good-bye."

Straightening things that had already been straightened, Rebecca heard someone coming in the open door. She turned and saw Frank openly studying her, and she felt uneasy under his perusal. He released a deep sigh, approaching her.

"Jake told me to come tell you good-bye." He shook his head slowly, examining the floor as though he thought it might open up and stop her from going. He knew it was unmanly, but he loved Jake, and he hated to see him hurt. And he knew he was hurting. "I don't know how you can do this to him." His eyes shot up to hers. "He loves you more than I've ever seen any man love a woman, and he's a hell of a good man. How can you not love him?"

"We can't control our hearts, Frank. I'd think you of all people would understand that."

"Well, I think I'd sure as hell try—"

"You're supposed to be telling her good-bye and wishing her well, Frank," Jake said from the doorway, irritation in his voice.

Frank looked guiltily over his shoulder and nodded before turning back to Rebecca.

"Good luck, Reb."

Her arms went around his neck as she whispered, "Take good care of him for me, Frank."

"If you gave a damn, you wouldn't be leaving." He pulled free of her hug. "Bye, Reb," he said to the floor before he stomped out.

Jake stepped in, shaking his head. "The innocence of youth. Everything appears so simple when you're young. What all are you taking?"

"Just that bag." She pointed to a carpet bag sitting by the door. "Seems everything else belongs here."

Everything but you and your son, he thought. He picked up the bag. "Well, let's go."

After tossing the bag into the wagon, he took Jacob from her and helped her up onto the seat before returning her son to her arms. Rebecca scanned the area one last time as he flicked his wrist and set the horses in motion.

They rode along in silence for some time, Rebecca watching the passing scenery, wondering how different Montana would be, wondering how different this place would look after the years had taken their toll. How different the man beside her would be. If his hair would turn silver or white. If the wrinkles that would add character to his features in later years would be brought on by joy or sadness.

"About your cattle," Jake said.

Abruptly brought out of her reverie, her head snapped around. "I thought I'd just leave them with you. I don't have a need for them and they'd be so much trouble to move."

"I was thinking the same thing." He reached into the pocket of his shirt and with two fingers pulled out a folded piece of paper. "I had a draft drawn up at the bank. This is about what I figure the cattle would be worth if we took them to market." He moved his hand towards her, extending the slip of paper.

"I don't want you to pay me for the cattle. I just want you to have them."

"I'd prefer to pay you. You don't know what you'll find in Montana, and I don't want you leaving here without anything. Take the draft, and if something happens and you need the money, you have it. And if you don't need it, you can put it in the bank for Jacob when he grows up."

She took the bank draft from him, slipping it into her reticule. "I'll put it in the bank for Jacob."

He nodded and they continued the journey in silence.

In the middle of town, they pulled up in front of the square building whose shingle boasted proudly, "Doyle

Thomas, Attorney-at-Law.'' The wooden door of the wooden building groaned in protest at being disturbed so early in the day as Jake pushed it open and Rebecca preceded him into the room.

Doyle Thomas looked up from his work and removed the spectacles from his nose. ''Well, I know it's bad for business, but I was hoping I wouldn't see you this morning, Jake.''

''Have you got those papers ready for us to sign?''

''Sure have.'' Doyle stood up and retrieved some papers from a drawer in a cabinet he kept in the corner of his one-room office. That drawer was the only aspect of his life to have any order to it.

He laid the papers on the desk, shuffling other papers aside until he located his pen and dipped it into a bottle of ink. ''Need you both to sign in four places.'' He indicated the places with his well-manicured finger.

Jake signed first and handed the pen to Rebecca. He took Jacob out of her arms. She looked from one man to the other, then leaned over, applying pressure to the pen to stop the squiggly lines from revealing her nervousness. She was ending her marriage to Jake, and all it took was her signature in four places. How simple. How complex.

''When you know how I can get in touch with you, Mrs. Burnett, you just send me a letter. As soon as everything is final, I'll let you know,'' Doyle said. Then he took the money Jake offered him and shook the man's hand.

After they walked out of the office, Jake retrieved Rebecca's bag from the wagon. As they crossed the street to the hotel, Rebecca was holding Jacob so tightly that he wailed a protest, forcing her to loosen her grip on him. In the lobby, Jake set the bag down at her feet.

''Wait here. I'll go find out which room he's in.''

She watched Jake remove his hat as he approached the front desk. Then he turned and walked back to her, his Adam's apple visibly moving up and down.

''He's in a room at the top of those stairs.'' He nodded towards the stairs behind her. ''End of the hall, last door on the right.''

Rebecca glanced over her shoulder and then her gaze came back to Jake.

"Well, so long, little fella," he said as his hand rested on Jacob's head. The child smiled at him. Jake didn't think he'd be able to leave. He forced his eyes away from the child, bringing them to rest on Rebecca.

Taking a deep breath he said, "I want to thank you for being such a fine wife. I was right proud to have you by my side, and I know Brett will be, too. If you or your family ever need anything, you just let me know. Take care of yourself, Reb."

The words had tumbled out, one after another, the last said in a thick voice. Rebecca felt his lips brush her cheek and then watched as he turned and walked quickly out of the hotel, out of her life. He hadn't given her a chance to say good-bye, and she had so much she wanted to tell him. She wanted to run after him and hold him and tell him she was sorry until the world ended.

Instead, she picked up her bag and walked to the stairs. Her burdens suddenly seemed heavier, and she didn't think she'd be able to climb up the stairs. The man she loved was up there waiting for her. The man who had fathered her child, who had made love to her on a moonless night, spoken words of love and then searched the country until he found her. She blinked back the tears and went up the stairs wondering why it was so damn hard to go to him.

She tapped lightly on the door at the far end of the hall, hearing a curse thrown out before the door was flung open. Then he was standing before her, shirtless, barefoot, his hair tousled. He pulled her into the room, enfolding her in his embrace.

"Damn, woman, but I had almost given up on you."

He released her and stalked across the room, his hand coming down hard on a lump in the center of the bed. The covers were thrown back, and a blond woman with fiery green eyes glared at him.

"What the hell was that for?" the blond woman asked in a throaty voice.

"It's time for you to leave, Luce."

Without preamble she got out of the bed. Rebecca turned her eyes away from the naked woman as she got dressed. When the woman had flounced out, Rebecca turned to Brett.

"You had a woman in here?"

He took Jacob from her and set the boy down on the floor before he put his arms around her, looking down into her blue eyes. "I was lonely, and I didn't know if you'd come. You didn't expect me to remain celibate while I waited, did you?"

Actually, she supposed she had, but she didn't say anything as his mouth came down on hers, burning. He lifted her up into his arms and carried her to the bed. "But now that you're here, you're the only woman I'll ever need."

His lips were searing her flesh, and she moaned as his mouth traveled down her neck and then drew her breast in for a taste. Her breath caught, her eyes flew open, and she stared down at him. When had he unbuttoned her dress? Her hands went to his shoulders and she pushed him away.

"I'm still married. It'll be two months before the divorce is final. And until then I intend to honor the vows I made with Jake."

Blue eyes bored into blue eyes. "What the hell does that mean?"

"It means I'll go to Montana with you, I'll live with you, I'll hold you, I'll kiss you, but I won't make love to you. I've hurt Jake enough, and until the divorce is final I don't intend to do anything that might cause him further pain."

Brett came up off the bed, running his hands through his hair. He turned, facing her. "Two months? Do you have any idea how bad I want you? I want you so bad I ache."

"And how much do you love me, Brett?"

He released a great gust of air. "Enough to take you with me and not touch you. But damn, it's going to be hard, woman. I hope you realize that."

She watched as he sullenly packed up his things, this man she had first loved, the man who had first made love to her. Tall, dark, with facial features that were the envy of men and the joy of women. He was the man she had wanted to marry a year ago. She picked her son up and began preparing him for their journey. They were a family, mother, father, son, joined by blood and flesh. Why wasn't her heart singing with joy?

Night had fallen by the time Jake pulled the wagon into the barn. Frank stepped out of the empty stall where he had been sitting, awaiting Jake's return.

"I was hoping she might change her mind," Frank said.

Jake turned to him and shook his head. "No. I knew she wouldn't."

"You shouldn't have let her go," Frank blurted out, his frustration with the situation having eaten at him all day.

Jake sighed, wishing he could make Frank understand. "I grew up being someplace I didn't want to be. I couldn't ask Reb to grow old doing the same thing." He began to move up to the lead horse.

"Here, I'll unhitch 'em for you. You've had a long day."

"Thanks," Jake said, before heading out of the barn. He hesitated by the tub of water. Old habits were hard to break, but he continued on without washing up. He didn't take his boots off outside the door either. There was no one for his noisy feet to wake up. He closed the door behind him and dropped the bar across it. Then he walked to the table, placed his hands under it and shoved it, sending it crashing to the hard wooden floor. Its vibrations echoed throughout the house, drowning out his low wail of agony.

He pressed his back up against a far wall and slid down to the floor, wrapping his arms around himself, laying his head on his uplifted knees. Never in his entire life had he felt such intense physical pain. He thought for sure his heart was dying. He released an anguished cry, then a desperate sob as all the tears he'd been holding in since Brett's arrival gushed forth.

"Damn ugly bastard! What the hell ever made you think she could love you!"

The pain of lost love increased until it consumed him. He wished he'd never made love to her, never told her he loved her, never kissed her, never brought her to Texas, never asked her to marry him. He dropped his head back and it banged against the wall, jolting him to his senses. He released a ragged breath. No, he thought, it would have been worse to have died without ever knowing. For a short time, he had held in his arms the woman he loved. Some men never even had that.

Wearily, he brought himself to his feet and walked to the bed, dropping down on top of the covers. He brought her pillow out from beneath the quilt and buried his face in it, inhaling deeply, wondering if she'd meant to leave the scent of roses behind.

# Chapter Seventeen

Montana Territory, 1884

STEPPING OUT OF the adjoining nursery into the final room on the ostentatious tour, Rebecca released a low whistle. The room alone was as large as the house she had shared with Jake.

The main house at the Pair of Aces ranch was finer than the house she had shared with her father. One room led to another; a living room, a kitchen, a dining room, a study, a nursery, and the bedroom she was now standing in were on the first floor. Wide sweeping stairs led up to the second floor and six other bedrooms, every room furnished in detail.

"Impressed?" Brett asked as he slipped his arms around her.

She tilted her head back to gaze into his blue eyes. "I can't help but be impressed. I never expected anything like this. How in the world did you afford it?"

He released a boisterous laugh, pride and humor competing for the right to grace his handsome face. "It cost me a pair of aces."

Rebecca's eyes widened. "A pair of aces? You mean you won it in a poker game?"

"Lock, stock, and barrel. The only thing I've changed is the name of the ranch. Seemed the appropriate thing to do."

"All this belonged to someone else?"

"Every bit of it."

"Some of these things must be heirlooms. You didn't let the owners take anything with them?"

"If the man didn't want to lose it, he shouldn't have put it on the table. He was bluffing. I called his bluff."

"This place has a definite woman's touch to it. You didn't even let the wife take anything?"

"Woman was stupid enough to marry him, she has to live with it, not me."

Rebecca supposed this acquisition of property was no different than Jake being given his land, but somehow it seemed different. It seemed very different.

Brett's fingers trailed up and down either side of her spine. "This will be our room when we're married. You can sleep here until then. I'll sleep in a room upstairs." He brought his lips down to hers. "Unless you'd rather I sleep here with you."

His mouth covered hers, his tongue seeking entrance, knowing it only had to seek to find, his hands pressing her body closer to his. She could feel his hardened frame against her body. He ran his hand down to press her hips against his, moving her pelvis back and forth against him.

She felt his heat through their clothes, her hips beginning to move on their own, her body straining against him. His mouth seared her neck, traveling slowly, leaving love bites in its wake.

"You make me feel like a piece of kindling, just flaring up," she said in a husky voice as her head dropped back.

"Burnett never made you feel like this, did he?"

"No," she sighed in remembrance. Brett's fire flared up and was quickly doused. It did not leave her with smoldering embers that even now, late at night when she woke up alone, could warm her with a thought. "Jake is more like a slow, roaring fire."

Roughly releasing her, Brett stomped away from the bed where he had tossed her. Rebecca looked up at him from her sprawled position. His face was hard, his blue eyes taking on a deeper hue.

"Do you have any idea how often you talk about that man?" he bellowed.

"You brought him up, not me!" Rebecca shouted as she heaved herself off the bed.

Pacing, Brett plowed his hands through his hair, not the first time he had done so since they'd left Pleasure. "I'm tired of hearing about him! Everything he did, everything he said, everything he thought!"

"I don't talk about him!"

"God, Rebecca. You talk about him all the time. On the train, every town we passed, there was something in it that reminded you of him. If you didn't mention it to me, you mentioned it to my son as though he could understand what the hell you were rambling about."

"Jake was an important part of my life for over a year." Longer than that if she considered the time before they were married, the times when they'd share confidences in low voices so as not to disturb the herd. "I can't just pretend he never existed. He's like a habit."

"Well, break it! And while you're at it, take the damn ring off."

"No! Not until my divorce papers get here."

"Why?"

"To remind me that I'm married, that I owe something to Jake until the divorce is final."

"Dammit!" He ran his fingers roughly through his hair again, his eyes boring into hers. "Jake is in Texas. I'm here. I'm the man you love; I'm the man you're going to marry."

Rebecca dropped down on the bed, willing the tears not to come. She couldn't recall ever mentioning Brett to Jake except when he'd proposed. She'd missed Brett when he had left, but his absence hadn't filled her with an emptiness that grew with each passing day. "I'm sorry. I . . . I didn't mean to bring him with us. Give me a couple of days to adjust to this big old place of yours, and I'll send him back to Texas."

Brett knelt down before her, taking her hands in his own, his voice smooth as silk. "It's going to be good here. You'll see. We'll have everything we ever dreamed of, everything we talked about."

She couldn't cite their dreams, but she didn't think now was the right time to mention that. She could recall vividly all of Jake's dreams, everything they had planned together, everything they had wanted. She gave Brett a small smile.

"Do you think the cook or the housekeeper could take care of Jacob for a few hours each day so I can ride the range?"

Brett stood up, once again furrowing deep tunnels through his hair. "I beg your pardon? You want the servants to care for my son so you can play cowhand?"

"I enjoy herding cattle."

Brett shook his head. "Look at this house." He waved his arm in a circle. "Look at this ranch. Look at me, for Christ's sake. This isn't some two-bit operation in Texas. I'm not going to have my wife parading around in a pair of men's britches looking like a cowhand. Jake may have needed you riding the range, but I don't. I can afford to hire enough men to do the work. Hell, woman! I only go out once or twice a week myself."

"Then what am I supposed to do? You have someone to clean, someone to cook."

"Be my wife. Dress like the wife of a wealthy rancher, meet with society ladies." He touched her cheek. "Please me."

Rebecca closed her eyes. "I don't want to be an ornament."

"You won't be. You have this home to manage and my son to raise. I'll handle the ranch."

She studied the face of the phantom that had haunted her since that moonless night so long ago. He was still a phantom.

Jake felt his breath leave his body as he pulled his horse up short beside the bedding hanging on the line. He jumped off his horse and took hold of a handful of quilt. Then he ran into the house, past Maura.

"Did you wash the bedding?" he asked as he moved behind the quilt and beheld the stripped bed. He dropped down on it bringing a pillow to his face, inhaling deeply.

It was all he had left of her, her scent mingled in the bedding. In bed, when he slept, she was still with him, comforting, warm.

"Thought it could use a good washing," Maura said as she came past the quilt. "Did I do something wrong?"

Dropping the pillow, Jake shot off the bed. "No, no. You're right. It needed to be washed."

Lord, he had to let go. It wasn't easing his ache any to hold on. "I reckon I don't need this hanging up anymore either." He yanked on the quilt suspended from the ceiling, bringing it to the floor. "It probably needs washing, too."

He looked around the house. What else was chaining memories to him?

"What's that little girl of yours sleeping in?" he asked.

"Bri picked up a crate at the general store last time he was in town. She's so tiny now, it'll do her for a while."

"Why don't you take that cradle?"

Maura glanced at the cradle, feeling guilty because she had thought many times of asking for it.

"Nah. I canna take it. You put a lot of love into the making of that fine cradle."

"I got no use for it. Take the rocker, too," he said as he headed out the door.

Maura ran her hand lovingly over the cradle, wondering how Rebecca could have left it. Her head jerked up when she heard Jake come back into the house, turning his hat in his hands.

"I changed my mind."

"Canna blame you for that," Maura said.

"Why don't you and Brian move in here? I got no need for a house. I'm seldom here, and I mostly watch the herd at night. All I need is a bed. Got plenty of those in the bunkhouse."

Maura rocked back on her heels. "But you're the owner, man. You canna sleep with the workers."

"Where I sleep won't change what I am. I want y'all to move in here. I should have built you a house as soon as I realized you were going to stay. Man and wife ought to have a house."

"I don't know what to say."

Jake shrugged. "Say yes." He set his hat on his head. "Thanks, Maura."

She wasn't sure exactly what the man was thanking her for. She was the one who should be thanking him.

As Jake walked out of the house, Frank pulled the wagon up in front of the barn and hopped down.

"Got the supplies!" he called out as he ambled over, his face beaming. "Got this, too." He held out an envelope.

Jake took the worn envelope from him, handling it carefully. He read it before casually slipping it into his pocket.

"It's from Reb," Frank explained.

"I can see that."

"Maybe she's writing because she wants to come back and needs some money," he said hopefully.

Jake shook his head. "I gave her money when she left."

"Ain't you even going to read it?"

"Later," Jake said as he reached for the reins of his horse.

Frank grabbed his arm, then released it, and began an intense study of the soil beneath his feet. He looked back up, meeting Jake's questioning gaze squarely. "I was wondering . . . well . . . I asked Arlene to marry me and, hot damn, she said yes. We'll be getting married at the end of the month, and I was wondering if you'd stand with me."

Jake quirked a brow, a small smile on his face. "Hot damn?"

Frank turned red, obliterating the freckles that covered his face. "Yeah. Her eyes turn brown otherwise. I figured out I need to keep those eyes green if I want her to be happy."

Jake's smile broadened. "I'd be honored to stand with you. Are you planning on staying on here?"

"Reckon so. Don't know how to do anything else, and been spending my money, so I can't buy us a spread yet."

"Why don't you take Arlene for a ride, find a spot the two of you like, and I'll build you a house."

"Goddamn! I mean, hot damn! You mean it?"

Jake's smile grew into a grin. It was going to be a while

before Frank could keep those eyes green. "Yes. And take
Maura and Brian with you. Let them pick out a spot." He
decided Maura and Brian's brood would need a bigger
place than his. "Guess if we're going to have all these
families here, I'd best start providing them with decent
places to live."

Frank took Jake's hand, shaking it so fiercely that Jake
thought Frank might have dislocated his shoulder. The
young man went to unload the supplies and Jake rode off
to visit a place he hadn't been to since Rebecca had left.

Sitting on the hillside, Jake removed the envelope from
his pocket, turning it over and over in his hand, weighing
it, trying to decide whether he really wanted to know what
was inside. He tore open the end, reached in, and pulled
out the single sheet of paper.

Dear Jake,
    Thought you might want to know we arrived safely in
Montana. So much was left unsaid. And a letter is not
the place to say it. Know only that I was more than proud
to be your wife, and I will always cherish the time we
had together.
    Reb

He ran his finger over her smudged signature before carefully folding the letter back up and slipping it into his
pocket, over his heart. She was in Montana, and he was
here, and the chasm separating them was widening with
each passing day.

Studying the man sitting before her, Rebecca was often
reminded of her father. Brett wore a woolen suit every day,
even when he rode the range. She couldn't recall ever seeing him actually get down off his horse and put in any hard
labor on the ranch in Kentucky either. He hadn't worn a
suit then, but she remembered him barking out orders even
though he had only been at the Lazy A a few months. And
she remembered men jumping to do his bidding. He simply
had a mien that spoke authority. She tried to remember
when it was that she first decided she loved him, and more

and more often she found herself wondering exactly why it was she loved him. She inhaled deeply, ignoring the fluttering in her stomach. "How would you feel if I was pregnant?"

Brett's fork halted halfway to his opened mouth as his eyes snapped from the plate to her. Slowly he lowered his fork, his mouth closing tightly, his jaws working to unclench.

"To be honest with you, Rebecca, I wouldn't like it much. Do you think Jake would come and take it after it was born?"

The invariable *it* again.

"I'm sure he would," Rebecca said. "But I'm not sure I'd want him to. Part of the baby would be me."

Brett looked down at his plate, moving the beans from one side to the other and then back again.

"I could never love it. I could never accept it as my own." His eyes came up to hers. "But I'd never abuse it. When's it due?"

"It's not. I'm not pregnant."

"Then why the hell did you ask such a damn fool question?" he bellowed.

"Because Jake accepted your child as his long before it was born, and I was just wondering if all men would do the same or if Jake was just special."

Brett held up his fork, pointing it in her direction.

"I'll tell you what Jake Burnett is—a fool. He was married to you and he let you go. Let me assure you now, Rebecca, I'll never let you go. I love you too much. Once you're mine, you're staying mine."

"Even if it would make me happier to leave?"

"I love you more than Burnett ever did, could, or would love you. I'm telling you now, woman, once we're married, it's for life. I love you too damn much to ever let you go."

And Jake had loved her too much to ever make her stay. She wondered which love was the strongest.

Brett walked into the foyer. Rebecca gave a low whistle, coming to stand before him, running her hands up his white shirt.

"Don't you look nice? Are we doing something special this evening?"

He averted his eyes. "I'm going into town."

Removing her hands from his chest, she said, "It's too late to buy supplies. And it's a Saturday night. What are you going into town for?"

He released a short breath. "Look, Rebecca, you have a need to remain faithful to Jake until those damn divorce papers get here. I understand that. You gotta understand that I have needs, too, and there's a little blonde in town that'll take care of my needs."

"I see. And how much does she charge you?"

"Charge me? Darling, women don't charge me anything. As you are well aware, it is an honor and a privilege to have me make love to a woman. Hell, some of them have even offered to pay me." He hesitated, judging the wisdom of his next words. "But I'll stay here if you'll unlock your bedroom door to me."

Rebecca was shocked, realizing that the only way he could have known her door was locked was if he'd tried to open it after she'd gone to bed. "And why were you trying the lock on my door?" she asked.

"Because I love you, and I want you so much it hurts, and I'm getting damned tired of waiting!" He looked contrite. "Should I stay?"

"No, but I appreciate the opportunity to compete with the whore."

He brushed his lips against hers. "Don't wait up. I probably won't be back until morning."

She knew she had no right to be upset. She wasn't giving him anything, and men did have powerful urges to mate. She squeezed her eyes tight, forbidding the tears to come. So he had never had to pay a woman to want him.

She walked to her bedroom, undressed herself, and slipped into bed, wrapping her arms around a pillow. She wondered what Jake was doing this Saturday night, if he was watching the herd so all the other men could go into town for a little recreation. Time was passing much too slowly up here in Montana. She shouldn't be thinking of

Jake at all, but she did, every night before she went to sleep. And she missed him terribly.

The flaming red curtains whispered in the open window, the red satin pillows thrown hither and thither around the room. A solitary candle sought to provide an intimacy to an intimate act which under the circumstances was anything but intimate.

"You can just set the two dollars on the dresser there, darlin'," Velvet directed the man standing uncertainly beside the door, looking as though he might dart out if she moved too quickly. If she hadn't closed the door, he wouldn't even be in the room.

Looking at the lace doily resting on top of the scarred wooden dresser, the only decoration in the room that he thought was homey, he dug down into the pocket of his pants and brought out the two required coins, laying them quietly on the dresser.

"Did you take a bath before you came? The madam insists that our patrons be clean."

For the first time since she had started flirting with him downstairs, he met her gaze squarely. She had never before seen such beautiful eyes on a man.

"Yes, ma'am, I did."

"Then come here, darlin'."

Torn between putting off the inevitable and rushing to get it over with, Jake walked over to Velvet, her red corset laced so tight he wondered how she could breathe. The woman wasted no time in placing her hands on his shoulders, turning him slightly and pushing him gently down on the bed. She swung a leg over his lap, presenting her firm backside as she lifted his foot and grabbed his boot.

"Just put your foot on my butt and give me a little shove, darlin'."

Jake closed his eyes, taking a deep breath, wondering why the hell he had come, knowing full well why.

"I'd rather not, ma'am. I can take them off."

Velvet glanced over her shoulder. "It won't hurt me."

"I can take them off."

She shrugged, swinging her leg high and turning to clear

his lap. She had once danced the cancan in fancy saloons, but the money wasn't as good and men were always pawing her. She had figured then she might as well get paid for their pawing. She stood back, watching the man slowly removing his boots. She never asked her clients their names—she didn't want to know them. They'd never speak if their paths crossed on the street anyway. And Velvet wasn't her real name, so what did it matter if she didn't know their names?

"This your first time, darlin'?" she asked.

Jake set the boot down and looked up at the buxom redhead, her breasts straining to break free of the material keeping them imprisoned. She had pretty violet eyes, and he figured that was the only color on her that she had been born with. Nature couldn't make hair that red or skin that white.

"No, ma'am."

His eyes left her as he set about removing the other boot, and she studied him. Men came to see her for all kinds of reasons: they were lonely, hurting, missing someone special. He was here for all those reasons and more. Sometimes men would jump on her as soon as the door closed, be done in less than a minute. This man was not one of them.

"Was she pretty?" Velvet asked in a soft, understanding voice.

The brown eyes snapped up to hers, the pain reflected in them making her hate a woman she didn't even know.

"I'd rather not talk about her, if you don't mind," he said, easing his shirt out of his pants and beginning to undo the buttons.

Velvet shoved herself away from the wall. She straddled his lap, placing warm hands on the back of his neck, kneading his muscles.

"No, darlin', I don't mind. It's your money. You just tell Velvet what you want."

He looked away from her, gauging his answer. Then his eyes met hers, his voice hoarse. "I want . . . I want you to want me."

She pressed him down on the bed, laying her body on

top of his. "I do, darlin', I do want you," she said in the sultry voice she had perfected over the years.

It wasn't unusual for men to be depressed, sad, just plain down when they stepped into Velvet's room, but they usually didn't step out that way. She had the distinct impression that the man lying on top of her was feeling worse now than he had before. He had called out a name, and she was certain it was the name of the woman who had hurt him. She didn't like to care about the men who came to see her; it just wasn't good for business. But she was finding it increasingly difficult not to care about this one. His trembling stopped, and she ran her hands along his firm back.

"Since you're already here, darlin', if you'd like, I'll want you again for a dollar."

Jake lifted his head from where it had been buried in her flaming red hair. "No, ma'am." He eased himself off of her and began putting his clothes back on. "But thank you anyway."

Velvet pulled herself to a sitting position, her back against the red velvet headboard that had been specially made and ordered out of New Orleans. She drew her knees up to her chest, wrapping her arms tightly around her legs, resting her chin on her knees.

"You sure are a polite one," she said.

He turned his head slightly, giving her a small smile. "So I've been told."

His smile tore at her heart and she wondered how anyone could have ever hurt him.

Jake stood, tucking the ends of his shirt back into his pants before setting his hat down low on his head and walking to the door. He stopped beside the dresser, shoved a hand down into his pocket and brought up two more dollars to set down beside the first two. What a hell of a way for a woman to make a living, having to take whatever man was standing next in line.

"Thank you, ma'am," he said as he opened the door.

"You come back and see me, darlin'."

Jake tipped his hat slightly before closing the door behind him, knowing he would never come back. He was not certain if it had been worse than he'd remembered or if it was just that he had experienced something so much finer with Reb, something that went deeper than the physical act. For the remainder of his life everything else would pale in comparison.

# Chapter Eighteen

SITTING IN THE center of the bed, Rebecca watched as Jacob pulled himself up to his feet and peered over the edge of the mattress, smiling at her. He cocked his head at the sound of approaching boots hitting the floor outside the room, then scurried hand over hand, foot over foot around the bed. He was positioned so Rebecca had a clear view of his face when the door opened. She felt an ache in her heart as his smile faded and he drew his dark brows together, a habit he had acquired which meant he was thinking hard, trying to fathom some unknown part of his world. He crawled across the room, pulling himself back up to his feet before the window and flattening his nose against the pane.

Brett dropped a package at Rebecca's feet, and her attention was diverted from her son. The white paper was wrapped tightly over the box, the paper's edges crisp and sharp at the corners, coming together perfectly. A large red satin bow rested in the middle of the package, streamers flowing out from it.

"Well, come on, open it," Brett commanded, and Rebecca could not disobey, the temptation to see what lay in the perfectly wrapped box too great.

The wrapping came off, followed by the top of the box. She moved tissue aside to reveal a white blouse with delicately embroidered flowers around the collar and down the front. Beneath the blouse was a split riding skirt with the same flowers embroidered around the hem.

"And what am I do with this," she asked, "when I'm forbidden to ride?" She used the word "forbidden" teasingly. Brett did not.

"You're not forbidden to ride, only to act like a cowhand. Try it on and we'll see if it works."

She arched a brow and he feigned a look of defeat.

"All right, I'll leave this time. But once we're married, you'll have to dress and undress in front of me every day."

He walked out, and Rebecca moved to crouch down beside her son. "Who are you looking for, Jacob? Who is it that you miss so much?" She gazed out the window along with her son, thinking it ironic that this particular window faced south. "I miss him, too," she whispered.

Donning the new clothes, she was surprised to find them a perfect fit. She looked at her slim figure in the mirror. Her breasts had returned to her pre-pregnancy size, her milk having dried up when she left Pleasure, no doubt a result of the emotional turmoil she had put herself through. It had made for a cranky Jacob on the train and prevented Brett from forming a close bond with his son in those first few days. Or at least that's what Rebecca blamed Brett's aloofness on. In truth, she knew Brett's interests did not include children. From afar, he adored his son, but up close he was tolerant and not overly affectionate.

She ran her hand along her flat stomach. Shortly after they'd arrived in Montana, she'd discovered she wasn't pregnant. An emptiness, an aching disappointment had assailed her. Not until that moment had she realized how much she was hoping that she was indeed carrying Jake's child. She shook away the unsettling thought. She would have other children.

But none would have brown eyes. None would wear a lopsided smile.

When she stepped out of the house, she found herself in a strong embrace, twirled around, set down, and glanced upon appraisingly.

"Lord, Rebecca, you are beautiful. And now to go with that new outfit, you need a horse." He bowed, extending an arm, and Rebecca followed the direction of his hand.

Standing before them, saddled and ready to ride, was Brett's brown stallion and a white mare.

"White for the purity of your body when I first met you," Brett explained as he helped her mount. The thoroughbred animal was beautiful, Rebecca had to admit to herself. Still, she preferred a black horse, but didn't have the heart to tell him.

They rode at an easy canter across his land until he led her up a tree-covered rise. From their position, they could see all that was his, his cattle in the distance, his land, even his home as the sun reflected off of it. Rebecca dismounted, tethered her horse, and leaned back against the rough bark of a tree. It was a beautiful sight, the deep blue sky coming down to meet the deep green earth.

Brett came to stand before her, bracing an arm above her head, running a finger down her cheek.

"I've seen too much sadness in your eyes since you've been here, Rebecca. Do you miss Kentucky?"

Kentucky? She hadn't missed Kentucky since she had left the state. But Texas, she missed Texas. No, it wasn't even Texas she missed. She shook her head.

"No."

His knuckles brushed her cheek, his face full of concern. "Was it hard on you when I left?"

"For a while," she responded honestly. Until Jake had taken her in his embrace.

"I would have taken you with me if I'd known," he said. "I love you, Rebecca." He slipped his arms around her, bringing her up against his hardened frame. She put her arms around his neck, her lips pressing against his as his tongue sought to mate with hers. His chest and shoulders were broader, sturdier than Jake's, his straight hair clipped shorter so when she ran her fingers up through it, no curls possessively wrapped around her fingers. The kiss ended and she pressed her forehead against his chest, wishing just once she could be with him and not think of Jake.

He moved, one arm staying around her as he led her to the quilt he had laid down earlier, food scattered at one end of it. Gratefully, she sat down, anticipating a picnic. They ate in silence, watching the serene scene surrounding them. From time to time, he would reach over and touch her, her hand, her cheek, her hair. When they finished eating, he put everything away and then, stretching out on his side, he reached into his pocket and brought out another perfectly wrapped gift and handed it to her.

"What's this?" she asked.

He laughed. "If I'd wanted you to know right away, I wouldn't have gone to the trouble of having it wrapped, now would I? Open it."

Inside, she found a ring of diamonds and emeralds nestled together in a tiny cluster. She looked from the ring to his face, seeing his love for her reflected in his eyes. Love in eyes of blue, somehow different from love in eyes of brown. He sat up.

"It occurred to me that my telling you to meet me at the hotel or never see me again was anything but romantic." He took her hand. "I love you, Rebecca. Will you marry me?"

There had been no intake of a shaky breath, no lowering of his voice so if she were offended they could both pretend the words had never been spoken. She saw no doubt in his eyes as to what her answer would be, saw that he really required no answer. The question was stated simply so in later years she would have the memory of his asking.

"Sometimes," Rebecca said softly, "I'm not sure it is me you love. Sometimes, I think you love the girl you left in Kentucky."

"They're one in the same."

"No, Brett, they're not. The girl you left in Kentucky had grown up surrounded by nothing but love and kindness. As much as Father prepared me to take over the running of his ranch, he protected me from the ugliness in the world. In the past year, I've known my father's unforgiving anger. I've seen a young man branded because we put barbed wire around our land, a man die for a brother he once hated."

"But the ugliness is all in the past. Look around you, darling, all there is, all you can see for miles is the future.

Our future. Slip your ring on one of those beautiful fingers of yours."

She slid it onto the finger of her right hand. Brett squeezed her hand. "It's supposed to go on your left hand so it's close to your heart."

"Not until I'm officially divorced."

"You are a stubborn woman, Rebecca. The divorce is inevitable. You set the wheels in motion for it before you left Texas. Just as our marriage is inevitable. Just as our making love that night so long ago was inevitable. Just as this is inevitable." He cupped her cheek in his hand, bringing his lips to hers, laying her down in the process.

His mouth covered hers possessively, his tongue claiming the regions that another's had dared to touch. He wanted to cleanse the image of Jake Burnett from her memory. How had the man managed to get such a hold on her? Why wouldn't she let him go?

His labored breathing resounded near her ear. "I want you so badly, Rebecca. Please, love, don't deny me this time."

She heard the want, the desire, the pleading tone in his voice, and she wondered if he had ever pleaded with any woman. Her lips ached from his passionate kiss, her body trembled from his closeness, so she was surprised the words came out with such ease.

"No, Brett. Not this time."

His body collapsed in defeat upon hers, and he wondered if she was even aware of the real reason why she continued to deny him. "But it's all inevitable. Why can't you accept that? Why can't you let go of the past today and let us begin the future?"

"Because I'm not the girl you left in Kentucky."

He lifted his head from where he had buried it in her hair and, gazing deeply into eyes of blue, he said, "I love you anyway."

Frank stood before the altar, afraid he'd suffocate before the ceremony was over. He had never worn a suit before, and he wouldn't be wearing one now if Arlene hadn't looked at him with blue eyes. Her eyes had taken to turning

blue of late, and the expression she carried within them
melted him until he'd do any damn thing she wanted. He
stretched his neck, trying to ease his discomfort, grateful
Jake was beside him just in case he passed out.

The organ music began, and Ruth Reading began walking slowly down the aisle of the church. Ironically, she and
Arlene had become the best of friends, but Frank barely
paid her a glance. His eyes were fixed on the woman who
was following Ruth. Arlene walked with her arm wrapped
around her father's, her white dress flowing along behind
her, her eyes a deep blue. Frank forgot all about his promise
to himself to stand staid and serious and not appear to be
some overanxious boy, and his face broke out into a broad
smile. Arlene returned his smile, and he forgot all about
the uncomfortable suit he was wearing, wanting only to
make her proud of him.

Standing just behind Frank, Jake thought of Rebecca
wearing her mother's wedding dress. Too many things still
reminded him of her, but he supposed they always would.
All he could do was learn to accept the memories and enjoy
them whenever they showed up unexpectedly. He listened
to the couple as they exchanged their vows, similar to but
different from the ones he had taken: theirs wouldn't be
broken. He handed Frank the gold band and watched as he
placed the ring on Arlene's slender finger and enfolded her
in his embrace, kissing her tenderly as the minister proclaimed them man and wife.

Following the service, Jake went to retrieve the buggy
for Frank. He came around the corner of the church building, stopping short at the sight of four women, tipping his
hat towards the one he recognized.

"Miss Velvet."

"Lord, darlin'. You're the only man in this state who
would tip his hat to a whore." She ushered the other
women along and stopped beside Jake. "You haven't been
back to see me, darlin'."

"No, ma'am."

"You won't be coming back to see me, will you?"

He shook his head. "No, ma'am. I won't."

She smiled, a warm, pretty smile. "It's just as well. A man like you, darlin', shouldn't have to pay a woman. You take care of yourself now, you hear?"

He returned her smile. "Yes, ma'am. I will."

She reached out, touching the raised corner of his mouth with the tip of her finger. "Lord, darlin', I don't know how any woman could walk away from that smile."

The inside of the barn was geared to a celebration. At one end band members were tuning their instruments. Jake smiled as Maura approached.

"I canna thank you enough for this fine celebration you're a-giving my Arlene and her Frank."

"It was the least I could do. Frank's a good man. We've been through a lot together."

"Aye. A good man, he is. My Bri wouldn't have given his blessing had the boy not been deserving of it."

The band began the first tune, and Frank led his wife out into the center of the barn and began waltzing her around. Jake nodded towards Maura.

"I think Brian is looking for you."

Maura laughed. "I haven't danced in so long, don't know if I remember how to move my feet." But when Brian took her in his arms, she did remember.

Jake stepped back against the wall, watching the couples dance, feeling the acute absence of a hand into which he could slip his.

He wandered outside to the corral. The horses pranced, seemingly in time to the music that was filtering outside.

"Frank's me brother now."

Jake looked down at the young cowboy who had followed him. "Reckon he is at that," he said as he bent his long legs to get to Sean's height so he could gaze through the same slats as his young friend.

Sean kicked the dirt beneath his boots. "If I tell you a secret, will you promise not to tell me mum?"

Jake studied the boy. "I'm not so sure it's a good idea to keep secrets from your mother."

The boy nodded acceptance of the truth and took to studying the horses with great intensity.

"But this time I'll keep your secret," Jake said, watching relief wash over Sean's face.

"I miss Jacob," he said quietly.

Jake felt a tug at his heart, realizing no one except Frank had mentioned Reb or Jacob to him since they'd left.

"I miss him, too, but that's hardly a secret," Jake said.

"Me mum said I wasn't to mention Jacob or his mother to you because it would make you sad. Did it?"

"A little, but it sorta warms me inside to think about him."

"When's he coming back?" Sean asked.

"He's not. He and his mother went to live with a man who could make them happy."

"Thought they was happy here."

"Only on the outside, Sean. This man can make them happy on the inside, too, and that's more important."

Sean nodded. "Do you think Jacob misses his wagon?"

"Oh, I imagine he has a new one by now. Hard part will be finding a friend to pull him."

"When I grow up, I'm going to go to Montana and visit him."

"Sean O'Hennessy! Your mother's looking for you!" Carrie called out as she trudged towards the two who were wearing guilty expressions.

"It's our secret, right?" Sean whispered.

"Our secret. And anytime you want to talk about him, you just let me know."

Sean held out a hand and Jake shook it before the boy ran off.

"Never took Rebecca for a fool," Carrie said as she approached the fence.

Unfurling his body, Jake turned his attention to the ponies. "Don't reckon she was."

"You trying to tell me she had two good men fall in love with her when most of us are lucky if we get just one?"

Jake's reply was silence.

"Have you heard from her?" she asked softly.

"Only that she arrived safely."

Carrie placed a weathered hand on his back. "You're a

special man, Jake Burnett. Don't you ever forget that.''

She walked away, leaving him alone to watch the horses.

Lifting his bride into his arms, Frank carried her across the threshold of their new home, straight into their bedroom. He set Arlene down, bringing his arms around her, his lips locking onto hers. Abruptly he ended the kiss, leaning back to study her.

''You're trembling. Are you afraid?''

She moved her head slowly from side to side. ''I could never be frightened of you, man. But I'm a wee bit nervous. I want to please you, Frank, but I don't know how.''

He smiled. ''I'll teach you everything you need to know.'' Drawing her close, he said, ''All you have to do is remember how much we love each other.''

And it turned out to be that simple.

Walking through the house, Rebecca felt the way she had after Jacob had been born, when tears came without warning. She stopped beside the large front window. Nature reflected her mood, as the rain fell in torrents. Although it was early afternoon, the clouds were so dark that the day resembled early evening.

Brett came charging out of the study. ''Got a rider coming in,'' he said as he brushed past her, depositing a quick kiss on her lips.

Stepping out onto the veranda, he waited while the man drew to a halt, handed him a parcel and headed back out. He studied it intently before stepping back into the house, his broad smile lifting up the corners of his dark mustache.

''It's for you,'' he said as he ripped open the end of the envelope, dumping the contents in his hand.

''Brett!'' she cried, reaching for it.

He held it away, high above his head as he gave a cursory glance to the top sheet of paper. Then shoving the papers into her hands, he lifted her up, spinning them both around.

''Thank God! It's your divorce! It's final!'' He lowered her, and his lips came down hard on hers, consuming her, as his hands ran rampant over her breasts and back. He stilled, drawing her back. "We'll get married tomorrow."

Holding the papers in a trembling hand, she said, "I need time."

Disbelieving, Brett released her, his eyes filled with anger. "What the hell do you mean you need time? You've had almost three months!"

"I need time to get ready. I want to look my best. I want it to be a moment we'll remember. Can't we do it Saturday?"

Pulling her into his arms, he said, "Saturday it is." Gently, he brushed his lips against hers. "I know it's been difficult since we left Texas, but everything will be all right now. You'll see. You'll be the happiest woman in the world."

Grabbing his black slicker off the hook by the door, he turned back to face her. "I'm going into town to get all the arrangements made."

"In this weather?"

"I don't think you understand how much I love you. How much I want you to be my wife. I'd brave all the elements of nature at once to have you."

Tears sprung to her eyes as she looked at the handsome man standing before her. He opened the door. "On Saturday, when we change your name, we'll be changing my son's name."

Rebecca had expected that. She knew he'd want Jacob's last name changed from Burnett to Meier.

"Pick out a name you like."

Taken aback, she asked, "You want his first name changed?"

"I do. I want no ghosts from Texas haunting our lives here. And when I get back, I want that damn ring off your finger as well." He closed the door behind him without another word.

Rebecca went inside her son's room, watching as he slept peacefully through the rain, knowing he would wake up soon from his afternoon nap. For the life of her, she could think of nothing else she wanted to call him.

She walked to her own room, closed the door behind

her, and drew a chair up beside the window. The curtains were pulled back, and the rain was hitting the glass and sliding down into a puddle on the ground. Shifting through the papers in her hands, she sought out the letter she had spied when Brett had shoved her mail into her hand, wanting desperately for the letter to be from Jake. With trembling fingers she pulled it out, her eyes scanning for the signature, disappointment reeling through her to realize it was from Doyle Thomas. But then why would Jake write? She began to read the letter:

Dear Rebecca,

As you can see, the divorce has gone through all the proper channels and is now valid and legal and you are free to marry again. I wish you the best of luck. Should you ever need my services, do not hesitate to call upon me.

Yesterday, I drew up Jake's will. It is his desire that upon his death, all his holdings be given to your children. I advised him against this action as he is still a young man and may have children of his own at some future date, but considering the reason for the divorce, I realize this highly unlikely—

The reason for the divorce? She had never looked beyond the lines where she'd applied her signature. She hadn't realized they'd given a reason for wanting a divorce. Hurriedly, she searched the papers. When she found the reason, she was assaulted by a physical pain. Jake had given the one reason with which no one would argue, the one reason that would guarantee Rebecca her divorce—husband's impotency.

"Oh, Jake, how you must have felt saying that to a man, knowing other men would read it. Why didn't you put the blame for our failed marriage on me?"

With a heavy heart, she went back to the letter.

Please keep me apprised of any future children you bear and when the little ones grow up and leave the nest, please keep me informed as to their whereabouts. Based

on the ranch's current reputation, I have little doubt, your
children will receive a considerable inheritance.

Your servant,
Doyle Thomas, Attorney-at-Law
P.S. I was asked to tell you Maura gave birth to a girl,
and Frank and Arlene are getting married.

Dropping the papers on her lap, she leaned her head
against the pane, feeling the rain beating down on the glass.
Out of the corner of her eye, she saw a small slip of paper
float down to the floor. She recognized the handwriting
before she picked it up, having seen it many times on lists
of supplies that were needed. She ran her fingers over the
lettering.

~~Dearest Reb~~
~~Dear Rebecca~~
~~Reb~~
      Thank you for letting me know you got to Montana
safe. Thought you'd want to know Maura gave birth to
a girl. Tiny little thing. Brian's chest is so puffed out
with pride, he doesn't need his bellows in the forge to
heat his fires. Frank and Arlene are getting married—
probably be married by the time you get this letter. I'm
building a house for them and ordered some furniture for
you to give them. Thought you'd want to do that for
Frank after all the two of you had been through together.
      ~~I think of you and Jacob often.~~
      ~~I miss~~
      ~~My love~~
      ~~Love~~
      Your friend

She read the letter until she could see it with her eyes
closed, every word written, every word scratched out for
fear he'd reveal more than he wanted her to know. Finally,
unable to decide on the best words, he must have given the
scrap of paper to Doyle Thomas so he could convey the
message. She could envision Doyle, who would lose his
glasses if they slipped to the end of his nose, adding Jake's

thoughts to the end of his own letter and then shoving Jake's note into the envelope along with the other papers.

She watched the papers wither where her tears splashed upon them. Her marriage to Jake was truly over. Her life in Texas, her marriage to the man with the velvet brown eyes and the endearing smile, was now in her past. It was time for her to begin her new life, her life with Brett. Come Saturday, she would marry Brett Meier, the man she had fallen in love with so long ago, who had made love to her beneath the stars on a moonless night, who had given her a son and searched the country until he found her. It was time to sever all ties, all memories of Jake. She lifted her hand, grasping the ring as her face mirrored the pane beside her, the tears of Mother Nature, the tears of a woman washing away the pain.

In the early morning hours it was difficult to believe that before the sun set that evening, it would attempt to scorch every living thing on the earth, green, brown, or otherwise, plants and animals alike. It had been trying all summer with a great deal of success since rain had been scarce. Jake's cattle had been spared suffering because the barbed wire fencing had protected his waterholes from marauders, and his windmills drew the precious liquid out of the earth.

Lying on the hill that had once been blue, leaning up on an elbow, Jake pulled a reed of grass out of the earth and inserted it between his teeth, gnawing absently, tasting the bitter and the sweet. He didn't think he'd ever be free of the ache in his heart, but at least it had lessened. Having Doyle Thomas draw up his will had helped considerably, given him a reason to climb out of bed in the mornings. He hoped one of Rebecca's children would see fit to run the ranch, but even if they sold it, he had no reason to complain. He wanted his years of work to be worth something to someone when he was gone, and he could think of no one else that meant as much to him.

He smiled, wondering if Rebecca was already carrying another child. He imagined she was pregnant five minutes after she stepped into Brett's hotel room. After all, she loved the man, she had no reason to deny him. He assumed she was not carrying his own child since he had only heard from her the one time. There were moments, usually late at night when he heard a lonesome howl, that he regretted denying her his seed that last night. But then he would feel the dull pain associated with thoughts of Jacob, wondering if he was walking, if he had spoken his first word, if it had been "Papa" directed towards Brett, and he would be grateful that there were no other children.

Removing the grass from between his teeth, he stood, lifting his arms up and stretching his lean frame, squinting as the sun hit his eyes. He mounted his horse, deciding to ride along the fence line. He had experienced little trouble of late, but still, it didn't hurt to check. He couldn't afford to have cattle wandering off. With the heat spell, he wanted to keep them close to known watering holes.

Spotting an unfamiliar group of longhorns, their hides rangy from lack of care, he slowed his horse and cautiously approached the band that was lazing around before a small grove of trees. To their right lay his fence, part of it cut, part of it torn down, but he could see no one minding the cattle. He retrieved his rifle and dismounted, then ran a hand over the flank of one of the steers. No brands marked the cattle. Moving to the fence, he swore under his breath. The fence was used to keep the cattle from going into the ravine that ran along the land. He'd have to find the owner of the cattle and tell him to get the cattle off his land or sell them to him. And he'd have to get the fence fixed immediately. He had already had three cattle wander off down this ravine and fall, injuring themselves. His men had been forced to shoot the animals to relieve their suffering.

The sound of a rifle being cocked caused Jake to curse himself as he slowly turned around. The last person he wanted to see was Ethan Truscott, and there he was, with half a dozen men behind him.

"It's against the law to cut fences," Jake said.

"Only if you're caught."

"Look, Ethan. I don't want any trouble. Just get your cattle off my land, and I'll overlook the mess you made here."

"I'm not moving my cattle. By all rights, this land should be mine. Now, you just set your rifle down and remove the holster, and I'll think about letting you live."

Jake slowly shook his head. "Ethan—"

"Take him!" Ethan shouted.

Jake had no opportunity to defend himself before he was battled to the ground. Once subdued, he was lifted back up to his feet, two burly men holding onto him.

Ethan smiled. "Take his shirt off."

Jake was like a madman as he broke free, taking a great deal of satisfaction in feeling his fist land squarely on Ethan's nose. It took four men to pull Jake off as Ethan came up spitting blood and holding his hand over his face, the blood trailing down his arm.

"You broke my nose, you bastard! You're going to regret that. Get his shirt off!" He stomped over to the fence and began yanking on the barbed wire, his thick gloves protecting his hands. When he had a lengthy piece pulled free, he extracted a pair of cutters from his hip pocket, and clipped the wire free, dragging it behind him as he moved towards Jake.

Brown eyes met brown.

"You've been wrapping barbed wire around your land without giving any thought as to how the land feels. Well, now, you're going to find out."

He brought his fist up into Jake's ribs knocking the wind out of him. While Jake struggled to breathe, Ethan pressed the tip of a barb into Jake's flesh to secure it and began wrapping the remaining length of wire around him. Jake clenched his jaw against the tiny shards of pain, alone not much to bother a man, but increasing in number until the sharp bite of one barb became indistinguishable from the other.

"Maybe I ought to brand you. Wonder if you'd yell as much as that red-haired kid did." Ethan laughed. "No, I reckon you wouldn't. You wouldn't even holler when Father took the strap to you. Get me some more wire!" he yelled back to one of his men.

"Come on, Ethan, you've done enough."

Ethan spun around. "Get me some more wire."

The man had never seen so much hate in his life, and he wondered if Ethan were sane.

"You can release him."

As soon as the men released him, Jake gathered what little strength he had left and threw himself against Ethan. With his arms pinned to his sides, his movements were hampered and he could do little more than knock Ethan down. Ethan scrambled out from beneath him and delivered a series of blows to Jake's already battered body, driving the barbs deeper into his flesh.

Then Ethan snapped the barbed wire that was handed to him and bent down, wrapping it securely around Jake, taking pleasure in watching him break out in a sweat as he clenched his jaws tighter. When he was finished, he stood up, placing a foot on Jake's chest and pressing him back to the ground, standing over him.

"You're going to die, Jake Burnett. Not by my hand, but by the hand of God. You're a child of sin, and when Satan has welcomed you into Hell, I'll claim this land as mine. I'll tear down your fences and make it open range." He increased the pressure of his boot bearing down on Jake's chest until he was satisfied with the grunt Jake emitted.

"Throw him down the ravine," he ordered his men.

Not one man moved.

"Bastards!" he yelled as he hauled Jake to his feet and threw him so he rolled down the steep incline.

Jake had no way to halt his progress down the slope, stopping only when it leveled off. He was unable to move as the pain intensified. The sun beat down on his back. The blood trickled over and down his flesh. The insects came to inspect the open wounds. His mouth dried like sawdust. Closing his eyes, he saw every smile that Rebecca had ever directed his way and knew a pang of regret. He would have liked to have held her in his arms one last time before he died.

# Chapter Nineteen

HE WAS IN Hell, just as Ethan had promised. And the fiery flames licked at his body unmercifully. He opened his eyes, not expecting to find Hell such a dark place, with only one solitary light illuminating the region. Why didn't the fires of Hell brighten the place up?

He felt a cool hand, small palm, slender fingers touch his cheek. A woman's hand? His mother's hand? She had touched his cheek when he had smallpox. Had his mother come for him? She had always managed to take away the pain when he was a child. He hoped she could take it away now, because the more aware he became of her soothing palm on his cheek, the more aware he became of the pain spreading through his body, the flames consuming him.

He heard a soft voice calling him and turned towards it, trying to focus the vision before him. It wasn't his mother. If he weren't so tired, he would have smiled. He hadn't expected to find an angel in Hell.

The angel, her image blurred, a whiteness surrounding her, would understand. The angel would know.

"Why couldn't she love me?" he asked. The angel's answer was garbled. He strained to understand the words, but all his senses failed him as he slipped back into the abyss on the edge of Hell.

And the angel knelt down beside the bed and wept.

Jake struggled to open his eyes, to wade through the thickness surrounding his mind. Maura was sitting in a chair beside the bed, his bed, in his home. So he wasn't in

Hell after all. Wouldn't Ethan be disappointed? Maura
looked so pretty sitting there, her face filled with love and
concern. Her hair was braided, the braid draped over her
shoulder. He had never seen her wear a braid before. She
didn't look like herself.

"Maura, you look like Reb when you wear your hair
like that," he croaked.

"It is Reb, darling," the sweet voice said.

He lifted his head, studying the woman before him, before dropping back down to the pillow. "Just take what
you need. Don't wait on me to get well." He now knew
there were two kinds of hell. He could deal with the physical burning, but not the other one. Gratefully, he allowed
the black abyss to engulf him.

Leaning forward, wiping the sweat from his brow, Rebecca whispered, "I need you, Jake. Please don't leave me
now." She brushed a kiss on his cheek, then laid her cool
cheek next to his fevered one, wishing she could do more
to break his fever, to ensure his survival.

Brett had returned home that rainy afternoon to find her
sitting on the sofa, Jacob in her arms, her packed bag at
her feet.

"What the hell is going on here, Rebecca?" he had
asked.

"I'm going back to Jake."

"The hell you are!"

Rebecca had moved her head slowly from side to side.
"Whatever I felt for you long ago is like the dwindling
flame on a candle. It's been flickering since that night, at-
tracting me, diverting my heart. I had to come to Montana,
I had to touch the flame, but when I did it sputtered and
died. And I hurt a good man doing it."

"When I got back to Kentucky," he had said, "when I
learned you had gotten married, I ranted and raved at myself for having ever left you in the first place. I had planned
to come back here and begin again. But I couldn't. I had
to see you, even if only from a distance. When I finally
found you and saw how you were living, I knew I had to
at least try to get you back. You deserve all I have to offer
you. You deserve to be married to a gentleman."

"I was married to a gentle man."

"You were married to a cowhand, and not a very charming or handsome one at that."

"Is that what you see when you look at Jake?"

"That and the fact that he doesn't deserve you."

"He doesn't deserve me only because I'm unworthy of him. Let me tell you, charming, handsome man, what I see when I look at Jake. I see a man who suffered smallpox as a child and survived, a man who took the love his mother gave him and held on to it like a lifeline when he was thrown into a sea of hatred, a man who would give his coat to another if he thought that man needed it half as much as he did, a man who married me knowing I carried another's child and never once condemned me for it, who brought my child into this world and called him son. He didn't give me a big house, but he gave me a home. He didn't give me gifts wrapped perfectly in beautiful paper and ribbons . . . but, oh, he did give me beautiful gifts, and I carry them all in my heart."

"I won't let you take my son."

She'd had no intention of leaving Jacob, but neither had she wanted to spend any more time arguing over her decision. Calling his bluff, praying he wouldn't call hers, Rebecca had deposited the child in Brett's arms and had begun emptying her bag.

"What the hell are you doing?" he had bellowed.

She had faced him with innocence. "You'll need Jacob's things."

"You love my son so little?"

"I love Jake so much."

"Dammit, woman! You know I'm bluffing."

Her gaze had become intense, blue eyes delving deeply into blue. "I'm not," she had said calmly.

And so she had returned to Texas, with her son and her heart. As soon as she had arrived in Pleasure, she had stopped off at Doyle Thomas's office. Overjoyed to see her, he'd hitched up his buggy and driven her out to the ranch.

They had arrived just as Frank and Lee were hauling Jake off a horse. Rebecca had felt her stomach lurch at the sight of his swollen, bloodied body. No one had acted surprised to see her, no one had questioned the orders she had barked out. She had handed her son over to Arlene. She had sent every man out riding the fences with orders to bring any fence-cutters to her. She would have ridden out herself, but she didn't want to spend time in prison after just coming back to Jake. And she knew she would go to prison, because if she so much as caught sight of Ethan Truscott she would kill the man. She'd prefer a slow death for him, but she'd make it a quick one if he wouldn't oblige her.

Since her return, she had been battling Jake's fever, the worst moments coming when his fever was the highest. He had rolled to his side, curling up into a ball, holding his stomach, saying how bad it hurt. He said things in his fever that tore at Rebecca's heart. The pain causing his anguish was not the result of the barbs that had been embedded in his flesh, but the wounds she had inflicted carelessly to his heart. For the first time since leaving Montana, she realized there was a good chance he would just as soon see her in Hell as see her in his house again.

The sweat poured profusely from Jake's fevered skin, the chills traveling throughout his body as Rebecca alternately bathed him and wrapped him in warm blankets, hoping his fever would break by morning. Her back ached from the bent-over position she had maintained for much of her vigil, her hands were raw from trying to soothe his fevered flesh, from dipping constantly into cool water that quickly turned warm.

She touched his cheek and felt the absence of heat. Finally, the heat was gone. She sponged him down and changed the bedding.

Sitting in a hard chair beside the bed, she rested her cheek on his upturned palm. For the first time since she'd arrived, she felt if she slept, when she woke up, he wouldn't be gone.

The slight movement of fingers beneath her cheek caused her to wake up. She opened her eyes to find deep brown hesitantly searching hers.

"Thought I was dreaming," he croaked, each word an

effort so sapped was his strength.

"Wish it had been a dream, but it was a nightmare. You've been very sick. It's been five days since Frank and Lee found you. Frank thinks you were out there for at least two days."

"Frank shouldn't have sent for you."

"He didn't. I came back on my own. Decided Montana wasn't where I belonged."

She touched his cheek, and he flinched as though he had been burned. "We'll talk about it when you're stronger. Right now, you need to rest. You have a lot of healing to do."

Rebecca longed to crawl into bed beside him, to feel his arms around her, to know he still loved her, but she had seen the look in his eyes when she'd touched him. His heart needed healing as much as his body, and she was no longer certain she knew how to care for his heart.

Gazing out the open window, feeling the warm breeze caress his skin, Jake wondered why Rebecca had returned. She had been sitting by his side every time he had awakened. He remembered her voice crooning to him, her touch on his fevered brow.

He had ignored her, feigned sleep and fatigue to avoid discussing why she had returned, mostly because he wasn't sure he wanted to know, but more because he couldn't let her stay if she didn't love him. To lose her again would kill him.

Carrying in a plate heaped with food, she gave him a hesitant smile.

"Are you feeling up to eating some breakfast?" she asked.

He nodded and she brought him the plate, plumped up his pillows, and sat down in the chair beside the bed.

"How are you feeling this morning?" she asked.

"Sore."

"I imagine that's an understatement."

She stared out the window while he ate, wondering where to begin, how to tell him what she felt, wondering if now was the time to broach the subject of her return. She glanced over at him. As though reading her thoughts, Jake held out the plate. ''I'm tired right now.''

She took the plate, and he rolled over presenting her with his back.

''I'll leave you be, then,'' she said softly as she quietly got up and left the house.


Rebecca returned to Frank's house after leaving orders with Lee to take a plate in to Jake at lunch and dinner. She had been ignoring her son since they had returned, although he failed to notice now that he had his friend Sean to make him laugh. She took a hot bath and washed her hair. She was too tired to deal with Jake. What she needed was a good night's sleep. And what he needed was some time without her.

She spent the night stretched out in Frank's loft with Jacob curled up in a ball nestled beside her. She had been foolish to think she could come back and have Jake welcome her with open arms. She could see so clearly now the last time they had sat together on the hill. Why had she thought he'd said ''When the man who loves you has come for you.'' And when did she realize he'd said ''the man you love.'' Had she given so little to him? Yes, she had to admit to herself that she had.

The following morning, Jacob clambered into his wagon and Rebecca pulled him in front of Frank's house. Sean soon replaced her, and she sat watching the smile stretching across her son's face. And she began to wonder where she would go if she didn't stay here.

As afternoon approached, she knew she could stay away from Jake no longer. She needed to talk with him, even if the conversation was only one-sided. She walked into the house and stopped. Jake was tucking his shirt into his pants.

''What are you doing?'' she asked.

''Gotta take a look at the ranch.'' Before she had stepped through the door, his plan had been to go search for her and make certain she was all right. But now that he saw her, he didn't want her to know he was concerned about her. Instead, he wanted her to think it was his ranch that concerned him. Picking up his hat, he moved past her.

She grabbed his arm and he winced. "I'm sorry," she said, pulling her hand back. "I don't think you should be going out."

"I have a ranch to run."

"Jake, sometime we need to talk. Maybe it'll be easier for you if you know that while I was with Brett, I never . . . he and I never made love. I honored the vows I made with you. I remained faithful."

"I didn't." Bringing his hat down low over his brow, he walked out of the house.

Rebecca's legs went weak, her breathing becoming labored. What had ever made her think he wouldn't find another woman? A woman who was not blind to everything Jake had to offer. God, but she felt the fool. She pressed the heels of her hands into her eyes.

Then, without realizing why, she walked outside and headed towards a small area of land that was shaded by several large oak trees, a white picket fence enclosing the space that served as a memorial to one. She read the words carved on the headstone and then knelt down beside the grave.

"Oh, Zach," she whispered. "You wanted to be his brother so badly, and in the end he called you 'brother.' What in God's name can I do to make him want to call me 'wife'?"

Sitting under the lingering shade of the oak tree overlooking the still pond, its blue water resembling a mirror as it reflected the early evening clouds, Jake wondered what in the hell had possessed him to say what he had to Reb. He had wanted to hurt her as badly as she had hurt him. And he had succeeded. Flinching inwardly, he remembered the pain that had deepened the blue hue of her eyes and, just like the fight he had with Ethan all those many years ago, he had found no satisfaction in his action or its result. If he could, he would take back every word spoken that afternoon.

His eyes scanned the slight incline and he saw the sight his heart ached to see. Rebecca was cantering toward him. She dismounted and slowly walked through the coarse grasses until she stood even with him.

Dropping down, Rebecca too stared out at the little pond, gathering courage for the question she wasn't sure she wanted answered. She had sacrificed the right to let the answer matter when she had left with Brett. She was beginning to feel that she had sacrificed everything for a haunting dream. She turned to study the rugged profile that man and nature had carved without care. "Do you love her, then?"

Jake's eyes narrowed as he continued to watch the inactive pond. "No. I had to . . . I paid her."

Rebecca returned her attention to the pond, relief washing over her like a soft summer rain, his answer filling her with undeserved hope. She lifted her eyes to the autumn sunset, thinking back on so many others she had watched with the man who was sitting by her now. She felt as though the brilliant hues streaking across the azure sky were a reflection of her feelings for Jake, and she wondered how she could tell him what was in her heart. How had he ever found the courage to tell her? It should be the simplest thing in the world, but she didn't want to just blurt her feelings out, not after all this time.

Jake studied the landscape, a little voice inside his head telling him to just accept the fact she'd returned to him and to try to rebuild the life Brett's arrival had shattered. But a little voice inside his heart had to know the truth.

He turned his steady gaze towards her and asked in a soft tone, "Why did you come back? What happened in Montana?"

Slowly she turned her attention away from the horizon, her eyes reflecting an emotion that had never been directed his way, a warm smile gracing her countenance.

"Actually, it's not what happened in Montana that made me come back. It's what happened here." Reaching up, she brushed the hair from his brow, her eyes delving into his. "I fell in love with you."

Jake hadn't expected those words, and though they were spoken quietly, they hit him with the force of an iron ball being blasted from a cannon.

"I thought you loved Brett."

"So did I," she said. "But when you walked out of that hotel, I felt an ache in my heart that I didn't understand. The man I loved was waiting for me at the top of those stairs. All I had to do was go to him to find all the love and happiness I ever wanted. I couldn't understand why those stairs were so damn hard to climb.

"The ache grew when we left Texas. In Montana, I thought it would consume me. I kept thinking the ache would go away once our divorce was final, once Brett and I got married. Then I got the divorce papers. It was the saddest day of my life. I thought my heart was going to die, and that's the moment when I knew. The man I loved hadn't been waiting at the top of the stairs; he had walked out the front door of that hotel."

Jake had studied her intently while she spoke, and he wasn't quite able to believe what she was saying. How could she choose him with all his imperfections over Brett Meier who was flawless?

"I love you, Jake, with all my heart I do." She took his hand, one of the few places she could touch him without hurting him. "If Brett hadn't left, if I'd married him, I'm sure I would have spent my life content. But he did leave, and I married you. After being your wife for a year, how could I ever settle for less?" She pressed his palm to her cheek and then to her lips. "And marriage to anyone else would be less. I know I hurt you badly, and I don't deserve your forgiveness or your willingness to take me back, but if you'll do either, I promise I'll do everything within my power to make sure you never regret it."

She watched the emotions cross his features as he waged a silent war within himself, and the one emotion she longed for was losing out to fear and pain.

"I hurt you so awfully much," she whispered, "more than Ethan ever did. I'll do anything to take the pain out of your eyes. Just tell me . . . tell me what I can do?"

He closed his eyes, his head slowly moving from side to side. She released her hold on his hand, and he brought it in close to his body, pressing the tight ball of his fist into the center of his stomach. Rebecca felt the world she wanted slipping away. She had hurt him once. She wouldn't do it again.

"I can't blame you for not wanting me now. I'm sorry if I've caused you any further grief by coming back. I'll leave tomorrow."

She wasn't certain her legs would be able to sustain the heavy weight of her heart as she clumsily brought herself to her feet. His hand unfurled and sought hers with the speed of lightning streaking across a tempestuous sky. His fingers squeezed her hand, and she looked down into the velvet brown eyes she loved.

"I don't want you to go," he said hoarsely, and she dropped back down to her knees.

"But you're not certain you want me to stay?"

Imprisoning her face between his hands, his brown eyes bored into hers of blue. "I don't know. I know I should be grateful as hell that you're back. I let you go because I didn't want you spending the rest of your life looking towards Montana wondering what might have been. I wanted you here, Reb, looking at me. When you looked at me, when you touched me, when you gave me a smile . . . Lord, I had everything I ever wanted." He dropped his head down, closing his eyes and releasing a sigh. "I don't know if it can be the same now, Reb."

She placed her palm against his cheek. "It won't be the same, Jake. But that doesn't mean it won't be better." She tilted his head up until he was looking at her. "We could give it a try, even if only for a little while, a few weeks, a couple of months, whatever you're comfortable with. And if at the end of that time you're still not sure, I'll leave."

"That doesn't seem fair to you. Not to commit myself to you."

"I'll accept life with you on any terms, Jake."

"What about the divorce?"

She smiled at him. "The divorce is null and void since it was based on a bold-faced lie."

The corner of Jake's mouth turned up. "First time in my life I ever told a lie. But I'd do anything to see that you're happy."

"Then give me a chance to prove to you that you can trust me and that I can make you as happy as you make me."

"Did you bring Jacob back with you?"

Her eyes softened. "Yes. I left him with Arlene because I was afraid it might upset him to see you when you were so ill . . . and then I wasn't sure we'd be staying long, so I didn't want to get his hopes up."

"Do you think he remembers me?"

"You're a hard man to forget, Jake Burnett."

Tentatively, almost afraid that if he touched her she'd disappear, he pressed his lips to hers, his tongue sweeping the familiar caverns, hot and moist, her tongue eagerly greeting his. Pulling back, his velvet brown eyes delved into deep blue. "Then let's go get him and go home."

Jacob clutched the side of the sofa, his blue eyes warily studying the opening at the front of the house. The door, several feet away from him, was ajar. Outside, the dimming sunlight beckoned to him. He glanced towards Arlene as she worked at the table, pounding the bread dough. Then he glanced back towards the door. He released his hold on the sofa and swayed as his equilibrium faltered, forcing him once again to hold the side of the sofa.

A shadow passed before the opening, and his mother stepped inside the house. Jacob smiled up at her. Then another shadow crossed before him, and his eyes traveled ever upward, his tiny heart beginning to beat furiously in his chest. He caught sight of the man's face. Squealing, he released his tenuous hold on the sofa, teetering towards the tall figure. He took three steps before gravity came to claim him and drag him down, but the man beat gravity at its game. His large hands lifted Jacob into the air. Jacob wrapped his small arms around the man's neck, snuggling his nose against the man's throat. At last, they had come home.

Rocking slowly, Jake held Jacob curled up on his lap. The boy snored softly, his tiny hands balled up around

Jake's shirt as though he were afraid Jake might leave him, or worse, he would be taken away again. Her feet curled under her, Rebecca sat on the bed, brushing out her hair. Jake watched as she parted it and began to braid it.

"Will you leave it loose?" he asked.

She looked up from her lap and smiled at him, releasing her hair and pulling the brush through it once again to erase the parts she had created.

"I don't want you riding out alone."

Stilling the brush, she lifted her eyes to her husband.

"Just until I've settled things with Ethan."

"Do you know where he is?"

"No, but I intend to start searching for him."

"Maybe he'll leave you alone now. What more can he do?"

"He wants this land. I don't want to have to worry about you or Jacob. I'm going to organize the men tomorrow, maybe hire a few extra until I find Ethan. Just until then, stay close to the house."

Jacob shifted his body. Jake pulled the boy closer, turning his attention from his wife to the sleeping child. Never in his life had he felt such love directed his way. He had been overcome with emotion standing in Frank's house feeling Jacob nestling against him, so glad to see him. Jake closed his eyes, listening to his son's soft breathing. His son. If there had been any doubt in his heart before, Jacob's reaction to seeing him this evening had chased it all away.

His body jerked as he felt Jacob being taken from him. He opened his eyes, trying to remember where he was. It had been a long time since he had been in his house in the evening. He usually didn't stomp in until the late hours, when he was so tired he could do no more than fall down on the bed and let sleep overtake him.

"You fell asleep," Rebecca said softly. "Just move to the bed and I'll undress you after I've put Jacob down."

She laid Jacob on a thick pallet on the floor. Even if Maura hadn't had the cradle, Jacob had grown too much to use it since they'd left. They'd have to get a real bed and a room for him soon. She covered her son and moved back to the bed where she helped Jake undress. Then she tucked the covers around him before moving through the solitary room that was their home, lowering the flames in the lanterns. Not for one minute did she miss the many rooms she had aimlessly walked through for months.

"Reb?"

"What?"

"Where are you planning on sleeping?"

"Where do you want me to sleep?"

"With me."

She dimmed the flame in the final lantern and moved to the bed, lifted the covers and slipped inside.

"Then this is where I'll sleep."

Jake lifted an arm and she moved in closer to his side, refraining from snuggling as close as she would have liked for fear of causing him discomfort.

"I should take all these bandages off tomorrow," she said as she lightly trailed a finger over his covered chest. At his lack of response, she tilted her head up and looked upon his sleeping face. Gingerly, so as not to disturb him, she brought herself up on an elbow. In the shadows cast by one low-burning lantern, she watched him sleep.

Rebecca felt strands of hair tickle her face as they were moved away. Languorously, she opened her eyes, the dawning sun filtering into the room, across the bed. She was greeted by deep brown eyes gazing down at her.

"I didn't mean to fall asleep last night. That wasn't much of a welcome home."

"You're still healing. It's more important for you to get fully recovered."

His lips came down on hers and she welcomed him. His hand moved slowly up her midriff, cupping and caressing a small breast beneath her cotton gown. She stopped the kiss when she felt his smile and drew back, searching his eyes.

"You left something in Montana," Jake said, his eyes teasing. It warmed Rebecca to the roots of her soul to see something besides pain reflected in his eyes. Perhaps earning his trust wouldn't be so hard a task to accomplish after all.

"No, I left it here. My milk dried up after we left Pleasure. But I warned you before—"

"I'm not complaining," he said as his mouth descended on hers.

A tug on the covers and a pounding on the bed caused the kiss to once again end. Jake looked over his shoulder to behold Jacob's beaming face. Reaching down, he pulled Jacob up onto the bed. The child snuggled down in between his parents, kicking at the covers and rolling from side to side until he gave them no choice but to get out of bed and begin the day.

# Chapter Twenty

CAREFULLY WITHDRAWING THE cinnamon-scented apple pie from the oven, Rebecca inhaled the savory aroma and let the steam warm the tip of her nose. It created a homey scent which helped with the mood she was hoping to create. Inside the house, she knew she was home, and yet she felt as though she weren't home. Jake, always polite, was more polite, more cautious, watching her in ways he didn't watch Jacob, trusting Jacob's love in ways he didn't trust hers. It had been three days since they'd brought Jacob back to the house, three nights that she had slept in Jake's arms. Though he was still healing physically, she knew it wasn't his physical pain that prevented Jake from making love to her.

Every morning, he was up with the sun, riding out to check the ranch and cattle, and each evening he came home exhausted. He had failed to locate Ethan or the cattle that had been with him the day Jake had last run across him.

Conversations she shared with Jake revolved around the weather, Jacob's activities, and the cattle. She constantly felt as though she were trying to breach a wall or crawl through a thick barbed-wire fence without cutters. She knew she should expect the distance between them, knew he needed to learn to trust her again. But she needed him, needed more than he was willing to give to her at the moment. And to obtain what she needed, what she knew they both needed, she had to make him trust her.

With a three-man escort, she had taken Jacob over to

Arlene early in the afternoon. She had spent the remainder of the day preparing for her evening with Jake. She set the pie on the table beside an assortment of vegetables. It had actually turned out well if the aroma filling the house was any indication. She placed two thick candles on the table.

Humming to herself, she bathed and slipped on her finest blue dress, her hair hanging loosely over her shoulders. Beneath the dress, she wore nothing at all. Inside her pocket, she carried a gift she had picked up for Jake when she and Jacob had begun their journey back to Texas. She had been trying to find an opportune moment to give it to him and having decided the right moment would never arrive, she had decided to create it.

She heard Jake's horse whinny in anticipation of receiving his oats. She stepped outside onto the porch as her husband reined in his horse. Her bare feet lifted the dust as she walked out to him. As he dismounted she slid her hands up his chest and she wrapped her arms about his neck, her body pressing against his as he pressed his lips against hers.

"I have something special planned for this evening," she said seductively as their lips parted.

His warm eyes traveled appreciatively over her. "Let me see to my horse. I won't be long," he promised. He led his horse towards the barn as Rebecca returned to the house.

She lit the candles and uncovered the warm dishes that graced the table. She brushed her hair until it caught the candle light. Then she began walking back and forth, waiting. Waiting. She brought herself up on her toes and set herself back down. And waited.

She frowned. He had promised he would not keep her waiting a long time. Was he playing a game with her? Did he really not want her back? Feeling like a fool, she clenched her fists into tight balls at her sides as she strode towards the door. Then she halted as though she had slammed into a brick wall. Jake wasn't one to play games. Panic replaced hurt, and she retrieved her gun, loaded it, and stormed out of the house.

*  *  *

Jake had hefted the saddle off his horse before he felt the dull pain at the back of his head and the world turned black.

When he came to, he was aware of two things: the hard ground beneath his sprawled body and the cold unforgiving steel edge of the bowie knife laid against his throat, leaving no doubts in his mind as to its sharpness or who he'd find wielding it.

"Before you get any stupid notions, let me go ahead and warn you now that I've got that boy of yours."

Jake broke out in a cold sweat and his breathing came with increased difficulty. He had little doubt that Ethan was telling the truth. Jake nodded his acceptance of his position.

"Get up," the hoarse voice commanded. Before Jake was fully upright, he was thrown back against the wall. The knife was once again pressed against his throat. Brown eyes met brown, intense emotions raging.

"Your wife coming back has messed things up for me. Killing you now won't do me any good. She'll get the land. So I'd have to kill her and then the boy." Ethan looked off in the distance. "Too much blood." He shook his head and then looked back at Jake.

"Now, I want you to listen real careful. I want you to go into town tomorrow and get the deed to this ranch put in my name. Then you deliver that deed to me. I'll be at that shack you built on the north end. You know the one I mean?"

Jake nodded.

A wicked, knowing grin crept across Ethan's face. "Did you forget? You say 'yes, sir' to me."

For Jacob's sake, Jake swallowed his pride. "Yes, sir."

Ethan nodded with satisfaction. "I'll give you back the boy then. You come alone. If you bring anyone, I'll kill him."

"I'll do what you want without the threat. Bring him back tonight."

Ethan smiled, a hard smile, a smile that never touched his eyes. "He's my guarantee. I'll keep him. Whether or not I return him alive will depend on you."

"Decided it was time to join your father in Hell?" a menacing feminine voice asked.

Ethan turned around quickly, a careless move that left him virtually open and unprotected.

"Reb! No!" Jake cried, throwing himself in front of Ethan as the harsh sound of gunfire filled the barn.

Ethan stumbled back. Jake dropped to the ground with a sickening thud. Rebecca would have fired another shot at Ethan, but Jake's actions shocked and frightened her. Why would he protect Ethan? She stood rooted to the spot, her mind screaming. All she could see was crimson blood spreading quickly over Jake's back before she felt the dull pain at the back of her head.

Rebecca's mind was still screaming when she opened her eyes. She was lying on the bed, a cool cloth on her forehead, a painful throbbing at the back of her head. She lifted the cloth from her face and searched the house. Jake was sitting backwards in a chair while Lee stitched up his shoulder.

"If you ain't the unluckiest man I know," Lee said as he pierced Jake's flesh with the needle, pulling the thread through the bleeding wound. The bullet had grazed his shoulder, taking with it a hunk of his flesh.

"I'm still alive. I'd say I was pretty lucky."

Lee finished up his handiwork on Jake's shoulder and left the house.

Rebecca dropped her unsteady feet onto the floor and Jake's head snapped around. She moved towards him in a confused daze.

"Why did you stop me?"

"He has Jacob."

"No," she said, unable, unwilling to believe the words that were spoken with such certainty. "I left Jacob with Arlene this afternoon."

"I got no reason to think he's lying, Reb. You'd best go over to Frank's and check. Take four men with you."

After she changed into pants, Jake took her hand, pressing it to his lips.

"He won't hurt Jacob as long as I do what he wants. I

won't do anything to endanger your son.''

"He's your son, too.''

He squeezed her hand. "He'll be all right. We'll have him back tomorrow.''

She nodded and hurried out the door.

Before she'd gone too far, Rebecca saw a small rider bumping along the path, frantically waving his hand. It was Sean.

"He got Jacob!'' he yelled at the top of his lungs and Rebecca felt her heart sinking.

"Sean, you shouldn't be riding out here alone,'' she chastised, her worry equal to his.

"Me mum sent me. Some man took Jacob and I was s'posed to come tell you.''

"Is your sister all right?''

Sean shook his head sadly. Rebecca followed him back to Frank's house.

Frank was sitting on the porch, his elbows digging into his knees, his chin digging into his hands, his face blank. He didn't look up until Rebecca knelt down before him.

"She tried to stop him,'' he said in a voice hoarse with emotion.

"Is she going to be all right?''

Frank gave a slight nod. "She lost the baby, but Maura said she won't die. She's with her now.''

Rebecca's heart lurched. "Oh, Frank, I'm so sorry. I didn't know—''

He forced a small smile. "No one did. There's been so much going on around here lately that we didn't have time to tell anyone.'' The smile left his face. "I'm going to kill him, Reb.''

"I'm afraid you'll have to get in line this time, Frank.''

"Frank?''

His head snapped around and he came to his feet.

"You can see her now,'' Maura said with kindness. The abrasive young man she had disliked that first night had turned out to be a wonderful husband to her daughter.

He gave Maura a brief hug before he stepped into his house. Rebecca followed him only to the door where she gave Maura a hug. She didn't want to impose on Frank's time with his wife but she wanted to catch a glimpse of Arlene to make certain she was all right. One side of her face was bruised and swollen. One arm was bandaged. Rebecca could only guess at what the rest of her body looked like, what other damage Ethan Truscott might have inflicted.

Frank knelt down by the bed, brushing his fingers along Arlene's brow, moving the damp strands of red hair off her face.

"I'm sorry, Frank," Arlene said in a weary voice.

He slowly shook his head. "Wasn't your fault." He brought her fingers to his lips. "I love you so much, girl. I thought I was going to lose you. Nothing means more to me than you do."

She brought his head to her shoulder and his arms went around her. Rebecca turned away from the door, tears in her eyes. It was difficult for her to look upon Frank now, to see a man in place of a gangling boy. A man who loved deeply the woman he had married.

Rebecca sat before the front window, looking out unseeing. Night had fallen, the moonless night reflecting her darkened mood as the tears began to trail slowly down her cheeks.

Jake watched her. After she had returned and explained what had happened at Frank's house, she had taken up her vigil by the window. She needed him and he knew it. He hadn't been fair since she'd returned from Montana. He had withheld his heart, afraid to let himself become vulnerable. He walked over and hunkered down beside her, taking her limp hand in his own strong one.

"Jacob will be all right, Reb."

She turned her head, her finely arched brows furrowed. "I'm not just worried about Jacob. I'm worried about you. Do you honestly think once you've handed that deed over that he's going to let you walk away?"

"He'll have what he wants."

She released a short laugh, shaking her head. "He has too much hatred." She brought her shaking fingers to her lips, releasing a sob, more tears rolling down her cheeks. "He'll kill you, Jake. And you and I both know it."

"I think he might try, but I won't give up without a struggle. He can have my land, but that's all he can have." He brushed his knuckles along her damp cheek. "The day I ran across Ethan at the fence line, he left me for dead. I thought I was going to die myself. Do you know what I was thinking while I was lying there in the hot sun?"

She slowly moved her head from side to side, her eyes never leaving his.

"How much I wanted to hold you one last time." Reaching around behind her, he pulled her braid forward, slowly combing out the crisscross of ebony strands until they were all free, hanging loosely. He filled his hand with the silky tresses and brought them to his face, inhaling rose scent, wondering what the night might have brought if Ethan hadn't come. "I sure do want to hold you in my arms."

"I want to be in your arms," she said quietly. He stood up, bringing her to her feet and leading her to the bed.

They undressed slowly, their minds not on the task. Rebecca climbed into bed. Jake blew out the lanterns and joined her. He lay on his side, keeping his aching shoulder off the bed, one arm around her, one hand rubbing her back.

"Was she pretty?"

Jake looked down on her, her face cast in shadows.

"Who?"

"The woman you paid."

"She had real pretty eyes. That's about all I remember." He gave her a small smile. "She asked me the same thing about you."

"About me?"

"Yeah. I guess she wasn't used to her customers being so quiet. Out of the blue, she asked 'Was she pretty?' "

"What did you say?"

He shrugged. "I lied and said yes."

"I don't believe you. What did you tell her?"

"That I didn't want to talk about you."

"Because you hated me?"

"Because I love you."

A comfortable silence surrounded them. It had been a while since they had felt the casual ease between them that had characterized their relationship before Brett's arrival.

''What was Montana like?'' Jake asked.

''Lonely.''

''Were you left alone?''

''No. We had a housekeeper and a cook. And . . . well . . . Brett seldom worked away from the house. But I missed you so much.''

''I missed you, too,'' he said quietly as his mouth descended to hers.

The kiss was warm and tender and all-consuming, like a slow roaring fire. And then it was as if someone threw a dry log on the fire and flames shot upward without warning. He wanted to go slowly, to worship her, to adore her, but he needed to possess her like he had never possessed anything in his life. And she felt the same need. There was nothing gentle in their lovemaking. It was as though they were battling death, clinging to each other as though there would never be another time. Jake ignored the pain caused by her hands pressing unmercifully down on him until her fingernails raked up his back, opening wounds that had only recently healed. He pulled her hands away from him, holding them in place on either side of her face, as he took possession, thrusting himself deep and hard. He released her hands, and she buried them in his hair, bringing his face down to hers, her mouth devouring his, her legs wrapped tightly around him. They both cried out with the force of their release, their bodies drenched in sweat, their breathing labored.

Jake rolled over to his side, bringing her up against him. He felt the shudder run through her body, followed by a trembling that had little to do with their lovemaking. He felt her tears, and then the hard sobs began to rack her body. He rolled her back over.

''Did I hurt you?'' he asked.

''No. I'm just so frightened. I know you too well, Jake. I know you'll put Jacob's life before your own. I can't bear to lose either of you.''

Jake pressed kisses over her face, tasting the salty tears, tears shed for him.

"I love you, Reb," he whispered. "I love you."

How easily she had left him the first time when the choice was hers. How difficult now to let him go when no choice was given her, when she wanted to lay in his arms until her hair turned silver and her skin wrinkled with age. For the remainder of the night, they held each other close in a futile effort to ward off death.

The line shack had been built in the midst of a grove of trees, nature's thicket providing protection from the hot sun in summer and the cold northern winds in winter. It also allowed Rebecca to follow Jake without being spotted. It took all her inner strength to stay hidden, watching the drama unfold before her, waiting for the moment when her presence would gain them the most.

Jake prodded his horse slowly into the area before dismounting and tethering the stallion to a post in front of the shack. His eyes scanned the small area that had been cleared of trees and he was not at all pleased with the sight that met his eyes.

"You can come in closer," Ethan said from his sprawled position on the ground, his back up against a tree. In his hand he held a rope, one end trailing behind him, the other end hanging up over a branch of a tree some distance away from him, wrapped securely under Jacob's arms as he dangled over a large wooden openmouthed barrel.

"Stop right there."

Jake did as he was ordered. He had worn his gun, and until Ethan told him otherwise, he had no intentions of removing it. He had no idea if he could outdraw Ethan if it came down to a show of guns, but he sure as hell was going to try. He gave Jacob a small smile, a smile that wasn't returned. The boy wore a deep frown, his blue eyes narrowed in thought, and Jake knew he would never be able to comprehend all that was happening before him. He could see no bruises or evidence that the boy had been treated harshly, and Jacob wasn't bellowing, so Jake had to assume he had been fed.

"Thought you might be entertaining ideas of killing me," Ethan said, and Jake looked back towards him, wondering how three men sired by the same man could have turned out so differently. "But if you do, I'll let go of this rope." He let two inches slip through his fingers and Jacob fell slightly, his eyes widening, before the slack of the rope tightened. The clatter of rattles echoed in the barrel.

Jake's eyes flew from Ethan to the barrel and back to Ethan. "You bastard," he said with more venom than the diamondback rattlesnakes that sat coiled, ready and waiting beneath Jacob.

"Now, you're wrong there, Jake. You're the bastard, not me. And as long as no one followed you, as long as I stay alive, as long as you do as I say, the boy stays in the air. Otherwise, he goes into the barrel. Do you understand?"

"He's not even my son, Ethan."

Ethan digested that piece of information as though it were a tender piece of sirloin, and then he began to laugh, a loud boisterous laugh. "So you weren't man enough for her, huh?"

"She was pregnant when I married her. Do you really think a woman like Rebecca would marry me if she wasn't desperate?"

"No. Never could figure out how you got her." His lips spread in a wide smile. "I like knowing that bit of information. But it don't change the boy's position. Now, you got the deed?"

Jake removed it from his pocket and held it out.

"Bring it here."

Ethan was now holding a gun in the same hand as the rope, brandishing both at Jake as he leaned over and handed Ethan the title to his land.

"Move on back," Ethan said, waving the gun loosely in the air.

Cautiously, Jake moved back, easing his way closer to Jacob, stopping when he was even with the barrel. Ethan flicked the paper open and read its contents.

"Everything looks legal." His eyes narrowed. "He's not your son, but you'd give up your land to save him." His eyes came to stare hard on Jake. "Why don't I trust you?" He released the rope.

Jake cried out as he made a lunge for Jacob, catching the boy before he fell into the open mouth of the wooden barrel, Jake's body slamming into the barrel and toppling it over. Jake froze with Jacob clinging desperately to his neck. He felt the first rattler strike and didn't dare move, his breathing shallow, his entire body feeling as though it were only raw nerves. He was aware of the pounding of Jacob's tiny heart against his chest, the pounding of his own heart within his chest. Somewhere in the distance he was vaguely aware of a man's screams. A second rattler struck, and Jake felt the milky venom dripping down his leg. The first rattler had targeted his boot. The second had struck higher, catching his fangs on the top of Jake's boot. The rattler's body swished from side to side as it struggled to free itself. Slowly, Jake lifted his revolver out of his holster, and taking careful aim, shot the rattler in half. Studying the area surrounding him, he saw no signs of any remaining vipers. He shoved his gun back into his holster before reaching down to pull the lifeless head from its hold on his boot and tossing it aside. Then he righted the barrel so the flat bottom was facing the sky and he sat Jacob down on top of it. The boy's eyes were wide, his mouth puckered, quivering, trapping inside the wailing cry he was too frightened to release. Jake put his arms back around the child.

"You're a very brave boy. And I love you very much. You'll be all right now. But I don't want you to move off this barrel." He reached into his pocket and pulled out a sarsaparilla stick. Jacob's lips stopped quivering, and his eyes widened in delight as he took the offering.

Jake moved towards Ethan who was still lying prostrate on the ground. Ethan raised the gun with a shaking hand. "Just stay where you are," he ordered.

Jake halted. "Let me help you."

Ethan laughed. "I counted at least four strikes. Not much you can do."

Jake took another step and Ethan pointed the gun towards the barrel. "You set the boy up so he makes an easy target."

Jake stopped, dreading the idea of watching the man die from snake poisoning, but he wasn't going to risk Jacob's life. He took a step back. If he could manage it, he was going to retrieve Jacob and ride out without another word being spoken between the two men.

"Father loved you best," a quiet voice said, and Jake's eyes snapped to the man on the ground. He had lowered the gun until his hand was lying by his side.

Jake was going to comment on the absurdity of that statement, but he realized the man looking up at him with sadness believed the words he'd spoken.

"I saw 'em, you know . . . Father and Aunt Emily. I was playing up in the hayloft when I heard 'em. They were in a back stall. I pushed the hay aside and I looked down through the slats. He was telling her how much he loved her. She was crying, telling him it was wrong. But he wouldn't listen. If only he'd listened," Ethan said, the pain from the memory engulfing him. "He whispered your name with his dying breath. That's what killed our mother . . . knowing how he truly felt about you. I never could forgive him for that . . . or you."

Jake saw Ethan's strength waning. Then with a swiftness Jake never would have expected, Ethan brought the gun up and fired. Ethan's body jerked as a bullet slammed into his chest. The rattlesnake laying at Jake's feet ceased its coiling as Ethan's bullet struck it.

Jake rushed over to Ethan, dropping down to his knees, pressing his hands against Ethan's chest, trying to staunch the flow of bright red blood that was gushing forth.

"Too late, little brother."

Jake's eyes flew from his blood-soaked hands to Ethan's face as the life went out of his eyes. Somehow, in death, his eyes seemed warmer.

Rebecca dropped down to the ground, laying her hand over Jake's.

"I thought he was going to shoot you," she said, quietly.

Jake could only nod before reaching up to close his brother's eyes, an unnatural lump in his throat preventing him from speaking. The last thing he had ever expected of Ethan Truscott was for the man to save his life.

Rebecca and Jake stood alone in a silent moment of reflection before the grave resting beside Zach's. The wooden marker was simple, deeply carved letters depicting Ethan's name, date of birth, and date of death. Whatever endearments he may have earned during his lifetime had perished with him. Rebecca wondered how Thomas Truscott would feel to know how his actions of so long ago had brought two of his son's lives to an untimely end. For when all was said and done, Rebecca could find no one else to blame.

After a few moments, Jake turned away from the grave. "I need some time to myself," he said quietly.

Rebecca had watched Jake mount his horse and gallop away, giving him some time alone before she followed. She'd known where to find him. She moved silently through the tall, dry grasses before dropping down beside him. Jake shook his head.

"Why'd Truscott ever come for me, Reb? Why didn't he just leave me where I was? He didn't want me."

She brushed the hair off his brow.

"I don't know, Jake. I don't know."

He dropped his head down, a shudder running through his body. He felt a need to cry, but he wasn't sure who it was he wanted to cry for. He lifted his head, his gaze falling upon his land. As far as he could see, it was all his. And without Rebecca it was nothing.

"This thing that we're doing," he said quietly, "this waiting to see if things'll work out . . . it's not working for me."

He turned his steady gaze her way, and Rebecca thought her heart would stop beating. After all that had happened during the past two days, she felt closer to him than she had ever felt in her entire life, and she had assumed he felt the same. She had allowed her feelings for him to give her a false sense of security. She should have realized that he might not be feeling what she felt. She wanted to beg him to give her a while longer to prove her love to him, but she had no right to ask anything of him. She nodded. "Jacob and I will leave in the morning."

The hurt in her eyes tore at his heart. He hadn't meant to cause her pain. "No," he said softly.

"Tonight then."

Shaking his head, he gave her a small smile. He brushed away the loose strands of hair that the gentle breeze was blowing across her delicate features. "That's not what I meant . . . or what I want."

Confused, she studied him. And then he spoke, his voice a gentle caress.

"I got some land, a few head of cattle, and I'm planning on building a house at the top of the rise that overlooks the log house. The house'll have turrets and bay windows, a porch going all the way around, and my bedroom will have French doors that lead out onto a balcony. I'd be real honored if you'd share it with me as my wife."

Tears sprang to her eyes. "The honor, Jake Burnett, will be all mine."

He cupped her face in his hands. "I want you to understand what I'm asking, Reb. I want it for the rest of my life. I have to know it's for the rest of my life. I've been holding my heart at bay since you came back, and I don't want to do that. But if I set it free and you leave again, it'll kill me. And that's a hell of a burden to put on someone."

"Long ago before you ever asked me to marry you, you were my friend. Then you became my husband, the father to my child, my lover. But it took me going to Montana to make me realize that you were my love. My only love. My true love."

She reached into the pocket of her skirt, bringing out a gold band.

"I picked this up for you when Jacob and I started back. I had it engraved."

She held it up for Jake's perusal. Squinting, he read the tiny letters carved within the circle of the band: "To the one I love."

Lovingly, his eyes fell on her.

"I was hoping you'd wear it," she whispered. Taking his hand in her own, she slipped the ring onto the third finger of his left hand and then said softly, "I, Rebecca, take thee, Jake, to honor and cherish . . . and above all else to love as long as I live."

One by one, she felt him give freedom to her buttons. Piece by piece she felt him removing her clothing, his own following hers. Gently, he lay her down among the tall grasses, her hands running up into his hair. She ached to pull him close, to run her hands over his body.

"I think I hurt you last night," she said. "I don't want to do that this evening," she whispered.

Moving a stray strand of hair from her face, he gave her an endearing grin. "I don't think you'll ever hurt me again."

She lovingly touched the raised corner of his mouth. "Lord, how I missed your smiles." Her finger trailed up until it rested beside the corner of his eye. "And your beautiful eyes, their depth of feeling. And you," she said as his mouth swooped down to capture hers.

Her heart released its hold on the image of love that it had clung to so tenaciously over the past year, embracing instead the love of a man that would last a lifetime. She gave Jake all of her heart, all of her soul as he slowly, passionately joined his body with hers. What had passed between them before this moment of true commitment could not compare with what was happening between them now. Rebecca held nothing in check, her emotions, her body, her love—physically and emotionally—were given freely and absolutely to the man whose arms encircled her. And Jake, knowing beyond a doubt that she loved him, gave more of himself to her than he had ever given to her, never before realizing that he had only given a portion of himself. Their hands, their mouths, their bodies paid tribute to each other, to their love until together they reached a resplendent fulfillment that melded their hearts and their souls.

Looking down on her, Jake saw the depth of his own love reflected in eyes of blue. "I love you," he whispered.

And his words were returned in a soft, sweet voice. "I love you . . . so much . . . so very much."

# *E*pilogue

### Texas, 1886

THE BLUE EYES diligently scanned the far horizons with experience that came from countless years of looking across a vast expanse of land and judging its merits. Brown and white cattle dotted the landscape, many more than he had expected to see after he had received the reports. Two years of drought and a bitter cold winter had forced many established ranchers to give up the business, only a few of the hardier breed remaining to try again. He had feared he had waited too long to come, that he should have offered aid before now. It pained him to think of Rebecca hungry or cold or doing without.

The man tugged on the reins of his horse, heading in the direction he had been instructed by a gangling youth with red hair. The miniature horse carrying the miniature saddle trudged along beside him. He came up over the rise, not expecting to see a large house nearing completion on the next rise, turrets pointed towards the sky, large bay windows framing the front, porches stretching around the lower portion of the house and balconies the upper. He smiled for the first time in three years. Rebecca would insist on porches and balconies and so many windows he wondered why she even bothered with walls.

For half a century, he had stood straight and erect against all obstacles that man, nature, or he, himself, had thrown in his path. Only recently had his shoulders begun to slump forward, only recently had he taken on the hated mien of defeat. Regret could do that to a man, had done it to him. Swallowing his pride, ignoring the bitter taste it left deep within him, he straightened his spine with increasing difficulty and prodded his horse forward.

The squeal resounded and echoed throughout the barn as two tiny legs churned in an attempt to escape the encroaching predator. The small boy got as far as the barn door before his father's large hands came around him, tossing him up, turning and catching him. The boy's arms tightened around his father's sturdy neck.

"I love you, Pa!" Jacob said in the sweet lilt of a child who knows nothing but love and security.

"I love you more," the tall man said, and Jacob shook his head vehemently, separating his arms from their secure position and throwing them back.

"I love you to here!"

"And I love you." The boy felt the hold on him loosen and he threw his arms back around his father's neck before the hold tightened again. "Enough not to let you go," Jake said as he began walking towards the house, stopping short as he caught sight of the man sitting astride a grand stallion.

Each man studied the other, past words, past actions, past feelings, bringing forth a tidal wave of emotions until finally Jake spoke.

"Mr. Anderson."

John Anderson nodded, uncomfortable with the way he'd treated the man, a feeling he had seldom found himself confronted with in the past. He cleared his throat.

"I'd heard hard times had hit the ranchers of this state. I . . . I wanted to make sure Rebecca was not suffering because of it."

"We were fortunate," Jake said.

"Fortunate, hell! Fortune had nothing to do with it. I'm not a fool, boy. I've ridden across this land of yours. I've seen the barbed wire that kept your cattle from ending up in Oklahoma frozen to death like so many others. I've seen your fields of hay that give you fodder for the beasts. I've seen your windmills drawing water out of the stingy earth."

John's face relaxed somewhat when he had finished the tirade. "You have an innate ability when it comes to ranching." He gave a curt nod. "That was the reason I asked you to marry Rebecca."

Jake smiled. "Reb's inside the house. I'll tell her you're here."

He strode across the yard and set Jacob down on the porch. The boy hunkered down by the post watching the white-haired man dismount rather slowly, he thought, for a man. His pa never got off a horse that slow.

John held the reins in his hands, studying the boy who was studying him. Even if Rebecca hadn't told him who had sired the boy, he would have known. The raven-colored hair, the deep blue eyes that for one so young were remarkably penetrating. John had been surprised to see the obvious affection Burnett showered on the boy, he himself knowing he could never bring forth those feelings for another man's child, wondering how Burnett did. And then the obvious hit him, the reason the man hadn't blinked an eye at the thought of marrying a pregnant woman. He couldn't sire his own. He wondered if Burnett were only sterile or if he were impotent. Impotent. Dear God, his passionate daughter chained to impotency. He never should have tried to rule her life.

Rebecca dropped the last of the items into the second of two baskets resting on the table. She leaned back as her husband's arms enfolded her and his lips pressed against the sensitive spot behind her ear. She turned, putting her arms around his neck in the same manner as her son had only moments before, her mouth welcoming the sweetness of his kiss, the flames of desire lingering after the kiss had ended. She searched his eyes as his fingers trailed lovingly up into her hair.

"What's the matter?" she asked, for the first time uncertain of the emotion he carried in his eyes.

"Your father's outside."

"My father?" Rebecca felt her heart pounding in her chest as it moved slowly up to her throat. She forcibly swallowed, breathing deeply to still her trembling. Her father's heated words still tore at her heart, after all this time still able to hurt her. "I hope you told him he wasn't welcome here."

"No, ma'am. I didn't."

"You're too tender-hearted, Jake Burnett." Rebecca removed her apron, shoving herself away from her husband with determination. "I'll be happy to tell him," she said as she stormed out of the house.

Reaching down into the second basket, a smile spreading across his features, he picked up his three-month-old son, brown eyes delving into brown. How any woman could be so thrilled to see a child coming into the world looking like Jake, Jake could not fathom, but Rebecca had. And the first time the boy had smiled, Rebecca's heart had swelled to overflowing with joy as only one side of his tiny mouth tilted up. Shaking his head in wonder even now with the realization that his wife truly loved him, he nestled his son into the crook of his arm.

"Come on, Zach. As hard-hearted as your mother sounds, I imagine you're going to be meeting your grandpa before this day is over."

Squinting against the sun, Rebecca stepped out onto the porch, her fists clenched as tightly as her heart. She looked towards the man, whose blue eyes sought hers. "He looks so old," she whispered as she ran off the porch, straight into his arms.

"I'm sorry, girl," John said through a thick voice. "I'm so sorry."

"It's all right, Daddy," Rebecca whispered hoarsely, the tears washing down her cheeks.

"I've missed you, girl. Lord, how I've missed you." John leaned back, taking a swipe at his eyes. "Got some dust in my eyes when I was riding," he said. "I brought a present for the child. This tiny horse over here. He won't get any bigger."

"And which child is this horse for?" Rebecca asked.

"Hell, girl. Are you trying to be difficult? It's for the boy you had."

"Which one?" she asked.

"Which one? Hell, the one hunkered down over there."
John turned and pointed his finger towards the porch. His
eyes widened at the sight of Jake holding a child in one
arm, his other arm holding Jacob close against his side.

"You got two?"

"We have two."

"Both boys?"

"Both boys."

"Well, I'll be damned." He studied his daughter.
"You're happy, aren't you, girl?"

"I'm very happy," she said. "We were just getting
ready to go on a picnic. Will you join us? It would give
you an opportunity to get to know your grandsons."

"Grandsons," he whispered. "I'll be damned. Hell, yes,
I want to join you." And then he winked at her and a smile
she hadn't seen since that fateful night crept over his face.
"How else can I teach them what they need to know about
ranching?"

Coating the small hill in blue, the bluebonnets had burst
forth in abundance despite the winter snowstorm and the
absence of water the year before. John led the small pony
around the tiny pond while Jacob held on tightly to the
pommel the way his father had shown him. Zach lay com-
fortably in the crook of the old man's shoulder, listening
to his grandfather's resonant voice as he recounted a tale
about his daughter's first experience with a horse. John
glanced over his shoulder wondering where his daughter
and her husband had disappeared to, and then chuckling to
himself, he turned his attention back to his grandsons.

Nestled among the bluebonnets, Rebecca sighed as
Jake's lips left hers to follow a familiar trail along her
throat. A cool breeze wafted across the land stirring to life
all that surrounded them. She opened her eyes to watch
billowing white clouds glide across the blue sky. Her father's appearance had forced her to think about things she
had repressed for so long, so many things she had often
wondered but not dared to ask.

"Do you ever wish, Jake, that you had been the only one?"

Slowly, Jake lifted his head to gaze down on her.

"I mean . . . do you ever wish there had been no man before you?" She watched the emotions light across his features, almost as though they played tag with one another.

"No," he replied in all honesty. He removed from her face the stray strands of hair that the gently blowing wind had toyed with. "I could never have given us Jacob. And as odd as it seems, Jacob gave me you."

Tears welled up in her eyes as the truth of his words touched her heart.

"I love you," she whispered just before his mouth returned to reclaim hers.

She knew they would return to this hillside at another time when her father's voice wasn't being carried on the wind and her sons' laughter wasn't filling the air. Zach had been conceived here among the bluebonnets on a warm spring day, and in the years to come, other children would follow. But for now, Rebecca was content to lie in Jake's tender embrace until it was time to return home.